KRISTEN BAILEY

Published by Accent Press Ltd 2016

Paperback ISBN: 9781786150998
Ebook ISBN: 9781786150677

ACKNOWLEDGEMENTS

A huge thank you to everyone at Accent Press for all their hard work ... my fantastic editor, Alex Davies in particular.

Thank you to Ruth and Jacob Sealey for giving me all their insider knowledge about what it's like to be little and have appendicitis.

Huge thanks always to N, J, T, O & M for the inspiration, the cups of tea, the hugs, the laughs.

And to all the 'souper' friends and family in my life for their support and love.

For my Souper Mum, Lauren, who always had me coming back for second helpings ...

One day, I hope to be able to cook like you. You can stop laughing now.

PROLOGUE

As a general rule, I don't like being urinated on when I'm asleep. For those of you worried about my husband's bedroom activity of choice, fear not – this was not Matt's doing. No, the urine in question belongs to a little person, ginger of hair and whose nappies are too small for her now. Millie. Thanks for that. I look over at the clock. 5.56 a.m. If I wake her now, she'll cry, she'll wake everyone up, setting us up for a day of misery.

Balls.

I'm not sure what's worse: the fact I can't remember when she came into our bed, the fact Matt is also covered in piss but managing to sleep through it, or that I now have a sodden duvet which I'll have to launder. I sit up and watch the slate-grey sky outside. The same pigeon who has taunted me since the day we moved in sits outside. How old are you, Mr Pigeon? You must be ancient. Is he even the same pigeon? Perhaps he's one of many who are stalking me. Maybe they take it in turns. He pecks at the ledge. I should name him. Peter? Paul? Pierre! He has a smug Continental look about him, proven when he craps on the windowsill and flies off. Can't Matt smell the pee? It smells like we're in the stairwell of a car park. These are the times I truly resent Matt's ability to sleep through anything. Do we have any Febreze? We'd better have Febreze. I roll my sticky side of the duvet off and tuck a couple of pillows around Millie who looks lighter – unburdened, shall we say – since depositing the contents of her bladder about my bed. She still has that cherubic baby podge that makes her thighs squidgy, but is getting to that stage where her hair is making her look like a little version of Mick Hucknall. She talks now. My favourite thing she does is following her father around the house calling him 'Matt'.

'But I'm Daddy,' he replies.

'Matt' she says, toddling off, waving her breadsticks in the air.

I go to the bathroom, where a small part of me realises this morning has just got a crap load better. I pull down my knickers and sigh a small breath of pure meh. Period. Meh. They're well timed now. Always on a Monday, always before I make a pact with myself that I'm going to start a fitness regime which will involve hot yoga and jogging around the park gearing myself up for a local 5K race. I sit on the toilet for longer than I need to, cramping slightly and thinking about the pros of this situation. At least I'm not pregnant. Was that even feasible this month? We did it on the sofa a couple of Fridays ago after a takeaway, but a child arose from their bed using the creaky second step on the stairs as an alarm and we had to withdraw from the situation quickly. There was the Tuesday before that, on the landing because Millie had invaded our bed again. That wasn't comfortable. Or sexy. If that session had produced a baby I'd be bitterly disappointed. No child needed to be created under such circumstances. I roll my memory back as far as I can at that time of the morning and realise that's it. Twice this month? That's not a good law of averages. I scramble under the sink to find a tampon and sort myself out. But I'm not pregnant, so this is good. I think.

I let myself out of the bedroom and sneak a peek at the twins, sleeping in symmetrical star shapes in their bunks as Hannah curls up like a cat in the bedroom next to theirs I still have a good hour of peace before the jungle stirs so

I opt for tea and BBC News. I won't lie, the house is different since the events of eighteen months ago, when I became a celebrity of sorts, and a cooking one at that. Now Matt runs this house. Clothes don't lie strewn along the stairs anymore, used nappies don't sit on the landing waiting to find the bin. Toys are sorted. Someone with OCD tendencies (Matt) even sorted the Lego. Blocks organised into colour, dimension, and cross-sectioned by usage. Don't laugh at my system, he said. I made fun, but I can't deny there have been far fewer barefoot Lego injuries and children fighting about someone hogging all the wheels. That was always going to be the joy of having extra manpower around the house – there was finally time to sort out all the menial stuff that usually lay abandoned and waiting. Ironing, for example. Matt loved this: that for the first time in ten years, my cookbook could pay the mortgage and he could be a bigger part of this family. It wasn't some fancy idyll of us all skipping down streets together, though. It was still going to be shepherding four kids through their formative years and the manic palaver that came with it. It was just going to be easier with extra sheepdogs.

Downstairs, Matt has been squirreling away. The lunches are made, bowls are set up to receive Cheerios, and uniforms hang from the door. I grimace thinking how much better he is at doing this than I ever was. I remember desperate times trying to smooth down crinkly polo shirts with bare, sweaty palms. On the table, Matt has been doodling again. The dream at the moment is the extension. Matt draws it out in crayon on craft paper with the kids, bad depictions of two floors added to the house, a large, light living space with kitchen islands, another bedroom, a goddamn utility room. With a tumble dryer as big as the moon, baby. On the back, leading out to the garden, concertinas of paper that are supposed to resemble the ultimate badge of middle-class success: the bi-fold door. Matt being Matt, he's scribbled down the maths next to his drawings to prove it's attainable. There are even stick figures which I've always approved of, given how skinny they make me look. I stare at them for a while, stirring sugar into my tea and riding the wave of a nasty cramp. The thing is, it is perfect. Look at those sage coloured units he's taken the time to colour in, at my fancy 3D doors and extra bedroom so Millie won't have to sleep in the cupboard under the stairs. But another feeling overrides.

Last week, Luella rang with the offer for me to write another cookbook. She'd come up with a name (*Second Helpings*), she'd given me exact details of a press tour and dates of release. I can't, I told her. I wasn't sure why. Neither was she. But the fact was, the first time 'fame' came round, it was not a hugely pleasant experience. It nearly tore me and Matt apart, my life was placed under a microscope, and people got hurt. This, what I had now, was enough. Just to be financially buoyant, to have a small measure of success that wasn't too invasive. This was all right. I wasn't sure what Luella said next, but it was very loud and very quick. The first cookbook had done all right but it was going to stop paying the bills soon. It will slide down the charts, new cooks will come on the scene. People will forget. And soon after, you'll be walking through some car boot sale in a leisure centre car park and you'll see your book propped up by an old candelabra and a novelty mug that came free with an Easter egg. 50p (O.N.O). Thanks, Luella. That's not to say it didn't send a wave of panic over me. This would come to an end sooner than I imagined, and where would that leave us? Matt going back to a job he hates? Extension-less. Worse, back to me holding down the fort and Lego everywhere, out of its box, scattered pieces of mayhem.

I hear a key in the front door and arch my back around the chair. He sees me sitting in my onesie and I shake my head.

'What time do you call this?'

He looks at his watch. '6.14a.m., dearest sister.'

I beckon him to the kitchen. When I mentioned manpower, there was another adult in the house making this work. Ben. Six months after graduating, work as an actor/dramatist was low on the ground and London had out-priced him. Adam had moved to some unchartered territory outside the M25 with a ladyfriend in tow (Cathy; we liked her. She wore big earrings) and Dad's little retirement flat didn't have the space, so our sofa it was. There were rules: no guests, no drugs, no random sex toys lying around. And in return, he was to be our live-in babysitter and accompany the children to the cinema to watch films involving Minions and dragons that Matt and I couldn't face. Mostly it was warming to have him around – Ben was a cuddler and generally quite hilarious. He allowed for a certain level of humour and artistry in the house that had been missing. But sometimes, like this morning, he'd creep in at some ungodly hour as a reminder of how dull my life was.

'I am hanging.' I smile at him to suggest I care very little for his woes.

'Who throws a party on a Sunday? That's a very unsociable day to have a gathering.'

He looks at me. 'Young people.' I throw a tea towel at him. Ben and his young bohemian friends who listen to electronica, wear dress shoes without socks, and languidly recite poetry to each other while sipping absinthe.

'Do you have anything for breakfast that isn't cereal? Bacon?'

I shake my head at him, trying to figure out if that was

a vague suggestion that I am expected to fry this boy a cooked breakfast.

'Cheerios, Shredded Wheat, Corn Flakes. I suggest a big glass of water.'

He retches a little. 'I need a crappy breakfast: runny eggs, thick, sliced bread, baked beans, those really cheap sausages that melt in your mouth.'

'Insert your own pun.'

He laughs his Ben laugh and I hush him in case he wakes the rest of the house. 'I am never drinking Jäger again – that shit is lethal.' Again, sympathy is lacking. He goes to the sink and drinks straight from the tap.

'BEN! GLASS!'

'You're not my mother!'

'YES, I AM!' I screech in an East End accent. He laughs. Adam never liked that joke because it hit a nerve but Ben and I act the scene out perfectly. I look at the clock again. Forty-five minutes till children start jumping out of beds and the circus that is getting them ready for school starts. I look at Ben and his parched mouth, greying complexion. The echo of his stomach churns in time with the central heating. I smell of wee. The painters are in. Needs must. I grab my purse and car keys off the table.

'Come on.'

Ben looks at me, eyebrows raised. 'For where, dear sis, doth we go this fair morn?'

'McDonalds, you idiot. My treat.' He goes to high-five me. I might high-five him back.

* * *

Fifteen minutes later, we've scooched past the drive-thru and are currently in possession of two sausage McMuffins, two coffees, an orange juice, and four, yes, four hash browns. I've parked and ordered that Ben eat everything because a) I can't bring any evidence home that I've been to the Golden Arches and b) I'm in a onesie and I've left home without a bra on. Ben snogs his McMuffin, holding the sandwich in two hands and making unsettling semi-orgasmic noises.

'Have I ever told you how much I love you?'

'All the time … now gimme my hash browns.' I won't lie, I am drooling in a slightly feral way. In my eyes, bar a Gregg's sausage roll and a packet of Percy Pigs, there is very little that can compare with the joy of a hot, freshly fried McDonald's hash brown. Food snobs will turn their noses up. 'Deep-fried filth! Has she not seen the videos of the pink slime? I would never tarnish my innards with that crap much less feed it to my kids.' Are you done yet? All I can say is that leaves more hash browns for me. Thank you.

Because McDonalds – yes, you contain a lot of fat and a lot of sugar and if I ate you every day, I would be fat, stupid, and probably constipated on a regular basis. But the fact is, I don't eat you every day. My visits are not some badge of honour; they're reserved for emergencies – interminable car journeys where children are physically beating each other black and blue in the back seat and are feral with hunger. On those days, your golden arches have shone like a beacon through the rain, the darkness, and the traffic and made my heart leap with joy. You have given me quick food, free toys, and handy boxes to store the rubbish. Stomachs have been filled, children have been tamed. On days like those, and days like today where hungover brothers need to be tempered, I give full authorisation that they are allowed.

'How do they get the eggs so round?'

'They fry them in rings.'

'You really are a fountain of food-based knowledge, aren't you?'

'Of course.' I add milk and sugar to our coffees as I watch Ben scoff two hash browns in quick succession. The boy has always had that ability to devour like a locust and still be able to pull off skinny jeans. If we didn't share genes, I'd hate him.

'So, I can assume from the time you returned this morning, that sexual congress was achieved last night?'

Ben eyeballs me, sipping his coffee. 'Maybe.'

'Don't I get details?' Ben's eyes open even further. 'Not like that, you perv. Name, for a start?'

That was another good thing about Ben living with us. Dad would never delve for such information so it was left to me to press him over his love life and to make sure he was taking care of himself.

'His name is Lars. He's a student. It was fun.' I shake my head and purse my lips at his diva-like curtness.

'And you know … Lars and you were sensible and you know … used protection.'

Ben can always see a good chance to rile me up. 'This coming from the old lady in the shoe and her five gazillion babies.'

I smile slyly. 'Will we be meeting Lars?'

'No, definitely not.'

My heart sinks a little. It's been the same since Ben graduated – a string of faceless affairs, random sex, and early morning walks of shame. It was very reminiscent of early Adam but a little more heart-breaking, as deep down you knew Ben was the sort of person who wanted more, who needed to be scooped into someone's arms and held like a fuzzy bear.

'You know, I never judge but maybe it's time to … you know, not give yourself so easily.'

'Wait for that special someone to give my flower to …?'

I shake my head and down my coffee, noticing egg

smothered down my onesie. I lick my thumb and try to scrape it off. 'Or just find out their last names?'

He fake laughs but a look of confusion comes over him.

'What, like that guy?'

He smiles, looking at someone behind me. I look over my shoulder. True enough, a man in a white Transit van sits there with a breakfast, waving. There's no other way of saying it: the fella is a beast. Tattoo sleeves, arms like basted turkey joints, neck decidedly absent. Please, Ben. There are classier places to pick up blokes, and not with your sister in tow.

'He's mouthing something ... wind down your window.'

Do I have to? I press the button.

'I knew it was you. Campbell, right? The one with the cookbook?'

Ben seems annoyed. I beam, trying to smooth down my hair.

'Yeah, it's me ... caught red-handed.' I put my hand out and he grabs it, shaking it so it reverbs through my shoulder.

'Love you. Missus loves your book. She'll be proper made up I met you. I'm Tony ... I do roofs.'

'That's very kind, Tony.' He positions his phone in the space between our cars.

'I can do that.' Ben reaches over to grab his phone. I scowl, knowing now is not the time for photos.

'Right, lovely. After three ... everyone say "Happy Meal!"'

Tony bellows with laughter. I urge Ben to move the camera up to avoid my midriff/boob area. 'I'm messaging her this now, she'll be so jel.'

I laugh, my arms folded over my unsupported boobs.

'Oh ... did you see?' He stuffs a newspaper through

my window and Ben and I glance over it. It's an article, with a photo of Kitty McCoy riding a jet ski, on holiday in Barbados, wearing a crochet monokini and pressing her boobs against her new beau, a Kardashian cousin. Next to her picture is one of Tommy McCoy leaving a Robert Dyas and holding a plastic bag full of gaffer tape. His hair's unwashed, he's wearing tracksuit bottoms and some unfortunate flip-flops usually reserved for swimming pools. I smile at Tony who does roofs.

'That's some comeuppance, eh? Prick.'

I look at Tommy's picture again and feel a weird mixture in my stomach. Hate is replaced by something sadder: pity, maybe.

'How the mighty have fallen.'

Of course, he could be in a much better place in the world. He could be sitting in a McDonald's car park on a Monday morning, in his pyjamas, scoffing his second hash brown. I hand the newspaper back.

'It was lovely to meet you, Tony. Got to rush but really, take care.' He winks at me, giving me a thumbs up while Ben giggles.

'Oooh, get you. Jools Campbell – celeb spotted!' I hit him with a serviette.

'Are you done?' I look at the car clock. 6.49 a.m. Time to swing by the Co-op, buy milk, go home, and pretend that was the reason I had to leave the house. We clear the car of debris and start driving with the windows open to get rid of that sweet deep-fried smell.

When I get home, I can hear the squawking and familiar cries of children. Millie in particular does not seem enthralled. I open the door and it's bedlam. Matt is, of course, running about upstairs screaming merry hell about sodden sheets and having been left to deal with them. This was your choice, Matt Campbell. You give up work, you're going to have to deal with urine.

'Mummymummymummy … DADDY! She's home!'

As soon as I step inside, I know something is awry. The air is different. Why is the house so cold? I'm used to bedlam but Hannah's voice is frantic, the sort she uses when a child has gone down and drawn significant amounts of blood. The boys stand next to her, perfectly still. And slightly ashen. Vomit? Hannah holds onto a half-naked Millie who, as always, look nonplussed – this is her norm. I panic. Upstairs, I hear Matt stomping around.

'JOOLS! SHIT!' Ben herds the kids into the front room as I leap up the stairs, my heart in my mouth.

Jesus, mother of arse and buggery pile of … WHAT?

What I'm faced with beggars comprehension. Matt is OK. There's no blood, no bodily fluid to have to deal with. He just stands there with his hands over his head. I look up at the ceiling over my bed.

A hole. A bloody big hole. And daylight. Water drips onto our bed through broken shards of wood. I'll give him this much, he's allowed to scream merry hell. Matt looks at me.

'Where were you? Why didn't you take your phone?'

'Milk. I went to … milk.'

I'm half surprised I have the capacity to still lie. It's not just a hole, either. It's feathers. Feathers everywhere. They are definitely not from our duvet. I spy the body of a dead pigeon on the floor. Christ, is that Pierre the smug pigeon? What the hell did you do, Pierre?

'Are you all right?'

'I got up. Millie had pissed the bed. Jesus, we could have been lying there, Jools.'

Plaster, tiles, and dust cloud the room. Some of the contents of the loft lie strewn on the floor including a box of Christmas baubles and a crap load of tinsel. I think about Tony who does roofs. Ben appears at the doorframe, his eyes wide. Little heads pop up behind him.

'It was like thunder, Mummy! Was it an asteroid? Don't touch it, it might be radioactive.'

I walk over to embrace a worried-looking Hannah.

'It's OK, Han ... no one's hurt.' She wraps her arms around my midriff. Millie continues to stare at the hole. Is that drizzle? I can feel Matt look at me and I catch his eye. Where does this rate in the greater scheme of things? It's a roof. It's not a pregnancy in your early twenties. It's not paparazzi chasing after you and your kids in the street. It's a roof with a big hole in it, possibly caused by a kamikaze pigeon. We'll get through this. We always do. He smiles at me and I smile back. We all stand in silence to survey the damage. I kick the dead pigeon under the bed. Ted starts sniffing.

'What's that smell, Mummy?'

All the kids prick their noses up like bloodhounds. Ben looks down to the floor.

'It's McDonalds!' And just like that, the smile from Matt's face is gone.

CHAPTER ONE

'Where are you?' It's Matt. That's not his happy voice.

'We're just pulling out of Euston, why?'

I know exactly what face he's pulling: lips pursed to the side, allowing for faint whispers of unmentionable swear words. I also hear rattling and the opening and closing of the dodgy drawer on the bottom left.

'Because it seems we have five gazillion Tupperware but none of the sodding lids fit. Why do we have a Walls ice cream tub from the seventies? Why do we have these plastic circle things? What are they? Can I throw them?'

'NO!' I raise my voice a little too loudly for the man sat next to me, who crumples his newspaper in fright. 'Don't you dare, they're adaptors for the bottles.'

'For the baby who doesn't drink from bottles anymore … seriously, I'm binning them.'

'Matt, don't you dare.' There is colourful swearing. The Tupperware have probably never heard such language.

'This is the problem when you buy all that cheap IKEA crap – none of it matches up. Jesus Christ.'

I sit there wondering how this warranted a call. I'm not sure how much help I can be over the phone. Yes, that lid. Try the big squarish one. Does that one not fit? Better try that long one then. But secretly, I know he wants me to bear witness to his rage because in forty-eight hours, once I walk through the door, he'll have forgotten and it's like he doesn't want me to miss out. I don't want to tell him that seventy-five per cent of our Tupperware actually belongs to his mother, Gia, and the numerous delights she'd cook for us on her trips down. The Walls ice cream tub, I keep out of nostalgia. I love how rubbery and tough it is. Sure, it's lost its colour and is possibly made out of carcinogenic fluorocarbons, but back in the day Dad used to pack it to the brim with jam sandwiches and we'd scoff them all the way to Bournemouth in the back of his Astra.

'Why do we have straws in the shape of penises?'

'Some hen do I went on.' He's doing his shocked and haughty face now, I know it.

'Daddy, what are they? Can I have one?' I hear scuffling and a little voice: Ted, from the sounds of it. 'It's not for you.' I can see Ted's face now. Ummm, yes it is? It's fluorescent green and bright and it's a straw. 'Is it a parrot? Why are its eyes so big?' At this point, I'm guffawing. Luella looks at me, half shaking her head. That is not an attractive face, Campbell.

'Ted, I want that back! TED!'

'Ahoy, m'hearties! This be my parrot sword!'

I hear footsteps running down the corridor. 'I blame you.'

'You blame me for everything.'

'Everything … there's a mum down the school who sells Tupperware. Clickable lids and this no-stain technology.'

I pause for a moment. 'I love when you talk dirty to me.' Luella shifts me another look. The man next to us pretends to feign interest in the FTSE.

Matt does his silent laugh thing where there is no sound bar the phone rubbing against his cheek as he laughs. It's a laugh you see. His cheeks rise, his eyes crease. 'I'm ordering three new sets. And I'm throwing away those rings. You're a hoarder. Hoarder, woman!'

'Mummy's a hoar … Mummy's a hoar!' I hear echoing in the corridor. From my seven-year-old son brandishing his penis straw.

'IT'S HOAR – DER! HOARDER!' I hear the doorbell ring in the background.

'Balls, the builders are here. TED! Give me the sodding straw!'

'Love you.'

'Hoarder ...' The line goes dead. I should have told him we have biscuits under the stairs for the builders, hidden in re-usuable shopping bags so the kids couldn't get to them first. Ted is also going for tea with Arun after school and Hannah needs a new swimming cap but not one of those rubber ones because she has too much hair for them. Will he remember? Do I remind him to the point of nagging? What if he forgets about Ted? What if the builders don't get their Bourbons? There'll be mutiny. They'll botch the roof and pee all over the toilet seat.

'Can you relax? Matt's got this.' Luella pushes a heavily sugared coffee in my direction. 'He's one of the most capable fathers I know. Breathe.' Luella has tagged along to be my centre of calm and feed me caffeine and wisdom. She adds another sugar to my coffee, knowing I prefer demerara and bans me from using lids now because I sound like a hoover as I suck my coffee through them. She smiles and encourages me to take deep cleansing breaths. 'Ungrit the teeth, Campbell. Feel your chakras.' I laugh. She shakes her head. How did this happen? Why am I here? This was Luella's fault. Mainly.

It started with the roof. After it collapsed (caused by rotten joists, not pigeons with a death wish), Matt and I went into panic mode. The insurance demanded a sizeable excess payment, money was running out, we needed a roof over our heads. Literally. We sat down, did the sums. We asked a proper architect to turn Matt's drawings into plans. We borrowed money. We discussed how this was

3

going to pan out. I sensed Matt's apprehension at going back to work. I say sensed, I caught him crying in the kitchen about how it would kill a part of his soul. He'd loved spending time with the kids but he needed more time to work out his own life. He couldn't go back. It broke me. I would lay in bed at night, staring at a roof patched up with strips of wood and plastic sheeting. I gave serious consideration to the future, to how I could help make this right. I rang Luella. What was that about a second book?

Luella worked like the clappers to get everything off the ground. She got me sitting next to Susanna Reid on some morning TV cooking segment wearing a giant necklace. She told my publisher I was good for three more books. The next week saw me do three magazine interviews, talking about everything from birthing four children (yeah, stretch marks city) to what I thought about taxes on hot food (it's ridiculous, it's those of us who eat at Greggs that suffer). That was when Luella became priceless. She did exactly what was needed to put me back in the public consciousness so I could squeeze every last drop of money there was in this game to pay for my roof. Of course, I was pretty sure the first book had exhausted most of my cooking know-how, but Luella knew exactly how this ship would sail. I just hoped somewhere down the line, she'd let me look at the map. So today, like every day, I follow suit. You're doing the Good Food Show in Manchester! Got you a live segment after Mary Berry. OK. It's like getting back on the rollercoaster. I wasn't sure how much I enjoyed the ride the first time round but I'm doing it for the good of the kids, who want to stay in this theme park a bit longer.

Luella has been a permanent fixture in my life since the McCoy drama. Of course, before her only incentive was revenge – cold and sweet – but now, I pay her and something tells me she almost likes hanging out with me; like I'm a pet project she likes to show off. There's also a maternal side to her. I like the way she storms into my house, engages in chat with all my kids, and always asks if I've eaten. Case in point, she digs through a bag and pushes a cereal bar my way.

'This one has yuzu and flaxseed. Five times more Vitamin C than an orange,' she reads off the label. I want to ask if she has anything with chocolate chips but know the answer. I take a bite. It's strangely salty, like it should be something that gives me bag loads of energy, but I know will be destined to have me checking my teeth all day. I wait for health to radiate through me. Luella watches me closely. 'They're all samples. I also have green tea and pumpkin seed. They're looking for endorsements ... Look how small they are.' She holds one up like a perfume sample. I laugh. 'It's all right, a nice alternative to a Penguin.' The truth is, this would be the uneaten part of my kids' packed lunches.

'Do we have a better quote?'

'They taste like health?'

The man next to us laughs. Luella scribbles something down. I hope that's not the quote she's going with. She sips something green and thick from a flask. Even though Luella has always supported me and my half-arsed cookery attempts, she always hid that she is actually quite the health nut. It was probably why she was so slim and her hair shone like lacquer. It's probably down to the French husband too, but she's fussy about wine and doesn't shy away from an endive on a menu (What even is an endive? Isn't it just posh lettuce?).

'That looks interesting.'

She pushes it towards me. 'Try some; it's a new thing Remy and I are trying. We've bought a new machine called a Fruit Ninja – makes the most awesome smoothies.' I take a sip. I was wrong. *This* tastes like health. Or cold vegetable soup. 'Kale, beetroot, apple, and wheat germ … yummy, right?' I nod, grabbing at my mocha to wash the taste away. 'You know I have a ton of stuff lined up for you … We should really think about starting you on a health kick to up your energy. Lots of late nights and travelling – it wouldn't go amiss.' I nod enthusiastically despite knowing that half the fun of these trips on one's own is going into a coffee shop and eating sandwiches and coffees without having to drag an entourage of children around and having to share your flapjacks.

'I've booked us in at the Holiday Inn. You have your lunchbox workshop at 2 p.m., which is a good crowd … everyone will have eaten by then and not be hangry. Then photos and signings and the rest of the day is yours. Day #2 is an appearance at Waterstones, late morning so we can get you home for dinner. How does that sound?'

I nod, man with newspaper taking more of an interest in me now.

'Do I have time to get a bit of shopping in?'

'Always … and you and I are having dinner tonight so I can go over some things for the next month. Any requests?'

I desperately want to say Nando's. 'Let's just get a Wagamama,' comes out of my mouth, knowing the presence of edamame will placate her.

'I'll book it now.' Like always, she moves her fingers over her touch screen like furious ninjas. I smile, thinking how it takes me twice as long just to get to my messages and then I spend twenty minutes picking emojis.

'Next month? There are plans?' Luella is one of those 'think ahead' kind of people. I know she's already got her order down at Wagamama. She probably hangs out her outfits the night before and knows what shoes she'll wear. I am not one of those people. I pore over menus and annoy waiting staff, I wear what's clean. The comfort of ballet flats vs heels vs trainers is a dilemma that has eaten into much of my life.

'Oh, you know … if we're going to look into a second book then I want it to be just right. I don't want it to feel like we're cashing in, so I have some ideas I want to run past you. Then I want to look at the calendar and you can tell me what you want to do. This frozen food brand is looking for a new face …'

'I don't think so.'

'Surrey County Council want someone to head cookery workshops in local schools …'

'Yes …'

'Panto?'

'No …'

'That *Bake Off* spin off show with Jo Brand, they're looking for a panellist …'

'But my baking is a little …'

'I think that's part of the appeal.'

'Then why not?'

Luella has a spreadsheet that's colour coded, which she ticks and crosses in appropriate places. The list is about fifty items long and I see the words 'sugar-free workshops' and 'personalised mugs'. I widen my eyes in what is either confusion or horror.

'You are OK with this, right? When you told me you wanted to capitalise on everything, I assumed you wanted to go at it … full bore, right?'

I nod unconvincingly. She picks up on it.

'C'mon, thoughts.'

Luella often speaks to me like this, in a shorthand that appears curt but which I like; she likes to get down to business, no bullshit.

'It's just … it's all moved up a gear quite quickly. I'm throwing myself back into the lions' den. I'm just …'

Luella eyes me curiously.

'Scared?'

I nod.

'Love, this won't be like last time. McCoy completely ambushed you. It was a baptism by fire if ever I saw one. Now the public like you … I think you underestimate by how much. You're verging on media darling status.'

I cringe a little as she unfolds a programme. It's a map of an arena.

'Look, this is your stall – A5, next to the stage and food tasting areas. This is a sweet spot, heavy traffic all day and I've told the organisers you're not going to be trollied in like some A-lister, wave at everyone, and eff off. You're there to stay, chat, mingle with Joe Public.'

She highlights another stall towards the back of the stadium.

'Et voila … stall W27. It's near the toilets and facing an emergency exit, little to no traffic and I know that rental comes with only a fold out table and two chairs.'

'And?'

'That's where McCoy is.' My eyes widen at the thought. I haven't seen McCoy since our infamous cook-off: the one which rather spectacularly ended his career and, one could argue, started mine.

'Seriously?' Luella does her special smile, the evil cat one where she knows she's won. I think it should come with its own special cackle.

'Jools, he's only there because he's endorsing a new multi-peel/grate tool, one of those tatty things you can buy off the telly. He is there to literally peel carrots. The organisers wouldn't touch him. He's bad news these days. How he treated you, the whole Kitty debacle …'

And then that feeling overwhelms me again. It's the same feeling I had when I was outside McDonalds looking at a newspaper article of him in bad flip-flops. Luella feels it too but is still confused as to why I shouldn't be waving my fists about victoriously.

'I can only 100% promise to take care of you in all this. It will be fine.'

I smile. The truth is, Luella has always done that, like a really well-dressed fairy godmother. She puts her manicured hand into mine.

'And things with Matt ...'

Still good. I'll admit, a year ago, with newfound fame and Richie Colman in the mix, our lives became complicated. We questioned everything about our relationship, our family ... but we laid ourselves bare. Matt became the constant in my life I hadn't realised made the most perfect sense. It was the most edifying of conclusions. He gave me a ring, a proper ring (promptly extracted from Ted's poo two days after Christmas and three trips to A&E later) and one day, when all the kids were bundled in our bed, Hannah asked if we were going to have another wedding. Why not, Matt said. It'll be fun. I was so taken aback by Matt's willingness, I fell out of said bed.

'... are good ... fine. Better than fine. Why?'

'Because I had some ideas about the wedding ...' That's not to say Luella hasn't been tickled pink by the idea too. Hannah told her. Luella squealed, clapping her hands like a seal, and started texting maniacally. Since then, it creeps into conversation every so often. She turns to the purple section of her folder and reveals mood boards and magazine clippings.

'I also have a Pinterest board. I'll give you access. This could go two ways ... I have this amazing idea of a city wedding. Ceremony on the London Eye and a double decker to take you to a vintage tea party in Regent's Park ...'

'Will I be wearing a Union Jack dress?'

'Very funny. Or we could go country Italian ... destination wedding. You looking all *La Dolce Vita* and then a big Italian feast like out of *The Godfather*. Gia will love it.'

Or she'll think we're taking the piss. My expression tells Luella that much. I'm also not sure if she understands the efforts it would take for me to transform into an Italian siren; there'd be a darn load of corsetry, filler, and hair dye required. She flicks back to the London idea with me in a Philip Treacy piece of millinery that looks like the Shard, and Matt dressed up like a Beefeater.

'He loves all that Brit rock stuff, he'll look like a Libertine!'

My immediate thought is to send this to him in an effort to cheer him up over mismatched Tupperware. I smile to appear polite, knowing the effort this must have taken. The problem is, she wants this to be big, marketable, and magazine worthy, whereas Matt and I just want some sort of party to placate the kids: something involving white dresses, dancing, and cake. My eyes land on a picture of a row of children dressed as woodland creatures, including a boy with a squirrel tail and jodhpurs. I can see Jake's face already.

'Really?' I say, laughing. 'I thought you knew my kids better than this. Zoo animals are far more apt.'

Luella laughs, knocking her head back. 'I liked the corduroy.' I sip at my mocha. 'Saying that, we could have a London Zoo wedding, they do that now! We could have you in ostrich feathers, it would be ...' Mocha flies out of my nose. The man next to us is chuckling. Luella can't resist.

'I'm sorry, help me out ... you know who this is,

right?' I grimace as Luella makes it sound self-important, bordering on obnoxious. I kick her under the seats. The man glances over the top of his *FT*. Most likely not, given his newspaper of choice.

'You're Jools Campbell. The cooking lady. I bought my wife your book for Christmas.'

I put my hand out to shake his. 'I'm sorry, we didn't mean to disturb you.'

'Oh no, far more interesting to hear about your ostrich feathers than read about collapsing shares. I'm sorry, but you are married, right?'

'Vow renewal.'

'How wonderful ... I vote for the Beefeater wedding, full horse and carriage, swans, dress like a giant croquembouche ...' He smiles, letting me know it's all in jest. Luella, however, is scribbling everything down.

'And just to let you know, my wife bought that thing McCoy is peddling. It's called a Greel. And it's the shittest thing she's ever spent money on. If you see him, please tell him that.'

Luella collapses in laughter. I smile back. 'Will do. Sorry, I didn't catch your name.'

'Charles ... a pleasure.'

'No, lovely to meet you, Charles. My regards to your wife.' He stops for a moment then smiles back. I can't put my finger on it but it doesn't sit right. He stares a moment too long before going back to his newspaper.

CHAPTER TWO

What is it about people and free food? I see it all the time. You're in a supermarket and there's a little old lady reheating soup in a slow cooker and people gather like flies around poo. Trolleys veer dangerously off route, people listen intently about the product they're trying, shoppers feel it their duty to inform complete strangers what's waiting for them around the corner. Of course, the soup could taste like watered down wee and you're not in the least bit interested in buying it, but that's not the point. It's free.

So when you come to these food exhibitions, it's like that. Except five gazillion times better. People queue for little polystyrene pots of shredded chicken. People who hate curry and hate queuing but man, this food is free and there for the taking. Case in point, the lady stood in front of me with two carrier bags filled to the brim with Schwartz stir-in sauces, everything from pasta bake to Thai curries. She has that look about her that says 'I am here to get my money's worth, I am here for the free food.' Not that I'm judgemental. I applaud your skills, good woman.

It takes me back to when Matt and I were students and first dating. We were poor, young, reckless. Life hadn't become serious and pregnant yet, so we spent most days watching *Neighbours* (twice; those were the omnibus days), drinking pints, and eating rubbish; the days when I got taken out for a kebab and considered it haute cuisine. I considered Matt a fling until that point. A very kind fling with good hair and taste in coats. And because we were both juggling loans and finances, I forsook all the presents that come with the initial throes of courtship, settling instead for gestures: tea in bed, him giving me his last Rolo, and what I had thought at the time to be the most gallant and impressive thing a boy had ever done for me – when we crashed the Freshers' Fair and he walked three circuits of the Student Union so he could acquire us fourteen free Pot Noodles. I remember Matt handing them to me the same way a parent gives their children Haribo; 'I'm not sure what I'm giving you has any nutritional value but I've never seen you so ruddy happy. Have them, don't eat them all at once.' I remember feeling impressed by his bravado, his resourcefulness, thinking this was someone to hold onto. To note, I did eat them all that week – I'm not sure my taste buds have ever recovered. I know my skin didn't; zits the size of flying saucers appeared on my chin in protest. I'm surprised it didn't scare Matt off.

'It's Tina.' Schwartz lady is beaming at me and I'm brought back to the room. I smile and scribble my name over my book. Not only has she Schwartz sauces but I also see a rucksack on her back filled with noodles, yoghurts, crisps, and most importantly, a wine glass in the place where a water bottle should be. This woman is armed and ready. I've decided I like Tina, so I put a couple of kisses after my name. 'I love your book. You doing any telly soon? I'd watch you over that Nigella bird – posh up-her-own, you know?' I laugh but not too loudly as I have a feeling Nigella is in the building somewhere.

'Oooh, I don't know … watch this space. Not sure telly's ready for me yet.' She laughs. She hasn't let go of her bag of sauces, not once. She reaches in for a hug and a selfie. Luella intervenes.

'Remember to hashtag JoolsCampbellGoodFood.'

Tina disappears to a stall giving out focaccia samples, on a mission, with my cookbook in hand as I watch another face appear behind her.

'Oh my god, I love you!' She comes in for the hug. 'Can you make it out to Lauren?' Lauren has a wine glass in her hand. Obviously she's not as prepared as Tina and lined her stomach with samples as she seems overly excited to see little ol' me. But I can forgive someone who likes a tipple. She gets kisses too.

I've been here all day. My lunchbox demo was at 2, where I showed people how to make their own muffins. How did it go? Well, apparently I swear too much. You just can't tell the public to get any old crap from the bottom of the fridge, toss it in batter, and make muffins with it. Nor can you say, '... cupcakes! Which ruddy child wouldn't like a cupcake for lunch?' Lying. Also frowned upon when it comes to children. 'Just don't tell them there's mushrooms in it. Half the time, I lie to get them to eat. Courgettes? Hot cucumbers!'

But Luella says it makes me personable and funny. While a lot of the chefs come here preaching about their organics and presenting high style food cooked in record time, I'm doing what 90% of cooks do. I'm telling people to stick with cheddar (it's safe, it won't let you down). I'm picking bits of shell out of my cracked eggs. I'm swearing at an oven door because it's spring loaded. That was the worst bit, actually. According to Luella, you can't call inanimate objects, 'cheeky feckers'.

So now I sign books in my corner of this cavernous hall as the sound of other chefs' voices echo over the loudspeaker. People flurry past and point and take photos from a safe distance. Others queue to get their ten seconds chance to speak to me and I answer truly inane questions: where are my children? What's your favourite colour? Do you own a spiralizer? (At home; yellow; no, but I think I have a Play Doh attachment that could achieve the same results), and I pose for photos, trying to perfect my toothless, sincere smile and watching Luella as she gestures for me to turn my head to the left and lift my double chin. The admiration is humbling, embarrassing, and almost confusing. To think people look at you and like you, that they've spent time reading your books and listening to what you have to say. I'm just me – little ol' South London mum, me. I am no different to you, bar the fact my publicist has chosen my outfit. The fact these people want to listen is a true surprise. I've spent nigh on ten years trying to get four people much smaller to listen to me. And nothing.

Lauren, in front of me, is rosy, young, and I suspect has come here on a lunch break to get sloshed. Free alcohol, that's surely one-up on free food. Luella and I should know. Since we got here, people have been awesomely kind with their free wares and products. I now have my first Le Creuset casserole (possibly heavier than my four kids combined), knives with different coloured handles, and a personalised apron I'll never wear but will possibly bring out for barbeques. And the food. Wagamama can wait for tonight as we are stuffed. I've had sushi, goat curry, jerk chicken, satay, macarons, and wine. All the wine. Luella pushes another glass in front of me.

'This is a lovely rosé from our friends at Le Château de Papeneuve.' We clink glasses.

'*A votre santé*!' We are that tipsy that Luella is speaking French. It slides down a treat as I sign my book for my next fan and friend, George.

'Like Peppa's brother?' Not that there is any other way to spell George but he laughs and goes with it and I draw a strangely conceived smiley face. Everyone is nice. They're all getting kisses. Luella notices that I'm losing control of my Sharpie and bends over to police our selfie before I forget how to use my face.

'Here, have some of these puff pastry thingies, soak up the alcohol a bit.' I give a thumbs up. I'm presented with a serviette and canapé type objects I only ever see at weddings and I down three at once.

'Hmmm, yum! What are they?' Luella shrugs. They could be some newly conceived bite involving sheep placenta but they are very tasty and lining my stomach a treat. I eat two more.

'Pastry! Gluten! Got to love it!'

A new face appears, not holding a book. I bite on my bottom lip knowing it's covered in puff pastry confetti. She puts her hand out.

'Jools, a real pleasure.' I reluctantly put my serviette down.

'Likewise?'

She smiles. 'I'm ...'

'Maggie Matthews,' interrupts Luella. She stares at her in a weird fangirl way, the same way I stared at Mary Berry earlier, quietly and with the look of someone dangerous until her security whisked her away. I look between them as they share handshakes.

'I won't keep you, but I loved your show. I think I might have a project lined up that we'd love you to be part of. Are you free later for a chat?' Luella may as well take my chin and nod up my head for me.

'Perhaps the Lanson tent? We could have a drink.' This is why I have Luella here. I would have suggested the Ben & Jerry's concession. Maggie nods and saunters away, dressed in a camel coloured coat, white shirt, and the sort of skinny tailoring reserved for people with money and non-existent hips. Luella is doing a little dance, the most animated I've seen her since I told her Tommy and Kitty had split up. I laugh, watching as her lacquered bob jigs up and down. She hugs me from the back and kisses my head.

'Errr, what just happened?'

'Maggie Matthews. You know who Maggie Matthews is, right?'

'Bernard Matthews' wife?'

Luella, who normally doesn't rise to my rubbish sense of humour, thinks this is hilarious, which makes me think I have a project lined up involving turkey.

'You, Mrs Campbell, have just been headhunted by the Head of BBC programming. She is the dog's danglies – big fan of female representation in the media. People listen to her. If she wants you then we are talking big, big stuff. This is the motherload.'

Funny, but when she talks load I still take it back to laundry. I think about cooking for half hour show segments in my pastel kitchen, my stuff separated into little bowls. It was everything I took the piss out of the first time round. But now they want me? How is this happening? Maybe it's a bloopers show. That, or it's one of those antique/property/lifestyle shows they show mid-morning when no one's really bothered. I'm a little confused, possibly a lot drunk. I look around as fans line up, take pictures, and a mum encourages her daughter to wave. I wave back. I think of my own kids. What's happening here? A project? For me. I revert back to my canapés in a bid to quell my stomach's somersaults. From excitement, nausea? I don't know. One minute I was happy to let it be; it was just a book and I was going to disappear into obscurity. But then my roof caved in and I've jumped right back into the pool. There are fewer sharks this time. The waters are calmer, clearer, like a warm bath. Crap, am I enjoying this? Well, there is wine – what's not to like?

'I knew it!' Luella cups my cheeks and gives me a

huge smacker on the lips. The next person in line doesn't know where to look as she puts my book in front of me.

'Ignore her! She's on the wine.'

'Aren't we all? Please could you make it out to Jackie?' she replies. I smile, listening to Luella making a call to someone at her office and waxing lyrical about my big break. Before, I was just someone capitalising on a small amount of fame; now the BBC are knocking.

'Are you married to Nicky Campbell, the radio DJ?' Inane question #645 of the day.

'Afraid not. My husband is Matt. He is Scottish, though.'

This seems to satisfy her curiosity and she goes in for the selfie and then disappears. I realise someone's missing from this picture. The only person in the world I want to share this semi-exciting news with isn't here and I feel it in the pit of my stomach. I look up, trying not to let alcohol and this sudden sadness consume me.

Then I see someone in the corner of my eye It's a wonder I do given the number of people, but I see him standing behind a dried fruit and nuts concession. It's slightly unnerving the way he's half hiding behind the stall gazebo but I find myself looking back and catch his eye. He looks different. It's possible he dyed his hair before because now there are touches of grey to the sides. He's definitely less trendy but something else is also very much missing. That jump in his stride, the colour in his face, the cheekiness in his eyes. McCoy, what the hell happened? I'm not sure why, but I go to wave. I put my hand in the air but as soon as he sees it he pulls a hat over his head and walks away.

'And then Mikey hit him on the head with his book bag and he got sent onto red ...' The screen freezes so I don't hear the last of that sentence. It makes it sound like little

Mikey got sent to Reading, which seems quite an overzealous punishment for some book bag pelting. The exhibition finished an hour ago so it's a quick return to the luxury of the Holiday Inn to spend some quality digital time with my children before bed. Before, I used to hear about their days as they sat in the back of my car – usually all at once. They spoke over each other, they ate crisps like farmyard animals, and kicked the back of my seat as they told me what they had had for lunch, which teacher was having a baby, and who got sent to the school office that day. Now it's all done via Facetime while I sit in a hotel room and they show me intricate close-ups of their nostrils and intermittently jump around the sofa so they look like huge fur-balls of hair in matching school uniforms. I pictured this scenario differently – Apple always advertise these chats of children sitting still, being read bedtime stories, and doing cute hand gestures to signal how much they miss their mum. I see Jake's hand gesture and there is nothing cute about it as he wafts what I assume to be a fart towards his big sister's face.

'I HATE YOU! Daaaaaddd!'

I haven't seen Matt's face since this call started. He's mainly been a flurry of limbs trying to keep Millie on screen and separate warring siblings. I hear a series of thuds behind everyone.

'The builder's still there?' I'm shocked by the man's commitment and industry, it's nearing 6.30 and I expected him to be a half a day kind of man.

'He's called Phil. His bum hangs out a lot.' The children all agree this is hilarious, the twins especially, who hang their trousers from their hips. Matt grabs control of the iPad.

'Right, all of you upstairs. Bath time and no fighting over the loo. Girls first. Go!'

I hear the thunder of footsteps as Matt grabs Millie and

puts her on his knee. She sees my face and claws at the screen.

'Phil and his unfortunately hairy crack had to stay behind tonight. The foundations are waterlogged.' My skin tightens. What does that mean? Is the house sinking like the Titanic? How much will this cost? Matt reads the worry in my face.

'Don't worry, it's just pissing it down. He needs to bail out the groundwater.' I breathe a little more lightly. 'So, tell me what you know.'

'Too much … I saw McCoy today.' I'm not sure why I lead with this. There are far more exciting things to mention, but seeing his face today reminded me why I was here in the first place, of everything that's happened in the past eighteen months that have snowballed into me being here, entertaining the idea of being a very minor but real celebrity.

'Bothered. Unless he looked like he'd suffered a major, life-changing injury.' Matt's lack of sympathy is jarring but understandable given McCoy's complete disregard for my privacy and family, something Matt was, and still is, so fiercely protective of. 'He looks like he'd lost some hair.'

'It's a start. I want to hear about Maggie Matthews and her tailoring.' I smile. Since meeting her, all I've wanted to do is tell Matt. So far it's just been me sending him a string of incomprehensible texts:

MEETING WOMAN FROM THE BBC!
GOOGLE MAGGIE MATTHEWS!
SHE'S WEARING SHOULDER PADS!
THEY HAVE FREE KATSU CURRY HERE!
YOU'D BE IN YOUR ELEMENT!

21

This used to be our thing; some mum would be a cow at the school gate, they'd forget to collect our bins, I'd meet a celebrity chef in the supermarket and he'd be the first person I'd think to call. He always used to listen to the dull minutiae of my existence and take it all in, regardless of how interesting or relevant it was to him. I miss that. I miss him, just being next to me. I remember the days when I used to think being on my own in a hotel room, sat in a dressing gown on a bed not laden with muslins and sheets that hadn't been changed in a fortnight would have been bliss: a proper night's sleep, space. Now it's the quietest, most clinically dull place in the world.

'So, I had champagne and got royally schmoozed ...' I inform him.

'That's such a Luella word.'

I laugh. 'They want me to be a judge on a cooking show.'

Matt can hardly control his giggles. 'You? But ...' I can't be offended when that was my reaction, too. How the hell does someone with amateurish cooking skills at best judge others in that same arena?

'Unless they're replacing that bloke from *Masterchef*?'

'Nope, it's kids cooking. It's a show called *Little Chefs* and they want me to be the nice maternal one who hugs the kids when they burn stuff and cry.'

Matt nods his head from side to side – this sounds more like my area of expertise, doling out sympathy for bad cooking. 'What do you think? Could be all right? What are the terms?'

This is why everyone should have a Luella. Had I been left to my own devices, drunk and loved up, I would probably have dared to hug Maggie Matthews, agreed to do it there and then and probably would have declined payment. But Luella stepped in, she wanted me to have to work a four-day week at most with the option to decline

22

publicity, and negotiated a contract there and then. A proper contract with proper money attached to it. For me. And all I had to do was try food and hug sad children.

'Well, let's just say when I thought the cookbook could keep the children in shoes, now this might just pay for a bit more.'

Matt sits up as I repeat to him the figure Luella wrote on a Lanson serviette. He jumps up, surprisingly high for someone holding a baby and electronic device and half embedded in the sofa.

'Fucking hell, Jools, that is ... what the ...!'

I couldn't believe it at the time. I still don't now. Matt rolls around on the sofa with the baby, giggling like he's done some rounds in the Lanson tent. Seeing him so happy is warming. This is why I was doing this, right? To lighten that financial load and look after my family. But I know that Matt knowing he might not have to return to work may have healed a part of his soul. I want to celebrate with him. We need to hug this out. I look closer at him as he rolls around on the sofa.

'Why are you wearing a shell suit?'

'Oh, we have a development. I've been asked to coach Jake and Ted's football team.'

'So you bought a shell suit?'

'It's the club uniform.' He looks like a very early nineties' David Beckham. I'm not sure if I find that attractive at all. But even so, he is over there and I am up here.

'It's nothing, just me telling small boys to share a ball and not run in the wrong direction in the park.' He'd be good at that, and I beam thinking about how him being at home means he has the time to get involved in this and be with his twinnies.

'It's awesome.'

'Scary more like! Do you know Michelle Richmond?'

'Silver Renault Scenic?'

'Think so. Big lass, arms like legs of lamb.'

I'm not sure Michelle would be so fond of the description but I nod.

'She's a piece of work … ideas above her station. Thinks her son should try out for Chelsea.'

'And why not?'

'Because the kid's got an attitude. Obviously from the mother. I've met dog turds with more charisma.'

'Matt!'

I suddenly remember Matt's amazing candour and lack of people skills. I've encountered Michelle Richmond before, when she barked at me for taking her parking space outside the school. At least she'll have a worthy adversary in Matt. I laugh.

'Isn't this weird? It used to be me telling you about the mums and you in your hotel room after an audit.'

He smiles. 'This time round you're doing something far more interesting than I ever did. I am so proud of you, you know. This is … it's amazing news. You're happy, right?'

Matt asks me this a lot now. When this started, when I had my huge crises of who I was and where I was supposed to be in life, Matt gauged this as a measure of how happy I was. I hated how he thought I wasn't happy. I was. I just hadn't realised it. But today, I can't not be over the moon to see him, to hear him like that. And of course, Luella and I totally lost our cool when we signed on that bottom line. We danced about like loons in a totally undignified fashion that may have involved a little bit of co-ordinated thrusting. But after the ink had dried, they started clearing up that huge exhibition hall, chairs were folded, and people started to leave. And I was left holding a contract, still missing the one person I wanted to hold tightly in celebration. I touch his screen on the face.

'I'm back on the rollercoaster.'

'But this time, you're in charge. People are going to get to know the real you and fall in love with you.'

'Like you did?'

'I kind of got stuck with you. I've learned to love it.' I laugh, ear to ear, head knocked back. 'What are you doing tonight? Are you out celebrating?'

I nod but he knows I'm lying. 'I dropped Luella back to her room about an hour ago. Apparently, she can't mix wine and bubbles.' I left her in the recovery position on the floor of her room, bolstered with dressing gowns, pillows, and towels after she curled up in a heap and I realised I was too much of a weakling to get her into bed.

'It's a big deal. You should celebrate. Does the hotel have a bar? Go get a drink.'

'You should be here.'

'I know.'

There's a pause as neither of us know what to do next. Being apart is a new one. In fact, in over ten years together I've recently worked out we've never spent more than two nights apart. Whether this is immensely sad or romantic, it does feel that maybe we're meant to stay in close proximity to one another or the universe doesn't really work. Millie seems to register surprise at seeing my face again and puts her little chubby fingers on the screen. I'm missing bath time. I'm missing the cuddles, the smell of strawberry shampoo, pyjama time. That said, so is Matt.

'You better go and monitor baths. You know Ted likes to overfill the tub.'

He salutes me. 'Big love, Mrs C.' He waves Millie's hand about. 'Come find us tomorrow. We miss your face.' And he hangs up. It's what Matt does, he doesn't draw out goodbyes, mainly because it's not his style and because he doesn't like to see me crying.

CHAPTER THREE

I'll let you in on a secret. I like to drink by myself. Whether that makes me slightly weird and depressive, I don't know but I think it's a result of four children and a husband who used to be so washed out from a working day commuting into London that I used to spend most nights cuddling a bottle of wine, a box set involving love triangles and hospitals, and a small mountain's worth of ironing. I once met a mother who told me she didn't drink; she didn't like losing control, the hangovers, the taste. It was a deal breaker. I knew that I would never be friends with that mother because I used to love cheeky glasses of wine on my own. I'd hold that glass (sometimes a mug; I was lazy like that) to my face with both hands and sup at it like communion wine. I was owed this. For the sleeplessness, the constant insanity, for all the daily incidents that involved wee, poo, and snot – maybe all three. This was mine. I wasn't going to share. I was going to drink it all myself until I passed out on the sofa, usually having ironed nothing but mumbling to myself that they never should have killed off McSteamy. Me, and my five-pound bottle of wine that would have cost three times as much if I were drinking it in public. Where I'd probably have to share it with someone and only get two and a half glasses worth. And worse, had I had to drink this outside of these four walls, I'd have to *gasp* get changed: into clothes with actual form and fitted waistbands.

I'm thinking about those bottles of wine now as I start on my £5.25 glass of Chardonnay in the Holiday Inn bar.

Ouch. I made it to the bar in the end, mainly because I have that voice in my head that dissuades me from drinking cans of Coke from the minibar but also because staying in my room felt sad. Not that I've suddenly become some swish bar-drinking sort. I did change into my hotel slippers. Classy yet comfortable. I didn't have the nerve to ask for the bottle, mainly because I knew I might end up swigging from it (which I did all the time at home – less washing up), but I think about what this glass means. This isn't wine in response to the twins beating each other up over badly divided pizza. No one is ill and downing Calpol. No one has had a meltdown because I won't let them watch another episode of *iCarly*. This glass of wine is for me, because something awesome has happened. I want to high-five myself. I don't, of course, but I fiddle with my coaster and take another large sip. Well done, Campbell. The BBC are building you a project. Whatever that means.

'Are you the woman ... you know, the cooking one?'

The barkeeper is a young girl with too much eyeliner but I like the way she wears black bobbly tights like me. *Hi! I'm Orla!* says her name badge. I nod and smile.

'Is there something going on in town? We've had all you cooking sorts about.'

'There was a food exhibition.'

'Where they exhibit food? What, like a gallery?'

I laugh and almost feel like I need to educate the girl.

'It's like a big event where there are lots of chefs and food samples and wine ... free wine.' Orla smiles at me as I'm definitely still a walking advert for the free wine. Is it the slippers? Or maybe the fact I've let my hair down, so I look like a banshee caught in a stiff breeze.

'Sounds all right, I guess.' I like Orla's soft Mancunian accent but doubt her sincerity. You wait till you're on a budget and free food samples are the only thing to lift your day. She goes to serve someone at the end of the bar: a businessman who scans me up and down, gets to the footwear, and knows to steer well clear. This is not someone who wants an illicit encounter with a stranger in a bar. This is a woman drinking for comfort. He smiles, raises his drink, but makes a swift exit towards the group of women by the veranda who are too uniformly pretty to be normal. I assume they're airline stewardesses.

I won't lie, as far as bars go, it's a bit dull. The sort of place you go to start an evening as a meeting point. The lighting is turned down way low in an attempt to make us ignore the green upholstery and matching carpet. There's some panpipe muzak coming from somewhere, and ads bandied about telling us of impending deals for Christmas functions. There's a couple sat behind me who seem to be having a cheeky drink before they head out. Or maybe they're on their way in. Is that a nightcap? I look at my watch: 8.30 p.m. If it is, that's a bit sad. The couple look like they're on a break together. I can imagine the scene now: *Martin, let's go for a romantic break away. Manchester Holiday Inn have some deals on? Perfect. I'll pack the sex toys now.* I laugh to myself, which makes Orla at the end of the bar curious and a little worried as I teeter on my stool. Further along, the random businessman seems to be having a laugh with his bevy of girls. I spy a wedding ring, you cad.

At the opposite end, three men eat burger remains and discuss the contents of each other's laptop screens, their ties pulled down low, bags under their eyes. That was Matt once. Matt who'd stare at computer screens filled with numbers and charts. He hated it but it paid well and it kept his kids in fish fingers. I want to go over and hug them but know better. I signal to Orla.

'Hun, can you send three bottles of Corona to the gentlemen over there?' I point over my shoulder badly so it looks like I'm suggesting she send it to the chandelier light fittings. 'Don't let them know they're from me. It's just ... they look a bit frazzled.'

Orla smiles. 'Bless you. Do you know them?' I shake my head. She goes to the fridge for the beer then comes back, looking over my shoulder. 'Who did you say again?' Her face looks stern and anxious. 'Gentlemen or man?' I turn round.

'Those three blokes over ... oh ...'

She awaits my instructions but I'm speechless. There's a man sat behind me, nestled away in a hidden armchair. He raises his glass to mine. I fall off my bar stool, quite literally flat on my frigging face. What the fuck? How the hell did I not see him? I suddenly feel two arms around me helping me to my feet. One of them belongs to Orla, the other to Tommy McCoy, the man who was nestled in that armchair. My first instinct is to shrug him off, walk away, hold up a hand to signal no communication. Orla reacts shocked, like what she says next may be instrumental in how the rest of this episode should pan out. We all stand there in perfect silence as I smooth down my trousers.

'Hi.'

'Hi.' I reply.

Orla giggles nervously.

'Are you all right? I'm not sure, do I need to call my manager? You might have to fill out an incident form.'

It's my turn to laugh. 'I'm fine, just me and swizzly chairs and alcohol. Not a good combo.'

His face doesn't show anything. No worry, no hate, no concern that I may have just scraped half my face off. At once, I wonder what he thinks about me. Maybe he's come via the cutlery stand and has a steak knife hidden up his sleeve. He'll stab me in the stomach so I'll die slowly and he'll stand over me telling me how I took his life, how I ruined him. *They found her in hotel room slippers with an extraordinary amount of wine in her veins.*

'Maybe I can get you two a drink? On me. Not every day I have two celebrity chefs in my bar.'

I'm torn between accepting free alcohol and the idea that the alcohol presented would most likely have to be consumed in his presence. He speaks first.

'Two gin and tonics. They're on me, bill them to my room.'

'What number, Mr McCoy?'

'442.'

I nod to signal my approval. We've moved onto hard liquor. Balls. If my experiences with alcohol have taught me anything, spirits make me pass out in strange places and give me hangovers from hell. But I'll play this game. The mood is still strangely silent.

'Thank you.' He pulls a chair up next to mine and sits down. Maybe this is one of those assassination attempts with added tension built in for drama's sake. Like from *The Godfather*, we'll have a half hour of monologues before he pulls that steak knife on me. I look down and notice his footwear. Hotel slippers. The fact we match is hugely disconcerting. Orla pours our drinks but studies us closely. Who will be first to crack? Will glass be broken? Don't make me get out the hoover.

'I saw you at the Good Food Show.'

He nods, slowly scratching his neck. Up close, the things I noticed before are definitely gone. His face is pale and drawn and the eyes look lost. What are noticeably absent are the wanky clothes and accessories: the neon trainers, the weirdly conceived denim. Instead he's in plain 501s and a white tee.

'Ladies and gentlemen, I present to you the Greel. Not just a grater and not just a peeler. It takes microscopic layers off your veg and can be folded into the size of a pen so you can take it out with you.'

'Why would you need to take it out with you?'

'Some git asked me the same thing today.'

'People often have carrot based emergencies …'

I'm not sure if he finds it funny but he picks up his drink and downs it, including chewing the lemon slice. I mouth quietly to Orla at the bar, how many? She puts five fingers up then slowly backs away.

'Barkeep, another when you're ready!' My eyes open. Do I do what I always do, bring him down a peg or two and tell him to stop? Pedantry can wait. Orla awaits my permission and I nod that she is allowed to proceed. Tommy sings some song about the Greel. It rhymes with peel, steal, and deal and seems to have the tune of a nineties' pop anthem by D:Ream. I find myself bopping along to try and ease the tension.

'Greel. It's one letter away from gruel. I don't know why I put myself through it.'

'Why did you?'

He laughs.

'Something called child maintenance, Mrs Campbell. Some of us have to earn a living to keep their ex-wives in foreign holidays and handbags.'

His drink ready, he clinks my glass and takes a gulp. I sip mine politely. I think back to when my dad used to drink gin every Friday night, slumped in an arm-chair, slightly morose about the fact his wife had run off with the beardy geography teacher and he hadn't the slightest clue what he was going to do with three kids on his own.

'I … I thought you were just separated.'

He looks at me then looks away.

'Oh no, the divorce was signed a month ago. She is free to do as she wants, climb that celebrity ladder to find the next sod who'll have her. The next stupid, stupid sod … You have to know I didn't hit her. I would never hit her.'

He looks into the distance, a tear in his eye, to such an extent that I think I may believe him. It was the saddest thing to come out of this situation, that Kitty was indeed as shallow as we all guessed she really was. Because when the human bankroll that was Tommy stopped providing her with the lifestyle she was used to, she left, trying to masquerade her departure with rumours that Tommy had hit her and left her with a black eye. From egg beater to wife beater, the papers said. It broke Tommy; none more so than when she walked out that door with their kids and restricted his access to them. I put a hand into his and squeeze it, I'm not sure why.

'Do you get to see your kids?'

'I'm allowed supervised visits. In a room with no sharp edges. They may as well put me in a cage.'

The sarcasm levels in his voice are rising, as is the volume. The couple sat behind us finally have a reason to be here: real life entertainment. Let's sit here with our boring, over-priced drinks and watch the fall of a once (semi) great man.

'I haven't held my daughter for over a month now. She's scared of me. Kitty said some goddawful things and now she thinks I am scary. Me? AM I SCARY?'

In a word, now, at this very moment, yes, you are scaring the frigging Jesus out of me. I know what this is all leading up to. I know why you feel this anger towards the whole situation.

'No. You're not scary. I've never found you scary.'

He laughs under his breath.

'Touché.' He squeezes my hand that bit tighter. 'You … it all started with you.'

I hold my breath for a moment to try and compose

myself. His implication is that I've broken up a family, I've deprived children of a father, I was the culprit in making this happen. It's heartbreaking but I can't take this lying down. Neither can he. Because, for some reason, he is now down on the floor on one knee and taking my hand.

'Oh, gentle crusader, defender of all mothers across the land who doth have a hard life. Tell me what is next for me. You started this, tell me how I should finish this shitstorm of a life.'

I look down at him. 'Get up, you twat.' He's shocked by my candour and steadies himself up, grabbing at my knee as he does. I push him off.

'Sorry, so sorry.'

'Tommy, you married a cow. And you married her long before you ever met me.'

I stare at him long and hard because he should appreciate that I also know about the circumstances under which they got together. The bare truth is that he was dating Luella and then tossed her aside to be with blonde Kitty who fitted in much better with his brand image.

'Oooh, sanctimony! You sit there all precious but you and me are alike. We met our spouses under less than traditional circumstances from which four children were born. Yes, my wife was a cow, but I stuck around because I had kids, because I had a family to look after and you … rug, pulled, feet …'

He downs the rest of his drink. I notice the mockney best mate act has disappeared and he almost sounds normal.

'Shots. Whisky. Now'

Orla does as she's told. I stare at him.

'It was a charade, Tommy. She used you to get ahead and dumped you when the chips were down. That is not a measure of a person. I bloody saved your bacon.'

34

He laughs under his breath. 'Two food analogies in one sentence ... we'll make a chef out of you yet.'

He tries to point at me but doesn't as he's clearly had far too much to drink. Instead, he points at the menu beside me then to the bar.

'And my kids? They were no charade. I miss them, I miss them so bloody much.'

At this point, knowing how just two nights away from my brood has me tearing up, I squeeze his hand again. We sit there in awkward silence. On the one hand, maybe I did do this. I pre-empted a family split that's left a man without a career and a family. On the other hand, he tried to set my family asunder. He paraded me around the media as his adversary, tore me apart, and questioned my marriage in the public arena. I squeeze a bit harder, hoping my nail might pierce skin. The dichotomy of emotion I'm feeling brews away with the copious amounts of alcohol I've consumed. What the hell are we doing here? I'm not sure what I'm supposed to say. 'I'm sorry' sounds trite. He made his bed, he must lay in it. But the part of me that is human – a mother, and someone who understands celebrity a little bit better now – knows he's been stripped apart and laid bare. He's at an all-time low.

'She called me a failure. She didn't even walk out on me, I was out at a meeting with some bloke about olive oil promotion and she left when I was gone. That's not even walking out, that's just disappearing ... poof ...'

He blows into the air like a magician, bar the fact there is a lot of spit involved. He also drools slightly out of the left side of his mouth.

'And her new man friend?'

'Oh. Jaiden. He was waiting in the wings, lined up to take her in his tattooed arms and rescue her from the terrible life I'd left her with ... the life she'd always wanted, that she'd pushed for … the magazines, the stupid merchandising deals. That stupid yoghurt ad?'

I know the ad of which he speaks. It involves a trampoline, matching white linen, and giant juggling spoons. At this point, he rubs his eyes like a small orphaned bear, leaving the skin all red and blotchy.

'For better or for worse, for richer or for poorer, for celebrity or lack thereof …'

I turn to patting him on the back in the same way a man friend who'd been screwed over by a woman might do. I've been screwed over by women – school gate mums, my own mother … I know a slight variation of what you've been feeling. Pat, pat, pat. My hand lingers a moment too long and I snatch it away. Drink, all the drink. I knock the rest of my gin back wondering how low this conversation can get. The gin won't help. Must lighten mood.

'You need to tell me one thing.'

Tommy looks at me curiously.

'Did she really make her own crisps?' Tommy laughs, gurning at the same time. It's the sort of face you think looks vaguely attractive when you're drunk but someone takes a picture of it for posterity and you look like you have a second row of teeth.

'Did she fuck! We had this lovely little Filipino woman called Marigold who used to make them. Kits would have her there all day with the ruddy mandolin. Marigold did the fricking cooking when I wasn't there. Kitty would be on one of her weird diets and she'd freak out and not be able to touch food because it'd displace her mental resistance so she would be languishing while Marigold would feed the kids.'

'That's an amazing name.'

'She was amazing. Kitty took her too.'

I'm not sure what else there is I can say. I am

heartened by the fact that all this time, when I imagined Kitty doing amazing things with heritage potatoes while I just reached for a bag of Squares, it was all a lie. I feel slightly better about my existence. But McCoy doesn't care, he's starting to rock gently in time to the muzak in the room. Is that panpipe Taylor Swift? Kill me now.

'But you can rebuild? It's not like you to go down without a fight. Maybe your marriage is broken but you could go back to cooking, work things from a different angle?'

He gives me a look, the same look Matt gives me when I put the milk in before the teabags. That's just ridiculous.

'Have you not heard what I've just said? I don't care about the money. I care about my children. I love those kids.'

'Then show them, work to get them back. This, here, this is not the father they need at the moment with the self-pity and the anger. You've got to ...'

I need to tell him to grow a pair, but instead of saying the words I seem to gesticulate the meaning instead, which piques the interest of onlookers. I stop. And before I have the time to react, to respond and tell him to show how much he loves them, fight for them, it starts. Man tears. Big fat man tears. If there's one thing that always stakes at the very heart of me, it's men crying. Phil Mitchell in *EastEnders*, my dad when we told him he was a grandfather, Olympic athletes who thank their mothers.

'She's right, I am a mess.'

And with that he lies himself across the bar and I see his shoulders shudder against the shiny surface, tears running down the bridge of his nose and landing like raindrops. I shake my head.

'She's the fool.' He looks at me.

'I don't need your condescension today, Campbell.'

37

'She's a nasty piece of work. The truth will come out.'

'And to think I loved her.'

The tears still roll, out of loss, pity, or plain old drunken emotionality, I'm not sure but I continue to pat his back. For a while it would seem, as even Orla looks at me not quite knowing how to help. Could she go to the loo for me, perhaps? I look around and the bar seems to have emptied. Fifteen minutes of a once famous TV chef crying onto a bar top is far less interesting than once thought. Pat, pat, pat. When do I stop? The tears seem to have stopped and there is a glazed expression about him. There is snot dribbling from his nose. The mother of young boys in me wants to wipe it. I won't. Shit, wait. Is he breathing? Have I killed him? I think about things like alcohol poisoning, drug overdoses with me in the frame. I put my hand by his mouth. Definitely breathing. Orla looks at me.

'He's passed out. He did this last night.'

She comes over and pats him slightly on the head.

'Mr McCoy. Come on now. Time to go upstairs.'

'Last night?'

She nods. 'He was here with another bloke, looked like a work thing. They got slaughtered. He made it to the lifts last night, though. Mr McCoy, come on, wakey wakey!'

McCoy mumbles something under his breath to let us know he's still in the land of the living. Orla looks like this is part of her job description and starts to wipe the counter around his head, looking at her watch.

'Umm, we close in half an hour. Do you know anyone we can call to come get him?'

Like his wife? I hate to think. She'd surely arrive here with an entourage of photographers to kick him when he was down. I don't know if he's here with anyone and the only other person I think could help us in this situation (Luella) doesn't like McCoy very much herself and is also currently sparko upstairs.

'Tell me, Orla. What does one currently do in these situations? Do you have security?'

'It's a Holiday Inn. Not usually much need for it.'

McCoy's body starts to lean, his arms propped against my shoulder. What would be the thing to do? Leave him on the Holiday Inn floor? It's comfortable enough. The cleaners could hoover around him, I could use one of the sofa cushions to rest his little head on. He'd wake in the morning and get himself back to his room. No one would be any the wiser. Orla doesn't look too bothered, she's texting and obviously has plans for after her shift that don't include the moving and resituating of a drunken mess. I notice a couple of front-of-house staff come in to gawp. One gets their phone out and I try to position myself so his face is obscured. I remember the time someone caught us on their camera phones at my worst, my most combative, and started a feud that would change us forever. I think about that video. I replay it in my head. I think about grainy pictures that made their way into magazines, newspapers, and televisions. I think about his kids seeing those photos. I hook my hand under his armpit.

'Orla, was that room 442?'

She nods. 'Fourth floor.

'C'mon McCoy, walk with me … let's get you back to your room.'

Orla seems pleased I'm doing her housekeeping for her though I am disappointed she's not seeing it through with me. It makes me think I'll take off a star on my post-stay questionnaire. Tommy slumps against his stool and mumbles something about slippers. I notice he's kicked them off, and I bend down to put them back on him. I think about how I normally do this for little people who've got their shoes on the wrong feet and have tied their laces together. He arises, wobbly, slightly fragrant, but he leans against my shoulder and we take pigeon steps to the lift. I think about how this is the second drunken person I have held against my meagre frame this evening. Normally, I am carrying small children from sofa to bed. Surely tonight's exercise burns me far more calories. When we get to the lift, he falls to the floor and curls up into a ball like a small cat.

'McCoy, please. C'mon, just to your room.'

'I'll sleep here.'

'Going up and down all night, you'll throw up.' The lift pings open and I pull him by the arms, holding the door open with my sizeable arse. It's another throwback to university: helping drunk people home, hearing them cry about loves lost and lives ruined, battling with cab drivers shouting at you about fouling charges. Strangely, it makes me crave chips.

McCoy is the worst sort of drunk, the one whose body turns rock solid when still, arms droopy and lifeless, legs without bone to make them function as working limbs. At least Luella half danced her way back to her hotel room. By the time he's out of the lift, he's crawling along the carpet at a snail's rate. I walk beside him, coaxing him along like a faithful pet. He stops outside his door, face down in a star shape. I go in his back pocket and retrieve his wallet to find his key card.

'Jools. Rhymes with mules.' He laughs at his own joke.

'And fools.' Who's the fool now? I push his door open. He stumbles in. I put his key card into the wall and go to the bathroom to get him a glass of water. The mirror shows me in a scarily bright light, my hair on edge and eye make-up blotchy, far from the preened and perfect cooking lady we'd showed off at the Good Food show this morning. The taps out of focus, I also realise I am incredibly drunk; probably proved when I had the superhuman strength to drag a grown man out of a lift.

I use the facilities, take a few large gulps of water straight from the tap, and return to the room. In my absence, McCoy has removed his clothes and lies spread-eagle on the bed in pants and mismatched socks. Not that I have thought much about it, but it's what I remember from when I saw his oily chest at our cook-off: toning, some hair, but the fake tan hasn't been topped up in a while. Poor excuse for an arse, nice legs though. I divert my eyes as best I can and put the water next to his bed along with the bin. Do I tuck him in? No, but I survey the room: sandwich wrappers, old pants lying around, and like some type of sadistic torture, magazines and newspapers featuring Kitty. It's a little morose. I'm not sure what to do, so I hang some of the used clothes on the back of a chair.

'Bye then. That was ...'

I'd say painful. My back is telling me that much. But looking at him at his most vulnerable, I'm starting to think we've cleared a bit of that fog between us. I'm starting to see a human side to you that never existed. He mumbles something to me. It's of no discernible meaning but I know what he's saying. It's the international sound that tells me to lunge over to the bin by his bed and save him the hotel cleaning charge.

CHAPTER FOUR

Matt always used to tell me, the best part of being away from us was that moment you were standing in front of your house again, looking at all the windows lit up amber, and realising you were home. You were safe again. I always thought he was mad but I understand now. It's been a long forty-eight hours and I know what I want. I want long cuddles smelling the tops of heads. I want tea out of my mug with the yellow hearts. I want to embrace my husband. I want to wash the strange vomit smell out of my hair.

I stayed in McCoy's room for fifteen minutes after he threw up and the practical mum streak in me rinsed out the hotel room bin. I watched him drool into the sheets, pass wind, and hug the life out of a pillow asking it not to leave him ever again. There's little to do when you watch someone purge themselves of their stomach contents bar holding the receptacle they are vomiting into and giving them tissues to wipe their mouth. I have watched many people of different sizes vomit. I've watched a small person throw up into a full tub of Celebrations (I cried), and a full size woman (Annie) vomit outside a Boots in Leeds, making us think we'd be caught on CCTV and never allowed in again. 'Where would we buy our make up?' she wailed. But I stayed with McCoy out of some misplaced sympathy, thinking I could help, that my presence there was of some comfort. To be honest, I'm not sure he knew I was there. There was a point where he looked up at me and asked me if the kids were all right, he was sorry he'd not been around that day to help. That was when I realised he thought I was Kitty. That was when I left.

When Luella showed up at my door the next morning, I didn't allude to it, mainly because it would have riled her and because she showed up at 9.30 a.m., perky as you like, hair where it was supposed to be, face made up, clothes immaculate and preened. For a moment, she deserved my intense loathing especially as I looked like roadkill and the inside of my mouth felt like a badger's arse.

'Oh dear, look at you! Breakfast?' I shook my head. 'I assume it was you who helped me back to my room. You're a star. What did you get up to last night?'

I didn't so much reply as grunt at her.

'Haha, you little alky! Good for you! C'mon, Waterstone's in an hour and a half.'

And that was that. I did my part at the book signing; I smiled and posed and answered questions but then I got on that train and slept all the way back. Unattractive sleeping, Luella said. No one needs to count your fillings while you nap.

Standing on my doorstep, I want to put my surreal incident with McCoy behind me. I want normal and safe. The door opens before I have the chance to put the key in it.

'Mummmmmmmmmy!' It's Jake, with the best hug he's ever given me. I know now why Matt liked this. He's in his pyjamas, freshly bathed. Hannah and Ted follow suit.

'Are there presents?'

It feels wrong that they should be on the lookout for gifts as some reward for having survived without me, but they know I like to collect and hoard. There will be something about my person they can have and claim as their own.

'In my grey bag, there are colouring sets from the yoghurt people.'

'There were people made out of yoghurt?' asks Ted.

'Yes, with bananas for hair.'

They smile as Hannah comes over to study my face. She does this a lot, almost as if to ensure I am the same person, that I haven't been replaced by a robot, alien, or mother of lesser quality. She smiles and kisses my forehead. Ben appears from the front room where I can see they've been watching old *Doctor Who* on Watch, back when the Doctor was young and floppy-haired.

'Aaaah, she returns victorious. Do I get a present too?' the little brother enquires.

'Bottle of wine in my backpack.'

'That'll do. Ted tells me I should be the next Doctor.' I nod. 'I could bring back the tweed. The Doctor always looked best in tweed.' He looks at himself in the downstairs mirror, gurning and perfecting Doctorly poses. He catches sight of me looking less than enthusiastic.

'You OK, sis?' He turns around to give me one of his Ben hugs.

'Just a weird trip.' I take him to one side, thinking out of anyone he'd be glad for the gossip and could provide counsel on the matter. 'McCoy was there.' He does his comedy eyebrows and drags me into the living room.

'Matt told me ... but nothing happened, right? Shit, did he speak to you? Did you tell him where to go? Jesus Christ, I hope you wore a bra this time.'

He is half excited, half waiting with bated breath. His eyes speak that he wants drama: rugby tackling, high intensity fisticuffs.

'It was bizarre. Turns out we were staying in the same hotel. I was having a Chardonnay on my lonesome and he ended up at the bar.'

'Awkward.'

45

'Yeah. But no. We talked. There were moments of weirdness, some finger pointing. But turns out he's in a pretty shit place in his life. He laid it all out for me. Then he cried and passed out.'

'As you do.'

It sounds like a non-event. There's a part of me that feels culpable, partly to blame for his demise. I think back to a half-naked man in his bed, delirious with sadness, and I feel for the fella, I really do. But then I think of people in far worse situations and live in hope, in expectation that this is not the end for him. This is a blip. In the greater scheme of things, he'd claw his way back. Ben studies the confusion and angst in my face.

'Did he chunder?'

'Back in his room.'

'And what were you doing in his room?'

The story unfurls further, leading Ben to nod slowly to understand each strange chapter. His fists are clenched. I'm not sure what he's expecting me to say.

'I took him back to his room. I couldn't leave him in a heap in the bar, he was completely out of it. He chundered in the bin. I left him and what was left of his dignity alone.'

He studies my face curiously until I realise what he must have been thinking.

'You little sod! You thought I was in his room for other sordid reasons? Really?'

I proceed to get the sofa cushions and hit him around the head. He protects himself with a copy of *Room on the Broom*.

'I wasn't, you silly mare. I know you'd never do that, not with him as well. But a man and a woman going to a hotel room. Did anyone see you? That might look a bit dodge.'

It didn't even occur to me at the time. My greatest

worry was just making sure he got to the sanctity of his own room without anyone else seeing him all drunk and messy. We were alone in the lift, definitely. I think. I'm not sure I was so drunk that I wouldn't have noticed another person. Ben senses me recanting the scenario in my head.

'Did you see him naked?'

'Oh, you are such a tart. I saw him in his pants.'

Ben pulls a face. 'Did you disrobe him?!'

'God, no. Enough talk of him. It was just something that happened.' Ben takes my hand.

'But it obviously has affected you … you're a bit pensive.'

'It's just, you know. He has no wife, no kids, no career. I feel like me, rug, pulled.'

I pause as I realise I'm repeating verbatim the very words he used to chastise me in the bar. I did this to him. I brought a man to his knees and ruined his life. Ben takes my hands.

'He did it, love. We all saw it, the way he manipulated you: the cook-off, the bribery, the arrogance. I just can't believe you'd help him, many wouldn't have … but then you wouldn't be my sister if you left him there to rot.'

I take that as a compliment and squeeze his hands.

'Look, go and see Matt. We can talk more about this later. I want to know what he looks like in his pants. But first I need a cup of tea.' I pull another face and push him into the sofa cushions. 'Or wine. Where's my wine at?'

I leave him to forage through my bags as I make my way upstairs. I peek inside the kids' rooms and see they have found the colouring books as promised. The twins seem to have also found the Lindt samples stashed away in there too. Little sods. I smile, watching them plant the wrappers in their Lego boxes to hide. In our bedroom, two surprises. A toddler sits on the bed in her yellow onesie, clapping her hands to see me. I pick her up and twirl her around.

'Milli Vanilli! Oh, I've missed your little ginger face.' I am allowed to call her ginger as I'm her mother and she seems to know this. Anyone else define her by her hair colour or mock the locks and it is sorely frowned upon. Surprise two is what lies above me. We have a roof. Not one held together by tarpaulin, bits of plywood, and broken tiles: a proper vaulted roof.

'They need to board and plaster the ceiling up but we're watertight and they're going to start brickwork out the back soon.'

We both look up at the intricate joinery holding the roof over our heads, then at each other.

'You all right?'

'Better to be here.' He wraps his arms around Millie and me and I exhale, deep and calm. I would maintain this hold for the rest of the evening but Matt lets go and grabs the baby.

'Right, missy. Teeth time.' She giggles to be whisked away and I watch them closely as he props her on the bathroom sink and she bares her teeth for him.

'KIDS! Teeth! Uncle Ben hasn't brushed them already, don't try and get one over on me.'

I perch myself on the bed as I watch him tackle each one in turn. It's something I never tire of, watching him with them. Not that I've not seen it a gazillion times but ever since our dynamic changed and he's been here more, there seems to be greater clarity attached to every time he holds them, builds a Duplo house, or reads a book with them. You can tell this is all part of a new daily routine, one that had become mundane and stressful to me is now his every day and he loves it. Ben appears at the top of the stairs with tea for two and a tray of food for me.

'Han, Twinnies, Mills, we have a date with Uncle Ben

and *The BFG*.'

This is where Ben pays for himself. Matt trades kids for trays. I inspect the food.

'I made minestrone, my mum's recipe.' He knows it's my favourite and that the only other time I get to enjoy minestrone is as a Cup-a-Soup. He made it, proper.

'You're wearing that tracksuit again. Is this to be a new daily occurrence?'

'We had a practice tonight. Look at this.'

He runs over and produces a little whiteboard from the side of the bed with blue and red fridge magnets.

'It's a tactics board. The parents gave it to me. And look, I have my initials on my T-shirt.'

I smile broadly. These were the little things that were missing before.

'You know when you told me about those mums, I thought you were dramatising. Christ alive, they are feral.'

'Now you can bear witness to the bedlam that is the school gate. Who was it now? Paula Jordan?'

She of the gluten-free variety of children, who had media shamed me but also herself when it turned out she'd used the kids' teacher, Mr Pringle, to divulge secrets about her marriage. We don't see her much these days and are pleased to report we never have to see Jen Tyrrell, her BFF and my other arch-nemesis, since she moved her kids out of the school.

'Geez, no, I don't know half their names. I spend most of my time hidden behind that tree by the gate. But they do this queen bee thing where they stand there aggrandising their lives and the bitchery is horrific. Also, do you know a woman called Miranda Scott?'

'Mousey, always in Uggs.'

'Yep, well you'll love this. She left her husband, nice bloke called Tim who's an accountant like me, and she

49

has gone buckwild. Like she's on Tinder and she wears wet look jeggings on the pick-up. And well, there's no easy way of saying this but her son's on the football team.' He pauses '... She made a pass at me.'

There's a feeling in my gut not unlike nausea. Firstly, due to Matt's candour and his need to not hide any of this from me, but also thinking about Miranda Scott flaunting her wares about. I went to a class drinks with her once. She used to talk candidly about her sex life (Tim liked role play) and flashed her tits at the bar. Lovely pair, I should add but there is a time and definitely a place. I think about Tim. Tim who used to drop the kids at school in his Passat and was never seen without a striped shirt. Was it one role play too far? Maybe the boob flashing got too much. But the pass, I have to go back to the pass.

'She didn't flash her tits at you, did she?'

'Wait, was she the one from the pub that time?' I nod. He pulls a face which makes me glad he also thought it crass and uncalled for.

'She made a joke about my balls, then she grabbed my arm and told me she liked my accent ...'

'It is a winner.'

'Why, thank you.' He sips his tea. I won't lie, the accent was what got me into bed with him the first couple of times. I never tell him in case he thinks I'll jump any old Scottish man who comes my way, but it's very old Bond meets James McAvoy.

'So, she's got a great rack. Tempted?'

'It'd be like shagging a bouncy castle.' He smiles. I smile back.

'You're supposed to say something about steak and hamburgers at this point.'

'You and your foodie vernacular ... leave it in the kitchen. I missed you.'

'You seemed to have it covered.' I sip and signal at my

50

minestrone, quietly noticing all the vegetables and bacon cut into cubes exactly the same size.

'You know what I mean. Anything else happen while you were away? You didn't call last night to say good night.'

This is where I should tell him. He's gone full disclosure. This is my chance. Oh yeah, McCoy. We spoke. We drank. He eats whole lemon slices. I carried him to his room instead of leaving him on the floor of a Holiday Inn bar, I used his loo and left him there. In his pants.

'I have a confession ... I may have got a little bit drunk.'

Time to wimp out. Maybe it's because I know the reaction that divulging such information would illicit right now. He'd state how he was a complete tit to us, to our family (correct), that he deserves everything he's living through (kind of correct), and that I should hate him, that I should share in Matt's rage for everything he did to try and rip us apart. It would lead to a fight about how I shouldn't have been anywhere near his room or him, for that matter.

I think back to when we had these monumental fights about McCoy, about how celebrity claimed us as her bitch and nearly ruined us. And we haven't fought since. Yes, we've had our rows about teabags in the sink (this is still ongoing), bedtime flatulence, and leaving the garage open, but nothing on the scale of eight months ago. I like it. I like this acerbic edge to our conversations and the fact we can say very little to each other but know exactly what the other is thinking. I like how we can joke about Miranda Scott's boobs and know they can never come between us.

'Atta girl.' He lies down on the bed and I snuggle next to him. We've talked about McCoy in bursts since the cook-off and the incidents of yesteryear (e.g. Me: 'Look, this article says he's had to sell his farm.' Matt: 'Hahahahahaha.') But I'm learning that maybe McCoy was my blip. He was something from my past that needs to stay there. To have him in my life leads to stuff I don't want or need to confront anymore. I'm done with him. Toodle pip.

I'm awoken that evening by voices in the hallway. The clock reads 4.45 a.m. and I can only assume it's a child in need of assurance, a drink, or Ben still awake and binge-watching *Scandal*. I lie in bed, staring at the woodwork of my new roof and notice Matt is oblivious to the noise. I tiptoe outside and notice all the kids are in bed, safely ensconced to the early hour. Damn that brother of mine. I head downstairs and notice the voices sound more heated; one of those is definitely Ben's. Is he re-enacting scenes by himself again? Hang on, that's not Olivia Pope. Luella? I open the door slowly to see her waving a newspaper about, looking less like herself: no make-up and her hair scooped under a beanie.

'Jools, I've explained it to her. She stormed over. I warned her about waking the kids.'

I look at the paper and close my eyes slowly. Shit. Again? I sit down on a sofa.

'This was important. This was something you tell me, your publicist, about. "Oh, by the way Lu, when you were drunk, passed out on your bedroom floor, I was floozying it up with my mortal enemy and we had a little how's-your-father afterwards ..."'

I shake my head.

'There was none of that, thank you. I escorted a blind drunk back to the safety of his room. I didn't say anything because ...' I circle my index finger around, '... this ...'

She looks hurt, a little insulted. 'Seriously, you don't

think Holiday Inn were all over this?' She opens up the newspaper at a series of CCTV images collaged together. 'This one? Is he proposing to you? Why is he on all fours like a dog? This looks like some kinky foreplay thing.' Ben looks over at this point and pulls a face.

'He was drunk, he was crawling back to his room.'

'And you patting his arse?'

'Going in his back pocket to get his key card.'

Ben stares at the picture. 'Geez, Jools, hotel slippers?' I giggle a little, which does not impress Luella. Granted, the newspapers have done what they do best, they have taken every part of our interaction and focussed on those moments that hardly meant anything. When he was talking about losing his kids and I held his hand. When I patted his back while he sobbed – they look like moments of genuine affection. The moment I am propping him up when he collapsed off his stool looks like he is trying to mount me. It's unfortunate but just a fiction of the media's making. I have a clear conscience. If anything, I'm just a bit stupid not to think they would already have me in their sights and twist this out of sense and proportion. Luella reads the article closely.

'Look at the time codes on these pictures, why the hell were you in his room for sixteen minutes?'

For a moment I stare at Luella, wondering where this anger is from. Is it borne from serious concern about my celebrity and how this could affect my career? Or is it more personal? I know how McCoy is the most mortal of enemies to her, a love lost – is this a betrayal?

'He threw up. I helped him out. Please don't insinuate any further, Luella. It's really insulting.'

There is still disdain there. There is the fact she was not privy to our conversation or even aware of it, and some resentment that I do not share in her bilious rage towards him. I should introduce her to Matt. They could sit there and make voodoo dolls together.

'You know what? He was in that bar and we talked, like human beings do. And you know what I found out? He's at an all-time low, he has nothing. I helped him and offered him a shoulder to cry on. Shoot me. Shame on the papers for twisting this but if you think I'd go so low and desperate as to sleep with Tommy McCoy then I don't think you know me very well at all.'

And with that, the living room door opens, Matt standing there in his sea-green dressing gown. That is not a happy face.

CHAPTER FIVE

'We need full disclosure from you, Mrs Campbell. This part of the document alludes to your past. This is a family show so we need to know about instances of drug-taking, arrests, lawful convictions, and public nudity that could make their way to a public forum. Section 3.1 talks of how if we were to find out about such incidents after this contract is signed by yourself then this would void the contract entirely and expenses would be recouped with interest.'

That could very well be in French for all that was said. All I heard was 'public nudity' and I think about the time I was rooting through the laundry pile to see my last bra on the washing line and went outside to retrieve it in just my pants, the ones with the tartan Scottie dogs. I used to smoke the odd spliff at university. Matt smoked far more. He told me he took coke once at a party but ended up not sleeping for twenty-three hours. He never did it again. I once got a speeding ticket for doing forty-two mph in a thirty zone. I'm not sure when I should be opening my mouth. Luella sits next to me but studies my face.

Full disclosure.

We've been talking a lot about what this meant in recent weeks. For her, it's everything. If I so much as switch tampon brands, then she needs to know. Not because she is nosey and intrusive, but to protect me. She can't shield me from vultures if she doesn't know that I've let them out of the cage. McCoy was stupidity. I thought I was being human, decent. But apparently, there is no room for such things anymore. If I am going to be BBC, then I need to think more tactically, I need to realise that every time I wear new shoes, comb my parting in a different way, or change supermarkets I am going to gain the interest of paps and media columnists who need to fill their inches with such triviality. It was horrible to hear that my life was going to turn into this but at the back of my mind, I knew I had to think practically. About my kids, my marriage, about the roof literally only just pitched over our heads.

Matt's reaction to the McCoy CCTV scandal was far calmer than I had imagined. There was a look of pure horror but it was more directed towards the media, to the intrusive nature of the pictures. They were back in our lives, like the moths who had invaded the cupboard under the stairs. I remember when I found them the first time, the larvae, the way they flew at my face like some Hitchcockian nightmare. Then we got rid of them. They came back. Only this time we knew what to expect, I handled those mini-beasts with far more grace. Matt flicked through the photos and kept looking into my eyes.

'You didn't think to tell me?' I shrugged.

'I didn't want bad blood. I was just trying to do the right thing.'

He knew I hadn't slept with him. He knew that would have been all sorts of wrong, bordering on cruel, on completely unfathomable. He knew that McCoy could have been anyone. Some random businessman, a tramp off the street, a wronged woman, a member of staff, but I would talk it out with anyone having a bad day. I would have carried any old Joe back to their rooms if it meant helping them out. It just happened to be McCoy. I could tell he wanted to fight about this even less than I did.

'You didn't think to take him out with the rubbish?' Luella fist-bumped him at this point.

'No.'

'Then it's all lies. Luella, this is your department. Sort it out.' And with that he escaped to the kitchen to make some tea. It was 5.22 a.m. We all needed tea. Tea would make it better.

Now I'm sat in some fancy schmancy lawyer's building, bashing out the last of my contract with BBC's *Little Chefs*. You know something is above and beyond your station when there are more windows in the room than people. That's a lot of Windolene. I look out over the London skyline like an excited tourist. I'm obviously the only person in here to which this is a novelty. St Paul's! I see St Paul's! Feed the birds, tuppence a bag! Luella gives me a look, telling me to get my head back in the room. She's still waiting for that full disclosure, there must be something I haven't told her, almost like she's waiting for me to tell her I ran an online prostitution ring when I was at university, dabble in a touch of international jewel theft. But there's nothing. I think.

'Rest assured, Mrs Campbell's history is squeaky clean, I should know. Bordering on boring if I say so myself.'

I don't only have my publicist fighting my corner today but the lovely Annie acting as counsel too, looking gorgeous and official. She should be on maternity leave but I have called her away for a one-off meeting, knowing she was one of the very few I trusted to be here today. I spy her phone on the table next to us and a screensaver of the fantastic new baby in her life, Finn, looks up at me. She smiles. I don't even care she knows my life is boring and is broadcasting it. Full disclosure – it's the unfortunate truth. The contract is long and had only been handed to us in the last half-hour. Annie has a serious look about her and she's brought her lawyer pen – the one she says she only uses because it's clicky, silver, and makes her look important.

'Please can we have section 4.2 taken out, Mrs Campbell is free to entertain the media and after recent instances, I think it prudent she retain the right to defend herself in case of scandalous and inaccurate claims made about her person.'

'With the proviso that she does not give the media any clues as to the workings of the competition and remains impartial?'

'Done.'

I feel like I'm on the set of *The Good Wife*. Luella reads the same contract but highlights parts of it and has Post-its to hand. I pretend to read mine but, like I say, this could be French or any other European language I don't really know (all of them). The lawyer opposite is official; hired for expertise as opposed to any sense of manly suave, proved when he keeps taking out his hanky and Vicks inhaler. He is flanked by the familiar Maggie Matthews and another BBC boss-type. They seem different today. Before, the demeanour was kindly and welcoming – come join our side! We'll look after you! You're fantastic! I took it all on. There was champagne, there were compliments. It was hard not to. Yet today, the atmosphere is bordering on tense as Luella and Annie make their way through the contracts, the deliberate way in which they are turning pages heard throughout the whole office. I keep smiling at them, but every time I do they find ways to distract themselves, making me nervous. I break off bits of biscuit to pass the time. You know you're not in Kansas anymore when the biscuits are some posh deli biscotti that contain huge shards of chocolate as opposed to regular chips.

I look over at Annie running her fingers across the lines of the contract. Motherhood has softened her face. Fatigue will do that anyway but she suffered so much to have Finn. I don't see her half as much as I should since she's had him. Geography plays a part, the mayhem of first-time motherhood a contributing factor, but in truth, I've been a terrible friend. For someone who was a rock for me during my early adventures in motherhood, I owe her so much more. Annie sits back in her chair and does the clicky pen thing. She looks flawless in a light grey suit and chunky jewellery.

'I don't understand section 5.9. I assumed her co-stars would be the children. Of course, Mrs Campbell has every intention of protecting them. I assumed that was one of the reasons you hired her – as a mother, she totally understands the need to safeguard the emotional welfare of children in general.'

Maggie Matthews looks to her lawyer. My eyes yo-yo between everyone in the room. Luella looks on edge.

'Oh, well, as much as we like Mrs Campbell here, it was always going to be safe to assume that there would be more than one judge.'

I nod. Of course: *Bake Off, Strictly, Masterchef, X-Factor* – no one did these things alone. I never for once assumed it would just be me playing mum to all these children. Half the fun was seeing judges disagree, seeing their faces screw up to hear someone else's opinion. Luella pipes up.

'You did mention it at the Good Food Show. There was talk of Jamie Oliver at one point.'

I sit up in my seat. He is so my people, my demographic – we could do the funky parent thing and shout words like 'pukka' to the kids in our trainers and give everyone high-fives.

'Oh, as you know, Jamie has deals with Channel 4 that he's committed to and is generally a very busy man so we had to look elsewhere and think about what would capture the imagination of the viewing public.'

I stare at Luella. I wonder if she's thinking the same as me. Are they going to sandwich me between the Hairy Bikers? Am I going to have to get my test-tubes out and play cooking science with Heston? Luella is staring Maggie Matthews out. She was all fan loved-up around her earlier. Now she's reading her face in the same way predators face off on savannahs.

'Luella?'

'Who's the other judge?' She holds her gaze incredibly well. I must remember to never take her on in a staring competition. I'm not understanding the tension – the Hairy Bikers would be a disappointment but I'd have fun. I think back to our chat at the Good Food Show – they threw all sorts of food royalty names at me. There was even talk of reinventing Delia in a Mary Berry kind of way. Bring back the twinset.

'We needed a pairing that would make our viewers tune in – you know half the battle is finding that perfect dynamic that works for television. There needs to be a bit of push and pull, a bit of …'

'It's McCoy, isn't it?' Luella interrupts.

Maggie nods. Annie drops her clicky pen. My lips go dry. I can't feel my face. Annie proceeds to flick through the rest of the contract manically.

'The second judge in the show, Thomas Alfred McCoy, to be known as Tommy McCoy …'

'No,' says Luella. 'When we agreed to this, McCoy was not on the table. He was not even a remote possibility. He was selling peelers, his star was done.' Luella is seething, close to projecting a fair amount of spit across the room. Annie reads for her life, I stare at her. Get-out clause, get-out clause.

'He was. But then Mrs Campbell and Mr McCoy had their encounter and it sparked the media's interest again. It's something we couldn't ignore.'

'We won't have it. This is an ambush, it's unprofessional and I won't stand for it. I thought better of you, Mrs Matthews.'

Maggie doesn't reply but directs her next comment to me.

'Mrs Campbell. You have the potential to be a star, one of the BBC's brightest. Mrs Bendicks here has spoken volumes about your natural on-air personality. You are down-to-earth, you're the sort of celebrity we want on our channel. This could be your making.'

The way that I'm sitting, behind this big, important desk, she feels like a headmistress giving me career advice. But Luella is right, this reeks of something sneakier, something I'm dubious I want to get involved in. I stand up.

'Well, I would have very gladly taken you up on that but the last time I worked with Tommy McCoy, it was horrific. It was media slanging at its very worst. I'm sad that you think it's cause for entertainment. I don't wish to be involved in that.'

I'm not sure how I plan to make some grand exit but Luella is smiling and nodding and stands with me. Annie remains seated, looking a little more ashen.

'But you have to, you signed the contract.' She shows me my drunken scrawl next to my name. I sit down again. We were semi-drunk, overexcited. It was the BBC. It was hard not get swept away in it and we were scared they'd run off and ask someone else. Luella closes her eyes. Publicist fail to let your client sign a contract you've not read, when you were drunk, and not had verified by anyone with a legal qualification.

'What do you mean?' I say out the side of my mouth.

'Hun, you put your name to this. I can argue that they did this in bad faith without the stipulations of your involvement fully disclosed but ...'

She urges all three of us to swivel our chairs so we're facing the back wall of the room.

'This is the BBC. I am a family lawyer on maternity leave whose trousers are currently held together with safety pins. You're asking me to take on *the BBC*. If you renege on this, they have grounds to sue.'

It just gets better. Like falling in quicksand but having an elephant land on your head.

'So I have to do this? Luella?' She looks at me in pain, actual physical pain that she has let me down and not thought this through properly. She wanted amazing things for me, to see my star surge and take off, but it seems this will not come without having to pay the price. I think about that night, how I waved McCoy out of my life. Every time he'd become part of my universe, it had brought confused and emotional times. I didn't need that. I didn't need it at all. I realise at this point we are still huddled over in our chairs, bordering on rudeness. I'm not sure I care. A knock on the door gets our attention and a man enters.

'I'm so sorry I'm late. Did I miss the big reveal?'

It's not McCoy (thank God) but another suit, another briefcase. He's smirking as he looks at us. He opens his briefcase and pulls out a contract similar to our own.

'All signed and verified by Mr McCoy and his legal representation. Articles that we are contesting have been circled but nothing we can't work around. He apologises that he and his lawyers couldn't be here today.'

His soft American accent immediately grates. But why do I know this man? Luella looks at me as well. Where have we seen him before?

'I'm sorry, ladies. How rude of me. Cam, Cam Jacobs. Of Jacobs Worldwide.'

On the train up to Manchester. The man on the train. Charles.

'You!' Luella stands up. He offers a hand but she may as well slap it out of the way. He didn't have that accent on the train, he put on an accent and spied on us from behind a newspaper like fricking Clouseau.

'Croquembouche!'

Luella nods at me. Everyone else in the room is wondering why I'm talking about pastry.

'When is that wedding happening? I hope your new co-star is getting an invite. Think of the photos!'

'Croquembouche!'

I'm in that much shock I say it again. This was a man who slagged off the Greel in front of us, who heard part of a conversation that alluded to my fears about being involved in this game again. When we pulled into Manchester, I offered him a Starburst. He took a green one. Annie can sense that the BBC bodies think I'm a little doolally.

'Mr Jacobs, can I ask who you are and how you are related to Mr McCoy?'

'Publicist. He flew me in from New York recently. I'm here to turn his fortunes around, win him back some of that public favour that Mrs Campbell stripped from him.'

'None of his own doing then?' Luella adds. There is a stand-off about to happen but both of them know to do it in front of BBC head honchos is not the place. They both bite their lips, yet continue to stare each other out. Annie grabs my hand from under the desk.

'Tommy is amazingly thrilled and looking forward to working on the show ... and with Mrs Campbell. After the events of the other evening, it is so encouraging to see that they have forged a relationship, a bond ...'

I turn my head about thirty degrees to the left. 'Woah there, Cam. Relationship?'

'I think the pictures spoke for themselves. You are both adults, free to do what you want ... I mean, there was always a spark there ...'

'Right, you can shut up now.' Luella looks to me. Remember whose company we are in. Annie also looks around but does a good job of showing Cam that she is riled and defensive.

'No, I am married and have children. I don't care how sketchy you want to be but those pictures insinuated something that didn't happen. Were they your work? Was McCoy in on it? This isn't the first time he's sold me down the river.'

At this point, I can't tell if the BBC bigwigs are horrified or enthralled – either way, this was a pairing that had the potential for fireworks. They may as well be rubbing their hands together under their desks. Cam looks at me.

'He told me you had a great evening together.'

'If you call propping up a semi-comatose drunk a good night out.'

Luella looks proud of me, Annie looks like that was what I did for her every other week day at university. Cam Jacobs, you are an absolute sodding wanker. What is he trying to do? Why in the hell would I participate in this conversation when nothing has happened? The smugness, the sarcasm makes me want to do horrible things to him.

'That was not the only thing you were propping up that evening.'

And with that, I lean over the table and slap him. Lawyers in the room freeze. I can hear Luella laughing. I stare at that contract and realise what I've just done.

CHAPTER SIX

I remember when I used to sit in my kitchen and it was like some cosy Hobbit hole where I could escape from the world. In a small house like this, the living room acted as some sort of social area/playroom. If I escaped into the bedroom, the likelihood would be that I would fall asleep and be in breach of good parenting rules. The only other room left to hide in would be the bathroom, so I always escaped to the kitchen, in the well-worn chair next to the door with the cat cushion. At least there was tea. I'm sat here now on a school night with Millie. The cosiness of this hole has now been knocked out as it's become slightly more cavernous, leading to our extended family space and Matt's new favourite room: the utility room. He was seen to jig on Monday when the cabinets were fitted. 'Look at this! We'll have a room for the laundry. You won't have to hang things off radiators anymore that causes damp patches and the wallpaper to peel!' That night I found him Googling compartmented laundry baskets. I wasn't sure if I found that strangely attractive.

However, the lighting, flooring, bells, and whistles have yet to be installed so for now, my kitchen speaks industrial chic. Millie doesn't look overly impressed and puts a yoghurty handprint on the table. Jesus, my kids fricking love squeezy yoghurts but they don't half make a mess. Millie is especially good at manhandling hers and squeezing it wherever is hardest to clean. That's usually her hair, where the yoghurt makes it look like she's experimenting with colour. She reaches over to put a hand on my boob to cover me as well. Well done, Mills. While she snacks on yoghurt, I have resorted to cereal. Coco Pops, to be exact. They are my go-to comfort food, I think because after all these years there is still some magic to be found when the milk goes chocolatey.

'Me? Some?'

I can never resist the youngest one when she asks so sweetly, so let her nibble from my spoon.

'Don't tell Daddy.' I put my finger to my lips which makes her giggle. Matt is a breakfast purist. When he sees me eat cereal any time after lunch he finds it irritating, in the same way he goes ballistic when the Christmas tree goes up in November. There is a time and a place. The kitchen door opens and Annie enters, holding little Finn like a rugby ball. She looks curiously at the cereal but knows it's Coco Pops and knows better than to criticise.

'Jesus, the poo. I used the last of your wipes, I am so sorry.'

Annie is here for tea and sympathy, something she can schedule in far easier these days due to maternity leave. I shrug and pull a face about the wipes. We have cupboards of the things now (that was mainly due to Matt's organisational skills). She, however, looks frazzled and chaotic. It's strange to see her so. The Annie I knew was contract signing Annie who always looked luxurious in suits and heels and far more preened than I ever was. Now she was playing mum, the style was very pumps, jeans, and T-shirts covered in posset. This was my kind of chic.

'Chill, lady. It's poo. Tea?'

'Coffee, strong … black.'

I nod as she goes to put Finn back in his car seat, surveying the colour charts in front of me.

'You're having an orange kitchen?'

'Right, it'll look like being inside a tangerine.'

'Or an Easyjet flight.'

We both giggle. I load her coffee up with sugar like a good friend and hand it over. She takes a huge gulp.

'So, before poo explosion, I was saying, I had a friend go through the contract and if you backed out now, you could face financial backlash. Of course, they could let it go and just find a replacement but personally, I'd not risk it.'

I sigh glumly like a child who's been told they have to go to bed. It's been five days since we found out I was going to be one of the judges on *Little Chefs* alongside Tommy blinking McCoy. Five days since I bitch slapped his publicist, five days of apologies from Luella, and five days of trying to work out if there was a way I could get out of this. Annie ran everything past her lawyer friends, trying to sift through the legal bullshit to get me out of this, but solutions look thin on the ground. I could run off. Pack my family up and move to the south of Spain where we could live on a boat. The twins like the water. Maybe I could change my name by deed poll. I always thought I looked more like a Catherine. Surely they couldn't sue for breach of contract if that person didn't exist anymore?

After my unfortunate dealings with Cam Jacobs, I've spent the last five days scanning the papers for word that I may have hit him. He would be the sort to come wired up with a camera in his lapel and would have sold that on. Damn him. So every day, I scanned the pictures for leaked pictures, those same black and white grainy ones I was so used to. But nothing. Nothing … yet. Finn is angsty in his car seat and Annie tries to rock him back and forth.

'It's this low-grade grizzle I don't get. Is he hungry? He ate like an hour ago but he could sit on my boobs all day if he wanted.'

I study his face and pick him up, jigging him around the room. My phone starts buzzing and Luella's name breaks my concentration. I hold one finger up to Annie to ask her to wait.

'Hello?' Finn burps in reply. Annie looks horrified at the pitch and volume.

'Christ, is this Ted again? Lovely, give the phone to Mummy.'

'Luella, I'm holding Annie's baby ... sorry.'

'I did wonder. Look, how are we? Are we still on for tomorrow?'

I still don't know how I feel about Luella. Since Holiday Inn-gate, she seems slightly more suspicious. The trust is lacking, but she has appeared truly repentant for her part in bringing me to where I am now. Tomorrow is my first rehearsal at the BBC studios for the show. I have to be there despite my reservations.

'Luella, it's fine. I'll get there myself and meet you at their offices.'

'I can always come to you. I can get a car.'

'This will save time and money so please ...'

She seems offended at the idea, at the fact that I may not want to spend the extra time with her, but in truth, I think I want to handle this my own way, prepare myself mentally for having to spend more time with McCoy. On my shoulder Finn's drifted off and I look over at Annie, who seems baffled. She hasn't learnt the secrets of baby naps yet. Rule number one: the baby will automatically nod off once handed to another person. I sit down and finish off my Coco Pops.

'What are you eating?' It's one of my bad habits, eating while on the phone. I'm not sure Luella wants to hear the truth about the giant bowl of sugar and full fat milk, most of which Millie is eating with her hands.

'A bowl of tofu and baby spinach?' This makes her laugh, thank Christ. The problem with Luella is that I'm not sure where our relationship stands. I'm very much the kind of person who is prone to blurring the line between

68

friendship and professionalism, which is why Matt asks me to leave the house when the window cleaner comes in, purely because I spend half thetime talking to him and Matt suspects he charges us an extra fiver for his time. Luella has steered me through challenging times; without her I'm not sure where I'd be. But we also pay her a percentage of what very little I earn, which makes Matt think we should maintain some sort of boundary. All I know is that I see or talk to her almost every day. I know her kids' names, I've met her tall, French husband, and know he shaves his chest (it came up one day in conversation, wine was involved). As for the wine, I've shared more bottles with her than I care to mention. Every time I see her, we hug. This is more than a client's relationship.

Millie and I finish the last of the cereal and I feed her the milk off a spoon while continuing to leaf through my newspaper.

'Do I have to wear make-up tomorrow?'

There's silence on the end of the phone.

'I'll take that as a yes.' I sigh, knowing it'll add another hour onto my getting ready time.

'It's a rehearsal so smart casual.'

'Jeans.'

'Skinny.'

'Trainers.'

'No. You'll look tiny next to McCoy. The last thing I want people to think is that you're one of his effing elves. Something with a heel but ones you can walk in otherwise you'll be sliding around the shop like Bambi on ice.'

I laugh. I hate that she knows my clumsiness so well.

'And if I haven't said it enough, I am sorry. You know that, right? I'm working around the clock to make sure Cam Jacobs doesn't get a look in.'

The Cam issue drives Luella mad. She was angry that

he managed to get his oar in but now she speaks of him with hesitation in her voice. It's a strange thing to hear. She's told me Jacobs is legendary but as some sort of evil myth you tell your clients about so they know to watch their backs. Normally she is ballsy, no-nonsense, and able to sift through bullshit in an instant, so there's something which tells me she is planning strategies, that this man is going to test her abilities more than ever before.

'But we've got this, Luella. You're the best in the game. I wouldn't have you by my side otherwise.'

'That is true. I'll run past Starbucks on the way to the studio. Green tea OK with you?'

I seem to have lured her away from her worry. However, she is still attempting to coax me into this healthy eating lark. Normally, she'd feed me caffeine and sugar with shots and whipped dairy stuff, now it's hot pond water.

'Could I at least get a muffin?' With streusel topping and a slice of cake on the side. She ignores me in the same way I do with my kids when they ask me what happened to their Easter chocolate.

'I'll see you tomorrow, love. Get a good night's rest. It all kicks off tomorrow.'

'I know. Tomorrow, 11 a.m. I'll see you then.'

I turn to Annie, who's finished her coffee in record time and sits there studying the papers that line my kitchen table.

'I'm sorry.'

'No biggie, look what I found.'

I study the newspaper and pause. Lo and behold, Cam Jacobs on the business pages, looking all smart casual on a stage, talking to a crowd of people like he's about to unveil an Apple product. Annie reads from the text.

'Cam Jacobs spoke at a conference on Monday on the topic of people management and media savvy.' She adopts

an authoritative tone. '*Cam Jacobs has single-handedly branched out, expanding his company beyond the US and is now taking on the European market. He is known for being ruthless, slightly underhand, but has shown his tactics to yield results, stealing column inches and earnings for his large client base. He has his sights set firmly on the UK market, and has turned his hand to a famous Italian film star, who most notably was recently caught in a brothel with drugs paraphernalia.*'

We both pause as she knows she may be hitting a nerve.

'He had a very slappable face. I was very close to slapping him myself, you just got there first.'

'With my quick slappy hands,' I say, trying to recreate a swift ninja move.

She laughs. I study the picture quietly. What was most aggravating was how he was sat right across from me on that train to Manchester. Luella said he'd grown a beard for the ruse, wore glasses, and put on an accent to fool us. But she was confused as to why McCoy would be so desperate to employ his services. He was Grade-A scum, smarmy, evil glint in the eye genius, the sort in a zombie apocalypse who'd be running away, leaving small children in his wake as bait to aid his escape. I spy Annie looking at her watch.

'All OK?'

'I was just thinking, if Finn sleeps now then he won't go down till late and if he wakes up in the night …'

Baby feeding maths. It's been two years since I had to do such calculations but I feel for her, especially as Annie's life is far more ordered and organised than mine. Her life would revolve around the routine.

'And then the 11 p.m. feed moves around to 1 and I'll be lucky if I can get him up for 6 for *that* feed.'

'Again, chill. It's really not that important at Finn's age.'

'But they tell me I should be aiming for some sort of routine.'

'Who are they? Just go with the flow. If he's tired, he'll sleep.'

She looks at me absurdly, as if I should know that is far from her style. And instantly, I read something in her eyes that I can't quite place. Almost as if she thinks I'm being flippant. There is silence between us, awkward and uncharacteristic for us. I want to dig. Did I offend her?

'Look, if I want to best the rush hour, I should probably leave.'

'Woah, did I say something? I wasn't jesting, I was ...'

'No, you're right. I need to chill. I need to sleep, that would be better.'

The loaded sarcasm takes me aback and I approach her to try and hug her, use some bodily contact to convey my apology, but the back door opens and Matt enters with the bigger kids and the cacophony of noise that seems to float about wherever they go. Ben, who's been picked up from the station en route, follows behind.

'Aunty Annie!' Hannah wraps herself around her. I've always loved how they call her their aunt. Hannah goes over to inspect Finn as everyone trades hugs and hellos. I try to catch Annie's eye.

'Talk about bad timing but Finny and I were just headed home,' she whispers to encourage everyone to keep their voices down. The twins look disappointed. Matt looks at me, knowing something has been said. I just can't work out what.

'We can't tempt you with chips?' he suggests.

'Maybe next time?' What pains me is that I've genuinely upset her. She looks on the verge of tears and smiles over at me faintly.

'We will catch up and don't worry about the McCoy thing, really. I'll replace the wipes …'

'Annie?' She gets up to gather her belongings and I walk her to the front door. 'There's no rush, stay and see the kids.' She looks at me and stops herself for a second.

'We'll plan something. Bye, lovely.' And with that she's gone. Matt comes into the corridor to find me.

'That was swift. You twose are all right?' I have a distinct look of sad confusion on my face, thinking about my friend. My friend who I can say anything to because we know each other so well. I am mortified and hurt in equal measure. She was amazing at my contract signing, assured and confident like usual. I feel I need to run down the path and find her, but am left staring at Matt instead.

'I don't blame her, our lot are a rowdy bunch. I'd escape too with a sleeping baby.'

I'm still quiet. He beckons me into the kitchen. 'Some chips will make it right.'

I don't argue and follow him through, still looking at my front door. What just happened there? Inside the kitchen, Ben, a mere child himself, has lost control of allocating chips to children and throws them at them like he's feeding penguins. Jake catches one to a round of applause.

Matt overhauled my swimming routine when he became my house husband. Whereas before I'd drag them to the pool, fish them out, and throw snacks at them to keep them quiet, he now showers them at the leisure centre, puts them in fleece onesies, and buys fish and chips that they get to eat in front of the television. I re-member one mum stopping me outside the school gate to tell me he even dries Hannah's hair and she was amazed at his plaiting skills, like it was something I should wear like a badge of honour. It's a routine that works all round (bribery via chips and TV is always a winner) so much so that I envy his ingenuity, thinking of the number of times the twins would melt down in the car park, hair dripping wet onto school uniforms as I dug around in the change bag for a stick of gum they could share.

I get up from my chair to start getting plates out as Matt makes gestures at Hannah.

'Go on, or am I going to have to tell her?'

'Daddy!' I look over at her in navy fleece with pink hearts and teddy bear ears as she smiles that crooked smile of hers.

'I got into the club swimming team. They want me to swim backstroke.'

'Han! That's amazing!' My mood immediately lightens and Ben's face also shines to hear the news. He seal claps as I embrace her and her yoghurty sister in a joint embrace. Matt, who is divvying up chips, interrupts.

'They'll want her at practice twice a week for longer but so good, right?' I nod enthusiastically. The twins think I'm not looking and their hands skim over the pile of chips. Ben is also party to this. I glare at them. Ted grabs two, dips them in ketchup, and makes vampire teeth. I glare while Ben giggles.

'OK, kiddies, you've earned chips in front of the telly. Use kitchen roll to wipe your hands, not the sofa. Go, go, go.' They all cheer in unison and depart from the kitchen, leaving the adults to eat from the paper and break open the wine.

'So, how did the audition go?'

Ben stuffs five chips into his mouth and I know the answer. I put a hand on his back as Matt pours him a large glass of white.

'Oh, not enough experience, limited CV. It's like I wasted my years doing that degree. Some of these people

74

have been doing this for years, building up a portfolio of work.'

'But street Shakespeare, really not you at all. I think we aren't aiming high enough.'

'Street like performing on a street or street as in "word to your mother"?' asks Matt.

This makes Ben laugh. It's all I need to hear.

'They were a performing troupe who'd act out scenes at fayres, festivals, weddings, it was a nice gig, a bit of travel, but que sera.'

It's been the latest audition of many not to have gone his way. I think we were up to thirty-one. Ben was a star, a strong actor with a love of Chaucer, hardworking, handsome, and likeable, but the industry was crowded, competitive, and a bit of a bitch. He was determined to give it a go, to try and break it rather than it break him, but every time he was turned away, you saw a bit of his soul get chipped away. I wondered if it was why he turned his hand to one-night stands – were these casual acquaintances his way of being validated? I give him some of my chips. That should work. There's comfort in carbs. Matt makes a suggestion.

'Well, what sort of experience are they looking for? You've got a sister about to break onto primetime TV on a Saturday night. Surely you could tag along, make contacts?'

To be honest, it's not an entirely stupid idea. I reach over the kitchen table to open the laptop and show Ben a copy of my timetable for the next week. Luella had it done to merge my schedule with that of the kids. It looks like something air traffic controllers would have to deal with.

'He's not wrong. You could be my PA?'

'I thought that's what Luella does ...'

'Nooo, she's all publicity, ringing magazines, and

organising contracts. Look at this schedule. I am rammed, I'm travelling to these things on my own. To have back-up, support, someone to put my outfits together, remind me where I am. I need that.'

He looks at me suspiciously. On the one hand, this is nepotism at its worst and far removed from where he really wants to be – on a stage, suffering for his craft. But on the other hand, this is work. Work he hasn't had in the longest time.

'What are the terms and conditions?'

'It's a shit wage and there's no pension. I'll pay for your food and lodgings.'

'You do that already.'

'You'll be there every day – there's free food and booze. I get a shopping allowance on clothes I can let you in on?'

'Done.' We shake hands and he hugs me. I look over the schedule and panic slightly.

'See? I've already failed. Tomorrow is Greek Day in Han's class and I was supposed to make her a costume. Fail.'

I think about which of our bed sheets is not stained with wee, old milk, or poo and could feasibly become a toga held together with safety pins. Matt laughs.

'Oh, she of poor needlework skills, we are one step ahead of you.' Matt goes to the cupboard under the stairs and retrieves a little Greek dress with gold accessories and a gold leaf headdress. I point to Matt, who laughs.

'Please, all Ben's work. Where would I get the idea to cut up gold lamé and make a leaf design along the edge?'

Ben nods; the costume module of his degree going to some use, then. I hold out my hand.

'Then congratulations, Mr Hartley, the job is yours with immediate effect. Your first task is to work out what I am wearing tomorrow. Luella wants me in smart casual.'

He salutes me, wine glass in hand. His eyes scan to the article.

'By the way, he's gay.'

'Jacobs?' Ben nods like this is common knowledge or that I should have at least known.

'It's a cliché I know but no straight man would accessorise patterns like that.' Matt nods in agreement. 'Not even the most metrosexual of gentlemen. Not my type at all but thought you should know.'

And with that, he escapes with his wine – his gallop up the stairs making me think he's more excited about this than he's let on. Matt sits next to me and kisses Millie on the forehead.

'Was everything all right with Annie?'

'I don't know. She asked me something and I think I was a bit glib.' I stare at the front door again. Matt doesn't seem too worried. He looks as though he thinks I may be over-thinking this, which usually isn't too far from the truth.

'Inspired thinking with Ben, by the way.'

'It's going to get him on his feet.' He feeds me a chip. 'But yes, I am a genius.'

I wrinkle my nose to suggest he acquire some modesty with that but he smiles smugly.

'In any case, perhaps you'll need reinforcements. This Jacobs fella ambushing you with the McCoy thing, it sounds like maybe you need that little entourage to have your back.'

He spies Jacobs' picture on the newspaper and skims the article. Matt has only heard second-hand about everything that's gone on with McCoy and Jacobs. He supported the slap but the shock of hearing how I'd be ascending through the ranks with McCoy by my side left him cold. His first instinct was that the public would never believe it. Having been pitted against each other for so long, he thought most fools would surely see through such a charade. I was inclined to believe him. But given everything that happened with the drinking and the hotel room, I was still reticent to talk about it to him fully. This was becoming a habit of ours, to brush it under the carpet and hope matters would resolve themselves or not even be that big a deal.

'I'm worried about tomorrow. I'm worried about losing my rag, not being able to deal with him. What if Jacobs has stuff up his sleeves?'

'Then you come back. It's what you've always done. Plus, I was reading the rundown of the show. It's kids, they're all Hannah's age – no way would McCoy employ dirty tactics around kids. What sort of publicity would that be?'

'True. How do you feel about things? McCoy and stuff. You've never quite told me.'

Is it the wine? Or the fact I've eaten too many chips? Why, oh why would I speak of he-who-shall-not-be-named at the worst possible time? Like when the baby needs to be doused in wipes, when the others need to be put to bed, and I need to prepare for tomorrow – all better things I could be involving myself in. Matt pretends that he needs to finish all the chips left in the room so as not carry on this conversation.

'You're never more attractive to me than when you have a mouth full of potato.'

He half laughs, spitting crumbs of chips everywhere and trying to swallow.

'Oh, Jools. I don't know. Half of me is excited for you, I think you'll be good for this, the money and the opportunity is fantastic but you know in *Gladiator* when Russell Crowe's in the stadium and suddenly all those tigers appear?'

It takes me a minute to realise he's not talking about

the nineties' Gladiators who used to fight with giant cotton buds.

'I feel like I'm letting you walk into the arena on your own.'

'Do I have a sword?'

'Yes, but I'm not sure you know exactly how to use it.'

I nod. The analogy is half making sense. Unless he thinks that my harvesting of body hair means I look a little like Russell Crowe. That is less kind.

'McCoy is the tiger?'

'There are lots of tigers, they take on many forms.'

I nod again. Given the toll four children has taken on our brains, I fear this may be the most philosophical conversation Matt and I have had in years.

'Russell dies at the end. He gets stabbed by Joaquin.'

'But he dies an honourable death, as a good man who fought for what was right.'

I roll my eyes to the back of my head to work out what that means. I can die on TV, but it will be OK as long as I regain my composure and remain good and honourable. Millie laughs to see me wrinkle my face.

'I mean, we've done this dance with McCoy before. I can't say I'm looking forward to this but I have faith in you. I know you're doing this for us.'

I look him in the eye. This is the first time he's mentioned this and I'm grateful, relieved that he realises that I'm not purely on some fame-thirsty climb to stardom, leaving my family in my wake for more column inches. No, that would be what Kitty McCoys are for. But I'm glad he knows that this is a chance to work, to provide for my family, and that every time I feel this niggle to return to the fold and hide, I remember we need to put food on the table, finish the extension, put money away for rainy days and children we may have to house for another thirty years given the current state of house prices.

'You did it for us. For ten years.'

I squeeze his hand. He purses his lips to the side.

'I put a suit on every day and did sums. This is different.'

Either way, we both made our sacrifices. I wonder if we are at some happy medium where we can reclaim ourselves; for so many years we got lost in the throes of early parenthood and that primordial need to keep our heads above water, never admitting to each other that we needed more. Now we can do as our hearts please, we can don highly unstylish tracksuits and teach our sons about the beautiful game. We can go on TV. Was that what my heart desired?

'Are you happy?' he asks.

I don't respond. Millie has gone to town with the yoghurt for a start so she looks a little ghostly. He reads my reticence.

'I'm happy if you're happy, if the kids are happy.'

'Seriously?' He shakes his head at my diplomacy.

'Serious answer, I am bricking it. Deep down, I know I can do this but you're right, I'm offering myself to the tigers. I'm properly shitting my pants.'

'Well, don't do that on live television. I'd disown you if you did.'

I laugh and try to get Millie to stop covering the open laptop in pink slime. Matt looks over my shoulder.

'Seriously, Jools, 1890 mails unread? What the actual hell?'

This is why I need a PA of sorts: to sort the spam from the magazine interview requests and genuine fan letters. I open my inbox to scan through it and learn about eBay's zero insertion fees, emails from the school telling me about nits epidemics, and several gazillion emails from Luella who forwards me every article or newspaper I've ever been in. Delete, send to trash, move, ignore. Then I stop. Dorothy Young. I don't recognise the surname but instinct tells me it's her. My mother. I open it and scan its contents. Apologies, well-wishes, but they are some weird lead-in to introduce my brothers to me. And some new business venture of some description that they are involved in and … I stop reading.

Search <Young>

Fifty-five messages unread from Dorothy, Scott, and Craig Young like some joint ambush to come into my life. I am impressed, almost shocked at how little emotion this stirs in me, just minor annoyance. I look over to Matt, who picks at the crispy bits of chip at the bottom of the white paper. He smiles at me, ketchup splodges on his stubbly chin. I look at Millie who spreads yoghurt on the underside of the dining room table.

Delete
Search <Dorothy Young>
Delete all?
Confirm
Block <Dorothy Young/Scott Young/Craig Young>
Confirm

CHAPTER SEVEN

I love Ben. I really do love my brother. Last night's minor event where I happened upon my other family makes me realise this. I haven't mentioned anything to him. 'Tis a glitch in the greater scheme of things and I know how emotional talk of the 'others' makes him, so it feels safest to just pretend it never happened and get back to appreciating the brothers I do have. However, as much as Ben means to me, I may have made quite a mistake asking him to be in charge of my wardrobe. I forget this is someone who is in his early twenties, whose body has not succumbed to childbirth or their thirty-something years, and who can carry off ironic chic – like those eighties' sweatshirts and ankle grazing trousers that make most men look wanky.

'What is this?'

'Chic. Very chic.'

Matt is in the kitchen sipping his coffee and laughing. Ben's vision for me seems to be Shoreditch via Paris. Black skinny jeans with a white blouse, a huge leopard skin cravat-style scarf tied around my neck, a giant pendant of the Eiffel Tower, and black heeled boots he seems to have Benjazzled with sparkly laces.

'You've done the scarf all wrong, drape it around your neck.'

'Then what's the point? It'll be a fire hazard, I'll bend over a pan and set myself alight.'

Ben throws his hands up. I am messing with his vision. I'm not even sure where he found these boots. They've lived under the stairs for years, I don't think I've worn them since university but that was back when combat trousers were in fashion and everyone thought they were a Pussycat Doll. Now they make my legs look stumpy. Matt looks me up and down.

'Wear your ballet pumps,' he suggests.

'But Luella told me they'd make me look short and dumpy.'

'Well, you can't do heels for sure. Better to look short than break your neck. And Ben's right – drape the scarf, take off the pendant.' I do as I'm told and shuffle around on the landing changing my footwear. I reappear. 'Perfect.'

I look at myself in the mirror.

'I look like Uma Thurman in *Pulp Fiction*.'

'You look normal … use the red handbag, tie your hair up and use those green square studs you have.'

Ben listens on slightly bemused as Matt points this out in the same dressing gown he's owned since university. Now he's not working and doesn't have to groom a short back and sides, he's let his hair grow out slightly. It's bushy, like Chris Martin in his early Gwyneth days.

'You leave a lot of magazines in the bathroom. If you go monochrome, you can add accents of colour to lift the look without drowning it.'

Hannah walks in at this point – a little vision as a Greek Goddess complete with Converse and spotty school bag.

'Daddy, are you plaiting my hair?'

My heart breaks a little to hear her go to someone else to do a job that was once mine.

'Yes, what are you thinking, Mummy? How are we liking the costume in action?'

Hannah twirls about and I'm taken back to World Book Day when I gave her a giant encyclopaedia and told

84

her she was Matilda. It's perfect.

'I think you and Ben are a dynamic duo. If you'd met him first and got together, you'd be quite the unstoppable force.'

'Except Daddy isn't gay and neither of them can have children,' adds Hannah.

Ben nods in agreement. Matt shakes his head.

'Come here, smarty pants. Two plaits or one?' I widen my eyes at him and go to kiss him on the cheek as I leave.

'Just don't shit your pants,' he whispers in my ear.

Ben and I decided to drive to the studio, mainly because I don't want to give the impression that I can't do it myself nor that I have delusions of grandeur about my status as a celebrity. It was nice to drive down the A3 without traffic or kids in the rear arguing about leg room and sharing sweets, less so to have to endure Ben's electronica selection.

When we got in, we were directed to my dressing room and I was suddenly thrown back to the cook-off. That was a perfectly good dressing room, I got a quality sandwich with posh crisps and Diet Coke. However, this one is on another level. For a start, there's a coffee machine with the pods. And it's not just a selection of crappy ones that no one drinks – there are ones with chocolate, syrups, and settings to froth your milk. The cups are red and shiny and have saucers, there's even a selection of biscuits and I find myself back in that strange foreign land where the biscuits carry pistachios and are the size of my face.

'High five, Julio.' I don't care. I high five back. Julio was Ben's nickname for me when he was little. It began with an aunt who loved Julio Iglesias and used to play him on loop when we went to her house for Saturday tea times. We used to dance around her living room and sing along. Of course, we didn't know Spanish or what the eff he was going on about but we had routines, the whole shebang. When the moon is high and the wine flows freely, he is our go to karaoke song. So, of course, the nickname stuck.

We go to the coffee machine, caress it slightly, press buttons, and marvel at our pod selection, Ben jumping up and down and doing a strange jig.

'What do we say to Aunty Luella?'

Luella appears at the door carrying a number of files and bags. Ben runs to help her.

'Thank you, Aunty Luella.'

'We were talking Starbucks last night and I thought we should be able to do one better. Ta-dah! Open the fridge.'

I bend down to my under-the-counter fridge, slightly apprehensive. Is it filled with goji berries and spelt? It is my turn to dance. Cheese. Lots of cheese. Eighteen months with this lady has taught her I like my cheese. I like cheddar that hasn't been messed about with. I have a very excellent relationship with brie. I am a food cretin so I like eating it on plain crackers, nothing else. I open the cupboards. Yes. We have crackers and crisps of the salt and vinegar variety. I give her a little hug.

'You can't say I didn't try to get something better inside you, but then I thought it best if you went out happy. Ben! Lovely to have you here.'

'Oh, Lu. Ben is coming on full-time as my PA of sorts.'

She smiles. 'Excellent! I've always liked you. Love the shoes.'

I look down. Distressed loafers without socks – it's very Ben, but I also know this kind of fashion is prone to foot odour and blisters. Her look turns to me.

'Though I must say, this look, Mrs Campbell, is fantastic. The right side of chic. Ben?'

'And Matt.'

This comes as no surprise to her and she high fives Ben. 'Have you seen him yet?' I open my eyes as Ben goes to make coffees, keeping his ear in the whole time.

'I haven't, but you know what he's like. Though I expected if he was with Cam he'd arrive on a fricking chariot – we'd have heard it by now.'

I remember the last time I encountered Tommy in one of these dressing rooms. I'd been ambushed, but he had bribed me to lose the cook-off with a sizeable cheque in order to keep his career and reputation intact. I refused the money. And I lost the cook-off. But as I sip on my freshly made mochaccino, that memory of not caring, of being morally on the high ground and coming off better overwhelms me. That was a warm, reassuring feeling. Boo-yah to you, McCoy. A knock on the door brings me back to the room. We all look to the face that comes around the door. She's tiny and in black, microphoned up to the hilt.

'Mrs Campbell, when you're ready … can we have you over in costume? We just want to run some outfit ideas by you for the live shows.'

I forget the best thing that I might get out of this is the free clothes. Luella has given them their brief; don't make her look too mumsy, she can't walk in anything with a heel over one inch, and she's clumsy so nothing on her wrists or anything she can strangle herself with. So with this in mind, I have high hopes for what costume have in store for me: well-fitted jeans, knitwear that isn't bobbly, proper knee-high boots. I get up from my chair with a spring in my step.

'Do you want to …?' I urge to Luella and Ben.

'You go first. Let me run through the timetable with Ben so he knows where we need to be today.' Code for 'we're not wasting these coffees.' I smile and leave them be, following the girl down the corridor. This girl is slender, verging on ill-skinny and seems harassed. I try to calm her down.

'I'm Jools. Do you work on the show?' She smiles.

'Bella. Production Manager. Yeah, I make sure everyone is where they are supposed to be. I'm sorry, it's a stressful day. What do they say about animals and kids? And kids come with parents so I'm refereeing them today and … nightmare …'

'I don't envy you. So will I get the chance to meet everyone today?'

She nods, that frantic look still in her eye.

'Yeah, eventually but … look, wardrobe don't need to see you for another ten minutes. It's just … I just thought it might be good for you to … well, they thought …'

'The directors?' As well as being frantic, she's starting to sound incomprehensible and I'm reminded of times when the twins have just run laps around the house and I can't get more than mere syllables out of them. She leads me into a room. I enter but am a little confused – it seems to be some centre of sound recording with a huge microphone and a little stool and for one small moment, I worry that I am here to sing the theme tune. She closes the door. I turn around. Or voice overs, they do that all the time on these cookery shows. I have a very pleasant tone to my voice.

I hear the door click. It's locked. And at that moment, I don't even have to turn around. I know.

'Jools.'

You shitbag. Again? When I do turn around, it's a McCoy I'm more familiar with. The McCoy I saw last had a bloat around his face, his eyes were sad and bloodshot, and the pallor made his skin white.

'Seriously? If you wanted to talk to me, you could have come to my dressing room. This?'

'Look, I didn't know how to get you away from Luella and that man you were with ...'

'My PA, Ben.'

'You've gone up in the world.'

I immediately act insulted.

'Look, no, it's just I felt I had to explain what happened in the Holiday Inn.'

'You set up a falsehood, a crock of lies to make it look like we spent some intimate evening together? It was low, even for you.'

I am strong, I am the tiger. I am not sure what needs explaining; he was obviously desperate for the media attention and set it up for his own means and purposes. He and Cam must have been following me that evening, watching lonely, sad me slink to the bar on my own and rubbed their hands in glee to see how they could manipulate that situation.

'Look, it was nothing like that. Cam set it up, I had no idea. He leaked the camera footage. He didn't even tell me he went to the press, I only found out when I saw it in the papers.'

I crease my face into what feels like a thousand lines.

'But you hired him? You knew he would monopolise on something like that.' I put my hand up, tired of hearing him talk. I try the door again.

'I told Bella to leave it locked until I said so.'

I turn back to him. 'Entrapment. Great. So tell me, he leaks all that bullshit and still you associate yourself with him. Why? The man is scum.'

'Because it did exactly what I needed it to do. It got me this job, it got me working again and in a better place to get my family back.'

'So you're doing this all, for your family.'

'For my family.'

I pause for a moment because isn't that why I'm here

too? Of course, his circumstances are different, a little more tragic. I'm merely here so we can start putting tiles on the extension and can continue to pay off the mortgage. But we love our families. We stare at each other a little too intently. I break his gaze and try the door again.

'Thank you. And thank you for that evening. The way you spoke to me, the things you said. I needed to hear them.'

Thanks. It's a weird thing to hear from McCoy. It's not spikey sarcasm, it's not biting criticism. It's hard to gauge its sincerity.

'We need to make this work, Jools. We've signed contracts to work together and do it well. I need this show to be a hit.'

I could stab him on TV, nothing death invoking. Maybe I could trip and get him in the shoulder. He's right to an extent. I've committed myself to this endeavour so I'll be professional and do it to the best of my abilities. However, I hadn't quite figured out how I was going to do that with McCoy in the picture. I assumed I could just pretend he wasn't there and talk to the kids.

'I'll be professional, it's what I'm being paid to do. But after everything, I'm not sure how you can expect me to like you.'

He comes a bit closer to me. I step back.

'We're going to be on set for eight hours a day, two days of the week. For three months. You're going to have to learn how to. I'm trying to make amends here. What happened at the Holiday Inn ...'

'Was nothing! I'm glad it was some lightbulb moment for you where you picked yourself up and decided to get your arse into gear, but stop making out like it was dalliance worth bringing up again.'

I start knocking on the door.

'Bella, Bella. Please can we come out please?' There is

silence. I think about my first port of call when I get out of here: fire Bella.

'Well, if you're going to be like that, I'm trying to be mature. But it's obvious what you think about me.' I keep knocking. He puts a hand to the door above my hand. The physical proximity is unnerving and I roll away from him.

'So tell me, if you dislike me that much then why didn't you leave me? You could have left me on the floor in a pile of my own vomit. Press would have had a field day.'

I don't say anything back. The implication he's making is that I helped him because I like him. I did it because I'm human, because I hadn't sunk to some level of depravity where I was going to kick him when he was already down. If he'd taught me anything, it was that I was nothing like him. It's time for a rant, it's brewing, but instead I think it's a good idea to run at the door. Obviously I bounce off it. McCoy laughs. This, of course, induces rage and I knock at it again, falling out of the room as it works this time. I turn around.

'Do that again and I'll go on live TV and knee you in the bollocks. Seriously, you are such a cock.'

Tommy looks over my shoulder. Stood there are a row of ten very tiny people, all wearing chef hats and matching aprons, their parents stood behind them, giving me looks: looks I know very well.

CHAPTER EIGHT

I'm writing. This is a big thing for me because feasibly the only things I ever write are sick notes, shopping lists, and birthday cards. Technology and lack of practice mean that when I put pen to paper, I sometimes forget how to even form words and end up sounding them out in some alien phonics fashion developed from having spent years reading nonsensical books with little people about children called Kipper. Why wasn't Kipper bullied? He was named after a smoked fish.

'Why are you growling?' asks Hannah.

'I'm not, I'm doing my R sound.'

'You mean *Rrrrrr.*' Of course I was. Hannah runs her fingers across the cards on the coffee table.

'Who are all these children?' She reads out the names on the list. 'Shaun, Jackson, Kai, Callum, Oscar, Erin, Lydia, Mimi, Tia, and Rosie. I have a Tia in my class.' She doodles on my list with smiley faces and bubble writing. Ah, they are only the top ten amateur chefs in the country under the age of twelve. And these are the I'm Sorry notes the production company have asked me to write to them after the 'incident' in the corridor where I swore quite loudly and profusely at my co-host in front of their small and receptive ears.

'They're the kids who'll be cooking in this TV show I'm in. I have to write them some notes.'

'Like invitations?'

'Kind of. I said some bad words in front of them and I

have to write to them and their mummies and daddies to say sorry.'

This makes Hannah smile broadly to know I've been in trouble. I stick my tongue out at her.

'Oooh, which words? The C-word?'

'Which C-word?'

'You mean there's more than one C-word?'

Hannah's been doing this a lot recently. Before, she'd give me looks to question whether I knew what I was doing. Now she actually asks questions, she backs me into corners to test whether I can wriggle out of them.

'One rhymes with tap.'

'Yes, I know that one. That's one of your favourites.' I smile wryly at her. The next part is the test. Does she know it yet? Matt and I are hardly angels but that word makes very rare appearances in this house. My mind filters rapidly through my mental lexicon of swear words.

'The other rhymes with lock.' Is that OK for a ten-year-old? Oh dear, this might be a huge parenting fail here. I picture her repeating it to someone in the playground. I need to backtrack. Crap crap crap.

'Mummy, clock is not a swear word.' And with that she smiles, digging through our pen box to retrieve some ink stamp pen to help me pretty up my letters. 'You're funny.' Well, at least she thinks so.

I thank Christ my crumby parenting skills can still be saved by her innocent mind. The same can't be said for the ten little children, my Little Chefs, whose minds I corrupted so terribly. I finish my last letter to Jackson, son of Lisa, who comes from Berkshire and whose star dish is a lasagne that contains five different vegetables. After my incident in the corridor, I was summoned into Maggie Matthews' office for a stern telling off. Given I've spent the last ten years without a boss, or at least one who wasn't under the age of ten, it was quite the experience to be read the riot act and told quite explicitly 'we thought more of you, Mrs Campbell.'

McCoy got nothing; for locking me in a room with him, for bribing one of the production managers (who still has her job) to set up the scenario, and for generally being an all-out smarmy twat. Nothing. Luella went nuclear at this point. There was shouting, there was stomping, there were threats to out that he'd obviously put in hair plugs to fix his receding hairline. In terms of one-upmanship, he'd won this round. I was the one who was in the head honcho's bad books. Some of her fury was directed to me: swearing! I told you to control the swearing! And in front of kids. But luckily there was Ben to calm her down: to make camomile infusions to soothe her angst, to remind her that this was all part of his game. We'd been through this before; tit for tat. We always rose above it and last time we won. Ben also said swearing was part of the reason people loved me, or that Ben did. Thank the universe for Ben.

But it made the rest of our rehearsals painful to say the least. When the stage was set and the lights were on, like a switch, McCoy turned on his Mockney best mate act and bounced around the studio like his undercrackers were on fire. The boys loved his energy and pally jokes.

Half the kids were wary of me: the crazy shouty lady who knew bad words and every time I went near little Tia, daughter of Zoe and whose star dish was seared tuna with pearl couscous, her bottom lip would quiver. But what was worse was the palpable tension between McCoy and I.

There is a segment at the end of each episode where we have to stand around an electronic board with the kids' faces on it and pick who we want to go into the next round. It's very hi-tec. Half the time it looks like a tractor beam is going to drop into the studio and suck the kids into outer space for their failure to deliver food worthy of our attention. During that time, we actually have to look each other in the eye and deliberate these kids' futures. Of course, it's all for the sake of good TV. We could just go, 'Yeah, send that one home. Pasta wasn't cooked.' But the whole decision-making process is drawn out to a three-minute segment where pictures are highlighted and the whole screen glows several shades of neon like it's been thrown up on by the eighties.

After that we have to talk about the food, the textures, the flavours, and that kid's general aptitude. It's a horrible exercise to put a young child under the microscope like that, one I've tried to tackle with as much kindness and tact as possible but it's hard having to look at McCoy's face at the same time and feign interest in what he's saying.

'Glitter pens might not cut it, maybe you just need to bite the bullet and slip them a fiver. Win favour via bribery.'

Matt comes in clutching tea, cake, and biscuits – party rings because we're classy like that – and takes a glimpse at the letters on the table. Hannah listens on.

'What do the kids win in the end?'

'They win a family holiday, a cooking course in Paris, and an iPad.'

'And they just have to cook?'

'Well, kind of. It's a game show so their families come in and help and it's against the clock and there are challenges and…'

The fact she has wrinkled up her face makes me think I'm not selling this very well, or at least that I should not be heading up the promotion campaign.

'So, will it be like before?' Matt immediately senses worry in her voice and pulls her up to the sofa for a cuddle.

'Oh, not at all, Han.' I twitch a little to hear Matt talk so casually about what the next few months have in store. We thought it might be an easier ride this time round but the last few weeks have proven that we don't have the control we thought we had. If anything, this could be another power struggle in the offing and I'm not entirely sure where it will take us. Matt continues with the comforting dad hugs.

'I mean, Mum is going to be out more, right? Like working?'

I nod. I still hadn't equated it to it being my job yet.

'I liked it when both of you were here. It was fun and everyone was less stressed. It was nice.'

I scrunch my mouth up at this point as she's right. If I could refer to that time in our lives when Matt packed in his job and we were all at home, co-managing the house, eating together, sharing the burdens, it was a golden era for us Campbells. Halcyon days of just four months ago when if you ever needed that pint of milk, it meant you didn't have to pack four kids into a car to get it. It worked. I can sympathise with how nostalgic she feels for those days.

'And Daddy does things differently to you.'

'In what way?' I ask. Matt's ears prick up. Since taking Ben and myself out of the equation, Matt has been manning this ship solo. That's not to say he's not done a grand job, he's pretty much acing it. He still does the chip run after swimming and plaits Hannah's hair. He runs his football team, shops, cleans, and juggles kids and dare I say it, does it far more efficiently that I ever did. But I know him, I know he will not take criticism lightly especially when it comes from a ten-year-old.

'Daddy will only let us listen to Radio 6 Music in the car. Sometimes even talking radio where there's no music.'

Matt nods. That's not as bad as he thought it might be.

'He says you poisoned our brains with generic pop and turned us into musical cretins.'

But maybe not a good review for me. I shift Matt a look.

'It's true. It worries me that Ted doesn't know how to add but knows all the words to *Uptown Funk*.'

I think about old car journeys where we had that song on repeat and the boys would sing about Uptown 'Fuck You Up' and I'd have a giggle to myself and join in. At least Hannah's accusation points to me being the more fun parent, the one who feels they need some immersion in popular culture so they know what their friends are going on about in the playground. Matt was always more intent on them being a bit more alternative and free-range.

'Anything else?'

'Daddy's a bit stricter. He shouts more than you did.'

I look at Matt, who is devastated by the accusation. I am confused because I thought that's what I did eighty per cent of the time.

'Oh, Mummy used to do that thing where her voice went high and her eyeballs bulged out. Then she'd tell us she was fed up and sit in the kitchen and drink tea.'

That I did. I don't even feel the need to deny it. However, I am glad that she thinks I was drinking tea. Just because it was in a mug didn't mean it was tea. Many a half hour has been spent in there downing Pinot Grigio under a ceramic disguise.

'Daddy does his Daddy voice. It's all deep and loud and he says stuff like, *I don't care, your mother's not here and I don't care for your attitude.*'

She does that last bit in Matt's Scottish tones, making him sound a bit like Shrek to make us smile, but I see what she's doing. It's comparative parenting in some clever ruse to see if it will induce conflict. Her eyes shift between the two of us.

'And he doesn't do play dates. I've asked to have Clara around five times now and he always says no.'

I look at Matt curiously. That bit's not hard. In fact, I used to relish the playdates as it meant everyone had company and occupied themselves better without my intervention. Ultimately, all it really meant was a few more fish fingers in the pan.

'It's more kids. It throws my routine. I have a set routine and if it gets thrown …'

I laugh, secretly knowing that I've found his weak points: more than four kids, veering away from the routine. It makes me want to throw spanners in the works to see if he's up to the challenge.

'Well, maybe one day Daddy can sort a playdate in the park. It's sometimes easier in the park.'

Matt wobbles his head from side to side. Hannah eyes him, unimpressed.

'And he's started a rota where we all have to tidy up.'

Case in point. I laugh under my breath to hear of Matt's slightly militant ways. Matt shakes his head as if to say I ran this state before under no sense of rule and the citizens ran riot as a consequence.

'It's called being part of a family, Han. If we all do our bit, then it's less work.'

'For you maybe … they call that slave labour in some countries. I don't even get paid.'

Matt and I look at each other. In part, she's being mildly amusing but this, what we have here, is sass. Our ten-year-old in her purple leggings and stripey tabard dress is giving us lip. And I think confusion reigns as we're not sure how we need to handle it.

'Polly in my class gets pocket money for doing chores. She gets a pound for making her bed. And she gets twenty

99

pence for every dish she dries up.'

'Well, Polly sounds like a little –'

'Matt!' I interrupt before he has time to let us know exactly what Polly sounds like. 'Maybe we can negotiate some rates for you … Matt?' He shrugs. I know what he'll do. He'll make a spreadsheet because that's what he does. Each child will have a coloured column and he'll laminate it. I can see his brain planning it out.

'Well, that's settled. Is there anything else Daddy does differently that worries you?'

She pauses for a moment. 'Well, it doesn't worry me but he definitely cooks better than you.'

And just like that, I see Matt punch the air and collapse into the sofa in silent giggles. Hannah gives me a look like she's quite happy to wind me up. I push her into her father.

'I hate you both. But I'll always make the best mac and cheese, right? Right?'

She smiles and nods.

'Yes, Daddy puts weird cheese in his.'

'It's called gruyere. See, you've turned them into cheese cretins too. All they know is Babybels and mild cheddar.' He shakes his head. 'I'm giving you an education, Han. Trust me.'

'I know other cheeses. I know mozzarella and brie and Cheestrings and that orangey cheese.' Matt nods. See? Remember who the food expert is in the house, Mr Campbell. The BBC are paying me good money to impart this kind of knowledge onto the next generation. But there is a look in his eyes, one which tells me it is on – he is going to take on my recipe. It's mac and cheese wars. Bring it on, Matteo.

'So it won't be like when Daddy went to work then? You'll still be here? Some of the time?'

I nod. Of course it won't be nine-to-five but I'll try my

best to make this all right for her. Matt senses my discomfort at not being able to give her firm responses and squeezes my hand.

'And when she's not here, she'll be on the television so it's like she's here ... in the living room, at least.' Like Max Headroom, I want to tell her, bar the fact she won't get the reference at all. Matt sips his tea and looks at his watch.

'What time was Annie supposed to get here?'

I look over at the timer on the DVD player (the only way I can tell the time in this house except for the broken Ikea clocks). Matt is right, she's over an hour late, and the tea and cakes he's prepared are starting to get cold and stale. Today was supposed to be a belated tea and catch up so the kids could play with Finn and I could update her with the McCoy shenanigans. After our last meeting ended sharply and possibly with little comments unresolved, it felt important to do this, to get back on a better level with her. Hannah grabs at a cupcake and disappears from the room, mainly so she can shake it in her brothers' faces.

'It's very unlike her.' I look at my phone; no texts or missed calls. I pick up the phone to call her. It goes to voicemail. I try again. This time someone picks up.

'Hello?' The voice is a faint whisper, telling me someone's in between naps.

'Annie, it's me. I'm sorry, did I wake you? I just ...'

'SHIT! What time is it? Jools, oh shit! I am so sorry. It's just Finn was up all night and the doctors think he's got this acid reflux thing and ... I am so sorry.'

'Hun, it's OK, we're just hanging out at home.' I hear hesitation in her voice as she goes to speak and I suspect she's a little tearful.

'I'm so annoyed. I wanted to see everyone and see you and ...'

101

'Ssssh, you're allowed to be asleep you know, you have a baby.'

It's very Annie. Ever since I first met her, she has always taken everything very seriously and is extremely hard on herself if things don't work out as she'd like. From her degree to her relationships, she always expected things to work out to a specific plan. It came as a huge shock to her when she was told she'd need intervention to have babies, and when her repeated attempts to make that happen failed to work, I saw her fall into a place she'd never been before. Whereas I thrived on the future being unpredictable and chaotic, she shuddered at the very thought.

'We had cake.'

'Of course, you did, I'd expect nothing less.'

'We can save you a piece? And one for Chris too?' She goes quiet for a moment. 'Oh, I ... Chris's away for work. I'm flying solo at the moment. It's just ... Finn's asleep and ...'

'You don't have to say another word. Go get some rest. We love you guys.'

I can sense she's still a little tearful so I don't expect her to reply but I quietly hear the phone click and go dead.

'No show?' I nod. 'Is she OK?'

'The joys of new parenthood.'

Matt dives into the cake now he knows he doesn't have to share it politely, so instead of cutting it he grabs handfuls. I would shudder at his incivility but know I've often eaten cake that way. Damn it, sometimes I've just bitten into the thing and licked the icing off like a dog.

'Wait, she called the other day when you were at rehearsals. I told her to call back but don't think she did? She sounded awful.'

I think back: the four month mark with Hannah. It was pure bedlam. Matt and I were still so young, we still had some of that arrogance and immaturity that came with your early twenties so when this little thing came along that deprived us of our sleep, we didn't take to it too kindly.

'You know, I always assumed she'd slide into baby routines and stuff so easily. She's been around for the four of ours, seen how it works.'

Matt wipes crumbs from the corners of his mouth, appearing confused.

'Yeah, but that's like saying a teacher should know kids because she's around thirty of them every day. It's different when it's your own, when you don't get to hand them back.'

I nod, reluctant to agree, but perhaps I thought Annie being older, more professional in everything she undertook, would just be a dab hand at this. It pains me to hear her so tired and confused. I think back to when she was last here and she had all those questions to which I didn't give her the answers.

'But she's Annie,' Matt adds. 'She's been waiting for this for so long and now it's here – whether the dream is measuring up against the expectation is another thing. She likes to be in control, she likes order. Babies don't allow for that.'

I think what to do next. Calling and stirring her from much needed sleep is not the best idea. Annie, my friend from university who took me and my baby under her wing, who used to make me jacket potatoes with cheese and coleslaw because that's all she knew how to make. I need to show that same level of due care and attention.

'Mills and I will take her some cake in the week,' adds Matt. 'She'll be fine. Remember, you cried for the first, what, nine months of having Hannah?'

'I did not.'

'You cried at a sofa advert once.'

I cannot deny that. 'So you think Annie's all right?' He nods. 'She just has to find her feet.'

He hands me a cupcake.

'Of course. Now eat before the twins get in here, Millie wakes up from her nap, and those sodding kids come in here like vultures. Eat.'

I eye him curiously as he stuffs a whole muffin in his mouth. Maybe I should call Annie back. I stare at the phone. It can wait I tell myself. Yes, wait.

CHAPTER NINE

'So how do you want me to stand?'

'At a forty-five-degree angle, one hand on your hip, shoulders back, chin at level angle with your elbow.'

It's like the world's worst game of Twister. The twins stand behind Luella on the sofa, pulling faces, and I can't help but giggle.

'Beavis! Butthead! Enough!' Of course, my boys don't know who they are but one of them has just been called Butthead. 'That's you!' I look over at Luella who is close to grabbing the boys and knocking their heads together. I always imagine her French hybrid children are far calmer, arty sorts. While my boys are rolling down the stairs on their stomachs, Xavi and Clio are painting abstract watercolours of stately homes in matching straw hats.

'I thought you were a TV cooking person, not a model, Mummy.' I look over and they are now striking model poses in their matching pyjamas, clearly influenced by Madonna's 'Vogue'. This has nothing to do with me so next time Matt accuses me of poisoning his children's brains with pop music, I may have to point him in Ben's direction. Ted smiles that special smile he does when he sees my face all made up and my hair blow dried; there's an appreciation and a look of awe at how a rather bland canvas is now transformed. He comes over to play with my dangly earrings. Thank you for thinking I might be a model. That is the one and only time anyone will ever think that.

'I'm not a model, little man. It's just there will be

people at this party who'll want to take my photo and it's important I stand properly.'

'Like when we take family photos and you tell me to stand with my legs together and not smile showing all my teeth.'

'Exactly,' interrupts Luella, who is expertly putting on mascara as Jake Gangnam Styles behind her. She, like any experienced mother, seems to manage despite the distraction. She comes over and reaches under my dress to pull the lining down. I normally wouldn't acquiesce to someone clawing up at my tights, but today I make the exception. Tonight is semi-big: the show's launch party, in some flash London eatery complete with bouncy castle and candy floss for the Little Chefs. The BBC are making a big hoo-hah out of this given they've realised shows involving food and cakes seem to be some of their biggest cash cows.

So today there will be press, there will be free alcohol, and there will be the chance to mingle, present myself to the media, and have my outfit snapped and torn apart by critics the following day. Today, against better judgement, Luella has me in what can only be described as Iron Man red with accessorises in black and gold. Given my legs don't really get many outings, she took one look at them and said 'tights', so they have been covered in as high a denier as possible. The dress is the higher end of high street. A strangely conceived neckline means it scoops to the back so I have a bra on that seems to wind its way around my stomach and down to my knicker line. My hair is doing glamorous things it hasn't done since … well, ever. I've spent the last ten years fashioning it into a style which would mean it doesn't get caught in saucepans and fly across my face in a crowded playground meaning I lose sight of my kids. Now a young girl called Ashleigh has literally brought it out of hibernation. She's curled it and sprayed it and it feels light and bouncy, so much so that I feel swish it around a lot. Luella shakes her head. Enough with the swishing.

'Not sure I've ever seen you look so fancy, love.'

Behind me, Dad stands with Millie in her onesie with the cow print. When in need of a babysitter, go to Dad. He will literally just throw them into bed once we're gone and drink all our tea but it's always comforting to have him here to remind me that even though tonight has the potential for much to go awry, there was always going to be a man in South West London dressed in corduroy who'd love me no matter what. Someone who I know will get into my extension and have a go at the sweeping, because that's what he does. He goes in to kiss me on the cheek and I see Luella squirm to see Millie's hands go to the dress. Being a large event, I also leave with an entourage today. Ben is in the kitchen making himself a piece of toast. I trot over. Trot not being too far off what I actually do – tonight requires heelage that makes me walk like I don't possess kneecaps.

'What are you doing?'

'Marmite on toast. We're drinking tonight, substantial amounts of free alcohol. One does not simply swan in with an empty stomach. One must line the stomach. Did university teach you nothing?'

'I was at university ten years ago.'

He feigns shock but then hands me a slice.

'Plus you are in those crazy heels … drunk and not in control of your limbs, tottering about … eat. Because I don't want to have to hold you up in those heels when you're vomming.'

'Lovely.'

Ben knows how to dress for such occasions. There's leather and denim with flashes of green and of course, it all comes together like it should. He's been a welcome

107

partner in all this madness, like a lucky mascot.

'Look in here. I have a man-bag of sorts. I'm going to run in between photos and make sure your lippy is still shining and your hair hasn't gone floppy.'

I also see he's packed Haribo and smile. Little brother done good. There was worry that this was beneath him but secretly I think he might be enjoying it.

'Why the johnnies?' He shrugs. Yes, this is a date night but not the sort that would see Matt and I escape into a broom cupboard for any sort of illicit sojourn. Has it come to this? Ben is now in charge of my contraception? But then I pause. They're not for me, are they? Before I have the chance to respond, there are footsteps on the stairs and a wolf-whistle from Dad. We collect in the hallway to see my date for the evening.

'Oh, doesn't he scrub up well.'

That he does. Of course, Luella has picked his outfit – a well-fitted suit, shirt, and pointy shoes. This is very out of his comfort zone, but after years of a white collar uniform that didn't fit him very well and shirts that were always a bit see-through, his face conveys shock at the feel and fit of quality tailoring. He jumps a few steps from the bottom and I marvel at how he may have taken product to his hair.

'Whit-whoo, Mr C!' Ben exclaims from behind me, toast still in hand. Luella smiles and nods at her handiwork. Ted strokes Matt's thighs, trying to work out what this soft, form-enhancing material is. Matt smiles broadly at me. You'll do. It's a strange feeling that after all these years, this might be the most dressed up we've ever been. Even on our wedding day, he had on a suit that didn't quite fit and I had on a white skater dress thing I'd only chosen as it didn't make me look too pregnant. In between, there have been date nights and weddings but there have always been sacrifices made to my appearance in some way. Whether it was eyeliner/nail polish hastily applied in the passenger seat, sale dresses that had an ill-fitting bodice or going with flat shoes because you'd be able to carry a baby better, looks always came second place to cost, time, and efficiency. I threw a pashmina over it, I tied my hair back, I wore great big pieces of costume jewellery to make me think I was carrying off some vintage, off-beat look.

So now, I see us both in our downstairs landing mirror and we look at each other to ask where these people have been hiding the whole time. Matt even touches the mirror in a scene not far off from *Face/Off* when John Travolta meets Nic Cage for the first time. Ben catches us and shakes his head.

'You vain twats. Car's here! I'm riding shotgun!' I see the boys gallop to the bay window.

'It's black, Mummy! It's really big!'

Hannah looks at me and smiles. 'Just don't shout at the kids again or say bad words and remember to put your shoulders back.' I stick them right back so my boobs bounce a little. She laughs and hugs my bottom half. Luella is frantic on the phone. Dad smiles and does a royal wave. I royal wave back. There's a feeling in the pit of my stomach, but it's not fear. Geez, is this excitement? Is this that Christmas morning feeling resurrected from days of old when Christmas was actually something to get excited about? Why aren't I scared? This is epic. I close my eyes and take a deep breath. Matt hooks his arm through mine and we leave.

'Jools! Jools! Here! Here!'

I've always seen those photos of celebs on red carpets and thought, what a pile of piss. The way they edge their way across the red carpet, stop to talk to journalists, and then stand for photos like pretty ponies. It's so difficult, they would say. It's my least favourite part of being famous, said another. Oh, boo-hoo, I used to think. Compare that to your average orphan living in a war-torn country, first world problems indeed.

So as I stand here, temporarily blinded by a dozen flashing lights, alone and in heels so tall I might stack it in front of hundreds of people, I keep this to the forefront of my mind. I could be that orphan. God, this is not pleasant. Where do I look? I can see the paper tomorrow – a million shots of my face looking like a stunned haddock. What do I do with my arms? One on the hips, or is it two? I try that for a moment then realise I look a little like Wonder Woman. I remember Hannah told me to put my shoulders back. I try that.

The smile.

The smile is ruddy awful – there'll be too much teeth and Luella is not keen on my bottom row. They've also been recently whitened at the dentist (a BBC requisite, apparently) so I am conscious that the camera flash will bounce off them and my face will glow. Ben and Matt stand to one side to let me have my moment and I watch them stand in that nervous default position one undertakes when next to a climbing frame and a young child is in situ – ready to catch. Then suddenly, the lights seem to double in intensity and I have a brief moment where I wonder if I'm having an existential crisis. I squint my eyes and out of the flurry of lights walks McCoy. He comes up to me and for a moment we stare at each other like we're about to enter a boxing ring or host a G8 summit. He comes to kiss my cheek and I smile – the same smile I do when faced with elderly relatives.

'You look great.' Do I return the compliment? Oh, you look all right too. Less of a drunk and fumbling look going on? I smile and let him put his arm around me. Matt's face has gone to serious and unimpressed. He looks like a bouncer. We turn to the cameras and he holds up a peace sign. I wave. There's a cacophony of noise. Contract, children, money, new roof. I mumble under my breath like a mantra to keep me focussed and smiley. People have endured far worse for money. This is not the indignity of a sex tape, a reality TV show in the jungle, or pantomime. This will be three months of your life. Contract, children, money, new roof. A bunch of kids run on and more photos are taken, even though I realise with all these smiling, over-excited children, Tommy and I look like we've inherited the Partridge Family. I look at Ben, who has immersed Matt in conversation to try and distract him. But I read the discomfort all over his face and I move away from McCoy and trip slightly. He catches me by grabbing my forearm. People gasp and laugh. Luella's eyes are closed. Holy potatoes.

'Thank you.'

'Any time.' I smile, relieved it didn't end in a proper face plant but knowing that some photo will make its way into a paper tomorrow. Damn. Or maybe not. As I straighten out my skirt, a figure lurks behind us.

'Tommy, honey. Can we get a photo?' I know of her vaguely. She's possibly a soap star turned musician turned underwear model who's wearing a dress that seems to be made out of serviettes and gift ribbon. Georgie Gale, that's her name, and I'll admit to liking her for an iota as it's clear she'll take some of the media flak off me tomorrow. I study her dress closely, envious of the stick-thin frame holding it up but also wondering how she's going to manage to sit down without tearing it.

'Oh my god, you're Jools from the show. It's so nice to meet you.'

She goes in for the hug and I am mindful of where I put my hands. Of course, our hug is short-lived because as soon as she hears her name, she bends over, shoulders arched, and pouts with a flick of her extensions. I look over at Tommy, who knows exactly where to put his hands and I feel desperately embarrassed for him. Seriously? It's Kitty 2.0 with a deeper mahogany tan. Is this really how you're going to reclaim your dignity? He plants a kiss on her cheek and there is a bit of light fondling before I also realise what a complete third wheel I look. I back away into Ben by the sidelines.

'Here, drink.' He puts a flute of something sparkling into my hand and I down it with efficient speed.

'Christ, maybe you should have worn that dress instead.'

'I'm not sure there's enough tit tape in the world to secure me in.'

Ben sniggers. 'I swear I saw her noo-nah before.'

It's my time to snigger and gracefully spit a bit of fizz out. 'Noo-nah?'

'Yup, and someone needs a wax.'

Matt sidles up between us. 'There were definite flashes of noo-nah. God, what a bunch of tits.' I give Matt a look. 'You know what I mean!' But the humour calms me down and we move further into the foyer of the restaurant hosting this evening's soiree. Wowsers. I'm not sure how to describe it; it's like a wedding reception without a bride or groom. Another tray passes and I replenish my drink. Luella speeds past me looking focussed and efficient.

'Chat to everyone, Jools. Ben, make sure you check her teeth. I'm off to schmooze but I'll be back. Check?' We all nod. Drink.

'Jools, *Radio Times* magazine. How are you this evening? Tell us about the show.'

Shit, that was to me. I smile and read her name badge: Anita. Luella said to be personable and call everyone by name. Think of why everyone likes Adele; yes, she's got a great set of pipes but she looks the sort who'd be a laugh and isn't too up her own backside.

'Hi, Anita!' She looks impressed.

'I'm just so excited, this is such a wonderful evening to introduce the show and the kids and I love the format. I like how it's promoting family cooking. It's fun, it harks back to the days of good, old-fashioned Saturday night entertainment.'

She nods and smiles and I remember what Luella said – praise the Beeb to the hilt, link it back to family. Talk about the show, not about you.

'I love it,' replies Anita. 'And tell me about your fellow judge, Mr McCoy. What's happening there? Can we expect the usual sparks flying when you two are in the same vicinity?'

I pause for a moment. Sparks like electricity caused by some physical attraction or sparks that could be flying off kitchen knives because we're about to stab each other? I swallow hard and smile nervously.

'Oh, watch this space, Anita. There will be drama, I'm sure of it.'

She waits for me to continue. I'm not sure how. I feel a hand reach to my side.

'A drink for the lady to toast the occasion? How about you, Anita?'

Ben. This is why you are here: to fuel awkward situations with alcohol. Anita takes a flute of pink champagne and clinks my glass. I turn to Matt who points to Ben behind his back and gestures that he may have downed a couple already, shrugging about what the best course of action is. But Ben seems to have this under control, completely distracting Anita with fruity alcohol and commenting on how fabulous her shoes are. Matt sidles up next to me.

'I feel like a lemon. A lemon in a suit. What do I do?'

'Drink, hold my hand.' His fingers grip mine tightly

and I down my drink, tiptoeing away from Ben as he continues to chat to Anita from the *Radio Times*. A face appears in front of mine.

'Cat from *Heat*. How are you today, Jools?' This is a great evening. And you must be Matt?'

It's Matt's turn to be the stunned haddock. He nods and shakes her hand which catches her unaware. At least it will be noted that my husband has manners.

'So, how do you feel about Jools' big judging job on the hottest new TV show in town?'

Matt looks at me, like I have the answer. I know better than to speak for him, knowing it would make him look like some henpecked, idiot husband but also because I am curious as to how he will respond.

'Umm, well … this is a whole new adventure for her. I think she'll rock it. She knows kids, she knows how families and food work. It's the perfect job for her.'

Cat from *Heat* smiles but I can see her scanning to my shoes and I wonder if she's scribbling down how I'm slightly pigeon-toed. Matt links his arm into mine and curls into me, the same way he does when we're standing in the kitchen making the last cup of tea of the day and trying to keep warm because the heating's off and the floor's like bloody ice. The flashback to us on that kitchen floor is soothing, warm.

'You've been out of the spotlight for a while, Jools. Since the cook-off and your book, was that a conscious decision or were you just waiting for the right project?'

Ooh, she's back to me.

'I think you're right. I wanted something really worthy to come along … and the right reasons to throw myself out of the frying pan, back into the fire.'

I've used a cooking analogy! Surely that speaks volumes about my suitability for this role.

'And this … it's a bold move … live TV, primetime

on a Saturday night … how will you cope?'

A tray of more champagne passes by me and I take a glass. This might be the answer, Cat from *Heat*. Copious amounts of alcohol, my lovable clumsy charms?

'It's not just me. The show is about the kids so the plan is to let them carry the show and be there to support them.'

Bring it back to the kids, show Cat from *Heat* that I believe they are the future. Wish them well and let them lead the way. Matt knows a savvy media move when he hears one and squeezes my hand again. Do I break out into song now?

'And what about your kids, are they here?'

I shake my head.

'And interrupt date night? Hell no! Like I say, the focus should be the kids in the show. They are all awesome. Like that little lady there.'

I point at Rosie across the room who notices me and looks slightly cautious. Is the judge lady going to swear loudly again? I urge her to come over. Her mother pushes her in my direction.

'This is Rosie from Bristol. Rosie, this is Cat. Rosie is one of our little chefs and she's awesome.'

'I am?' I nod at her and for a moment I think about Hannah, also ten. She can just about make toast and cereal but she's equally as awesome. These kids are ten years old, I'm not sure there's any other way to be at that age.

'So Rosie, what's your favourite dish to cook?'

'Ragu bolognaise. I make my own pasta.'

I gesture to Cat that surely this kid who knows her ragu from her spag bol and can understand the workings of a pasta machine is more worthy of her attentions. Cat knows I've dragged a young child over as some form of protective shield. She scribbles something down.

'And Rosie, what do you think about Jools here? Do

you like her?' she whispers out the corner of her mouth. Screw you, Cat. I look at Rosie. Will she out me for bad word usage? Can she read newspapers? I should have included sweets and fivers with those thank you notes. Rosie studies my face.

'She's nice ... don't tell anyone but during rehearsals the other day she helped me chop some parsley when I was running out of time.' I think she winks at me. It's true. I'm not one to watch children suffer for the sake of garnish. I'd do it for any one of them, propel them along so they don't get too downhearted if things go tits up in the kitchen. It truly is only food, not the end of the world.

'Isn't that an infringement of the rules?' she gasps jokingly.

I wink at Rosie. 'If the camera doesn't see then it never happened.' She smiles. I can tell Cat still wants to ask probing questions. 'I like your necklace, Cat.' And with that I have a distraction as Rosie starts to ask more questions and I manage to slink away and find Ben, armed with a whole tray of alcohol.

'These are raspberry champagne cocktails infused with passionfruit. Friggin' yum and they are part of your 5-a-day,' Ben explains. I laugh. That laugh gets Matt worried because it means I've obviously drunk one too many so I have lost control of my neck and my head swings about with wild abandon. Matt sips quietly from a continental European beer bottle, the drink of the sensible, slightly hipster dad. The full hipster dad would drink sloe gin with lavender draping out of the glass. He wouldn't wear socks and have man whiskers. I laugh to think about Matt with whiskers.

'Like a little mouse.' I realise I've said that out loud and am rubbing my husband's top lip. Ben finds this hilarious.

'Geez, you'd never think you two are related. You

have the exact same tolerance for alcohol and it's seems to have turned you both into giggling fools.'

Of course, this makes us laugh more and I slap Ben playfully on the arm to shush him. Matt stops someone sashaying past with a tray of canapés.

'Here, both of you … eat something. These look like they have carbs in them.'

They are indeed carbs – baby bagels stuffed with cream cheese, pastrami, and rocket i.e. the devil's salad. I pop one in my mouth and Matt shakes his head. That was a two bite job and you know it because the cream cheese is creeping out the sides of your mouth. He turns his back to the reporters behind me to shield me. Ben reaches at a bowl of passing popcorn.

'Have you tried this yet?'

I take a kernel from his palm and almost choke as it touches my tongue. Christ alive.

'Is that blue cheese?' Matt eyeballs me yet again. 'Don't you dare spit that out … swallow, Jools. Swallow that shit, Jools.' He gives Ben the evil eye, as if to say you know about your sister's aversion to soft cheeses with veins.

'Yes … swallow, Jools. Does Matt have to say that a lot, dear sister?'

Blue cheese buggery. I'm half laughing, half choking. Matt sniggers.

'Yes, Jools. Swallow … it's all protein.' His once serious, semi-hipster, nonchalant face creases into lines. I like it when we break him. I like how this has become date night on steroids. Before, we'd watch a movie and grab a Nando's and revel in the marvel that is free refills on soft drinks. Now it's become a night of fancy cocktails, ridiculous canapés, and tittering over fellatio puns. Luella is not so sure. She approaches us, sensible cocktail in hand with eyes that demand serious decorum.

'People! Is there any reason Jools is gurning?'

This makes Matt and Ben laugh even louder. It attracts curious onlookers who I hope assume we're just fun people to be around. I swallow.

'Lu, seriously ... blue cheese popcorn. Are you trying to kill me?'

She puts a few pieces in her mouth.

'Gobshite caterers. I did tell them. How's things? I saw you chatting with Cat from *Heat*. I forgot to say can you mention you're wearing earrings from Tatty Devine but only if they ask so you don't sound like a label brag. I did mini bagels. You like bagels?'

She says it at three times the normal speed for Luella which is motorsport fast and makes me think the cocktail in her hand is not as sensible as first thought and may be tainted with the free, fashionable vodka also on offer. She pushes some of the hair from my eyes.

'I love you. You know I love you, Jools Campbell. And I love your husband and your babies and this gorgeous brother of yours. We should all go to France and stay with Remy's mother. You'd love her ... she lives in a shack and drinks wine out of a jug. She reminds me of Gia.'

Jesus, and I thought I was drunk. Matt sobers up for a bit, realising if she's also gone then noone is steering this ship. There is a need for a rudder, for someone to guide Jools through these stormy, media-infested waters. But the skippers are drunk on free, trendy moonshine. The boat will run off-course. Worse, it may sink. I can still taste blue cheese in my mouth so I down the last of my drink.

'Hi, Jools. I'm Briony from *Good Food* magazine. May I have a few moments of your time?'

I smile wonkily.

'Of course, Briony.'

'It's just we've come up with a set of quick fire questions that will be a part of a mini featurette in our next edition. It's just a little bit of fun …'

Ben puts another glass in my hand.

'I'm all about the fun. Bring it on!' I realise I will answer these half-cut but because my senses are heightened and I am, of course, five times more hysterical than normal, this may make for some better answers.

'OK … trifle or torte?'

'Trifle, every time. I'm retro like that.' I try to remember what a torte is. Posh cake?

'Salt and vinegar or Cheese and Onion?'

'Salt and vinegar.' I grimace thinking about that popcorn. 'I prefer cheese I can see and sink my teeth into.'

'Coffee or tea?'

'Tea, every time. It keeps me sane. That and gin. But separately and when the children are not in the vicinity.'

Matt looks at me to alert me to the fact I may be rambling nonsense.

'Ketchup or brown sauce?'

'Ketchup on chips, brown sauce with a fry-up.'

She nods, pensive. 'Interesting.'

'How so?

'McCoy said the same thing.' I stop in my tracks and notice Matt trying to gauge my reaction too. Is she trying to fish for a reaction? Or is this coincidence?

'My husband would say the same too. Classic combos.' I say that to allay any tension she's trying to cause but secretly, I've also seen Matt dip his chips in mayonnaise which always makes me question the foundations of our relationship.

'And they have to be proper chips, not those weird skinny shoestring ones that are all floppy when you hold them.'

119

Of course, talk of floppy chips makes Ben, standing in earshot, erupt into giggles. There's a twitching at the corners of my mouth. Must not laugh in the kind reporter's face.

'Where I come from, they're called French fries.' I recognise that smarmy accent as soon as I hear it and roll my eyes at Matt. Of course, now is not the time for face-slapping or accusations and I'm far too merry for that in any case, so I make the unfathomable decision to embrace Cam and do the fake air-kiss. Luella reaches into the air as I do it, just in case a violent head-butt was my intent. As is usually the way, people hold their breaths to see what I will do/how I'll mess up.

'Cam Jacobs! How lovely to see to you.' Even he can't read the reason for my merriment and studies Matt and Ben's faces curiously. Matt, who's never met him before in the flesh, is very Matt. He can never hide his displeasure from anyone, so his face scrunches to a scowl. Ben can just about focus, let alone stand. Luella looks like a raven ready to protect her prey. A drunk raven.

'Cam, this is the lovely Briony from *Good Food* … Tell me, have you become accustomed to our strange eating ways over here?'

If I've learnt anything about Cam so far, he's about face. He'll dig and cast aspersions but if this is about him, he will do everything he can to make himself and his clients come across well. If alcohol does anything to me, it makes me chatty. I can handle this, probably better than if I was sober.

'Well, Tommy introduced me to something you guys call a "chip butty": deep-fried carbs on carbs. It's a wonder you're all still alive.'

I find this hilarious and shove him playfully in the shoulder to let him know. He knows I am drunk and laughs at me. I should add, 'at me' as opposed to 'with me' – he knows I'm within a razor's edge of doing something I shouldn't. Briony senses something is awry and stands there knowingly, grabbing a glass of cocktail from a nearby tray so she has something to sip as she watches the action.

'You're in fine fettle, Miss Campbell.'

'Mrs Campbell. He, over there in the suit … he put a ring on it.' And this is where I feel my body slip into a weird Beyoncé style dance move. Of course, I don't look like Beyoncé when I do it. I look like I'm screwing in a lightbulb. This makes Ben rhubarb with both shame and amazement. Luella looks like she could laser off my hand. I take a large gulp of drink.

'That he did …' He goes over to shake Matt's hand, almost as if to say to marry a person of such incompetence was a feat worthy of commiseration. Matt takes it cautiously.

'And, pray tell, where has Thomas got to this evening? My old TV buddy judging chum.'

I look out at the crowd of flashing lights and canapés.

'Oh, you know Tommy. He's chatting to some of the people from his foundation about his charity work with food banks. And he was on the bouncy castle with the kids before, he is a hoot! Did you meet Georgie? How cute did they look together?'

I nod. Of course he has a foundation. He was to win public favour back somehow. The only other way was to ride on horseback through towns flinging free food at the peasants. I didn't think I'd have to endure the indignity of a bouncy castle, though. The dress, hair, and pelvic floor would never have allowed for that. I smile to myself to think about that picture: me star jumping to reveal my giant knickers and a puddle of piss. This obviously appeals to Briony as well, who slinks away with her photographer in tow to capture this moment on film.

'But we need to get some more photos of you later, maybe a selfie? You guys and your TV family!'

Matt's nostrils are flared at this point and he looks at me as we have one of those conversations noone else is party to. Is this the publicity man-whore? Yup, pretty much. I smile and go to air-kiss him as my way of ending this charade. He whispers into my ear as our cheeks touch.

'Did you like the popcorn?'

Oh lordy, did this man infer he had something to do with attempting to poison me via the power of blue cheese? Smile, you have to smile.

'I loved it. How original, but then you are full of surprises, Mr Jacobs.'

'Oh ... my mates just call me Cam,' he says in a faux London accent.

I go to whisper in his ear.

'We're not friends you dodgy tosser.' Matt's eyebrows let me know I've sworn in a manner which is quite unlike me: through gritted teeth and with a vernacular that is usually reserved for his angry Scottish tones. He looks almost proud. Luella looks happy she's still standing and that I seem to have handled things. Who needs a skipper, eh? Cam smiles back and salutes, almost as if to tell me battle has commenced. There's a moment of eye contact as he disappears into the crowd again.

Ben appears, this time with shot glasses. 'So that's the famous Cam Jacobs? Hmmm ...' I can't tell what sort of sigh that is but who the hell cares when the brother is carrying shot glasses? I did well, I held my own, yay for me, so I pass the shots around and countdown from three. '3-2- ... Christ, Ben.'

'Sambuca?'

'It's old skool.' Matt looks like the alcohol has hit a nerve, making him recall cold, sticky university floors.

'Geez, Ben, that tasted like death.' Matt laughs.

Sambuca was possibly the liquor that sealed our fate. It got us so plastered that it led to our first bedroom meeting. It's like paint thinner lining my throat. Oh sweet Jesus. No, not now. Matt notices it first. When Matt needs to vom, he sways like he's on a boat. I'm different; colour drains from my face and I make a low-grade mumbling.

'Stay with me, Jools.' Don't speak or move your lips. Breathe deeply through the nostrils. I burp under my breath. It tastes like blue cheese. Matt quickly hooks an arm under mine and escorts me through the crowd.

'One foot in front of the other, Mrs Campbell.'

I giggle, humming a wedding march. Not before remembering I need to vom.

'Just not yet. We're nearly there.' But there's a queue. There's always a queue.

'I could vom in the sink?'

'Not on my watch.' He changes direction to the Gents and opens a cubicle for me, holding my hair back as I launch myself at the toilet. He shuts the door and rubs my back.

'Well, this is new. The last time I did this, you were pregnant with twins.'

I laugh and throw up at the same time. It's an unusual feeling. I see bits of pastrami floating in the loo. Matt looks away. I struggle to stand in this footwear and wobble about, using the walls of the cubicle to hold me up.

'What have I done, Matt? Seriously?' Matt shrugs.

'You've thrown up after downing five flutes of champagne, worse things have happened. You could have thrown up on a kid. Personally, I'd have liked to have seen you throw up on Georgie Gale so we could check out the absorbency of that dress.' I laugh and rest my head against his chest.

'Don't throw up on this, it's the most expensive outfit

123

I've ever had in my life. Here …'

He bends down and cleans a little bit of splash-back off my shoes, what every gallant husband should do. We hear someone come in the doors and he puts a finger to my lips. 'Ssssh!' I giggle and we wait. He unzips his trousers and relieves himself in front of me. Of course, this is nothing to me and I've seen far worse in ten years of marriage. We wait. I open the door to the cubicle. I wipe at the corners of my mouth and look up. A flash goes off in my face.

CHAPTER TEN

'Campbell! Oi, you dirty beast! Come 'ere!' Donna launches herself at me and locks me in an embrace. It feels warm, familiar, and I'll admit to having missed some of her candour. Since becoming a 'working mum' of sorts, I don't see her every day, twice a day and I miss our little chats outside the school gates, joshing about our fellow school mums and herding gangs of children around. Because in effect, it's these women that become your friends; not through choice but given you see them every day, they become some common denominator, faces that wave at you from their car windows and console you when your youngest throws herself in a puddle. So now I don't see their faces as often, I confess to missing them a little, this one in particular.

'You and Matt, eh? The magic is still there, you filthy puppies.'

I blush and look over my shoulder. What Donna is alluding to is the launch night and the rather unfortunate picture that found itself into the papers the following day; because the public weren't interested in the prodigious cooking children nor Georgie Gale and her noo-nah. No, the picture that caused all the fuss was 'family chef' Jools Campbell emerging from a cubicle in the gentlemen's loos with her husband, wiping her mouth while her husband looked to be adjusting his tackle.

Matt, of course, does not see the fuss. Given what was really happening, he laughed as such an activity is a rare treat at that, which I've never conducted in a toilet cubicle … well, ever. Luella and the BBC thought differently. This was the sort of picture that could void our contract, especially because there were children at that party and mothers 'like me' shouldn't be doing things like that. Luella argued differently: a married couple indulge in sexual activity. It's not a shock, it's not wrong. It's not even what she was doing, so scandalous hearsay. She won them round. But at the same time she was equally thrilled that my picture was top headlines instead of McCoy and his desperate attempts at clawing his way back into the limelight.

'We weren't doing what everyone thinks we were doing.'

Donna punches my arm playfully. 'Yeah, whatevs. You're allowed. The toilets in Wetherspoons have seen me and Dave plenty of times.' I'm open mouthed at the thought and laugh, clouds of cold air puffing out of my mouth, hoping the crowd of parents nearby didn't hear. Today is football day. Later, I will have to skedaddle to a studio and film the first episode of *Little Chefs,* so what better way to distract myself from my nerves than drag my arse out of bed at stupid o'clock to watch my twins and husband in action? Donna is here to watch Justin on the neighbouring pitch. I can't feel my toes. If I make the front pages tomorrow, it's because I had to have my feet amputated due to frostbite. Matt stands at the other side of the pitch in his now-famous tracksuit, old trainers, and a woolly hat, making rows of kids do star jumps to warm up. The tracksuit is not doing it for me in any way but it's better compared to the other manager who's wearing bleached white knee-length socks. I wave at one of the school mums further upfield but she eyes me curiously, smiles, and looks away.

'So, goss. Miranda Scott. I saw her around your Matt but from what I hear she's down the pub most nights trying to get it where she can so I wouldn't worry.'

I've scanned the field for her but she's smart and sits in her car with the heating on. Part of me feels slightly disappointed that she feels Matt is fair game but also that she seems to lack any sort of discernment when it comes to her selection process.

'But seriously, it's like the woman's on heat. Did you hear what she did? Just walked out, told that poor bloke of hers he was a saddo and boring … those poor kids. And now she's on Tinder, hooks up with complete strangers and has a go on them in the lay-by next to the services on the A3.'

This. This is what I've missed. But as she says it, I feel a pang of emotion run through me thinking about other mothers who did that once. My mother, who walked out on three young children with lame excuses, and rebuilt another life without them in it. Donna gets out her phone and scrolls to her Facebook profile.

'It was after she went on Slimming World and lost all that weight, look at her profile picture. If it's not pictures of her effing dinner, it's selfies of her arse in gym wear.'

I take the phone and turn it round several times, not sure if I'm looking at buttocks or boobs. I flick through several more pics involving selfies, alcohol, and one that seems to be her dry humping a lamp post.

'She's allowed to have fun, we all are, but she needs to tone it down and think about her bits. This is how you catch things.'

I hand Donna back her phone and catch that mum from across the field looking at me again. Lizzy, I think her name is. She's a governor at the school, one of those mums who has illusions of grandeur that she might run the place. I smile. Nothing. Across the way, I catch an opposition mum staring and pointing. I pull my scarf over my mouth.

'Haha, you got spotted! Can I get a pic? I can send it into the mags and get £50.' I pull a face.

'What's the deal with Lizzy, Charlie's mum? I'm getting vibes off her. She was always really nice.'

Donna shrugs. 'Love, school mums, football mums ... they're all the same. Catty as you like. I've given up trying to read some of them. You know she's the sort who has a thing about working mums, she's just miffed you're not one of us any more.'

The insinuation makes me stop in my tracks. When did I stop being a mum? I'm still here fifty per cent of the time and do at least two or three schools runs a week. She knows she's hit a nerve but Donna's not the sort to let a comment like that sit without explanation.

'Oh, you know. You're a celeb now, and you'll always be my mate ... just some of them won't understand it, they'll be jealous and weird about it but that's their thing, not yours ... RIGHT, C'MON, PANTHERS! LET'S BE 'AVING YA, BOYS!'

It's like standing in a wind tunnel. I wish that had come with some warning. She laughs.

'You'll love it. Morning, Frank! Nice fresh one, eh?'

I turn around and it's Dad with a Thermos and folding camp chair. He looks prepared for the Arctic. He holds a hand up to wave to Donna as she jogs along the pitch, shouting about kicking things up the line.

'You're here?'

'Why not? I did it for you three. Remember when you played hockey? God, you were awful.' He laughs to himself and I cradle his arm, thinking about how even if I didn't have a mum, I had another parent who covered her role, who came with the knowledge that tea made everything better. He unscrews his Thermos.

'You didn't bring tea, did you? Here, warm up.'

'No, but I brought half time oranges.'

128

Dad screws up his face. 'It's not the eighties, love. They'll want Lucozade and energy bars.' I still cuddle my Tupperware proudly. At least it's fruit? I sip my tea, watching as a ref who looks like a child himself blows a whistle. I'm not sure what that means but it seems to prompt twelve kids to run at a ball and follow it around in crowds like a magnet.

'Their team is called the Tigers, just in case you wanted to support them.' I smile at Dad, who knows I would've just shouted my kids' names sporadically and 'go, red team!' Matt stands there clapping but generally being quite nice for a coach. There's lots of support and calm, positive comments. Unlike the berk in the knee-high socks who's shouting on a very different level, making veins stick out of his neck like you'd see on a soft cheese. The thought makes me think back to launch night vomiting and I swallow slowly. Dad hasn't really commented on what's made the papers recently and the thought of what he's read makes me cringe.

'Why are the boys stood at the back?'

'They're in defence, love.' Figures. Ted seems to have taken the ball off someone. I think that was good. 'Go, Ted!' He smiles and waves. That wasn't too embarrassing, eh? I feel an arm on my shoulder.

'Oi, oi. Look who's emerged.' Donna's run over to tell me Miranda Scott's out of her car. She's gone over to chat to Matt and kisses him on the cheek. They seem to be talking and Matt points at me. I wave. She smiles awkwardly, looking aggrieved that I've made an appearance.

'I heard her proposition one of the dads the other day,' Dad pipes in. 'She told him she's got special ways she could keep him warm.' I love how Dad says that, completely incongruous, like he's heard it all before. Donna snarls slightly as Dad points him out. 'That one with the hat, hiding behind his wife.'

'Oh my Christ, Ginger Pete!' Of course, we never call him that to his face but Ginger Pete looks like Chris Evans in the nineties if he'd put in rollers every day. Lovely bloke with a penchant for outdoor wear and trapper hats, not someone I'd think about in that way, but each to their own. Donna's shaking her head.

'Like I say, she can have all the fun she wants but she starts flaunting it about with the marrieds then I've got a proper beef about that ... MARK UP, JUSTIN! '

Miranda positions herself by the goal, glancing over to the parents every so often. I half want to chat to her, to tell her to have some self-worth and stop ostracising herself from her womenfolk but the fact she is fully made-up, hair washed, and wearing two-inch heel boots makes me think I need to keep my distance. I pull my hood up, glancing down at the parka chic I've chosen to face this morning with. Dad and Matt are shouting.

'Go, Tigers!' Dad looks over at me. 'Dad, who's this Manon kid everyone keeps shouting for?' Dad gives me that look that questions if he knows me or not.

'Man. On. It's a football term, like there's someone behind you, so watch your back. Jesus, Jools ...'

'Well, they're six years old, surely it should be "boy on" ...' Dad sidesteps to dissociate himself from me.

'Do you know anything else about that Miranda woman? Apparently, she's been a bit flirty with Matt.' Dad looks at me out of the corner of his eye. He knows when I like to fish for information.

'Well, I'm glad Matt brought it up. She's got a way about her, eh? But, you know, your Matt is a catch. I've often wondered how much you know that ...'

It's my turn to give him the knowing looks. 'Well, he is my husband.'

'Yeah, but back last year when it was all kicking off

and that Colman kid made an appearance. I don't think you knew how lucky you were to have him. Look at him, half the mums here are giving him eyes. And it's worse at the school gate. I went to that drama festival last week and they were all over him like flies on shit.'

I stand back, watching my husband closely. He's always had that youthful grunge look about him like he should be an Arctic Monkey. There's some stubble, some lines around the eyes. I look at it daily, never comparatively, so I know I like it, it does me fine. I've never doubted he may be attractive to others but I've always thought there were little things about his person that I endured that were a complete turn-off to anyone but me: the constant need to complain and swear at inanimate objects, the klaxon-volume morning flatulence being two fine examples.

'Of course, he's really lucky to have me too, right?'

Dad shakes his head about. 'I was lucky. I offloaded you early. Found some mug who'd put up with you.' I punch him in the arm. He pours me another cup of tea. 'You don't realise, a house husband, a man at the school gate who can seemingly do all those things their own husbands can't … it's attractive.'

'You talk from experience?'

Dad nods. 'Back in the day, there was a mum called Yvonne. She used to take photos of herself in her pants, back before your digital nonsense. Back when you had to take a roll down Boots and collect your photos the next day. Yup, she was persistent.'

I can't stop laughing. 'She wanted a piece of Frank, eh?'

I can hardly breathe for laughing and Dad has to hold me upright and tell me to calm down to stop attracting onlookers.

'You weren't tempted?'

131

He goes quiet for a moment. 'Well, your mother broke me, eh? When you've had your heart broken, chewed up, and spat out, you think twice about going back for seconds.'

The giggling stops. 'Oh, Dad.'

'Especially to a woman in lilac cotton knickers who takes photos of herself in the bathroom on timer.' I smile but cuddle up next to him. Dad never says much about old Dot but he does reveal snippets of information now and then. In the middle of a windswept field is a strange place to divulge such emotion but it gives me another piece of the jigsaw.

'But you and Matt are different. It'll take more than a random old mare with her bosoms out to separate you two.'

I nod.

'What time you off for filming?'

'Car picks me up at lunch. You going to be watching?'

'Umm, stupid question? I've got a date night with Matt and your kids. I've made a fish pie. You'll be all right.'

I don't know if his last sentence was a question but I nod and repeat my mantra again: contract, children, money, new roof. I've done this before under far more stressful circumstances. I simply have to rock up and try some food. Dad's gaze sticks to mine for a moment longer than needed, because he knows I don't always have the answers, but he hopes he might be able to read it in my eyes. Do you have enough money? Will you cope with twins? How did your history exam go? I'll live. He smiles. But then my ears are distracted by Matt shouting from the other side of the pitch. I spy Jake near a goal, the ball goes near his feet. 'YES! GO, JAKE!' I'll admit to a smidgeon of excitement bubbling away inside of me. That's one of my babies. Go, go, go! And the ball hits the back of the net. I scream.

'Yes! Go, Jake! Woohoo!'

Why is Matt staring at me?

Dad whispers over my shoulder. 'Own goal, love. He scored for the other side.' Jake doesn't seem to care. He runs down the field and practises a goal celebration that involves robot dancing. The only part of today that has undoubtedly come from me. I pull my scarf over my face and let Matt handle this one. Lizzy stares at me again then whispers something to the mum next to her who raises her eyebrows. Dad catches wind of it too.

'Yup, there'll be plenty of that. Nothing worse than a gossipy school gate. I had one woman go round saying your mum had left me because I was a Quaker and had several other wives hidden away.'

'What the hell?'

'It was back when I used to teach that adult IT class out the meeting halls and she used to catch me coming out every Monday night.'

'I'd have slapped her.'

'Yeah, you're good at that.' He laughs and gives me a look. 'I tell you, for half of them, they live pretty mundane lives and the school gate is their soap opera – it's live and happening right in front of them. And it's all they have. Sad, really. So imagine, a mum like them suddenly breaking out the mould, on the TV and seemingly having it all …'

'Beware of the daggers.'

'Exactly.'

I look around as I suddenly notice half the eyes around the pitches are pointed at me, shifting me looks, taking notes as to what I'll do next. Has that person got a camera phone out? I stare at Lizzy to try and get her attention. I'm still like you, honest. But she looks out towards the boys, ignoring me.

CHAPTER ELEVEN

If motherhood has taught me anything in the last ten years, it's that I have picked up an innate understanding of when a child may be on the precipice of relieving themselves of bodily fluid.

'Kai, Kai honey, are you OK?' Kai jogs about on the spot like he's doing the wee dance. I know the wee dance. The poo dance involves crossed legs and a hand down the back of the waistband. This is wee. But then he looks as white as a sheet, could this be a double whammy? Someone is counting down quite ominously. Eight minutes.

'Hon, we could run to the loo and get back really quickly?' He nods, looking ashen.

'But we could be … I don't want to spoil things if I'm missing?' I take his hand and signal to Ben. He signals back that it's not my job but I'm not sure I care – saving this boy's blushes seems to be the priority. I signal I'll be back and he looks slightly panicked. We find the nearest ladies' and I duck in with him as he runs to a cubicle and leaves the door open. I'm reminded of my twins, who still gladly take a dump, swing their legs while they're sat there, and watch you take a bath. I turn around.

'All good?'

'Yes, thank you, Mrs Campbell.'

'Geez, Kai, I'm not your teacher. You can call me Jools.' He returns to wash his hands but still looks pale and sickly.

'Thank you, Jools. I have an aunty Jools.' I smile at

the kid trying to make small talk, but I know it's probably helping quell his nerves. I think back to my first foray into live television and how it really meant nothing, some cooking segment to save my name. All I had to do was remain standing and not burn down the place. But I guess when you're ten, the stakes are higher, the world seems a much larger place.

'Do you like *Star Wars*? When I was little, I had two brothers and they couldn't say my name properly so they called me Jewie, like Chewie.' I make a Wookiee sound but sound the way I do when I yawn first thing in the morning. He smiles.

'What if it goes wrong? I don't want to mess up.' I see his little face on the verge of tears and put a hand to his shoulder.

'Hey, did you see me on the cook-off I did a couple of years ago? I nearly chopped off a finger, I burnt the food … like really badly. And I'm still here, still standing. I won't let you mess up. You'll be fine.'

He takes a large gulp like he might not quite believe me.

'And anyway, if something goes wrong, I'll trip up McCoy and everyone can laugh at him instead.'

He laughs. 'You really don't like him, do you?'

I arch my eyebrows and watch as a smile broadens across his face and the colour returns to his cheeks.

'There you go. C'mon, they'll be looking for us.'

When we get back, Luella is frantically pacing the set and takes me to one side.

'Christ, you want to give me a heart attack. You can't disappear like that! Next time I can take the kid to the loo. We have interns for that. Ben, your own brother!' She's stress ranting. Most would be taken aback but I'm used to it and maintain calm. Children next to me marvel at the words per hour.

'Slow down, we're all good. This will be fine. Contract, children, money, new roof.'

I sound like the mad one now. 'What the hell?' she enquires.

'It's my mantra. It'll get me through this.'

'Bloody McCoy … have you seen him? He's wearing some stupid Adidas top. I suspect it's some high fashion shit because of the young girlfriend but he looks like a prize idiot. Grrrr.'

Yes, she really makes that noise. I always forget about Luella's past with Tommy. She hardly talks of the ins and outs of it but there's still bad blood where she won't forgive his betrayal. Of course, his massive fall from grace was cathartic and definitely made some headway into helping her achieve the revenge she wanted but I often wonder why she persists on this journey to ruin him. I take her hand and stroke it like a small kitten. She laughs.

'Just go out there and kill this.'

'THIRTY SECONDS TO TITLES, PEOPLE!'

'I think kill's the wrong word in this circumstance – there are knives and children in the vicinity.'

And with that I'm pushed out to the blinding lights of the studio and the sound of faint applause.

'Ten minutes left, kids. Time to start thinking about plating up and making everything look good. That's ten minutes.'

Because the giant clock in the middle of the room won't remind them, McCoy's voice echoes through the studio. He stands in the middle of the room with his arms behind his back. He's not how I thought he'd be. In rehearsals, there seemed to be general interest in the kids and their cooking. Today, he seems to be keeping them at arm's length and asks them questions to almost throw

137

them off. Poor Erin doesn't know about pollock and how it's a sustainable alternative to cod. It was thus left up to me to act as the go-between, the one who told them to keep going, to hug poor Jackson when his roux burnt, and to joke with Lydia about the size of her sweet potatoes. I kept looking over to McCoy to gauge what he was about.

This was primetime television and not just that, the spectators in the galleries were the kids' families, watching our every move and ready to pounce. This was not the time to change tack and be the surly judge no one likes. I continue to pace up and down the studio as the kids do their best to produce a one pot family dinner for under a tenner. They've raided the giant fridge/larder for their ingredients, they've brought on a family member to help with the prep (special mention to Callum's gran, Minnie in the Minion T-shirt), and they're all on track to receive the Head Chef award that McCoy and I will give out at the end of the show. It's the first episode so there'll be no eliminations, just praise and pats on backs. I get to Kai's worktop and he's frantically stirring a saucepan. I put a hand on his shoulder, conscious a cameraman is right in his face. He's back to ashen and scared.

'Kai, love. It's OK, tell me how I can help?'

'My stew, it's not thickening. It's like soup.'

'Well, maybe we can call it a soup.' I'm trying to make light of the situation, thinking about how I often have re-branded dishes based on whether my ineptitude has completely screwed them up, but he's not buying it.

'I think it needs more flour. Is it too late to put more flour in? I just …'

'Kai, breathe, it's fine. Let's turn the heat up and reduce it a bit.'

But he's panicking. He rushes over to the kilner jar on the counter and tosses a fair bit in. I gasp and watch as it forms cloudy balls in the stew gravy. I grab a whisk and

138

try to stir in as much as I can.

'Oh no, what have I done?' I swear my hand has never moved so fast in the hope that he hasn't seen how he's royally mucked up. The gravy is thickening now but far too fast. I turn off the heat, cover the pan, and watch as his face stiffens. Remember when I said I knew about children? I also know when they're going to cry. Please kid, don't cry. Not now. He tears up and uses the end of his sleeve to wipe his face. I see his mum stand in the gallery and I urge her to sit down. I put my hand over my microphone to the confusion of a floor manager who starts tapping at machinery.

'Come here.' I let him hide his face in my Monsoon jumper so noone can see him and feel his shoulders shudder.

'I messed up. I didn't want to mess up.'

I can feel myself tearing up. I look at him.

'Kai, how is this messing up? Coming on live TV and doing your best and doing something a huge number of kids your age don't know how to do. That's not messing up.'

Kai's mum is crying. I want to round kick this cameraman and tell him to get out of our faces but he persists in hovering over us.

'Kai, mate, for judging we're going to need something on a plate. Give us what you got.'

It's McCoy at the end of his worktop with a disappointed look about him. I instantly want to slap him.

'Tommy, give Kai a break. He's had a bit of a mishap.'

McCoy shrugs and walks off. Kai whispers to me. 'I guess I have to?'

'Not if you're not happy with it, Kai, we can improvise.' A floor manager is winding her finger at me from the sides and telling me I'm not standing in the right place. This is the point where Tommy and I are supposed to stand next to the giant clock and count down like it's New Year. I shake my head.

'Are you OK, Kai?' He nods at me, using a tea towel to wipe his face. I bend down to whisper in his ear.

'I'm going to trip him up, you watch.' He smiles at me. I join McCoy at the clock, who seems upset I've spoiled our major countdown moment.

'5-4-3-2-1 … and step away from your dishes!'

I, of course, leave that line to McCoy but stand there surveying the counters, encouraging everyone to clap and cheer. I look down at Kai and watch as his stew sits there in its casserole. His eyes peer over into the pot and I see a look of sheer terror like he's stumbled across roadkill. I am familiar with that look.

'So kids, thank you. Let's get trying some of these dishes then. Kai, we'll start with you.'

I look at Tommy. One, we are supposed to work our way alphabetically through the kids, but this is live and there's no telling him. He strides over and I follow.

'Kai, tell us what you've cooked for us today.'

'It's a chicken stew with flatbreads.'

Tommy takes a fork and pulls out a piece of chicken that he flakes onto the plate. He doesn't taste it but scratches at the meat. He then pulls out pieces of vegetables and cuts them with his fork.

'Well, everything is cooked through … but seriously, the gravy is congealed and like jelly. There are lumps running through it. This isn't great, I can't even eat this. I don't think I want to.'

The whole studio stops. Managers and directors are on the floor looking aghast, parents on the sidelines look murderous. Kids look like they've turned to stone. Young Kai looks like he wants the floor to swallow him up. I pick up my fork.

'Well, he can't but I'm going to give it a go. I saw your mum chopping the veggies – there's onion, carrot, and is it French beans?' I wave at Mum. He nods, trying hard to hold back more tears. Tommy continues to finger the bit of chicken on his plate.

'Did your mother never teach you not to play with your food, Tommy?' This makes some of the kids laugh. He gives me a look.

'I'm curious as to why he used breast. Thigh meat would have made this stew far more succulent.'

Kai is lost for words. I intervene. 'Well, whatever meat it is, this is really tasty. The thyme is a really nice touch and you made your own bread in the time, too. I'm super impressed.'

Tommy doesn't even look at him. I wait till the camera is on the move then elbow him in the ribs. Kai sees and giggles. Tommy reads my look but moves onto the next dish. We sample nine other dishes from tagines to soups to curries – all tasty, well-thought-out, and given they've come from the skills of children, I can't fault any of them. Given my shock at how adept they are, I thus lavish them all with praise, questioning the very reason I may be here as they certainly cook far better than I do.

And then it comes to my 'favourite' part of the show, where McCoy and I are led to our judging quarters: touchscreen central, watching lights and giant photos flash up. I hate how they're making me look directly into his face. It's like having a picture of Justin Bieber in front of me and not being allowed to slap it.

'So, top dishes were definitely the massaman curry and the risotto. Textures, flavours, and ingredient choice were top notch. I give them my vote.'

Tommy pulls up pictures of the final dishes, in case I've forgotten I only tasted them fifteen minutes ago. I scan through the photos. Of course, these were the standout dishes, one of those kids even made their own curry paste in a pestle and mortar. But I have the overwhelming need to disagree with him as I normally do.

'I liked the tagine. She was the only one who attempted fish and she did it really well. I liked the nuts in the couscous, it was different.'

He gives me a look; they're only giving us four minutes to decide. I'm the chef, I know what was good. Leave this to the professionals, love.

'And bottom of the pile, that chicken stew disaster, obviously.'

He's doing it, he's really doing it. I can't believe someone who's a father would do this to a child on live television. He knows the fallout will be epic. Does he not remember this is going out as it happens? Where is the compassion? Happy Tommy who went on the bouncy castle and high-fived all these kids like it was going out of fashion?

'Well, you didn't even try it so I don't know how you're fit to comment?'

'I wouldn't waste my time. The kid's obviously out of his depth.'

'The kid's called Kai and he's got this far. He can cook as well as most adults and frankly you're being way too harsh.' A camera lens zooms in on me but Tommy continues to ignore me.

'So, curry for the win. Let's go tell them?' And with that he returns to the studio, leaving me staring at the camera, mumbling something I probably shouldn't.

As soon as I'm where I'm supposed to be, the lights dim and there's a bizarre flash of lights. I look to the melee of people and for the first time notice Ben, taking it all in. He waves and pulls a face which makes me smile. Wait, it's me. It's my turn to announce the Head Chef. I look out at the sea of little faces. Kai's face is bright pink, that boy has been sobbing, proper full-out crying. I think for a moment.

'So, Little Chefs, we are so glad you cooked for us today and thanks to all of you for your efforts. When Tommy and I were thinking about who to give Head Chef to today, we thought about what this show and cooking is all about. You know, it's not all fancy recipes and stuff – the point is for kids like yourselves to come out and give it a go and when it doesn't go to plan, to be brave, pick yourselves up, and keep cooking. So both of us thought it was really important that Head Chef today goes to … Kai.'

The studio stops. Kai looks at me like I'm mad, so do the parents of Tia and her massaman curry. Tommy stares me down. He doesn't dare correct me as Kai's parents stand to applaud. I see Ben and Luella on the sides, smiling and nodding.

'Come and get your badge.' Kai will get to wear a pin on his apron all week now. He comes over confused and bends into me.

'Are you sure? Did you say the wrong name?'

'No, you're a great chef. Just believe in yourself a bit more, OK?' I shake his hand. He goes up to Tommy, who ignores him but reads from an autocue to bring the show to a close. I wink at Kai as he returns to his friends, who all congratulate him.

'ROLL CREDITS!' I'm not entirely sure what happens after this but Tommy glares at me from his spot on the studio floor. Kai's dad comes down to meet him.

'What the hell was that? What the …' He takes McCoy by the collar and I see Ben run on to get between them. I couldn't care less. The man deserves a punch. Just don't punch my brother. A producer walks on to try and keep the peace.

'I did not give permission for my son to come on here

143

and be made a fool of. That was out of order. He was a complete tosser to those kids.'

Parents stand in the galleries to start revolting against him. A little part of me revels in the fact I am no longer the bad guy who teaches the children bad words. But the part of me that once thought McCoy was worth helping? That part of me no longer exists, he deserves everything that comes to him. I see Cam Jacobs stride on.

'Parents of our Little Chefs, if you'd like to gather round. I think I can explain, please.'

Kai's dad shakes his head, gathers Kai up, and marches over to me.

'I'd like to shake your hand, Jools, 'cos you saved the show. You saved his arse. I want him out.'

I take his hand but have no response. I just look at Kai and know I've repaired what Tommy tried to tear to pieces. That was all I could do, it's what I'd hope anyone would do for my kids. Cam is in the corner of the studio preaching to parents who will no doubt fall for his spiel. Tommy strides over.

'That was not what we agreed. Kai?'

'We didn't agree anything.'

'I didn't come here to award mediocrity. You've made us look like fools.'

'Oh no, Tommy, you did that yourself.'

Eyes start to wander in our direction and I'm immediately brought back to a supermarket floor where I laid this man bare and tore him apart. It's all bubbling away, so much to say, but he doesn't give me a chance. He storms off to his dressing room. I follow him. What I have to say needs to be aired. I feel an arm on mine.

'Jools, let him be.' Luella looks at me, straight in the eye. 'You were awesome this evening. He's making his own bed.'

'But he forgets I'm in the same room, he's not

bringing me down with him.'

I shake her off and storm down the corridor towards his dressing room. I open the door.

'Get out! I don't need this!'

His dressing room is different to how I imagined it. Perhaps I thought after our encounter at the Holiday Inn, that something had changed. Cam had obviously given him some sort of lifeline where he'd found the spark to remember all that foodie wanker vernacular that had made him so famous in the first place. I assumed he'd just lifted himself out of the gutter, had a shower, put his show face back on. But this dressing room is a tip, rubbish lines the floors (I spot a Snickers bar wrapper, I am secretly thrilled) and it seems to contain rails of unworn clothes with their labels on. On the coffee table lies a million magazines and papers open at pages of articles about Kitty and his kids. The most damning headline reading: *KITTY MCCOY – PREGNANT WITH #5*. My voice and demeanour soften.

'What happened out there, Tommy?'

He shrugs, crestfallen and completely dazed.

'Rehearsals last week; you were the old mockney Tommy jumping around and today, you were a shit. There's no other way of saying it. You have kids, you know you don't talk to a kid like that.'

His head is in his hands and he's bent over on his sofa. I tread carefully but look around. There's no bathroom. I have an ensuite. I've won a minor battle here. I await his response but he's quiet. Do I stride out and slam the door? I've made my point. But then I hear it. Geez, Tommy. You've got to stop it with the man tears.

'It was Cam's idea. He thought if we changed direction, go down the Cowell, mean judge route, then it could bring up the ratings and … crap, I did that, didn't I?'

145

I'm half glad that he knows what he's done was harsh and worthy of displaying some emotion over, but I can't quite believe he'd allow Cam to puppeteer him in this way.

'But what we did in rehearsals was fine? It was better.'

'Cam said it was dull, he ran it past a test audience who said it was boring.'

'I'd rather be called dull than cruel.'

I sit down in an armchair and watch as he wipes his face on his sleeve. I think I've seen this man cry more than my own husband and I wonder if that makes Matt hardened and heartless. Or does it make Tommy a sap? Either way, I'm again affected, especially as I know this time it's not drunk crying (I think) and the amount of snot produced makes me think about Tommy as a seven-year-old boy, sobbing about something inconsequential, making my maternal side scream out to embrace him and tell him everything will be OK. He sees the concern in my face.

'You can go. I've fucked this up. I'll get fired and be back at square one. That'll teach me to put my faith and money in an American publicity tout.'

I stay where I am. He notices me scanning the table.

'Pregnant. The last insult. They're keeping it a surprise. They don't want to know what it is but if it's a girl they like Honey and Kale for a boy. Honey, stripper name.'

Because Ginger isn't?

'It was our thing, the foodie names. When she was pregnant with Baz, she was hooked on pesto and it just happened. Then he was born with the green eyes and it made sense.'

He has that look that someone has when they talk about their kids, that look of pure amazement, of a love that seizes the bones that you never thought

146

capable of feeling.

'Have you seen them recently?'

'Well, that's the only good thing about Cam – he has lawyers working things out for me. But it's totally fucked. Twice a week at most ...'

He's tearing up again. I don't know how to respond. My heartstrings have been pulled to hear him talk of his kids so fondly but he stands up against that cliff edge declaring all is lost and how he can't face the world. And all the while Cam Jacobs hovers over him like a lairy seagull, telling him to jump. Go on make a tit of yourself because it'll make for excellent TV, get everyone talking.

'Then fire Cam.'

Tommy looks at me, pensive.

'He got me this gig, I owe him.'

'Then pay what you owe him for his services. Seriously, he's asking you to feed people this charade about playing it mean and courting girls in see-through dresses. If all you want are your kids, then I don't think this is how you play things out. You're better than this.'

And with that, there's a knock on the door. I stand up to open it and find Maggie Matthews and Cam Jacobs, surprised to see me, though the look Cam has makes me think he may have heard the tail end of our conversation.

'Is he in here?'

I nod.

'I hope you've given him what for. By the way, you quite possibly saved my bacon with that last move, so thank you. I've just had Kai's parents threatening to sue. Can you leave us?'

Cam shakes his head apologetically but his duplicitous nature means he also glances over occasionally to give me evils. I nod but turn to give McCoy a last glance before leaving the room. This could be it, she could end this here and get on the phone to James Martin, but there's a look between us that has greater significance than ever before. Help me, please. I need you.

CHAPTER TWELVE

If there's anything that will bring you down to earth, put you in your place, and remind you that you really aren't very famous or important, it's the sight of a nearly two-year-old sat in the middle of your bed, filling her pants noisily, lifting her buttocks slightly so the smell can permeate through the room.

'I poo.'

'Yup, I guessed that, Mills.'

Millie doesn't care. She doesn't read the papers nor watch mid-morning television shows. She doesn't have Twitter nor take heed of things like ratings or chat rooms. Millie has this sorted. Be like Millie. Because since Saturday – only four days ago – life has taken quite the turn, for better or worse, I can't quite decide. I left the television building that day quietly happy at how *Little Chefs* had gone, for me at least. I'd done what I'd been paid to do, I'd boosted the self-esteem of some young people and put McCoy in his place. Even if they had taken the show off the air immediately, I had at least done good.

It'd been better than the time I'd nearly cut my finger off on live TV, that was for sure. So I went home. I hugged my children, my husband. I celebrated with some wine Matt had bought from Lidl (it topped taste tests, he told me, and was cheaper than a tin of beans). It went down surprisingly well and of course, as I always do when red wine is in the general vicinity, I spilled some on my new top. I'm not sure if I cared. I went to bed that night with a clear conscience and a tiny feeling of celebration in my soul. I'm not sure how I expected the next day to pan out. I expected the irritation of a sideways facing drizzle. Instead I got a storm. A shitstorm, if you will.

It turns out people actually watched it. *Little Chefs*. Me on their tellyboxes. It was reviewed, it was Tweeted about, it made the showbiz news. For the most part, people were kind about me: I was warm and relatable, mildly funny (only mildly), and endearing. But most of the media was reserved for McCoy and a lot of it was bad. Child hater! Terrible father! Emotional exploitation! What the hell happened to his mockney accent? Why was he wearing surgical scrubs? It was all deserved, not unexpected. I imagined Cam Jacobs out with an actual ruler measuring the column inches it was generating. However, I felt that pang of emotion to read it all. I understood this was part of the show, the manipulation of public feeling that would get him back into our consciousness, our screens, so he could worm his way back into our lives. However, now I understood that in amongst this was a man. Just a very confused man. A father.

'I poo.'

A child sitting in her own faeces brings me back to the room. I hear Matt downstairs making an almighty racket emptying the dishwasher (why does it sound like you're playing spoons?) and realise I can't fob this off on him. Shit, quite literally.

'C'mon, Mills, nappy time.'

'No.' Millie can talk now, in those defiant monosyllables that make you crave the times when she just used to stare at you, gabble nonsense, and dribble down her top. She is also mobile, so she gets up and runs towards the headboard. Of course, she trips over a pillow and lands head first into it. Cue inconsolable crying.

'What's happening?' Matt's voice echoes from the bottom of the stairs.

'Millie vs headboard! I've got it!' I cradle her in my arms, wrinkling my nose as her large mass of auburn hair tickles my nose.

'Sheeet.'

I look at her for a moment. She said that, didn't she? This was not a reference to bed linen but the fact she head-butted our solid oak headboard. Or maybe her nappy sitting squelchy against my jeans.

'Oh my god, what is that smell?' Hannah comes in with hair-bands and a brush. 'Millie's done a stinky.' This makes Millie laugh and Hannah pretends to brush her hair. Millie adores Hannah in the same way most children of her age worship pigs called Peppa. I think she finds sanctity in the fact she's not a twin boy that doesn't come with an off-switch. Hannah is older, wiser, and has better hair to play with. I let them have a moment to bond until Hannah stares in horror at my legs.

'Mum, we have a leaker.'

My first instinct is to look at the ceiling. Leaks and dodgy roofs will always be a terrible preoccupation of mine and I'm still not certain I trust Phil, he of the hairy crack who eats all my biscuits whenever he walks through the door.

'It's what daddy says, the poo, it's all over your jeans.'

I look at two patches of light brown excrement smeared down my thighs. Worse than that, it's on the bed where she rolled around after nutting the headboard. I hook Millie by the chest and hang her off my arm. This is suddenly very funny, to her at least.

'Clear the way!' I push Hannah aside and head for the bathroom, torpedoing little pooey bum into the tub. Hannah watches me curiously. She knows the drill – this has happened several hundred times already, but Matt and

I handle such episodes differently. While I react with mild panic, shower the wriggly toddler, and usually forget to enter the bathroom with a towel, Matt will be calmer, always have nappy sacks about his person, and not get poo all over the toddler's hair. I hear heavy footsteps on the stairs.

'Mills, I could smell that from downstairs!' Matt enters the bathroom. 'Here, let me take over.' He takes the showerhead from me.

'She shat all over the bed,' adds Hannah. Matt and I look at each other. Do we allow shat? On the one hand no, but on the other she could have said 'shitted' which sounds worse and is possibly grammatically wrong. We do what we always do, which is not to react and to power-shower the larger bits of poo that have stuck to her arse down the drain.

'It's five past eight, you'll need to be leaving soon. I made you another coffee downstairs. I'll deal with this.'

'But it's still early.'

'If you leave now, you can get the good parking spot.'

It's my turn to do the school run today and again, we do things very differently. Matt leaves early to get his regular parking spot. He reverses in so he can leave the school car park a little easier. He leaves the house in good time to avoid the traffic by the station and ensure the children are first in through the gate. His attention to precision parking is, frankly, a little sad, and I get a buzz from the burst of adrenaline that comes from sprinting before Mrs Whittaker closes the front gates. Matt is picking bits of poo out of Millie's hair and giving me looks. I hop out the bathroom, tripping on my skinnies as I try to roll them off my legs. Matt laughs under his breath while Hannah looks unimpressed.

'You're still coming, right, Mum?'

Since fame has come a-knocking, the school run has

usually been Matt's job. It seemed the fairest of trades after doing it for nearly every day of the week for seven-odd years. He still revels in the novelty of it – where every drop off and pick up involves hugs, asking them enthusiastically about their days, and skipping to the well-parked car. I think he needs a few incidents of torrential rain, lost jumpers, and dragging a buggy through a pile of dog crap to really rub the sheen off.

But today, the responsibility has fallen on me. I have a day off from *Little Chefs* and doing TV publicity type things and have promised Hannah I will go to the school assembly and see her get a certificate for being Star of the Week. That's if I can find a clean and suitable pair of trousers. Hannah looks at me from the landing like she's having a flashback to school runs of old, ones where I didn't wear bras and threw toast at them like Frisbees. She looks worried as I pick something which looks like old porridge off a pair of leggings.

'Of course, we have time. Where are your brothers?'

I hurdle downstairs and spy the twins in the living room, gawping at Steve Backshall talking to a tarantula. Ted stands in his socks and school trousers while Jake seems to just be wearing a polo shirt and pants. Were they to be just one boy, they'd be fully dressed.

'Boys, clothes!' They nod without muttering a word. I trot into the kitchen and jump to see Phil, staring into my freshly plastered but empty utility room. He smiles. I go to sip my third coffee of the morning.

'Jools, love, me and the missus saw you on Saturday. Good stuff! You put that tosser in his place. It's really good, like *Bake Off* mixed with the *Generation Game*. I told Al, the plasterer, it was you and he's asked if you can get us in the audience … or was that only family? Anyways, we love it and I can't believe I've done your house. Can I put it on my blog? By the way, do you have any biscuits?'

I've only encountered Phil a number of times. It seemed far more appropriate to let Matt and my dad choose the contractors responsible for our extension, as I was far more inclined to choose someone based on their looks or whether I liked the font in their company logo. He seemed friendly enough and structurally, the surrounding building work seems sound, but there are little things that annoy me about him. He doesn't wipe his feet when he enters a room, I've mentioned the biscuits, and for my life, the man can talk. I sip quietly at my lukewarm coffee and realise there were questions that needed to be answered.

'We'll see, of course, blog's fine just no pics of the kids. There are some malted milks next to the fruit bowl.' I've learnt to not buy biscuits with chocolate as they go far quicker. A young boy enters the room, still without trousers.

'Mr Phil! How are you?'

'Jakers!'

I'm not sure when these two became acquainted but Jake perches himself on the kitchen table. I put my hands up in the air and shake my head in disbelief.

'So, when can Logan come over to play?'

'Maybe when you've put some trousers on.'

'I can't find them.'

I frogmarch him back into the living room to see Ted straddling the sofa, still enthralled by Steve and his wildlife and still topless. Matt has obviously learned no new tricks to make these boys move any faster. 'Here, trousers on the sofa where you left them.' I turn the TV off and await the fallout.

'I can't believe you, Mum. Just because you're famous doesn't mean you can tell us what to do.' Jake has said that to me a couple of times since Saturday in an almost tongue-in-cheek way. I'm not entirely sure he enjoyed or understood what *Little Chefs* was about, but he's processing my increased involvement and testing the waters to see how much it's changed his world. Unlike Ted who's let this wash over him, Jake seems conflicted by the idea of me being around less and hasn't reacted too well to such circumstances.

'Well, before I was famous, I was your mother. I'll always be your mother. Put your ruddy trousers on ... and how the hell did you lose a sock?'

Jake shrugs and looks down at his now naked foot. Ted has one sock on. Are they sharing the pair? Ted is my sleepy baby. Every morning, he has a shell-shocked look like he's literally fallen out of a nest. His hair sticks out in several different directions, he yawns several times throughout the morning. He looks at me and smiles as words are not forthcoming yet.

'Daddy wouldn't swear at us. He'd let us watch till the end of the show.'

Unlike Jake who has all the words, all of them.

'Ruddy is not a swear word.'

'Hell is.'

He's doing this, isn't he? But I've had coffee. I am fuelled to win this battle of wits with a seven-year-old.

'Put the trousers on.'

'Make me.'

'Put it on or I will literally carry you and put you in the car half naked and drop you off at the gate so the whole world can see you are wearing Thor pants.'

He stares at me. Ted gets dressed quickly, secretly knowing if I were to follow through on that threat and apply it to both boys, he'd have to share in the humiliation which would involve him exposing his nipples to the world. Jake continues to stare me down. A battle of wills is brewing. I'm not unfamiliar with this situation but it

155

feels different this time, like he's trying to see how far he can push me. Almost like he's waiting for me to crack so he can have some collateral against me. We once did this on a pavement and it involved a coat. He told me he didn't need the coat. It was -1°C. He needed the coat. We stood there facing off as half the school watched us on their walks home. He wasn't going anywhere until he put that coat on. He put it on. I told him to put his zip up. He took it off and threw it on the floor. I got in the car and started the engine. Ted started crying because he thought I was following on all those empty threats of abandonment. I remember the engine running and Jake not moving a muscle, even when a mum knocked on the passenger window thinking I'd left one of them behind. He has the same look about him today – the boy is fearless. It's an amazing quality to have in someone so young, but at the same time it makes me want to wrestle him to the floor and squeeze his little legs into these trousers so I can feel I'm winning. Matt walks into the room with a freshly changed Millie and Hannah's hair in a French plait. I stare at her hair curiously.

'YouTube,' Matt tells me. 'What's going on here?'

'I want you to take me to school.'

'Mummy is taking you.'

'I don't like Mummy.' He looks me right in the eye when he says this. I pretend not to act offended but the truth is when any of my kids say this to my face – when I've denied them crisps, declared it's bath time, or told them off for using their clothes as napkins – it always breaks a little part of me because they say it with such unadulterated clarity. They mean it for that moment. Matt knows it always drives a stake through me and gathers the trousers from the sofa.

'Put these on and apologise to Mummy.'

He looks me in the eye, putting his beanpole legs

156

through his trousers. 'Sorry, Mummy.' He'll be lucky if I stop the car this morning when we get to school. When my dad sees particular acts of defiance like this, he reminds me of the days when you could slap that sort of insubordination out of a child. Matt and I don't subscribe to such methods, but the temptation is always there. I'm reminded that cruelty to someone so young is not only wrong, it's McCoy-esque. Matt tries to dissipate the brewing tension.

'Say sorry nicely or I'll tell Mummy to take her trousers off and she'll drop you at school in her knickers.' He cracks a smile for his father. I don't doubt that would be embarrassing, but surely not funny. It breaks down his defences. Ted looks relieved, Hannah looks impatient. I think Millie may have just done another poo.

'My name is Hannah Campbell and I am Star of the Week for my positive attitude to my work and friends and producing some great project work on the pyramids.'

I smile to see her face and name on the whiteboard. She looks over and waves and I flutter my fingers back. Hannah is now in double digits, taller, smarter, and all round just becoming a little person before my eyes. She's savvy, more keyed into people than her own mother, and she's growing into her features. She asks to carry cool teenager rucksacks to school adorned with multiple keyrings and I can't just buy her school shoes that have heart-shaped buckles in the supermarket any more. She goes back to sit with her friends while Mrs Whittaker moves on to the next stars awarded for the week. One of these stars is Charlie Farrow-Burns, son of Lizzy from football, who's being awarded for good manners and respecting his classmates. Matt would hate these awards for mediocrity (Look at little Jimmy, he put his shoes on the right feet – let's give him a piece of paper to celebrate!) but I like the sense of inclusion, the fact that every child is acknowledged in their own special way. Lizzy sits two seats away from me and as Charlie goes to the front of the hall, I look over and smile. And then it happens. She looks me straight in the eye and looks away. It's not quite rude but it's almost as if she looks right through me, like I'm not even there.

This is not uncommon. I've been a mother at this school for many a year and spent many a time stood outside the school gates like a lemon as groups of women shut me out of conversations, standing with their backs to me as they gassed on about their lives, their achievements, their infinitely more interesting lives. They would instantly dismiss you and move on to mothers they thought more worthy of their time, they'd be narked if you stood in their usual waiting spot, they'd make assumptions about who you were (youngish, of multiple kids, obviously a teen mother of minimal prospects). So when Lizzy Farrow-Burns does this, I question it, but I am not surprised.

Maybe I assumed too much that recent events gave me licence to at least be acknowledged, but maybe I was reaching too far. Maybe nothing has changed. Still, I clap my hands for Charlie because good manners should always be applauded, and continue to enjoy hearing about what the school has been up to. People are getting pens, badges for maths, and a flurry of other achievements. I see little people stand up, their faces aglow, and I think about my new job.

Maybe that's where it stems from, just being able to tell a child that they're getting on OK in the world. Hell, we all need that reassurance from time to time. I keep clapping and smiling but I can feel Lizzy Farrow-Burns looking over at me. I've done something, haven't I? Wait, did I brush my hair? Luella has demanded I cut it into something resembling more of a style, but old habits prevail and I still find myself bundling it into a bun that makes me look like an angry rooster. I didn't do make-up, not as a statement of vanity but because the baby crapped on the bed. I look over and smile and she raises her eyebrows. Dad's words echo in my ears – the daggers, they're everywhere.

As assembly ends, the children are herded away and I manage to catch Hannah's eye as she leaves and stick my tongue out at the boys.

'Can I just say, I watched the show on Saturday and I think you're great. I'm Emma, Lola's mum.'

I realise I still have my tongue stuck out and I'm not entirely sure who Lola is. Still, I smile – it's a lovely compliment and she seems genuine.

'That's really kind, thank you, Emma.'

She beams at me happily. 'You're, like, famous now, that's so cool. I keep telling everyone I know you're a mum at our school and they can't believe it.'

'To be honest, neither can I. It's all a bit crazy, really …'

She giggles. 'Can I get a quick pic on my phone? Just to show my mum?'

I'm bemused but can't be offended and smile away, just as the parents are escorted to the main atrium.

'Mrs Campbell, good to see you today.'

Mrs Whittaker and I are fast friends now, partly because two summers ago she was quick to stand up and defend my gay brother after Jen Tyrrell dared to insult him, and partly because after Jen tried to get her sacked, I defended her to the hilt. She is still ruddy complexioned and bosomy, the sort you know would give amazing hugs. I don't, of course.

'Mrs Whittaker, it's been nice to be able to come.'

'I watched it … on Saturday. How wonderful! I trust

we can call on you to do some work for the Christmas Fayre.'

'As long as I don't have to be Father Christmas?' Of course, she finds this hilarious and laughs a laugh fitting for someone of such a bosom, which makes some of the parents stop in their tracks. I like how Mrs Whittaker finds me funny.

'Well, I will keep watching …'

I smile, thinking about her with her Saturday night tikka masala balanced on her knee, swigging from a glass of red. In a onesie, perhaps. Across the way, another friend waves at me, Mr Pringle – not Hannah's teacher any more but still looking youthful, and it seems he's also discovered waistcoats, so looks like he should be a member of the Kaiser Chiefs. I exit the hall and quickly escape to the loos, mainly to empty my bladder but also because I'm paranoid about my hair and selfies where I may not have been looking my best. Cross fingers that Luella never sees them or she'll give me a bollocking. I find a cubicle and go to pull down my leggings, finding an encrusted patch of something orange, possibly sweet potato, on the knee. The outside doors fly open.

'Oh my god, I am hanging. That's the last time we do school night drinking.'

I tap my feet on the floor quietly, smiling to myself to hear mums doing what I do best. Her companion sniggers but sounds like she's fake retching into the junior school sinks.

'All the clapping, my ears are ringing. Whose idea was this again? Thursday drinking?'

'Grace's mum. The idea was we did the Year Two mums night out on the sly so we wouldn't have to invite some of them. You know, like Queen Jools …'

I pause for a moment, my feet mid-tap, wondering if they know I'm in the cubicle in possibly the most

160

vulnerable position a person can be in. One of them sniggers.

'Oh hello there Mrs Whittaker, schmooze, schmooze, schmooze, oh yes, I'll be at the Christmas Fayre flogging my book, signing pictures of my smug face …'

'She might bring McCoy though. That would be a coup.'

I am mid-stream. Do I stop and let it dribble out quietly so they don't know I'm here? I lean over to try and spy through the crack of the door so I can identify the culprits.

'Emma is such a succubus … oh, Jools – can I get a selfie?' I don't know who speaks but they have the affected and put-on accent down to a tee. Poor Emma, I only got excited and well-meaning from her – she definitely doesn't deserve this character assassination.

'Emma's girl still has ringworm, I reckon. She says it's eczema but I'm not buying it. Make sure you don't invite her to your party.'

Curiosity turns into anger as they start bringing children into this.

'Of course. I tell you that girl, she's not quite right. She licks the white board markers.'

The laughter that follows is pure witchcraft at its best, as the two of them revel in their perceived normality, their perfect children.

'I'm not inviting the Blackwell twins. Last time, the blonde one bit my entertainer. I thought I was going to get sued. And the other one is a greedy bastard, fills his pockets with cocktail sausages. But I guess that's what's going to happen when you don't toe the line with boys?'

As a mother of twins, this strikes a particular chord with me. The Blackwell twins are in another class in our year and I don't know their mum but we've traded looks in the playground. That look that says, people will never know. Twice the fun, twice the frigging energy; it's a different sort of parenting, one that sharpens the senses but can have you crying tears of torment. I don't deny that at one party I caught Ted licking the jam out of sandwiches and putting them back on the tray. One of the lady laughs, snorting as she agrees.

'Like the Campbell boys, really. Live wires ... but that's what will happen if you go off and abandon your kids. I mean, she's on my telly, she's everywhere, it's so boring.'

I go quiet to hear that bit about me abandoning my kids, my teeth grinding into each other. A nervous tic I seem to have developed, hearing the words 'mother' and 'abandonment' together it goes into overdrive.

'Do you think she's actually shagging McCoy like the papers say?'

'I would.' They both cackle like the witches that they are. I'm still weeing, fuelled by three cups of coffee this morning, feeling like the walls of this primary-colour cubicle are closing in on me.

'It's her husband I feel sorry for. He's such a nice bloke – he coaches the boys' football team and it's like she's left him for this job and totally dropped him in it: the kids, the house, the lot. You know he was totally flirting with Miranda Scott – I wouldn't be surprised if he was finding his kicks elsewhere.'

I know exactly who's speaking now but let her continue as her friend feigns horror.

'Miranda's another one ... I heard Tim threw her out because he caught her shagging someone who worked in her office who was on work experience.'

'NO! She is such a tart.'

'Well, not unlike Mrs Campbell, shagging McCoy behind her poor husband's back? What a bitch! So their marriage is basically a sham.'

162

'Yup. It's so selfish for a start ... I mean, those kids need a mother. I blank her when I see her. It's despicable behaviour. I was wondering whether to bring it up at the next governors' meeting?'

I'm stood up now, jeans up, T-shirt tucked in. Maybe I need to hear it all so I can know everything, but I just stare at the back of the door for a moment, at an old Childline sticker that's peeling at the edges. I laugh to think about when the Childline lady came to talk to the boys' class and do some sponsored shenanigans with them. You mean there is somewhere we can ring when Mummy is being mean to us and denying us sweets before bedtime? They came home and stuck their stickers next to the actual phone. I open the cubicle door. I spy their faces in the mirror first, both of them etched with horror. Lizzy Farrow-Burns and some mum I don't quite know but who always clogs up my Facebook feed trying to sell me Avon products.

'Ladies, as you were.'

I wash my hands quietly as Mrs Avon slinks into a cubicle to hide her embarrassment. Lizzy is defiantly unaffected, and thinks staring me out is the answer.

'Morning, Lizzy. Lovely to see Charlie get his award today.'

'It's his second this term.'

Do not slap her, do not slap her, do not slap her.

'That's great.'

Rise above this mum and her obnoxious gossip, lies, and tattling. Why do this to anyone, let alone children and another woman, someone you're supposed to be joined with in sisterhood? Then I remember you're talking about the school playground. Mothers don't stand in circles, congratulating each other and validating each other's experiences as people makers. No, the playground is a battlefield where egos fly about, competition reigns, and everyone is vying to be queen, hurdling over small children with book bags and hopscotch markings to prove they are better than everyone else. Queen Jools. I don't know who she is but in my mind, she wears a crown from Burger King. Lizzy stares at me in the mirror as I wash my hands with strange pink goo.

'No Matt today?' she asks. She's doing this, isn't she? Right here, to my face. Mrs Avon flushes the loo to try and break the tension. Part of me wants to throw inane gossip at her to fuel her sad life ... no, he's at home shagging the builder. When this is over, I'll go join them. I dry my hands on a paper towel.

'He's at home with our youngest. Last time I brought her along to one of these things, she tried to do a runner out the fire exits and set off the alarmed doors.'

It's true. It rates up there as one of my most embarrassing parental moments ever. She raises her eyebrows like I might be lying. The Campbells have failed to show up together for a school event and thus have pretty much declared their marriage to be over. I am calm. I am so calm. Go on, throw something else at me, you bloody cow. She stares at me some more. I roll my paper towel into a ball and throw it into a nearby bin. Of course, I miss.

'You're lucky to have him, he's a great dad. He's doing such a good job with the football team too. I mean you're both so busy ... it's a wonder you ever see each other.'

She's doing it again. Dig, dig, dig. I was there at the last football match too. Granted I was drinking tea, you ignored me, and I did spend fifteen minutes half asleep in a gazebo, but I was there. With my husband. What does she want me to say? Does she want me to validate her lies so she doesn't lose face in front of Mrs Avon? Christ, does she actually believe her own tripe? I'm biting my tongue, trying not to flare my nostrils. Calm, Jools. Think green tea and chakras and how you are bigger than this piece of poo mother in front of you.

'Indeed. I mean in between shagging McCoy and abandoning my family, it is a wonder.'

Lizzy's jaw drops slowly.

'Oh, you don't have to say anything, you're blanking me … I understand.'

I smile and walk out. If I was fitter, more flexible, and not in my kids' school, this is when I'd fist pump and jump, heel-clicking in a Gene Kelly-esque way.

Invigorated by taking Lizzy Farrow-Burns down, I drive home that little bit faster, feeling I've taken on the world and swung my middle finger up at every bitchy bitchface I've ever dared encounter in my lifetime and lost face to. I think of Katie whose-surname-I-can't-remember from Year Nine who said my hair was plain and my shoes looked like they served an orthopaedic function. I think about Kitty McCoy. I think about a woman in a Tesco car park once who claimed I stole the last trolley from her and called me a shit in front of three kids. I've always had problems with women who attack me, I find it gut-wrenching and usually don't know how to react. Perhaps the tide is turning. Look at me all eloquent and passive-aggressive and knowing exactly how to play things to my advantage. Maybe I've finally grown a pair.

My joy is short-lived as I walk through the door, hearing Matt ranting and raving in his dulcet Scottish tones, sounding not unlike Groundskeeper Willie. I walk into the kitchen and Phil is nowhere to be found. I hope this isn't a biscuit issue. Matt throws some papers at me.

'Look at this, it's a retrospective complaint from the neighbour about the extension. Because apparently when this was going through the council four months ago, it was fine. Now, they have problems. Light! We're stealing their fucking light!'

Millie sits on the concrete floor chewing an old bit of cable. I hope it's old. I finger the length to ensure it's not wired up to the mains. I take the paper but can't make head nor tail of the jargon – legal precedents, sunlight projections, restricted 45 degree angles.

'Read the bottom, the bit in red, it says all work has to cease with immediate effect until it can be resolved. Failure to do so may end up with legal injunctions being brought against us. I had to send Phil home and we still have to pay him for his time, he had the carpenter ready to do the counter-tops and everything.'

My heart sinks to hear it and I go to embrace Matt in some lame attempt to calm him down. Light simmer to rolling boil is how I'd describe him at the moment. I glance at the papers and see the name of our neighbour, Duncan Fox. You bastard. Him and his wife are our neighbours to the right, they only moved in nine months ago when Mrs Pattak moved out to live with her daughter. We never knew his surname but he had big, bouffant hair with giant sideburns to match, so the kids called him Wolverine.

'Surely he can't do this now, he needed to voice his concerns when planning was subject to public consultation?'

Matt is in the wild throes of looking like he's going to shatter things with his fists and declare he's ready to give up on the human race. I'm impressed that I have uttered a sentence that sounded like I knew what I was talking about. Matt shrugs, deep in his own disappointment.

'Remind me to get the boys home and allow them to bounce footballs off their bedroom wall for as fucking long as they want tonight.'

I don't want to add that that is probably why we're

dealing with this problem. Living next to a house with four children who wake up at six every Sunday and whose parents lose their shit with them every so often probably doesn't make for a kindly semi-detached living situation. This could be revenge.

'I mean, I saw him in the street the other day. I was putting out the recycling and we chatted and I gave him Phil's number as they're thinking of putting their own extension on the back, and then this?'

I sit down. I've had no time to tell him about Hannah's awards or my mini victory in the toilets but I think back to Lizzy Farrow-Burns and to a time when we'd be civil and say good morning to each other and that would be it. Now everything feels filled to the brim with resentment. This feels no different.

'You don't think he's trying to make a quick buck? It says here that he could sue us for not making our plans clear enough. Maybe he's seen me on TV and is trying to take advantage.'

Matt looks up and puts his hand in mine. He knows there may an element of truth to it.

'Either way, it's shitty. Even if we'd managed to build this through other financial means, this feels two-faced. It's not how I run my show.'

The Matt Show with his four minions and Queen Jools in her cardboard crown. Were our mornings always this eventful? I spy the fruit bowl to see the malted milks are gone. I don't even have biscuits to calm my fears. Damn you, Phil. I get up to make us a cup of tea.

'Breathe.' I am amazed by my calmness. Usually this situation is reversed; I am waxing lyrical about some unsolvable problem and Matt is the one with the tea and the back rubs. This morning has helped me find my zen. Matt studies the paper.

'I reckon it's his wife, I think she works for the

council. I'm going to go out tonight and study her car for council parking badges.'

'The boys have that crappy telescope from Christmas, you could use that.' Matt looks vaguely excited. He studies the bemusement in my face as I picture him in his tracksuit going *Rear Window* on our rubbish neighbours. I think about how his world has changed in the last eighteen months. Before, he wouldn't have had the energy to worry about such trivial matters.

'How was Han?'

'Star of the Week. I also had a little to-do …'

Matt sighs, as recently this has been more of a common occurrence. 'Who was it now? It wasn't a teacher, was it? A child?'

'Lizzy Farrow-Burns off the football team.'

Matt immediately looks confused. 'Lizzy, but she's nice enough. Her son is my star midfielder. You didn't cause a ruckus, did you?'

Matt has a look about him that suggests I've caused some disturbance to his formations. I shake my head.

'She's a cow. She was in the loos talking about me, about how I was shagging McCoy and our marriage was in trouble.'

'Cow. Did you deck her?'

I love how Matt thinks this is how I choose to defend my good name these days. 'Tempted, but no. It's just disappointing. You wonder how many people she's talking to, what else she's saying.' I clink spoons against cups and look at our half-finished kitchen counters. They're new, a lovely ash effect. Already covered in bits of playdoh and old tea stains.

'Well, maybe that's how the land is going to lie at the moment. Just peppered with hearsay and bitchbags who've nothing else to do.'

It's a clarifying statement and I nod in agreement, not

that it doesn't make it any easier to swallow, though.

'Remember the days when you could take Ben in and he'd give them what for?'

I smile. Ben did that at the height of the last McCoy scandal, after a school play. He was fantastic. Truth is, though, we rarely see Ben these days. Since he started this foray into television, he's made new friends and has started mingling in fashionable circles that involve us not seeing him in the morning or him scrambling in as soon as Matt and I are off to bed with mugs of Horlicks. I don't resent him, but I will admit to being the inquisitive older sister, hoping he's looking after his heart and his bits. There is someone he's been texting in all of this. I catch him with that after-text glow sometimes. It makes me smile, even if he'll never tell me the identity of this new mystery man. Please be someone cool, a film star. I see Ben married to a film star. Matt is still flicking through the letters.

'Back to people who have nothing else to do. They also mention we have to pay for a survey because we may be affecting their foundations. Give me strength, we had that engineer fella in, right?'

We did. Another biscuit thief but who asked for Earl Grey, not too strong with a splash of milk. I served it to him in a Captain America mug.

'Look, maybe I should ring Annie and get some advice about the legality of this? She can walk us through it.'

Matt makes a sucking noise through his lips which makes me turn around.

'Or not? Give Annie a break, I have a mate from Price Waterhouse I can ring up.'

I act surprised. We go to Annie for all our 'legal shit' because we know we can trust her implicitly and because she gives us excellent mates rates where we can pay her back in wine and Wahaca.

'Why not, Annie?'

'Because … she needs a break. She doesn't need our shit on top of her stuff.'

'Stuff?'

'Stuff.'

We look at each other blankly like we're speaking different languages.

'When was the last time you spoke to Annie?'

I think back. It was probably when she couldn't come round for tea that time. We're those sorts of friends who don't need to constantly text or phone but drop in and out of each others' lives when we need each other.

'Then you don't know?'

'Know what?'

'When she couldn't come for tea, Mills and I dropped round later that week with cupcakes. I'm sure I told you. I mean, she's completely struggling – Finn has reflux, she's not sleeping …'

I knew a little and immediately feel guilty for not having followed up to check on her. She had always been a solid fixture in my life when new babies came on the scene and I feel awful that I haven't reciprocated. I thought she was treading water at least, like we all were when very new babies were sprung upon us. My first instinct is to reach for my phone, to hell with light stealing for now. Matt studies my face.

'You really didn't know? I thought … I thought you'd be the first person she'd tell. I assumed you two spoke in private about these things.'

I shake my head because there seems to be more to this story. How could it get worse?

'Chris left her last month. He walked out.'

170

CHAPTER THIRTEEN

'So I love this top. Where's it from?'

I'll always be confused when people ask me this question. I used to adorn myself in an array of hoodies, misshapen T-shirts, and an old parka covered in snot and sweet remnants. Now people ask me fashion questions about where things are from and how they too can purchase them. I pause for a moment before answering.

'It's H&M ... my best friend bought it for me because she knows I like squirrels.'

I smile, hoping Annie heard, wherever she is. Since I found out Chris had left her, I've been on the phone, Facebook, emails, trying to get in touch. But nothing. The pain and guilt stakes through me in the worst possible way. How could she not tell me such a monumental fact? Have I neglected her? Was she hurting? Maybe she doesn't need me. Or she does and I've been unavailable. Oh, Annie. Maybe wearing this top will show her how much she means to me. The panel of women sat round the table in front of me pause to fawn over the top.

'Oh, and my socks match.'

In some moment of ridiculousness, I decide to raise my leg on the desk and show the panel my socks. I can't see Luella's face but I can envisage her shaking her head, eyes closed. One is no longer limber enough to attempt such a sitting position or straighten one's leg so one should not be doing this. Luckily, it raises a laugh from some of the panel and audience. I put my leg down, feeling grateful I've remembered to shave and not subjected the viewing public to my grass-like leg stubble. Today, I'm in a new studio and uncharacteristically being a bit of a Loose Woman. It's all publicity for the show, of course, the second episode of which went out two nights ago. It feels strange to be on my own, without the cover of clever cooking children and Tommy McCoy. One of the ladies in the panel doesn't laugh at my squirrel socks.

'Aren't squirrels classed as vermin now?'

Another panellist laughs nervously at the peculiarity of her statement. She jumps in to bring light to the situation. 'I think, actually, there are some high-class London restaurants that serve them. Isn't that right, Jools?'

I nod and smile, don't ask me for recipes, please. Roasted à la hazelnuts?

'I have no idea. But just to clarify, I only wear them in print. I do not advocate the wearing of real squirrel.'

People smile broadly. I look over at Vermin lady – a popstar turned West End star turned 'well-being' guru who also has an underwear collection based around ladies with boobs larger than a G cup. She looks at me suspiciously from across the way. Another of her colleagues intervenes.

'So, you need to run us through what happened at the weekend on *Little Chefs* because that was possibly the TV highlight of the year for some.'

I smile, looking at the audience. Rows of women watch me eagerly through shiny rows of lights. Last Saturday will now be referred to as Granita Gate. The show started off innocently enough. McCoy was still trying to make out that he was some hip icon of today's fashion circles and showed up in a utilitarian smock and stacked trainers. Kai was also back by some minor miracle that may have involved money and empty promises of fame that may or may not be forthcoming. It was desserts week and it started innocently enough, until

Oscar realise he'd left his lime granita in the freezer for too long and could no longer fork it. When it got to tasting, he produced us a modest bowl of what he'd been able to scrape off the container, that Tommy deemed completely unacceptable. Yes, he did it again. And this time with little Oscar who not only has eyes like a bush baby but was our show's standout sob story. He had turned to cooking after the unfortunate death of his father and so was the one contestant that everyone championed. And the fact was, the granita was fine; it was sharp and cold and everything it needed to be, but not for Tommy. So I picked up the bowl and tossed the contents over his head.

'Well, it was a moment of madness, but McCoy had it coming. You don't berate a child on live TV who's done nothing wrong except mess up a bit of cooking. We all do that, right?'

I'm encouraging a bit of audience participation and I hear people murmuring in agreement, shadowy heads moving up and down. Vermin lady arches her eyebrows. I look at her questioningly.

'You call him McCoy? That's a bit … personal, shall we say? Already referring to each other by nicknames?'

She's doing this. She's not going to stop at the squirrel remark. 'It's what a lot of people on set call him, not just me.'

'There is a spark between you two, though. Would some call that chemistry?'

'Sparks aren't always a good thing. No doubt, we have a relationship that people want to tune into – we bounce off each other, but not necessarily in a good way. People like to watch a fight.'

A fellow panellist pipes in. 'You should know about sparks … How many husbands have you had now?' Everyone laughs except her. Three, I think it is. She's well-known for putting her relationships on show, vociferous in her love and devotion until the paps catch her outside a pub having slanging matches with her lovers and then telling the magazines how badly she was treated.

'Well, I'm just saying what everyone thinks. You two obviously have something. These ratings that *Little Chefs* are pulling in are mental, they're beating ITV and the Beeb haven't had a hit like this since *Strictly* in that time slot. You'll see, people will assume you two are together after a while.'

I pause. A part of me is slightly happy as I have never thought of McCoy in that way. Maybe because most of our encounters have been bile-inducing, maybe because now I know what I know about him, I know he lacks balls, gumption – there is a strange indecision to how he acts and tackles life that is most off-putting and wildly unsexy. I wonder if this lady has been paid by Lizzy Farrow-Burns. Do I tackle this with searing sarcasm? I'm not sure if lunch time television could handle that. Time to act the diplomat.

'We have a working relationship. Many on-screen couples do and it's important to me to remain professional. I find what you're saying really disrespectful to my husband.'

The lead panellist can sense trouble is brewing and intervenes.

'And we have a picture of you and Matt here, aaaah …'

Granted, it's a selfie, and not entirely glamorous. I think it was taken in a beer garden, one we'd taken the kids to because there was outdoor play and they ate free. But it's non-pretentious. I haven't got my 'fifty shades of foundation' TV face on and we look like we might be genuinely happy. Of course, that may have been the Pimms.

174

'Yep, we've been married for ten years now. I think you double that in celebrity marriage terms.'

The panellists laugh, except one, of course.

'And I believe you're renewing vows later this year?'

I nod and this leads people to 'ooh' and clap and generally be more excited than me. It's something we've yet to plan. Every time it's brought to my attention, it's usually done by Luella, who prevails in trying to make this about designer frocks and matching macarons.

'We're going to have a thing, yeah.'

Vermin lady eyes me closely. 'A thing? Don't sound too excited then?'

It's the turn of the studio audience now to sharply intake their breaths and wait for more action to unfold. Zen, I am zen.

'Oh, don't mind her, someone's let the Botox go to her sense of manners.'

There is an obvious discontentment amongst the ladies around the table as they all eye each other closely. I'm not sure if this palpable tension was here before or whether I lured it out, but they stare daggers at each other through their fake eyelashes and designer glasses.

'I just think, Jools, I can't place my finger on what you do. You seem to be famous for being a celebrity mum. I am not sure why you're here today and why you're a judge on that show. Seriously?'

Daggers. Big fat pointy daggers. Even floor people are shaking their heads and slicing their hands under their throats. But she's not even vaguely close to being under my skin; she's a very annoying yet benign skin tag that I know is something I should deal with but which I know can sit there quite nicely without intervention. My wedding is a *thing* because it's really not important. It won't change my marriage, nor my relationship – it'll just be a party to celebrate the fact that we exist as a couple and give my children a chance to dress up. I don't need to justify that to anyone, especially this scab of a woman. Now she's starting with the celebrity qualification rant and all at once I am transported to a school toilet, listening to my name being part of the whispers. Breathe, Jools. The lead panellist sees me squirming and not intending to answer. Vermin lady looks like she's won a major victory.

'Well, someone's a tad bit jealous they weren't chosen to judge. I think that's it, right?'

Panellist number three once represented Great Britain in Eurovision and had an infamous role in *Hollyoaks* where she was killed off after she tried to kidnap her husband's twin and got blown off a cliff into the North Sea. I shift her a look.

'We all know you were desperate for that job. You auditioned but the Beeb didn't like the fact you've got three ex-husbands and you don't cook anything … you're on that stupid raw diet shit.'

Panellist number three realises she's thrown a bad word into daytime ITV but doesn't look like she cares. She and Vermin lady may as well sharpen their claws against the desktop and launch at each other. I'd pay to see that fight, hair extensions flying across the fake laminate floor.

'And woah, ladies …' Lead panellist in her geometric-shaped bodycon dress tries to keep the peace. I smile, knowing there are some ladies out here who have my back. I look over at Vermin lady. I took your job, I'd be peeved too, but I wouldn't do what you're doing here. 'So we're going to take a short break. When and if we return, we'll be looking at contouring and whether it's worth the hassle. So, Jools Campbell, *Little Chefs* on BBC 1, Saturdays at 5.30 p.m. Thank you, Jools.'

There's applause. And cut. Lead panellist exhales the words without pausing, probably on a command from someone on high and a desire to escape the tension. I nod and wave, wait for studio cameras to swing away and for Vermin lady to throw her mic to the floor and storm off. Panellist number three laughs.

'Prima donna, up her own jacksie. Lovely to meet you, by the way.' She winks at me and I have an inkling that her afternoon started with a few glasses of prosecco.

'Thank you for jumping to my defence.'

'Oh, any time. I like you. Her? Not so much. Don't tell anyone but I may have laughed when her latest fitness video only sold fifty-six copies, lol.'

She actually says the LOL, which makes me think she's definitely a little bit drunk, confirmed when she goes in for an air kiss and totally misses my face.

I am soon ushered back into my dressing room by the floor managers, who seem to have these things rented out by the hour as the next daytime TV chat show is lining up a whole new set of guests. Luella is with another client today, stuck in the middle of a Snapchat scandal and who requires her full attention. I like how she's leaving me to do these things on my own, like she may trust me a bit more. Don't think she'll have the same thinking when she sees that clip of me showing my socks with my legs akimbo. Anyway, for company, and to have someone help me carry my bags and help me accessorise, I have brought Ben and am expecting him to be there waiting with bottled water and hugs. Who awaits me is unexpected to say the least.

'You're not Ben.'

'Last time I looked.' It's McCoy in my dressing room, casually sipping from a lidded coffee cup. 'There weren't enough dressing rooms so they've put all us *Little Chef* folk in the same room.'

I can't hide my look of displeasure, especially given

how relaxed and comfortable he's made himself. I ache to see Ben, just to give me some sort of safety net. I pray he's not Tindering in the studio halls again.

'So, you're a Loose Woman for the day too?'

McCoy fake smiles at me. 'I'm doing some other filler show later in the afternoon. I'm actually cooking this time. I've been allowed back behind a hob.'

His eyes light up, looking slightly more excited than he did last Saturday, when I found him with his head against a wall, trying not to deck a producer who was telling him to record yet another soundbite for the show's online commercials. I look at what he's wearing.

'I'm glad you abandoned the minimalist smock chic thing.'

He laughs sardonically in reply. He seems to have reverted back to the jeans and colourful trainers and wears multiple rubber bracelets. He's obviously trying to get back to that persona he once inhabited that fought for all manner of foodie army causes like ethical pig farming and saving the plight of the near extinct iceberg lettuce. It seems more like him, but the more I think of it, the more I realise I don't know who he is at all – I'm not sure he does either. I go to make myself a cup of tea.

'Tea?'

I'm not sure why I offer. After a while I guess it becomes a reflex while stood next to a kettle.

'Oh, it's OK. I have a soy chai latte.'

Of course he does. The chocolate hob nobs are probably not organic enough for him, either. I wait for the kettle to boil, and as always, it takes far longer than it should. Where the hell is Ben?

'You did well out there. She's a piece of work, eh? Kitty was in the jungle with her. She's all out for self and that's saying something if you compare her to my ex-wife.'

He was watching? His eyes veer towards a small monitor in the room. I look over to see Vermin lady has chosen not to return to set and they've masked her absence with a potted plant.

'Well, the fern is far more charismatic than she was.'

Tommy laughs. He never laughs at my jokes so I shift him a look nervously. It doesn't pass me by that he's talked very casually about Kitty, referring to her as his ex and without the usual tears that accompany discussions of her. That said, I don't dig further.

'I can't believe they gave it a name. Granita-Gate.'

It's my turn to laugh. He shakes his head, smirking.

'You have good aim, I'll give you that. It went right down my back. I found some in my pants.'

'Serves you right. If that's the route you're sticking to, mean and unforgiving, then I am going to give you what for.'

'It's what keeps people watching.'

There's a moment of silence between us as we realise what's just been said. The show has been a real water-cooler success because of that tension between us: one brewed from past resentments but which McCoy has totally manipulated to give people what they want. We may have just found our formula. It feels underhand to be conning the public so, but it's what's working. I sip my tea to ponder this moment over.

'Do you think we made the right decision on Saturday?'

McCoy shrugs. In truth, I don't think he's too worried about the contestants we turn away, but I always feel responsible for them, worried we're scarring them for life by rejecting them and sending them on their way. This week it was Lydia and Rosie's week to say goodbye. Lydia's ice-cream didn't set. Rosie's mousse was too sweet (Was that a thing?).

I cried when Tommy announced their names but apparently that is also what draws people in, my insane ability to cry at anything.

'It's a competition. If we didn't send someone home, we'd be there forever,' adds McCoy almost callously. 'They've created a name for us.'

'You what?'

'Team McBell. There's an army of fans who want us to get together. They do fan art and shit.'

Tommy holds his phone up, showing a pencil drawing of us in a strange embrace next to a kitchen counter. It makes me feel slightly nauseous and Tommy reads it so, laughing heartily.

'Never.'

'In a month of Sundays.'

Well, at least that's been sorted.

'Anyways, how's Georgie?'

He shrugs. 'Orchestrated by Cam to get some column inches. It was very pleasant but trust me, I'm not what she's looking for.'

I look confused.

'She's aiming higher than me. And you know her teeth? Not her own. She's got this huge mouth of veneers. It was like snogging a bathroom splashback.'

It's my turn to laugh, but the laughter with us is always cut short; almost as if we won't allow ourselves to fully let go when we're in each other's company. Like there still remains a need to be overly cautious with each other.

'No Lu?'

It takes me a moment to work out he's not talking about an en-suite. I've never called her Lu in my life and it jars to refer to her so casually. It makes me remember why I'm so cautious with him, almost out of some loyalty to her.

'Nope. Where is your Mr Jacobs? I see you're still

keeping his questionable company?'

He ignores me and goes back to his fancy non-dairy coffee thing.

'You still don't trust him?' he asks me.

'As far as I can throw him, and you've seen my spindly arms.'

He laughs again. 'I'm signed up. I found out if we parted ways I'd owe him more money. It didn't make sense.'

Knowing too well the situation that led me to signing up for *Little Chefs* in the first place, I have no reply, trying to look less mocking than I am. We are trapped in these situations so we may as well play them out for as long as we can. My phone ringing breaks the tension.

'Hello?'

'You're not going to make it back, are you?' It's Matt, sounding resigned and disappointed and I scroll through today's events. Where the hell is Ben to remind me where I need to be? I know today is an INSET day, I know I had to pick up milk.

'Hannah's first swimming gala.' Shit. I look at the clock and factor in getting out of the car park and battling the traffic. He knows my response without having to answer. 'I didn't forget, but no ...' He's doing that thing where he's running his tongue across his teeth. Of course, the guilt settles in, but I can't help but feel riled knowing that when he was a nine-fiver, he missed many (if not most) of these events and I flew solo, having to explain that Daddy was at work.

'She'll be gutted.'

'Take Dad? There'll be other galas.' I can feel myself repeat exactly what he used to say.

'Yeah, look, Jake wants to talk to you.' His aloofness is too much to bear. I snarl, knowing McCoy is in the room and can hear everything.

181

'Mummy, it's Jake. Can I play on the Wii? Daddy says I can't until I've done my spellings.'

'Jake, Daddy is right. He's in charge when I'm not there. Listen to him.'

'You used to let me play on the Wii.'

Usually so I could have ten minutes of peace with a cup of tea/have a wee but I don't tell him that.

'Don't be a smart arse, Jake.'

'Daddy! Mummy called me an ARSE.'

The phone goes dead. It's a quiet room so I'm sure McCoy heard most of that, pretty much confirmed when he starts giggling. He stops.

'I remember those conversations. Baz was the king of smart arses. "Ten more minutes on the DS, Dad." I used to find him under the duvet like a crack addict.'

'I swear these things send out special waves that spin them into a trance.'

He laughs. Again. I gauge his reaction because we've started talking about kids and that usually pre-empts tears (again), but he is calm and engaged. I feel the need to dig a bit further out of sheer curiosity, but knowing very little bonds us besides being parents.

'How old's Baz?'

'Ten going on sixteen. I swear at that age I was dressed in Puma tracksuits and baseball caps. The kid's got me buying him Superdry.'

'Same age as Hannah. It's that age, they're teetering on tweendom.'

McCoy looks horrified at the prospect. It scares me in equal measure to know they are little people growing into monosyllabic cave-dwelling pockets of hormones. We stare into space to take it in. I think about how similar our journeys are: we must have both had children in our early twenties and gone through the same traps of young parenthood. We have many things to discuss, surely.

'We should get our kids together at some point.'

He throws that out like a grenade, waiting to see if it'll explode. I look at him curiously. That was a suggestion of social activity beyond seeing each other in studios and in front of glaring lights. It makes perfect sense: you have four, I have four. In any other circumstance, this would be perfectly normal. We'd go bowling or hang in a park and swap humorous anecdotes of what it's like to have a gaggle of children. Oh, there'd be stories and swapping tips about seven seater cars and how you feed that many children (rice, every time), and we'd laugh flightily knowing we wouldn't have it any other way. Still, what McCoy has suggested feels like a step too far. You are assuming a lot here: one, that we have crossed into some weird friend zone; two, that our kids and non-present spouses would consent to this. We look at each other strangely. It feels like this conversation has potential, that there are things to say. The door opening grabs our attention. Alas, it's not Ben but some crew member in black with the requisite headset.

'Mrs Campbell, we've just signed your brothers in. I've told them to come on through.'

He's too busy having a dual conversation with someone on his headset and checking things off a clipboard for me to question him. I pull a face, assuming Ben's locked himself out of the building.

'I only have one brother. He's in here already. He has a pass.'

Crew member shakes his head. 'No, him we know about. He's in the cafeteria. Your other brothers. Sorry, I have to run.'

He scoots out as I think through what he's just said. Adam is here? Why didn't he ring ahead, the idiot? He would have called. Unless he came with Matt. But I just spoke to Matt. It could be Dad. McCoy intervenes.

'Are you OK?' I look at him.

'Yeah, they got it wrong. I've got brothers but they've obviously thought my dad was my brother ... or Matt or ...'

Then it hits me. No. Not here. There's a knock on the door. Rooted to the spot, I can't seem to answer it so McCoy rises, intrigued. Please be Ben, please be Ben, please be Ben.

'Hi, we're here to see Jools? They told us to come on through.'

I'm at an angle to the door where they can't see me, which is good as I seem to be doing strange shaky things with my hands and some poorly conceived mime which is throwing McCoy for a loop. The half-brothers. They're really here. Why are they here? I blocked them, surely that meant they couldn't do this sort of thing? Is Dorothy with them? I might be sick. I will be sick. Oh, bollocky bollocks.

'Sorry, you are?'

'Sorry, mate. Firstly, it's so cool to meet you, we're huge fans. We're her half-brothers. I know she wasn't expecting us, but she wasn't answering any of our emails and we thought it best to just come down and ...'

McCoy is doing a very good job of blocking the door with his body so they can't step beyond the threshold. Meanwhile, I am backed into a wall having a mild panic attack. What the actual hell? They're here. In the building, within actual spitting distance. It's terrible. What are they doing here? Why? Since Dorothy mentioned their existence to me, I never gave them a second thought, only to remove them from my inbox. Perhaps it was cruel to not acknowledge people who were kin, but she left us. For them. Maybe there was a part of me that felt disdain, pure jealousy towards them, but for my own sanity, I needed to not let them be part of my universe. I can't even remember their names. I desperately want to see their faces. I'm imagining carbon copies of Adam and Ben, except my brothers are better.

'So to ambush her?'

'Not really, it's just ...'

I feel my head crane around the doorframe to hear the trailing end of his sentence. It's just ... is Mum ill again? They need a kidney and I'm the only match? Of course, I crane my head around too far and knock my forehead against the frame. Everyone behind the door freezes and I creep out.

'Hi, I'm Jools.'

As soon as I see them, there is relief. Adam and Ben *are* better, both sartorially and in terms of looks. HB #1 is tall and gangly like Ben, but facially I don't see anything I recognise. HB #2 is shorter and I am drawn to his face. Mainly because of the eyes. He has my eyes. This studying of faces draws out into silence. I don't know if I should be hugging them, so I hold my hand out.

'Craig.'

'Scott.'

Where the bleeding bellends is Ben? I smile at them, my eyes strained from having this thrown at me on my lonesome.

'You should come in. I'm not sure if this was the best way for us to meet but come in.'

McCoy signals to me but I shake my head and he reads the fear in my eyes.

'It's just, we tried emailing but you haven't replied.'

I lie. 'I didn't get anything. I'm sure I would have seen something?'

'The emails were under our corporation name, Crott Brothers.'

I desperately want to laugh. I want to say that's the worst name for a company ever. It rhymes with snot

185

and pronounced incorrectly it could rhyme with scrote. And all at once, the big sisterly need to tease is overwhelming. I guess the other option would have been Scag, which would have been worse. I need to share this with them. But I hold back. I'm still amazed by the eyes. Craig has my eyes, the bastard. Both brothers look at each other a lot, sharing that same mental space you do when you're siblings and you can read each other's minds. I'm not sure what they expect. How was this a suitable way to meet your sister for the first time? By stalking her to know where she'd be, invading a TV studio, and catching her unaware, then to sit in awkward silence knowing all parties are totally unprepared for this meeting?

'Tea, anyone?' asks McCoy. I smile at him.

'I'll take a water if you have one,' says Craig. McCoy bends down into the counter fridge.

'So, you found me, not that I was hiding but …'

'It's pretty easy using social media and stuff. Mum's been following you too. We told security we were Ben and Adam.'

I don't answer. It's a little unnerving that they know where to find me. That all this time, they've been lying in wait, whereas I've had no idea where they are or who they are. The time Mum told us about them, Ben and I did go on Facebook and have a nosey, but the whole thing left us cold, especially Ben, who couldn't deal with the fallout. This sounds like the whole situation was still hanging, but to me there was resolution. Dorothy was a stranger. She left and I had no space in my life and my heart to let her back in. Scott looks at me like he's disappointed, angry, or somewhere in between. I know exactly how he feels.

'Not that we've been stalking you or anything, it's just we've kept our distance. We didn't know how to approach you.'

186

I guess it could have been worse. They could have shown up at my door and confused my children. By the way, kiddos – two more uncles. Ta-dah! I don't want to tell them I had no intention of ever finding them. What do we do now? I'm still reticent to hug. A restaurant may have been better so I could have the opportunity to put something in my mouth, a park where I would have had the chance to leg it.

'Mum sends her best.'

'Thanks.' I don't return the gesture. 'So, where do you both live? What do you do?'

'With Mum and Dad.' Your dad. Not my dad. They are still sponging off their parents and I feel slightly superior, bar the fact one of my other brothers is living off my sofa.

'Dorothy lives in Kent, right?' It obviously jars with Craig to hear me call her by her first name.

'Yep, and we've both been working and trying to start up an internet thing, but ...'

'That's great.' Is it? It just seems like a reasonably placid answer. I don't know how to respond as they obviously know about my life and what I'm up to now. God, were they in the audience? Were they watching me, studying my every move? Silence. I hate Ben. Where are you, you wanker? I don't pay you in Starbucks to go AWOL.

'If you wanted to stick around, Ben is about, in the building somewhere. My brother ... and your brother too. But you knew that, eh?'

Both brothers smile politely. What do you want to do? See slideshow pictures of my kids? This is asking us to condense twenty-odd years of conversation into how long I have left to inhabit this dressing room. McCoy stands around. Inquisitiveness keeps him there but he almost adopts a protective stance. Do I have questions for the

187

brothers? So many. Do you know what my mum did? Do you know what she did to my dad, how she broke my heart? The confines of this dressing room is not the place. Such grand emotional statements deserve a better setting. My mind can't think beyond niceties. Maybe I used up all my sass with Vermin lady. I attempt to cut through the bullshit.

'So sorry … corporation? So you have an internet company?'

'Kind of … it's kind of why we wanted to approach you. Of course, we wanted to meet you too, but …'

Scott reaches into his rucksack (I stress that again, his *rucksack*) and pulls out some folders with information.

'Yeah, this is us.'

I pick up the paper and flick through it curiously, thinking as an opener into their lives. It's incredibly thorough. Will there be a Powerpoint presentation? At least it's not photos of her, them, and this parallel life that exists beyond my own. That wouldn't have been kind. There's a shit load of paper in front me, bound together like A-Level coursework. It's printed in dodgy Word letterhead paper and I flick through the papers with words bouncing out at me. Pyramid scheme, money, investments, financial gains. A bleak realisation dawns on me and I am silent.

'You can read it in your own time. Mum said you might be interested because we're family and …'

I look at them and inspect their clothing. They're in badly fitting chinos and crinkled shirts, the sort of clothes Matt used to live in back when he was a working week slave. If Ben is twenty-four then these boys must be in their early twenties, and I sit and feel disappointed for them. This is like a really bad episode of *Dragon's Den* where I am the lone dragon and they've walked in, sweaty, immature, and lacking any social grace. It's only taken them five minutes to hint that they are only here for one reason and it makes me slightly nauseous. Nice to meet you too, boys. They sit there awaiting an answer to a question they haven't asked. You could have worked your way up to this, you could have started with a mere hello, nice to meet you. But no, it's a thinly-veiled attempt to see if I have any money for some financially dubious project. I want to say it feels duplicitous and downright rude, but I am more embarrassed that they've chosen to do this here and now.

'I'll read it in my own time. Thanks.' I put the papers to one side and Scott studies my face. I'm stunned into silence and sit there waiting for him to dig further.

'You should give Mum a call, you know. She'd love to see you and the kids.'

Bingo. I pretend not to have heard him. Seriously? My children are mine, not that I feel I have strange ownership rights over them, but she lost her grandparental privileges a long time ago. Surely those are things you earn over time? I can see Scott get slowly riled and he immediately reminds me of Adam. Bring it on, you think I can't handle brothers. I have two.

'Ummm, look … we've just met and I don't want to lecture you, but we shouldn't talk about that, not here.' Not ever, but he seems determined.

'When you saw her last, you didn't even try to reach out to her. It took a lot of courage for her to do what she did.'

There is something brewing in me, bubbling over like something I would cook. It's boiling over, charred, and hard at the bottom of the pan. Smoke. There is smoke.

'You think it's brave to walk out on three young children?'

Craig tries to hold his brother back, almost as if he's trying to signal to the big pile of paper, reminding him

189

they have to think about their financial endeavours.

'She was duped into talking to the media, she was confused, and you didn't even give her a chance. She's so proud of everything you've achieved.'

'I'm sorry, please don't give me sanctimony here. She had a great chance of twelve years to reach out to us, to make her peace, to say she's proud of me. You're not allowed to be proud of someone you didn't raise.' My voice is slightly loud, but there is a tremble I am dying to control.

'Scott, leave it. I told you it was a bad idea.'

'You could just leave it in the past – make amends? It's your choice to be a bitch about it and not reach out to your family.'

My eyes immediately well up. I refuse to counter that. Oh, the stories I could tell you. The way that woman has scarred a piece of my heart and left it tinged in grey. I am quiet and finger through the papers on the desk like an old flick book, feeling pangs of sadness. If they'd come here and asked for love, acceptance, family – would I have been so cut-off, so unwilling to accept them into my life?

'Mum was right, maybe the fame has gone to your head.'

And it was going so well. Good luck squeezing any moolah out of me. Craig looks like he's lost control of the older, volatile brother. It's that same dynamic I see between Adam and Ben all the time. I hear a voice behind me, hands clapping.

'Bravo, so tell me, you little prick, did you come here to purely insult her, or to con her out of money?'

McCoy's words jolt me back into the room. He walks to the coffee table and takes the papers and flicks through them, before walking over and putting them in the bin. Craig looks speechless, staring daggers at his brother.

'Scott, it's time to go.'

The door opens. 'I tell you, I could have flown to Colombia and picked those coffee beans myself.' Ben walks in, juggling hot drinks and buns, and sees me totally crestfallen. 'Here, McCoy, grab my buns for me … oi, oi! Chin up, sis. I did tell you this show was a bad idea. Next time, we'll get you an angle and a blazer and get you on the Culture Show …'

He refers back to Vermin lady, but that is forgotten in comparison to what is going on here, now. 'Actually McCoy, what are you doing here? You're seriously obsessed with my sister, you need to let it go …' He laughs to himself but notices McCoy shaking his head and the mood not lightening in any way. He puts a hand out to Scott and Craig to introduce himself.

'Hi, manners, sorry. I'm Ben. If I'd known we were having a party, I'd have got more buns …' He takes Scott's hand and there is a moment when he looks at him and knows. It's those bloody eyes.

'Jools?'

'Ben, meet Scott and Craig.'

And with that, my confident, bright little brother reverts to some lost child, staring them down and into empty space. 'I don't understand.'

McCoy intervenes. 'And they were just leaving, weren't you, lads?'

Scott clearly hasn't had his last word yet. 'You're our sister, I expected some civility. You don't even know us.'

I know enough. Ben looks at me. This meeting of minds had started without him and things have obviously been said pertaining to our scattered life history. I fill him in with a look. *They're a bunch of tossers. I've been dealing with it while you've taken an age getting the beverages in.* McCoy opens the door and stands by it. Maybe he's dealing with it more. 'You're two chancers who've come in and tried it on. It's crass and it's rude.

191

You'd be better off staying clear of here.'

'Don't worry, mate.' He emphasises that last word with a sarcastic smile, which only underlines his youth and poor manners. I can only wonder if this is the product of having been raised by Dorothy with her own lack of propriety when it comes to people and relationships. With that they get up to leave, half arguing about how badly the meeting has gone and how they totally mishandled what happened. Ben stands confused and dazed. Craig goes to shake his hand, but he refuses. He looks up at me.

'Look, our details are on the emails and documents. Just get in touch, if you wa …'

McCoy shuts the door on them before they have time to finish. He looks at me on the sofa, still and pensive.

'I should make myself scarce if you need some space.' We don't answer. Did that just happen? Did I just meet my other brothers? That felt weird, almost surreal. One of those awkward moments in life I will replay in my head for years to come, where a better, more satisfying outcome was warranted. Did they really come in, have a go, and ask for money I don't have?

'Thank you,' I tell him. He's still surveying the situation, sitting down on a nearby armchair almost as if he's waiting to catch one of us.

'No, it's fine.'

I look over at Ben, nails in mouth, and urge him to come and sit with me. He puts a Chelsea bun in my lap, knowing gluten and sugar may be the answer.

'That was …'

'Yeah …'

'Here …'

'Yeah …'

I bite into my bun, shards of sugar falling down my top. It's stodgy and sickly sweet, stuck to the roof of my mouth. I've forgotten how to chew. I look over at Ben, his face creased and joyless to take it all in. I grab his hand. He squeezes it tightly and the three of us sit in that room, swimming in a thick, paralysing silence trying to work out what the hell just happened. McCoy studies my face for signs of life. I forget why you're here. But don't go, not yet.

CHAPTER FOURTEEN

So, tell us, have you ever met Jools?

Craig: No. That was the first time we'd met. It is such a shame things couldn't have gone more smoothly. We were really upset that she decided to just shut us out of her life. And not just us, her mother ... our mother too.

Scott: We just want to get to know her but she and Mr McCoy were rude and dismissive.

You mean Tommy McCoy was in her dressing room?

Scott: Yeah, it all looked a little too cosy. He was just like you see him on the television – real attitude about him.

Craig: They have a close relationship. It was ...

'Just stop reading it. It'll only make you more upset.' Matt grabs the magazine from my hands and throws it over his shoulder. I smile, he's right. I need to let go of their lies. It was only last week that Ben and I stood there in that dressing room, frozen, ambushed. We stood there for exactly two minutes holding hands after. What do you mean they emailed you? Why didn't you say anything? I did it to be kind, protective, but mostly because I thought that if I pushed the idea of our 'other' brothers out of my mind, they just wouldn't exist. They didn't exist.

But last week, they appeared like magic, in a poof of their own self-importance, only to slink away into the shadows. When would they pounce again? Well, in a Sunday morning magazine supplement, of course. Making the inevitable decision to go to the press in what I can only assume was a desperate attempt to fund their financial endeavours. The story came out a couple of days ago with the usual clap-trap: I'm rude and let fame go to my head, I've (yes, *me*) abandoned a whole arm of my family who are normal, sweet people with no agenda except that of love. To be honest, I feel nothing for the article but apathy – it's hard to feel affected by those for whom you have no genuine level of affection – but the front, the crassness, the barefaced cheek of their actions still stings. Matt sidles up to me.

'Adam called before and asked why one of you didn't deck them. They are welcome around his for a light beating any time of the day, week, or month.'

Maybe physical violence would have solved this. 'How is he?'

'OK. He's having cat issues. His ladyfriend's new cats don't like him. Apparently, they hide in the bath and spy on him when he's taking a dump. He finds it unnerving.'

I look at Matt curiously as this almost sounds like gossip, something quite alien to my husband. He looks unfazed. I smile and think about Adam fighting little kittens. Adam would have handled this situation a lot better, with the no-nonsense approach it needed. Maybe like McCoy did. I think about how he stepped into the situation and threw the half-brothers out when Ben and I were lacking meaningful words and grace. And again, just like that, he climbed up a few notches on that barometer which measures how I feel about him. Apparently, when he hit the big time, this was standard. People climbing out of the woodwork to try and monopolise on old friendships and tenuous family links. He was once asked by an elderly aunt's neighbour if he'd put his name to a home brew made out of potato peelings. But he was there and he spoke to Ben and I about these things in good faith which made me think he wanted to help, to heal the weird rift in our relationship. It didn't go unnoticed.

'Wine,' Matt suddenly shouts. 'Drink, woman, before I finish this bottle on my own.'

'You called me woman.' That way I know he's already a little half-cut.

'You love it.' I do. But I don't tell him that. I refill my glass and snuggle up close to him on the sofa, removing a giant dinosaur toy from behind my back.

Tonight is a good night. It feels safe, how things should be. Technically, it's a date night of sorts, but one of those ones of old, a two-star experience. Matt and I had our fancy five-star shenanigans at the programme launch a month ago. That evening ended in vomit, which I think made us realise we are not five-star people at all. Heels, fresh pants, and a delirious array of alcohol to choose from can only end in disaster, so we've reverted back to old ways. So today, the sheets are used, the bodily hair has not been removed nor will it be sculpted to a pleasing aesthetic, the wine was on offer, the dress code will be comfortable, bra optional. Most likely the date will be interrupted by a child who wants a drink/has filled their nappy/has kicked off their covers and won't get their lazy arse out of bed to fix this dilemma on their own. It's also a Sunday, to fit in with my new-found work schedule, which limits our television options. Jesus Christ, who decided to reserve all the depressing television for a Sunday night? Any right-minded person would put the light entertainment on Sundays to cheer us up in preparation for the week ahead. Instead, we have the option of costume dramas where people mumble about love, die of consumption, and end up alone, or depressing modern war dramas where people mumble about conspiracy, the torture is bloody and real, and people end up alone. Matt studies the television pensively as someone from the CIA harps on about moles and interrogations.

'I'm not sure I have the energy to think this one

197

through,' says Matt. I sigh, relieved, knowing that anything that asks me to juggle multiple storylines of misery in my head may give me an aneurysm. He flicks through the channels.

'We could start a box set. Do we want dragons and sex, prisons and sex, or the White House and sex?'

'Dragons?'

'Done.'

Matt is readying the Sky box when his phone buzzes. He quickly scooches off the sofa to the front door, reappearing with two brown paper bags.

'Is this some new-fangled doorbell system Wok Away are using now?'

Matt laughs, clearing the stack of sticker books and assorted Lego off the coffee table. 'No, it's a system I've got down with the takeaway; they text me when they're at the door and it means the doorbell doesn't ring and doesn't wake the kids who consequently don't come down and steal my pancakes.'

It's a logic so clarified I high-five my husband. We love our kids, we do, but when there is crispy aromatic duck in the vicinity, they become thieving bastards who leave us with bits of spring onion and little else. Matt does what he does best and unloads all the bags in an organised fashion. Little has changed in the ten years we've known each other. I like a wonton soup, he thinks they look like waterlogged bollocks in a puddle of piss. He will always bemoan the quality of the meat but inhale his crispy chilli beef. We both love crispy duck, a love of true meaning we have passed down to our offspring. We still haven't quite worked out the appeal of chicken balls or what chop suey actually is. When we do get a Chinese, I think back to when we were young, starving student parents.

Our local in Leeds did lunch specials which were huge so it meant we could share and it'd last us until dinner, can of free fizzy drink and all. It used to be our special Friday treat. Matt would come home from his sociology in development lecture and we'd walk down to the Golden Phoenix as this new, confused family unit. The lady who worked there never quite knew what to make of us; he was Northern, she was Southern – they were too young to have a baby, which was clearly evident from their choices of footwear and the fact he carried a wallet with a Velcro fastening. The pram looked new, though (it was – Matt's parents weren't going to have their only grandchild carted about in any old chariot) and hell, the baby was cute. So she gave us free prawn crackers. We'd eat them on the way back to our flat. Matt used to make Hannah laugh by balancing them on his tongue and flipping them around. At the time, I thought that was the mark of a great dad and used to beam at them, deliriously in love.

He doesn't do the prawn cracker thing any more, not around me at least, but over the years, he's developed better table manners and control over his chopsticks. He divides everything evenly, even counting out the pancakes so we both get the same number. He spies me looking.

'I got dumplings today. I thought we should go all out.'

I clap my hands like a seal in the same way any other normal woman might when presented with diamonds. There are five in the box, he gives me three and I link my arm into his. This is what love has become.

'So you think Ben has a new fancy man?' Ben has hardly been a fixture in the house recently. When he's not with me, he's off with his new mystery text man on what we assume is an array of dates in places far trendier and non-suburban than around these parts. That part of the world that plays dubstep and serves food on slabs of slate. Either way, this could be the start of something new and exciting for him, so I'm secretly pleased.

'He's been all over his phone and he always looks smug.'

'Like he's having way more sex than any person should be entitled to have?'

'Yep.' Matt laughs and dips his fingers into the hoisin. What was that I said about table manners? He tops up my wine knowing it'll appease me. He's not half wrong.

'You need to dig a bit more so we can find out about him. Tell the kids to do some eavesdropping. Ted is amazing at that.'

Matt gives me a look, like the one he gives me when we're at motorway services and I tell the kids to line their pockets with napkins and little packets of sugar and ketchup.

'Give the boy some room, he'll tell you when he's ready.' I build my pancake, smearing the hoisin on first like butter which I know annoys Matt.

'This is the dragon girl.'

'Is she fit?'

'Well, you wouldn't turn it down if it were in the room, eh?'

'I'm in the room.'

'Well, obviously I'd discuss it with you first.'

I throw a bit of flaccid cucumber at him, eyeing a rather hirsute if brooding young man on the screen dressed in fur. If he were in the room, maybe. Matt notices, laughs at me, and throws the cucumber back in my direction.

'What else is happening then?'

'I'm famous now. I was spotted in the Tesco Metro the other day.'

'Yeah, you told me about that. That was the day you missed Hannah's gala.'

Matt has had no problem reminding me about that over the past few days, almost as if to punish me. I am quick to reply. 'You need to cut me some slack with stuff. I was working ...'

Matt looks at me, wondering where this conversation is going.

'It was her first one.'

'You missed the twins' first day at school.'

'Touché.'

'It's the truth. I never once had a go at you for missing school stuff when you worked, and you missed a lot ...'

He looks at me and it almost makes me wish I'd tallied all those music recitals, special assemblies, and harvest masses up. I never once questioned that I should have been the active participant. Matt pauses, knowing he's halfway through his chilli beef and doesn't want to gun for a fight and the resulting indigestion.

'I found a lawyer to tackle the thing with the neighbour.' Change of subject. I play along.

'Not Annie?' Matt shakes his head. It's been two weeks since I found out about Annie's woes. Chris had left, the hows and whys were unclear, but in turn, the shame and loneliness had slowly seen Annie retreat into herself. It was Matt who managed to get some of the story out of her, but he told me she was at a low: one he assumed I had known about. I felt a tumult of emotion over the situation. There were selfish questions over why she'd never felt she could come to me, but also fear, sadness, anger over how it'd come to this – whether I'd been a bad friend and let this occur without intervention. So I called, I left messages. Go see her, Matt said. I said I was too busy, as he looked on disapprovingly. But the reality was, I was scared I wouldn't be able to prop her up when she was so low, that I'd let her down even more.

'Ring her, please. The longer you leave it, the harder it'll get to reach out to her.'

I try to gloss over the subject. 'So, the neighbour ...'

201

Given I've just lectured him about judging my new working parent persona, it feels like we're on an even keel. Do we open up these arguments and start digging through them? Or do we just drink more wine? I refill my glass. Matt shakes his head to signal his dismay at the Annie situation. I glare back at him. He knows to retreat.

'The neighbour is a dick. If his cat shits in our garden again, I'm going to jump over the fence and start pissing on their begonias.'

'Nice. Tell me when you're going to do it, I'll make sure I'm out.'

'Will do.'

I'm not following what's happening on the telly in much detail, but brooding hirsute man has his top off and is happily shagging some girl across a kitchen table. Wait, did she just slash his neck? Matt and I don't seem too dismayed. In fact, these days I think we crave the gratuitousness to balance out the amount of Mr Maker in our lives. The more naked arse and random shagging the better. Wait … isn't that his sister? Matt is transfixed, as any man is when pert, youthful bosoms are on show, and I debate whether our love life has ever been that vigorous or been practised with such wild abandon. I pour Matt some more wine to try and snap him out of his sex trance and comfort myself with a few dumplings, knowing I may never possess the body of dragon girl in my lifetime. Matt turns his head to the side. I notice he has a bit of hoisin smeared on the underside of his chin, the same spot where sauce always seems to stick, and I realise he may never look like hirsute man in fur either. Matt's gone into comfy Dad mode recently. When he's not rocking tracksuit chic, he lives in jeans and an array of hoodies, chunky trainers, and beanies. Sometimes, if I blur my eyes from across a room, he looks exactly how he did when we were at university.

'That's your lass that McCoy is shagging, the one from the party.'

True enough, it's Georgie Gale as some slave girl/prostitute wearing pretty much a suede version of what we saw her in last.

'Except they're not shagging …'

Matt gives me a look. 'Really?'

I stuff another dumpling in my mouth.

'Big showmance. I guess Cam set it up to give Georgie a bit of media coverage before she started being in this.'

Matt has a confused expression about him. I'm not sure if this is because he's wondering why McCoy didn't monopolise on the opportunity to shag the very attractive Georgie or over why I know these things.

'Luella told you?'

'No, McCoy and I were chatting in the dressing room before the Brothers Grimm made their appearance. We talked about the kids and Vermin lady, it was all very civil …'

I shift him a look through a mouthful of egg fried rice. I have nothing to feel guilty about, he'll know better than to believe any of the tattle trying to link us romantically.

'So you two are buddies then?' He says it with an edge in his voice, letting me know he disapproves. I eat more rice. I've attempted in small bursts to try and change Matt's feelings towards McCoy, but as I imagined, he is less than forgiving.

'You know, I think there's more to him than we first thought. I feel bad about Kitty and the kids and he was there when the brothers made their appearance. He was the only one who had the balls to kick them out and tell them where to go.'

Matt doesn't say a word, but fills his mouth with food to avoid what is obviously brewing. It's all rising to the surface. Not here, not on date night. We have wine to

203

finish. We have half an episode of something on the go. I don't sense jealousy but I feel he wants me to keep my distance. Luella is of the same feeling. No fraternising with the enemy. Neither of them have any forgiveness in their souls to gloss over events of yesteryear. Of course, Luella has greater reason to have some hatred for him given the sudden and cruel way he disposed of her. But for Matt, he'll always be the man who nearly broke us. I often think he looks upon his marital breakdown with some glee. But I've seen the man tears, I know there are kids involved, so I can't be so callous. He was also calm and helpful in the face of being ambushed. There are conversations there that beg to be finished, a desire to want to get to know him better, offer him the help he wants. I want to tell Matt, but he is still fuming about something. There is a moment of silence as someone on screen screams in Shakespearean tones about avenging their father and the awful ways in which they plan to spill blood. I feel the need to add to the conversation.

'He's a bit lost. Cam Jacobs is a twat and I'm not sure why but it seems he trusts me, confides in me …'

It's a strange feeling, to feel there is friendship brewing between us, but that's all it is, nothing more. Matt shakes his head, knowing he can't keep his feelings at bay.

'I just don't get it.'

I await the rant about him destroying our family, etc., etc.

'So you have time to speak to someone like McCoy and offer him a shoulder to lean on, but one of your oldest friends, who has been there for you for as long as I can remember, since Hannah and uni and all those times we were totally out of our depths and you're just …'

I am totally unprepared for this. He thinks I've prioritised who my friends are? He thinks I don't care about Annie? I shake my head and stop him mid-sentence.

'Look, I've tried to get in touch with Annie but she hasn't got back to me.'

'You're not trying hard enough.'

'I can't make her ring me.'

'No, you need to go over there and take control. She is drowning and she's too embarrassed to ask for help. You need to show up at her doorstep and tell her you are here, you're her friend, and you love her.' Tears are welling up in my eyes. 'Because friends is a term used too loosely. Annie is family. She always has been.'

I am quietly sullen, mainly because I know he's right and I don't want to let him know. I also know that on this sofa and with a MSG laden plate, I have been shamed. I think about how Annie used to come over unannounced, bearing arrays of useful gifts like nappy sacks and giant bars of Galaxy. She babysat Hannah as I took my final exams and I wore a pair of her heels on my wedding day. Matt's right. I need to work harder for her. From the moment I'd heard Chris had left her, I should have been at her side, but I've let it stew. I've assumed too much and not done enough. Matt puts an arm around me.

'I didn't mean to upset you, you silly mare, but ...'

'Yeah, I know.'

He hands me wine. I sip it but daren't look at him. He rakes through his rice the same way the twins do that annoys the hell out of me. He grabs my hand and I squeeze it back. There is that tiny bit of resentment to be told something so obvious. There's also that understanding that it's come from a place of knowing someone so well you can just put things out there in plain view without beating around the proverbial bush. This was definitely a better, clearer place to be in than say two years ago when everything was unsaid and brushed under

205

the rug. He pulls me in for a hug so I can fall into his fleecy sweatshirt and feel like this has been resolved.

'I usually hope our date nights can end in some sort of intercourse as opposed to one of my lectures.'

I laugh under my breath.

'Here, have a look at this.' And with that, he takes a prawn cracker and flips it around in his mouth. I laugh a bit unattractively. This is the most romance I'll be getting out of this evening. He remembered. And I figure this is the only person I want to be with right now, right here in our slovenly state, in our version of normality away from cameras, lights, and action. We've both had a fair bit of wine. Let's make this happen. He pushes the hair from my face and is about to make his move when we hear a key in the door. Damn you, little brother. He pokes his head around the door.

'Oooh, dumplings!' He comes over and nabs one, taking off his coat before realising what he's done.

'Shit, date night! I forgot. I can go over to Dad's or sleep on the floor in Hannah's room?'

Matt and I look at each other. We're used to date night coming with interruptions, albeit usually from people far smaller and needier.

'No, grab a plate and join us,' Matt adds, knowing we've over-ordered and knowing a shag will be forthcoming later, probably in the comfortable confines of our bed as opposed to the sofa with a Nerf Gun lodged against my shoulder.

Ben disappears into the kitchen. 'Did you have a nice evening?' I wink at Matt for digging for info. His voice echoes down the corridor.

'Yeah, I went to this new gin bar in London, three hundred types of gin and some amazing urban art installations.' I look down at myself, in pyjama bottoms, and wonder what the reaction would have been had I rocked up. Truth be told, it's very Tracey Emin. I'd fit right in.

'Did you go with anyone?' There's no response. His face reappears at the door.

'A friend.'

Matt laughs. I raise my eyebrows. 'Is that a special friend?'

'Fuck off,' he giggles. 'I forgot chopsticks.'

He escapes to the kitchen as I look at the coffee table and see his phone there, unlocked. I grab it quickly as Matt shakes his head and tries to grab it from me. I turn my back to him and he tries to reach around me as I hold it in the arm furthest away from him. Messages, messages. Nothing. WhatsApp. I hear footsteps in the hallway. Matt's eyes widen.

'Mate, better get another wineglass too.'

'And some kitchen roll.'

Matt's nostrils are flaring with disapproval as we continue our silent game of him trying to retain his brother-in-law's right to privacy from his nosey sister. WhatsApp? Messenger? What are the cool kids using these days? I flick through the menus. Photos! There'll be photos. There are photos. But then the phone starts to vibrate. I drop it in shock then pick it up again. The name of the dialler and a picture comes up. What the actual hell? Cam Jacobs calling.

CHAPTER FIFTEEN

'So, we're here today to run through a couple of things … just contractual matters, timetabling, promotional considerations and publicity, and then I'm going to throw the floor open to some questions … are we all OK for coffees? Iris, let's go for a pink grapefruit and Echinacea tea … people?'

I shake my head. They like their hot drinks at these things and I'm already on my second coffee, any more and I'll be peeing like a racehorse. We're in the offices of Maggie Matthews: all white with accents of lilies and yellow painted into the alcoves, pretty much as minimalist and ordered as you'd expect a head honcho's office to look. Part of me hopes that, like my drawers at home, you'd open them and odd paper clips and unpaid bills from last year would come fluttering out. I shift awkwardly on her leather sofa, knowing that every time I re-cross my legs or reach for a pastry, the material squeaks not unlike a small fart might sound. I bite into what I picked up from the table. Christ on an actual bike, that's not what I expected at all and not in a good way. It's filled with a deep red paste that's not jam and the bread part has birdseed in it and is greying slightly.

'Oh, they're sesame and red bean mocha. Lovely, right?' Luella tells me.

I feel like I've been ambushed by a baked good, a previous friend, an ally. It's like a stake to the side. Luella watches me curiously as I attempt to politely nibble it, giving me that look Dad used to give me when we went to aunty Sylvia's and she served her cast iron teacakes. Just bite and swallow, don't you dare spit that shit out.

But then Luella has been shifting me these looks quite a lot recently. It started after I was waylaid by the half-brothers. After McCoy ushered them out of our lives, Ben and I thought nothing more of it, even after the article went to print. But Luella was fuming. She needed to know. She could have blocked the story, she could have prepared my response, or just known. Instead, the brothers put out their version of events that most will know to take with a pinch of salt but some will take as truth. I'd gone against everything we'd discussed after the Holiday Inn incident, that part about full disclosure, warts and all. When the brothers' interview referred to McCoy being at our meeting, it stuck the knife in even further. We were friends now? Like in a nineties' sitcom way? I knew she felt betrayed, that I had crossed a line. I was supposed to be right by her side knowing the awful ways he had treated her and repaying debts for the fact she got me here. So a professional betrayal and a personal one too. I wasn't allowed to blur these lines, to forget so easily, to be some ruddy awful peacemaker in this perfectly played out tension. Luella sighs heavily beside me to signal her level of unease towards me of late and I chew at the gelatinous mochi thing.

'Iris, I might take another coffee if possible.' Iris is Maggie's assistant. She has a very harsh fringe and wears a short sleeved blouse which shows a tattoo of a geometric fox on her forearm. I'm not sure why but I have the overwhelming urge to colour it in. She looks the sort who spends her weekends with a retro camera partying it up in Berlin. She smiles and nods.

'I could have got that for you,' whispers the voice

behind me. Because I need the tension cranked up even more, I have Ben sat on a stool behind the sofa – here to take notes and create that façade of me having some sort of entourage. I'm not sure how I feel about Ben at the moment. Yes ... Ben is not just shagging but *dating* one Mr Cam Jacobs. Part of me wants to launch myself at him like we did when we were kids, tackle him to the floor, and try and put my fingers up his nose. Part of me wonders about his catastrophic levels of judgement. It's not like we live in a small England suburb where there are few gays in the village. For God's sake, him? He's a sleazeball at best, not one I can envisage ever liking or welcoming into my fold. They really get on, he told me. They have so much in common. I wasn't kind at this point. I may have mentioned bad words and loaded them with sarcasm. But then he retaliated with my lack of knowledge about him, his community, his lifestyle, and threw lines at me usually reserved for teenagers in the throes of love that they don't quite understand. I called him immature. He threw a spoon of hoisin at me. It killed date night.

It's not quite resolved between us. He gives me no clear indication about whether they are a couple and feels I am being preachy and intrusive into what should be a private matter. However, it feels like I'm being stabbed in the back. He knows all the ways in which Cam Jacobs has wormed his way into our lives – surely that gives him huge potential to be a sod when it comes to matters of the heart. But he refuses to listen. So I am being petty and moody in return and even though he still tags along beside me, I ignore him in that angsty teen way I can get away with treating a little brother.

That said, Jacobs is in the room and putting on all his usual airs and graces to impress the bigwigs. I want to stab him in the way you do when someone you don't like is having physical relations with someone you love, but part of me feels a slow and painful death is possibly more deserving, like maybe I could run him over and leave him in a ditch. McCoy reads my expression and makes faces from across the room. Why do you look murderous? He signals to the baked good in my hand and I laugh. Luella freezes to catch that moment between us.

'Iris darling, please can I get a carbonated water with a slice of lime, thank you honey. Mags, this array of desserts is inspired. I love the matcha.'

Cam smiles at Ben and I go murderous again. He's in full charm offensive, call-everyone-pet-names mode. I daydream about throwing the remnants of what's in my hands at the perfect space between his eyes to shock him into falling off his metal chair and looking like a twat. Sadly, I lack the aim and courage.

'A new Japanese bakery. Try the black sesame when you have a chance.'

'Oh, I will.' Schoomzy schmooze.

'So, first things first. I have some dates you need to blackout as per mentioned in your contract. First thing, I need you to represent the show at an awards show – you're to present an award so posh frocks, free champers, all that jazz.'

I nod in resigned agreement yet know there are probably harder things in life to contend with.

'And I've been asked by the honchos about you doing charity stuff – are you both that way inclined?'

Luella nods, though I wasn't sure I could answer in any other way. Oh no, I don't want to help starving kids and homeless people.

'There's some sporting stuff they need people for, bike rides, mountain climbing, all that jazz.'

The need to do jazz hands overwhelms me. I don't. 'Anything that involves marathon binge watching?' I laugh at my own joke and see McCoy smile. The rest of the room, Maggie included, don't. If Davina McCall can throw herself into a freezing lake, you young lady can shuffle up an Alp (or ideally something smaller). McCoy's smile turns into a snigger. Luella squirms in her seat again but this time Cam gets wind of it and smiles wryly.

'Maybe it's something you guys could do together. You could sail somewhere together, share a cabin ...'

Shit is being stirred. Luella scribbles in her notebook, tearing little holes into the paper with her biro. McCoy chips in, 'Or we could jog around Richmond Park?'

'Grab a Mr Whippy along the way,' I add. We both laugh. Christ, that is not Luella's happy face. Maggie Matthews tries to diffuse the tension.

'Well, I will mention something. Next, I've been going through the timetabling of the show and we've decided in weeks seven and eight we want to pre-film segments so they become double headers to build the tension. We'll ask the kids to prepare something that takes days – like a cake or something with jelly.'

It never struck me that Ms Matthews would be such a fountain of cooking knowledge. Tommy arches an eyebrow at the fact this hasn't been thought through in too much detail.

'It'll be another day of filming but we can combine it with some promotional stuff. We want a whole new set of commercials and there's some photos that need taking for next series?'

Luella perks up at this point. 'So this is under discussion?'

'Of course,' replies Maggie. 'It's a ratings hit and there's huge potential to sell the format overseas and have a whole off-shoot of merchandising, books. Discussions have been under way.'

Luella and Maggie seem to face off. There are pound signs in people's eyes; Luella knows I am a commodity and whereas the shiny BBC was like some holy grail that lured me in with sweet champagne and promises of grandeur, I have my feet under the rug and she's willing to negotiate me bigger stakes, higher fees. Frankly, I'd be glad for a DAB radio and a cosy fleece blanket so I can take naps on the sofa in between show segments.

'Then, if the floor is open, we'd like to be privy to these discussions.'

I nod but shift her worried looks as I am all too aware that she has spoken for me as opposed to this being a discussion where my feelings and worries have been acknowledged. Would I want to do a second series? At the moment, we are four episodes in and while it's been exhilarating in places to be live on TV and maybe actually enjoying it, it's too early to know where this may go. It may peter out into something very shit (like when *X-Factor* have those catastrophic finale shows and wheel out Westlife and their bar stools) or the media circus built around the show may die down and interest will wane. Cam Jacobs' Cheshire cat grin makes me think he has no intention of that ever happening.

'Us too, we'd definitely like to be in on those negotiations.'

It goes deathly silent as people eye each other up and try to read Ms Matthews' poker face. Do you still want me on your team or are you going to dump me for a younger model, someone actually licensed and qualified to deal with children and cooking? Maggie coughs.

'I'll let you know when this happens. So back to pre-filming, how are we set for next Friday? I need you on set by 7.30 a.m.'

'Millie has her music classes on Friday morning.'

Luella stares at me, biting her bottom lip in

214

disappointment. You're telling the BBC you're busy so you can go sing Old McDonald with your youngest and bash it out on a recorder? I realise I've said that out loud as Maggie studies my face. She has a family picture on her desk: three girls dressed in Burberry with impossibly perfect blonde curls. But still, she appears to not understand my dilemmas. I have yet to understand how I do that, cut myself off from being their mother. Of course, biology will always make me their mother, but before that role made those music classes, the assemblies, the walking around classrooms admiring pieces of art made from pasta my daily routine. Now, sat in a room with lily-white upholstery, I look back on my attendances of such things with a strange fondness. I have to do Jungle Jingles as Matt can't. He may be the perfect parent but we found out even he has his limits. A hand appears on my shoulder.

'I can cover that, I'm sure Matt could …' I look over my shoulder at Ben and shake my head. You're not allowed to talk yet. He removes his hand.

'Well, if we're doing individual segments … don't we have that piece where I go and see how broccoli is grown? Can't we reschedule so Jools can fulfil her parental responsibilities? I don't mind.'

It's time for Cam to stare McCoy down, questioning why he is facilitating the enemy. I smile at his gesture while Maggie ponders over a list.

'I guess that could work. But no later than lunchtime, Jools, please.'

'And in return, perhaps I can do that report Tommy was going to do about the microbrewery?'

'Oh, you'd love that, wouldn't you?'

We laugh in unison, scribbling down notes. I look up and everyone is silent. Cam laughs under his breath. 'Well, isn't that just sweet …' he mutters. Luella can't hide her disdain anymore and stares out of the window, glassy-eyed and gloomy. Cam smiles at Ben sat directly behind me, almost as if he's intentionally taunting me. It's my turn to brood. It's a tennis match of looks, silent in their delivery but loaded with emotion no one can seem to express in this soulless white room. Maggie's phone suddenly rings and Iris answers it, signalling that she needs to take it.

'Is it Len Goodman? Balls, I have to take this. I shan't be ten minutes. Iris, more drinks.' Her finger does a dance pointing to everyone before she slinks away to an adjoining room and Iris hovers over us clearing mugs and the leftovers of a matcha confection that might be mine. I fear who will speak first, but if you were going to hedge your bets, you knew who'd be first to pip in, with all the subtlety of a sledgehammer.

'Soooo, second series, that is exciting. Jools, what a massive step. Hey, you can finally get your extension finished. I have heard all about it …'

I turn to Ben. Great, so you're going at it hammer and tongs with your shiny American douche and telling him all about my home life. He reads my disappointment instantly and expresses to Cam how he should have kept his mouth shut, making me think about what other nonsense he's been divulging. Luella looks lost.

'Didn't you hear? Ben and Cam have been shagging.' Luella closes her eyes as if to say that word is barred at the BBC, didn't you know?

'Seriously, Ben? Seriously?' she adds. I clap my hands to acknowledge her support.

'It's more than shagging and I'm not sure when this crappy, unpaid job of mine came with the proviso that I couldn't have sex with who I wanted.'

'You live in my house, you know he's a complete twat.'

'Sat, right here ...' interjects Cam.

Tommy, who's been observing the action, has his say. 'You've been sleeping with Jools' brother?'

'We are two consenting adults, there is really no problem. The way I see it, we've all got it on in here, eh? You and Jools, Luella ...'

'Wait, just a minute, where the hell do you come off spouting shit like that?' I exclaim. I am snarling. Ben is red with shame. I look at Luella. I lied, that wasn't Luella's angry face earlier. She's wearing it now. It's that face reserved for ladies at Black Friday sales. But her stares seem to be purely reserved for McCoy because she knows this would have come from him, that this would have been mentioned casually in conversation to hurt her or us in some way. She's over it, she keeps telling me, but you can tell it still stings and Tommy's not had the comeuppance he deserves yet. No apologies seem forthcoming and even McCoy looks confused. He turns to Cam.

'How did you know? Did you research this? It has absolutely no bearing on this situation at all.'

Cam gestures and holds his hands up to Ben. I tell Ben everything. I go white with shame.

'Ben! For fuck's sake!'

Luella gets up and storms out of the room. I follow closely, dodging Iris who obviously thought we needed some self-blooming jasmine teas. Luella stands in the corridor of the offices looking like she's going to punch holes in the wall. She looks impeccable, as she always does: blazer with pointy shoulders, trousers that seem to wrap around her and drape beautifully around her midriff. She's plaited part of her bob behind her ear.

'Luella, you know me. I don't just spread tattle and speak about you so casually like that. I can't believe Ben ...'

She looks at me like I've totally missed the point. Disappointment reigns, slouching her pointy shoulders.

'Jools, that whole meeting. You just don't get it, do you?'

I stand there, silent.

'This, us. It has to be a partnership, you have to tell me everything. I don't care if you want to be friends with McCoy, knock yourself out, but I go in there and I don't know and you're cosying up to each other and you're making me look like a fool, like you're hiding this from me. When your stepbrothers ambush you, Ben, Cam ... I should have been the first person you called when you found out.'

'I know, you're my publicist.' I mutter casually like a sullen teen. She immediately looks insulted.

'Fuck off. You're my friend, I care about you. I wouldn't have come this far if I didn't care about what happens to you and your family. I have always been on your side and fought for you. So, you shutting me out, that speaks volumes.'

I shake my head, wishing I could take that insolence, that indifference back. Luella knows how much I appreciate and need her. We've shared wine and I've carried her back to hotel rooms. Have I prioritised other things over my consideration of her? I think about Annie all of a sudden. Maybe I've been a tool, maybe this has got too much and I've let the people who matter fall out of my circle, letting them teeter along the edge and pushing them off like I don't have time for them.

'Luella, I'm sorry.'

But apologies come too late to dull her rage. She goes back into the room to gather her handbag and files and leaves.

'Luella, please ...'

Cam, of course, can't hide his glee that I have to beg,

attempt to talk her out of this, but she goes for the dramatic exit as you'd predict her to do. Ben sneaks his head around the doorframe.

'Sis …'

'Don't sis me now. Jesus Christ, Ben! He's using you to get to me. How the hell did the subject of Luella come up? What right is it of yours to tell him, of all people, about it?'

Ben has tears in his eyes and he is right in the line of fire, like a bunny rabbit in a field, all wide-eyed and looking for a friend. But my anger bubbles away and the eleven-year-old sister inside me feels the need to push him, to make him cry, to feel like I've won something.

'Believe it or not, we don't just shag … we talk, we date, there's a connection …'

I hold my hand up, shaking my head. Eyes peer over desks at the BBC, leaning back in their swingy office chairs.

'What? You love him? Then you're a bigger idiot than I thought. Grow up and smell the fact that this little dalliance means nothing. It's desperate, it's laughable. I had you down as a complete manwhore but not a complete moron.'

And that's it. I've done it. He stares at me, longing for me to take it back, to hold him and apologise, but I don't. A lot of it is symptomatic of siblinghood, of practising arguments with someone since infancy so you know exactly how to have the upper hand. We'd be little and arguing over something small and mundane (toy ownership; sofa space) and I would say something unforgiveable that I knew would sting. It was usually about mum leaving and him being unlovable and it would hit that nerve. And it's done now. But I'm not eleven years old. I'm a grown woman, one of the few Ben knows to love him without conditions, and I'm now officially the

219

shittiest human being to have ever existed. A single tear rolls down his cheek and he closes the door on me. Well done Jools, well done.

CHAPTER SIXTEEN

When Hannah was first born, Matt and I didn't have money. We lived on student loans and handouts from Matt's parents. She slept in the same room as us until she was two, we lived off pasta and sauce (Matt doesn't bring this up, it was a culinary low point), and I remember we used to go to the local playground a lot. I'm not sure why. Hannah wouldn't have been big enough to go on any of the equipment until she was way into toddlerhood, but there seemed something safe and reassuring about being around other children, about thinking you were getting fresh air and hearing the squeals of children going down metal slides that were scalding hot on a summer's day. Matt and I did the swings a lot, almost as if parenthood had made us regress into our younger selves to prove to ourselves and others that having a little person in a carriage next to us didn't make us old and laden with responsibilities. The swings made life free and fun and we used to sit there showing the kids how it was done, how high we could go. Matt would show them tricks, I'd revel in the air rushing past my ears and tangling my unwashed hair until another parent would stare us down for hogging them and being far too old for the twelve-year-old age limit as stated on the notice on the front gate.

So when I mentioned to Annie about meeting up, the park felt like the obvious choice. It was safe, reassuring. We'd get some fresh air, I'd bring coffees, there were trees, ducks, sunshine – things that connect you to life and nature and provide you with some level of simple clarity.

But the truth is, I suggested the park because I was petrified about seeing her in a situation where it was just us. I wasn't sure I could handle the silence of a room where it was just us two, and me having to fill that silence with my poor excuses for apologies. I had been a rubbish friend to her recently, to a lot of people, and it was time to make amends. With Annie, there'd been awkward coffees, brief, almost tense, phone conversations, and a lot of it was down to us adjusting to this new hurdle in our friendship. I had lacked the sensitivity to look after her as she made her first forays into motherhood and abandoned her when it was obvious she needed me the most. I should have beaten down her door and forced my way in. In fact, the very definition of friend has been turned on its head recently. With Luella having stormed out on me and my relationship with McCoy no longer defined by hatred, possibly finding ourselves in a place where we had more in common than we thought, I was being asked to examine these new relationships I surrounded myself with and force myself to define their importance in my life. I tell you, life was far easier when it was just me, little people, and Mr Bloom and his vegetables who asked for nothing except me singing along about cabbages.

'Thank God you brought coffee.'

Annie ambushes me from behind the bench I've stationed myself on and I turn to greet her.

'Oh, Annie.'

She registers my surprise and suddenly seems embarrassed, pulling up the zip on her coat and tucking strands of hair around her woolly hat. She is still the Annie I knew, she has the tailoring and the sort of put-together style I crave. But today I see a face caved in from emotion; her eyes are dull, her hair crisp and flyaway. Fatigue will drain you, but emotionality out of your control can affect your whole disposition. This is no

Annie I've ever seen. Even when boyfriends left her, she failed job interviews, and her grandmother passed away.

'Well, if a look could tell me I look shit, I think I've found it.'

I want to laugh, without sounding cruel, because that's the sort of friends we are – there's a sarcasm that runs through what we say so neither of us could ever be offended, but that doesn't feel appropriate. Or does it? I'm not sure any more. Maybe now is the time to be light-hearted, humorous me and mask all that hurt and confusion with something funny, and then it'll all be gone, done and she won't look gaunt and ill with sadness. Her cheeks will fill out, the colour in her skin will brighten like flicking the contrast on a television set. I can make this better for her, I can be her cure. But instead I curl my body into hers and grasp her a little tighter to let her know this is more than a hug, this is me infusing all my love into her. She releases me to push the stroller with one hand as Finn stirs in his sleep.

'It's madness, he sleeps in these two hour stretches and then I have to feed him and hold him upright for half an hour afterwards because of the reflux. And he's so angry.'

'Chris?'

Her body freezes to hear his name, out there like the bad swear word I'm not supposed to say in front of the kids. It was too early to say it. Flowers wilt behind us.

'I meant Finn.'

'Oh.'

She pauses, looking at me, urging me not to bring up that subject, not without coffee anyway.

'His little body. Every time I put him down, he contorts and his little face from the reflux, it goes this strange pink. And I just can't seem to settle him, he gets no comfort from me.'

She stares down at the pram and pangs of a memory

223

and emotion once lived dart through me; of looking at this little helpless being arching its back in its cot at some ungodly hour. And you ache from fatigue, your face feels like it belongs to someone else, that it could literally melt away, but you have to keep going. You have to feed it and change it and stop it from crying and keep giving it life. But it keeps crying and pooing and needing you. And you want to throw it out of the window. You want it to stop. But you don't. You keep going. You don't know how, but you do.

'Hun, it's what the little feckers do.'

She looks at me and smiles, shaking her head. She hears me refer to my kids as certain words all the time and she always disapproves, but for once seems to recognise the truth. That said, her eyes bloat with emotion.

'You saw me at university, I was a wreck. I didn't sleep, eat. I didn't wash my hair for two weeks. Remember when we took it out of a hair tie and it stood up of its own accord?'

The anecdote does what it's supposed to and she laughs again. I have mountains of things that I could just feed her and it could put everything right. Instances of teething, nappy rash, mastitis, sicky bugs that last weeks on rotation: times when motherhood was my nemesis and the world felt on the point of implosion. But I realise this has to be about her, not trading stories tit for tat.

'But then, you were so young. You were barely out of your teens, you were still at university, for crap's sake. I've had ten years on you to sort this out – to grow up and be better than I am.'

I shake my head. There is potential to be offended but she'll know I can never feel that way about her. Whatever age you become a mother, it's a physical shock to the system that catches anyone unaware. I want to give her clichés: it will get better, you're doing great, but I know

224

it's not what she wants to hear and I know she sees my brood regularly enough to know the carousel never quite stops turning. She takes a large gulp of her coffee.

'Who said you're not doing a good job?'

'Me.'

'Because you're Annie – you need to let your standards drop. Seriously, you're wearing matching socks, the baby is dressed … in my eyes, this is coping, this is doing OK.'

She shakes her head at me, smiling.

'And you never told me about the baby group thing where they sit there and talk about their nipples and compete about whose baby is already holding their head up …'

I laugh. 'You missed out. I went to some special ones in Leeds meant for "young mothers" – there was a baby called Shakira, I shit you not.'

She smiles and downs the rest of her coffee. 'It's all they frigging talk about and they're judgy and when Finn sits there and cries, they look at me like I'm ruining their happy baby group vibe.'

'Then don't go. I never went for the twins. I barricaded myself in the house, it's probably why they're so manic, because they were under house arrest for the first six months of their life.'

'Then what do you do all day?'

I don't answer because she knows exactly what I did. With Hannah, I scraped past my exams and finished my degree but I let my career fall by the wayside and fell into this strange role of homemaker/mother where a large percentage of my time was spent doing the mundane; from cleaning to cooking to moving toys from A to B and daytime napping. Your mind is so sleep deprived it's not built for much else, but you're confined to this space for a while. Some break out of it, they take on the world and juggle it admirably, but some hide away into it just to feel like they're coping.

'But you and I, we talk about other things. Not just babies.'

'Because we've known each other forever. When you meet new mums, all that connects you are the babies.'

She rests her head on my shoulder. I think back to the time we first met. We were in halls together and she was someone definitely worth knowing as she'd arrived with her own sandwich toaster. But toasties aside, she was warm and forthright. She'd fight with cabbies taking us the wrong way and chat down men who'd been too handsy in clubs. She was the sort who herded us all together at the end of the night and made sure we got home safely. She'd show up for you whenever you needed her and I always felt safe under her wing. I wonder how she views me as a friend and whether her opinion of me is as glowing.

'I love him, Finn. You know I do and we fought so hard to have him but now it's here and it's …'

Chaotic? Overwhelming? Underwhelming? Manic? I don't want to fill in the gaps for her but let the sentence hang in the air as she stares into the space before her where children squeal and run about like loons. Maybe the playground was the wrong choice of venue – it will give her a glimpse into a future where she'll be wearing her trainers thin running ungainly around a roundabout.

'It's just the routine, it's draining and then when you meet these mums, they just want to talk about babies some more. I want to feel connected to something else.'

I put my hand in hers so she knows she's connected to me, here, but know there is truth to what she's said. It took me nearly ten years of motherhood to realise I needed something more, to feel like I was a person, a woman who had ideas and hopes above Tumble

Tots and school runs.

'Which makes you better than me, it took me an age to work out I needed to break out of the mummy mould. You have your career, you've worked out that this is a tough gig, but you tread water and you survive and you'll get there.'

She smiles.

'I used a cliché, didn't I?'

'Just remember when you asked me to be your legal rep at the BBC thing and I got out of the house for four hours. That felt right, it felt amazing to stand back from it for a while and use my brain. But at the same time I felt so incredibly …'

'Guilty.' Annie nods, looking at Finn and hoping he hasn't heard. 'Hun, it's been this way since I started this whole *Little Chefs* thing. About wanting more than just motherhood, about wanting something for yourself.'

It's strange because I've never been on that professional level with Annie before. She's always been the suit, I've always been the mum, and suddenly, after all this time, we find ourselves in the same unenviable position, pondering our own levels of maternal guilt. However, by that same token, it feels nice to be bonded to her in different ways now.

'Are you watching *Little Chefs*?'

'Well, of bloody course. Shaun's my favourite with the big trainers. Please let him win.'

I smile, 'He's not great with desserts though.'

'But he can roll sushi. It's made me realise I won't care if Finn can ever read. My child goals are to have him doing things with nori by age five.'

I laugh. It feels warming to know she's invested and that at least she's seen my face on her tellybox every week. Kai is still my favourite – I've always had a soft spot for the underdog.

'And Chris, do we talk about him yet?'

'Chocolate?'

I came prepared with Twix. She slides her fingers along the wrapper and pouts, not knowing where to start.

'Oh, he was just a fecking idiot. He used to tell me how tired he was and moan how it was affecting his work and I got sick of it. So he left, I pretty much packed his bags for him. I couldn't micro manage him too.'

I look at her in shock for possibly being overly harsh, but then I remember a time in early first-time motherhood where I may have thrown a loaded nappy at Matt for asking to go for a pint with my dad.

'I mean not left-left. He went to his mate's for a few weeks. He's back, we're getting through it. But I just wish he'd grow a pair, man up. Not make this about him.'

I am part relieved but slightly sad. Chris was the solid, dependable sort, but they had the sort of relationship that just bobbed away on the surface quite nicely without any major events looking to drag it under. A baby would test their waters and it's sad that Chris abandoned ship, even for the briefest of moments. It makes me think about Matt and for some reason, I imagine him as Captain Birdseye, at the wheel, weathering the storms.

'So, you're good.'

'We will be. I could throttle him, but you know how it is. I'll make it work. It's weird but we'll get through it.'

It's a glimmer of my Annie coming to the surface again for which I'm glad. Deep down there is a fighter, someone who won't be defeated though this is the first time in forever I've seen her come this close. I wink.

'You winked at me.'

'That was weird, wasn't it?'

'Yeah ...' she says, laughing. I open another Twix and Finn's eyes spring open as he looks straight into the clear sky, looking for a face to comfort him. Annie sighs and looks at her watch.

'One hour exactly. Finbo, seriously?'

I go to retrieve him from his pram and sit him up next to me, wondrous at how light he is compared to Millie who feels like a sack of rice most days.

'Good morning, Finn. It's me, Aunty Jools.'

I shake his little fingers and he studies my face, looking confused that I am not a breast and that the voice is not the one that usually greets him. He yawns a baby yawn and I have a brief two-second moment of broodiness before reality hits. Five kids would be my breaking point, my Titanic, that's a ship capsizing.

'So you need to sleep a bit more, can you do that? For me and mummy? I'll give you a fiver.'

Of course, if he closed his eyes there and then, it would have been a miracle, but he smiles like he has no intention of letting it be that easy and continues to stare at the sky, the trees, and everything that is far more interesting than my face.

'So, I'm sorry. I should have been there more when it was all a bit much. I wasn't there.'

Annie looks at me and I can't quite read her. Does she resent me? Have I gone down in her estimations because I didn't show up for her? I think of what she said about Chris and it pains me that perhaps I didn't do the same. At least it's out in the open. I've said what needed to be said, though waiting for her reaction makes me swell with emotion.

'Matt said it the other night. You're family. And I've felt like I wasn't there and I am sorry and I've just …'

And then the tears start to roll quite unfortunately onto Finn's head. Annie hands me a muslin. I feel awful as I don't want this to be about how I'm feeling.

'Oh, you div, don't cry. You know I pushed you away as well. That time I came round for coffee after the

229

contract signing?' I nod. 'I had all these questions and you fobbed them off like they weren't important. And it stung so I avoided you because I was embarrassed. You were like this big shiny reminder of someone who did motherhood really well, you juggle four and I only had one and was struggling. I think I hated you a bit.'

I laugh in surprise. She was allowed to hate me, I think I carried a little bit of resentment towards her for being that well put-together career woman I could have been. But I am also shamed for neglecting her feelings and forgetting so quickly what it was like to be new to this. We sit for a while to let these admissions to each other sink in.

'I juggle four ... sometimes I drop them. That's what all mothers do.'

'Is that why Millie's hair doesn't sit properly?'

I laugh and almost in an instant, all is forgiven. Annie's been witness to some of my particularly bad mummy moments to know how terribly bad I've been at motherhood.

'You have me, you know? You're not alone in this.' I say this to Finn, hoping Annie won't tell me off for more conversational clichés. She nods but knows this is also in part a reprimand – Annie will rally around her friends without question, but when in trouble, she likes to dig out of her holes herself, to admit that she needs help feels like failure to her – she's always liked to work under her own steam. We hug with Finn sandwiched in the middle. A small child in the distance falls off the end of a slide too quickly and there's a squeal. Both our heads swing round.

'Zinedine! Zinedine! Watch your sister!'

Annie and I look at each other wondering who'll be the first to burst into hysterics. The French World Cup was around the time we were at university and it was a time we made a brief foray into liking football to impress

230

boys. We see Zinedine sitting on a swing with a DS.

'Remember that Dutch bloke from uni who told you he was Dennis Bergkamp's brother so you slept with him?'

We were in a nightclub. It was novelty to hear an accent that wasn't coarse and Northern and Annie thought she was continental by shagging a foreigner, even though he was wearing double denim and had blond, bushy hair like a sea sponge. Annie can't contain her giggles.

'He was awful. Proper "come to fix your fridge" accent. Oh, he had Y-fronts ... tighty whiteys.'

I love how it takes a pair of men's undergarments to properly make us keel over with laughter. Finn looks at us like we're mad; who are you women? Why you laugh like lunatics? I see another part of the Annie that I love – the one who has shared this history with me, who knows those little stories that make us who we are. It's as close to a sister as I'll ever have. Yet immediately, it makes me think of Ben and I go quiet.

'Don't ever apologise to me, Mrs C. I've known you far too long for that bullshit. I know you're there if I need you. Likewise, I may be a big crappy mess at the moment but if you need my shoulder, I'm here too.'

I pat her shoulder in recognition that should the need ever present itself, I will use it.

'So getting back to normal stuff that isn't babies, give me some gossip, I want gossip.'

'Oh, there is so much to tell you.'

'Spill.'

'Ben moved out.' She doesn't seem surprised, but in my mind, it felt gargantuan, like a big shift in our relationship. Ben did it in the most dramatic way possible, of course: with the kids still in the house so he could hear them beg him not to leave, a flourish of a scarf, and the bang of a door. I'd gone a step too far and forgotten how to treat people. I wasn't his mother, he took great pride in reminding me. That was a stake to the heart. I told him to leave, good luck in his future career being Cam Jacobs' fuck buddy. The whole time, Matt observed this from the kitchen, shaking his head, knowing we were hurting each other in the worst ways we could think possible, but knowing the levels of immaturity on show could rival the twins. I act surprised at Annie's nonchalance at such news.

'He's Ben. He'll be back. I've known that kid since he was twelve. Remember, he used to write you long, rambling letters at university. He's more in love with you than anyone I know. He'll be back and this will all be fixed.'

She seems so certain. The fact is, I didn't realise how big a part Ben had become of our family until he left. There was noone to read *Matilda* to the kids anymore (apparently my Miss Trunchbull sounds constipated) and no one to provide the level of humour and hugs he'd dole out. At a time when our family was experimenting with new routines and roles, he seemed to level out the associated stress and worry. I missed him, but knowing he was making a catastrophic judgement when it came to Cam Jacobs made me want to swing for him.

'But at the same time, he always needed to move out. You got that, right? Ben a big boy now,' she mimics in a toddler voice. I smile because she knows I worry and baby him. Adam always had the emotional shields in place to protect himself from the outside world, but Ben was more fragile, kindlier, which left him a target for bullshit. It meant I worried about him like a child, my child, which was wrong, but left little hope for my actual children when they reached such an age and attempted to escape my clutches.

'And if he moves in with a complete twat who's using him for sex and not treating him in the way he deserves?'

'Then you let him be a grown up and make his own mistakes? It's how most of us learn.'

I scowl but know she's right, just like Matt and Dad were too. Damn them and their collective level-headed thinking.

'Just don't push him away. Not Ben. I caught that article about your other brothers, by the way. They should be the only reminder you need of how important Ben is. You need people around you who really matter, who really love you. Maybe that's the only way you'll work out where you belong.'

The emotional loading makes me think there's double meaning. We're both in a time in our lives when we need to find out how we fit into new roles, new lives, and it's only by surrounding ourselves with the opinions of those who matter, who really love us, that will we truly understand where we need to be. I feel philosophical but downright soppy with how I feel towards Annie now, though I'm not sure Finn is ready or willing to be sandwiched into another hug so soon.

'You're one of those people, one of the ones who matter,' I tell her in a haze of adulation.

Annie looks at me in all seriousness, her nose turned up.

'Too bloody right, you'll never be rid of me, ever.'

'Or me, and all those fecker children of mine. We know where you live.'

And of course, if anyone else said that, it'd be creepy and weird but it's not, it's us. Finn stares at me like he's still trying to work us out.

'But you only bought three Twixes? What the hell is that about, Campbell? I may have to reconsider this, you know?'

And we both laugh, comforted as we hook arms, balancing a baby on our collective knees, watching as

233

Zinedine hurls himself off the top ladder of the slide into what looks like a huge crater of rain water.

When I get home, I find the children lined up on the sofa, all wearing an array of shower caps that have been pilfered from various hotel rooms over the years; that and their pants. I've seen them in stranger get-ups (the twins went through stages of wearing my bras on their heads pretending they were fighter jet pilots) but now that Hannah is that bit older, I'd think her modesty would take priority. She notices me at the door.

'Ted had nits.'

Joy. She returns to the screen where Matt has opted for *Big Hero 6* which always leaves them transfixed. He appears at the top of the stairs with rubber gloves and a head torch on his head.

'Get up here when you have a moment. I'll check you. How did it go, by the way?'

'Good, yeah, good. I think we're both in a better place and Chris's back in her life and ... you know, she'll figure it out.'

I climb the stairs to find that Matt, efficient as always, has stripped the bed linen. The sink is full of brushes that look like they're being soaked in Dettol and he seems to have lined the bathroom floor with newspaper. This is a proper de-lousing session worthy of someone entering prison for the first time. He also wears a shower cap but scratches at his neckline.

'I was combing them through and found an egg in Jake's hair.'

'One egg? All this for one egg? It could have been fluff.'

I had a much more laissez-faire attitude towards nits that involved general resignation that they would feature as part of primary school existence. Matt freaks out at the very thought; parasitic infection is what he calls them. Little things living on his little things that could move on to other body parts covered in hair. He once gave himself hives from the psychosomatic scratching.

'This is how I deal with nits. Napalm those fuckers.'

'Napalm, lovely. Did you get that at Boots?'

'Yep, they do deals with North Korea now. Sit your arse down.'

I see Millie appear at the doorway with a little hair turban, grimacing at how her life has come to this. Matt starts with my ears and claws his way through my scalp.

'So Annie's good?'

'Yeah, she's getting there.'

Matt seems pleased he brought us back together. I am more at peace with the situation, knowing I have to work harder to maintain that relationship but revelling in time spent with someone I love. I spy something curious beside me.

'Why are all the hairbands floating in the bath?'

'I'm soaking them in tea tree solution. Ha, got something … what do you think?'

He picks out something and rolls it around on his finger.

'I think that might be dandruff.'

He laughs and I wonder if that's the reason the house is in lockdown, what he perceived to be a nit could have been a dry piece of bogey, knowing Ted. He tips my head down so I'm forced to look at the floor as he hums a tune that I realise is the theme tune to *Paw Patrol*. I smile. A small part of Matt likes this – to take control of his home from me, who really had no idea what she was doing and ran it into the ground. I think about adapting to changing roles and Matt finding a niche in his life that has finally made him happy: a life where he can wear his tracksuits and realise lifelong dreams to pretend he's Jose Mourinho and educate our children about real cheese. Maybe in years to come, this ennui may bore him, but for now he's around his little people and I see a pep in his step that certainly wasn't there when he had to board his commuter train every morning.

'Ouch, what are you doing?'

'It's my new nit comb. Hold still.'

That seems to be scalping me. To brave the pain, I try to read the newspaper he's laid out on the floor, today's no less. I notice a half-done crossword, offers on flights to Spain, and a wet image of the FTSE.

'Is this a good time to tell you I've found grey?'

'No, fuck off.' Millie laughs and goes running off. This will forever be known as the day romance died. Next he'll be telling me he wants to examine my pubes. Paranoid Matt is also thorough Matt.

'The shower cap is sexy by the way.'

'You know it.'

I look at the floor again. There's a fuzzy black and white picture to the left of the hand basin that catches my attention and I turn my face to see it. It's some soap star coming out of an eatery followed by an entourage of people. In that entourage is Cam Jacobs. I scowl to see his face and scan to his skinny jeans and loafers without socks combo. Then I see it. I drop to my knees and grab at the paper.

'Jools! Seriously! What are you doing?'

I hold it up to the light of Matt's head torch.

'Sit down, what the hell is it?'

It's Cam Jacobs coming out of a restaurant. Holding hands with another man. The caption: *Cam Jacobs with husband.*

236

CHAPTER SEVENTEEN

'So this is gelatine and you have to soak it and then you can make jelly with it.'

It's a sad day when you have a ten-year-old called Shaun and he's teaching you how to make jelly with actual gelatine as opposed to cubes of bright green rubber that you're used to chucking boiling water over. I nod like I know what he's talking about. McCoy is next to me, rubbing his chin. He stares at him, saying nothing. Shaun takes this as a sign that he's done something wrong. He looks at Callum at the end of the bench, also using gelatine. Callum shrugs and descends into a mild state of panic. I stare daggers at McCoy. Of course, he is used to this and assumes it's part of our stage act, but today the daggers are real. Did he know about Cam Jacobs' ways?

A quick Google and I found out Cam Jacobs was married and an oft-rumoured he-slut. Ben had been a pawn in his game, a shag. It made me murderous that night. In a shower cap, as Matt tried to calm me down and de-nit me (turns out I did have them, must stop hugging these bloody children). But pure sadness overwhelmed me as I remembered what it was to be an eleven-year-old. To hold information in your hand and flaunt it in front of the misinformed, to brag about it, to say I told him so. But the thirty-year-old in me couldn't revel in the misery. He'd find out in his own time. Hopefully before he caught anything untoward and that was when he'd need me. So I'd wait it out. I had to. But McCoy must have known. He spent so much time with him. He is nosying through Shaun's ingredients.

'And tell me about these berries you're using.'

'They're mulberries.'

'Like the people who make the handbags ...' Shaun looks at me like I'm a little mad. 'Or the song, la-di-dah the Mulberry Bush ...'

Yes, I sang. The cameraman shudders a little and the floor manager cuts the clip. McCoy looks at me like I'm a cretin.

'Umm, yup, I think we have what we need here.' The floor manager is Claudia and I swear she doesn't like me, almost as if she's the only person to know I'm an interloper and completely winging it. She totally knows I think wet gelatine looks like lubricant and gives me the jeebies. She leads McCoy away to film some other lead-in segment while I marvel at Shaun being able to make caramel. Like proper caramel. Not the normal stuff I see sandwiched in a chocolate bar.

Today is the pre-filmed section of week five and the Little Chefs are cooking uber-cakes that involve jelly, ice-cream, and two days of preparation. I am not sure on which planet anyone would need a cake of such grandeur unless they were preparing for a royal wedding, but there is joy to be had in knowing that in a day's time, I will get to feast on these creations and that they may taste way better than any cake I usually make, which is usually slathered in buttercream so it holds together. As I survey the room, children are hard at work with free-standing mixers and giant, fashionable kilner jars. Am I the only person who doesn't decant their flour but leaves it in a crinkled paper bag stuffed in the cupboard? I notice Mimi, who is our youngest contestant but the exact same size as one of our giant kilner jars and looks like she's about to topple over from carrying one. I shuffle over to assist.

'Mimi, let's give you a hand. If I pour it into the

scales, you tell me how much you need.'

Mimi, being the youngest and the tiniest, also hardly speaks, so she whispers 'three hundred' into my ear. I smile and do as I'm told and notice she is stood on a footstool to get to the counters. McCoy strides over to take a gander.

'What are you making, Mimi?'

Mimi has the demeanour of an innocent lamb so is thrown for a loop as she folds in her dry mixture, her eyeballs literally shaking in their sockets. The mixture of emotion I have for McCoy is still on a light churn and my instinct is to punch him in the knackers. Mimi whispers something as the cameras come along to join us.

'What was that?' She's going red in the face and I bend down to her level.

She leans into me.

'It's a banoffee Charlotte Russe,' she intimates.

I smile. I have no idea what that is but banoffee tells me there are bananas and toffee and it will be delicious. McCoy looks at me expectantly, trying to work it out himself using the ingredients laid out before him.

'So?' There's a tin of condensed milk on the counter top. I want to throw it at him.

'Well, it's a secret, you'll just have to see when Mimi makes it. But I think it sounds amazing.' Once I go home and Google it, of course. I put an arm around Mimi and squeeze her shoulder.

'Is she making sponge fingers?' guesses Tommy as he looks down at the piping bag and baking sheet all marked out. I see Mimi's hand shake. 'Did you use the whole egg? They'd be a lot lighter if she just used the whites.' She looks at me for reassurance.

'She sifted the flour twice, I saw her. And she doesn't want them too light or they won't be able to hold the filling.'

Thank you, Mary Berry. I knew all those months I spent in front of *Bake Off* would amount to something. McCoy looks surprised that I may have some cooking knowledge stored away in there.

'Still, a stodgy sponge finger, no one likes that.'

And he walks away. I bend down to Mimi. 'They're my favourite type. Keep going.'

I wink at her. I seem to wink a lot at these children and it always makes me think of Ted. Ted doesn't always chat to me or have a lot of words. I have a feeling that Jake speaks for him most of the time but we seem to have this habit of winking at each other from across tables. It's like our own Morse code so he can let me know all is well. I have a moment where I miss him, all of them. Would Jake and Ted be able to bake a Charlotte Russe? I smile. They'd probably put straws in the raw mixture and drink it before the thing had a chance to bake.

Admittedly, this segment of filming has been quite relaxing. There's less of the pressure of the live shows, where the kids always look a tad more petrified, and we had a leisurely start so I could go to Millie's Jungle Jingles class with her. It's a longer, more drawn-out day but there are large segments where I can go and sit and have a cup of tea and not have a perma-smile etched on my face. I look at little people staring inside ovens and running towards fridges trying to get things to set. Tomorrow they will nominate a family member to come and help them ice and decorate their creations, so today is all about the prep. Kai sits cross-legged in front of his oven, staring at it like a TV screen. Kai has redeemed himself since the chicken stew saga and has shown himself to be quite the … well … Little Chef. Of course, I put this down to my attempts to bolster his confidence. I go and sit with him.

'It doesn't bake any quicker if you stare at it.'

'I know, Julio. I know.' I shift him a look. 'I heard your brother call you that. I thought it was funny.' He waits to see if I have a sense of humour about it. I'm glad he is comfortable enough around me to try and crack a joke.

'I haven't seen him in a couple of weeks. We really liked him. He was nice.'

I stare at my reflection in the oven, knowing since Ben moved out, he hasn't been on set either or been accompanying me around to my weekly *Little Chefs* filmings or my other engagements surrounding it. I'd say he's quit but we didn't pay him. You can just say he stopped hanging around.

'He used to sneak us Haribo between takes. He was funny.'

'Ben is possibly the funniest person I know. My kids love him.'

Don't cry in front of Kai, squatting in front of an oven. I put an arm around him, wondering if Kai is my only ally in this. Luella still lingers, mainly out of contractual obligation, but our relationship is strained and I have no idea how to get that back on an even keel. I've sent her mochi, jokey texts with lines of cat emojis, and suggested sharing bottles of wine, but she seems less keen. Even today, she's left me to turn up on my own, carrying my own bags, and sit in my dressing room earlier on my tod with a coffee machine and no one to share it with.

I look over at McCoy, terrorising a young child about the colour of her sponges. It's Erin. I worry less about Erin because she's the sort who can handle herself, with her Breton stripes and high ponytail. But I worry what I've done. Have I got to the stage where McCoy is my only ally in this? What is he to me? A friend? This time two years ago I'd have swung for him. Even though I understand his act a bit better, we're still in the leagues of

241

early friendship where it's new and foundations have been laid but I wouldn't necessarily run into a burning building to save him. I can liken it to half the friendships I seem to make as a mother. They're born out of proximity. You see the same faces every day so alliances are built and the frequency of interaction builds what you have. Yet as soon as someone moves school or stops going to baby group, you see them less. Busy lives mean people don't have the time or energy to keep these friendships going, so they get relegated to Facebook where photos get liked, promises are made to keep in touch, but things never happen. In that way, he definitely isn't in the same league as Annie or Ben. Ben. I gaze over at McCoy. He knew, didn't he? He knew Cam was a walking erection and didn't think to warn me. A friend would have told me. Claudia, the floor manager, catches me looking at him, a wistful look in my eye, and nudges a cameraman to catch it on tape. Claudia can do one. I leave Kai by his oven and turn to get up, and realise my jeans are far too tight to simply squat and attempt such a manoeuvre, so end up on all fours while Kai pulls me up. Graceful, really graceful. I bet Claudia got that on tape too.

It's five o'clock by the time filming ends and the kids are ushered off home. I can't comment at this early stage but Erin's white chocolate sponges and Shaun's mulberry jelly flavoured with gin (Is that allowed?) look to be sealing the deal with me. People have come and cleared the set for tomorrow's stage of cake making and the hirsute man with the rope hanging from his waist has turned off the light rigs. I sometimes wonder what the rope is for. One day, will he descend on us like Tom Cruise in *Mission: Impossible*? Maybe it's something to do with lassoing. Either way, he's very friendly, always calls me Mrs Campbell and drinks tea from a Homer

Simpson mug. And he's not here. Just me.

I like these quiet, dark sets at night. I remember my first day of filming, I didn't have time to process anything so I returned to the set when everyone was gone, sat in an empty chair, and had a bit of a cry. Ben was there. He cried too because that's what Ben does. It was quite an enormous and profound situation I had gotten myself into and there never seemed to be a moment for me to digest what was going on. So that night, I had my cry. Luella found us fifteen minutes later with tissues.

Of course, the emotion has passed now. Everything's still bigger and crazier than I ever thought it would be, but I like having this moment to let the day wash over me. Today, I'm comforted by the buzz of the set fridges and I creep over to one housing three shelves of jelly, a Crème Pâtissière, and a mousse. It's like checking on whether my kids are still asleep. I open the door gently. Still there, still setting. I close the door and hear footsteps behind me. For some reason, I drop to the floor. A light comes on.

'Jools?'

It's McCoy. I look around, looking guiltier than I should. McCoy has a box of things with him. He puts it down on the counter and signals up to the audience area. 'Cheers, Harry!'

It's hirsute man with the rope, still about, still playing with the lights. I'm all too aware that my presence on set requires an explanation. McCoy gets in before me, laughing under his breath.

'Are you stealing cake?'

'Nooo!' I say, indignant but sounding guilty. 'I was checking the fridges were on.'

He nods. We stand there for a moment trying to suss each other out. I still don't know whether to confront him about Ben and Jacobs. I also have a bit of anger at how he made little Tia panic about over-whipped cream. Why is he holding a box?

'Are you OK?' he asks.

'Yes, why?'

'You seemed preoccupied today.'

There is a gap for me to confide in him. No. You're not that kind of friend. Not yet, I don't know if I trust you. He senses my hesitancy and looks embarrassed. I change the subject.

'Why are you here?' I ask. He pouts at me like he's not sure whether to trust me either. He comes over to the fridge I'm standing at and scans the shelves.

'Do you know who's making the mango mousse with the jelly?'

'I'm sure it's Callum.'

He nods and pulls a tray of dishes out of the fridge. I watch closely to see what he's going to do next. Unfortunately, given his manner on set and his constant talk of ratings, I worry he may be plotting some terrible act of sabotage so I hold my hands up to him. He senses my worry and shakes his head.

'Woah, really?' He looks insulted. I backtrack but watch him closely. What's he playing at?

'Look at this.' He beckons me over and holds a bowl to its side.

'It's an inspired idea, mango and pistachio – he's onto a winner, but he didn't use enough gelatine. This will be like soup in the morning and he needs it to set to create the centre of the cake or it'll collapse.'

I realise why he's here. I look over at the box on the counter and see three sunset coloured mangoes sat on the top. He's here to recover the situation, make it right.

'Seriously? You're going to do that? For him?'

McCoy smiles to know that my opinion of him has shifted ever so slightly and nods.

'I've made one kid cry this series and that was more

244

than enough for me. Like I said, it's all an act … I know you're no authority on gelatine but maybe you'd like to give me a hand so I can get home a bit quicker this evening too.'

I nod, still slightly in shock at the generosity of his gesture, but knowing it's even worthier given that tomorrow no one will be none the wiser and he'll still career around this set with his angry judge face on. Yes, perhaps we are fooling the judging public, but at the same time we are sparing a young boy his blushes when he overturns a dish tomorrow and a canary yellow river of goo turns his cake into a disaster. This change of tack makes me even more confused about him.

'Where do you need me?' McCoy signals over to the whisk and tells me to work on the cream. I do as I'm told, watching him make light work of the mangoes. There's the way he flicks his knife around and chops things uber-quickly that reminds me he's a chef. I forget that used to be his bread and butter, how he earned and made a living before books, TV shows, and wives turned him into a big media machine. When things were at their lowest, the restaurants he had went tits up and he had to sell two of them off. I forget that he possibly had an affinity to food, one I jested about but which essentially gave him everything he needed.

'Who taught you how to whisk then? That's stirring.'

'I normally use my electric thingy.'

'Cheat.'

I smile sardonically as he takes over my whipping duties and gets me to mash the mango.

'Not too well. Callum was aiming for texture.'

I salute him. He laughs. 'So this was your idea?'

'Well, it wasn't Cam's.' I raise my eyebrows and he knows he's hit a nerve. 'I had words with him, by the way. The whole carry-on with Ben was very unprofessional considering he's …'

McCoy leaves a gap to see if I know. I know he knows and my expressions shifts. He's not sure what to say. Given that I'm murdering this mango, he knows he needs to tread carefully.

'I mean, I don't know how his husband puts up with it.'

The mango. The poor mango is dying under my hands. I stop and look at him.

'You know his husband!' I exclaim loudly, looking up to the ceiling, resigned. I should have known better.

'I'm sorry.'

'Not your fault,' I say a little too dryly.

'But unprofessional for him to cross that line. Uncalled for, I told him …'

'You told him? But you didn't tell me?'

'I found out him and Ben were sleeping together at that meeting. I'm not sure it was my place to say anything else. I'm not sure it was my place to get involved.'

I stare at him. There may be truth in that statement, I'm just so angry about it and it's too easy to fire all my bullets at him. He comes over to take the mango and heat it in a pan, seeking distraction in cooking.

'So, play by play, we're going to heat the mango and stir through the gelatine till it melts. Can you do that?' He asks me like I'm a child. I nod, I'm sure I can just about manage that as long as I don't have to touch the gelatine. He's stood next to me now. It's a weird one but he definitely looks different to when I encountered him in that supermarket. I'm not sure if it's age or the fact he isn't caked in make-up, but he looks like he's aged a bit more and that's given his face a wizened sincerity. But I see through it, the act, that media persona that defined him. I shift him the same look I give Matt when I'm doing the washing-up and he throws a teaspoon in the bowl just to annoy me. He still looks defensive, like he's gearing himself up to duck in case my fists come flying out.

'How are things with Lu?'

I'm not sure how this will improve the conversation. I still can't get over how he calls her Lu. It jolts me and makes me think he's talking about someone else. I'm not sure her own husband calls her that. I've never spoken to McCoy about Luella, mainly out of devotion to her, but also because I don't know what happened. I can't gauge if he's indulging in idle chit-chat or wants to dig more into our relationship. I decide that shrugging is the best way to answer.

'She hates me, doesn't she?'

'You're not her favourite person in the world.'

'I don't doubt that for a second.'

He assumes I know what happened between them but truth be told, I know as much as she's let on over the two years of our relationship, but even when very, very wine-ified and slurring her words, she never gives me the total goss out of loyalty to the very tall and very French Remy and her kids. I don't push, I don't pretend to know how she feels, but obviously something went very awry.

'The thing to know about Lu is that she will throw everything, her whole being, behind people she cares about and her work. She's an all-or-nothing girl.'

I smile because that was always the impression I got of her; she'd worked hard for me in the time we'd been together and at every key moment had been there with tissues or hugs or wine and useable pens and made things happen. She made this happen. God, if it'd been down to me I'd be doing this gig for free or still signing books at foodie road shows.

'You're lucky to have her.'

'I am. So were you, you know.'

That was possibly a step too far and he scrunches up

his face. He puts his energy into whipping his cream and stares into space.

'I didn't know she was pregnant ... when I broke it off. I'm not sure what she's told you, but I didn't know.'

I stir the pan over the fire really slowly, feeling my ears redden and my face blush with what he's just divulged. What the actual fuck? My terrible poker face can't hide my confusion and his eyes widen.

'You didn't know?'

'I knew you left her for Kitty and your new shiny media life but I didn't know she was pregnant.'

He looks ashamed, maybe rightly so, but with something like that out in the open, he needs to explain what happened with better clarity and to fill in some gaps.

'She was early stages and I didn't know. I left, she lost the baby ...'

I hold a hand to my mouth in shock, in anger, but also complete sorrow. The good thing about Luella was that she was brassy as balls, but now I understood completely how she felt. Before, she used to display comedic levels of anger towards him, but now I know the real hurt from which it stemmed. She would have been grieving the end of a relationship as well as the loss of a child. I'm glad McCoy understands the level of contempt she holds towards him, but he still needs to feel the end of my wrath. I throw a mango seed at him. He stares into space.

'I was young. I was foolish and selfish and she was the one who got away. The one I treated badly ...'

'Despicably,' I add.

'Despicably. It will always be on my head and I'll take whatever comes my way.'

I think about how seeing him every day, spending all this time in his company must stir up so much bad feeling in her. She yo-yos between getting over it, understanding how it's part of her past and has shaped who she is now, and looking like she could knife him in broad daylight without remorse. I know that feeling. The way I feel about my own mother borders on similar levels. McCoy still stares into space and my mind starts to process everything I know about him. The mistakes he's made, the people he's hurt. How long before my patience and goodwill run out and I leave him here, alone. He takes my pan off the fire and stirs it slowly into the cream he's whipped. I am quiet, taking it in while he shifts me looks which seem to ask me if my opinion of him has gone from mousse-saving redeemer to pregnant-Luella deserter. I can't quite decide. I edge slowly away from him, thinking about mistakes I've made in my life – tiny in comparison – and whether there is any way he can come back from this in my estimations, whether he still falls in that friend category. He senses my judgement and looks at the floor, quickly resetting Callum's mousse in the fridge and closing the door slowly. We stand there, not looking at each other and wondering if there is anything else that needs to be said.

Footsteps, stompy and pacy, interrupt the scene. They belong to someone on a phone who bellows his conversation around the studio.

'I've tried her dressing room, seriously, I don't know where she is.'

I know that voice. Ben? He sees me, his eyes red and swollen and comes to a halt.

'Ben?'

'Where have you been?'

'I've been here on set for most of the day, I don't bring my phone it's not allowed ...' I trail off to see his face, his mouth agape and dry as he swallows before telling me what he needs to. Why has he been crying?

'We've been trying since two to get hold of you. Matt's been calling and he told me to come here and get you and drag you away.'

'Ben?'

He turns to McCoy like he's too scared to tell me.

'It's Ted. Ted's in the hospital.'

CHAPTER EIGHTEEN

I think I may have felt pure, unadulterated fear three times in my entire life. All these instances have involved my family. I remember when my Dad collapsed at home after a particularly bad bout of food poisoning. I remember when a car swerved away from Millie after she toddled into a supermarket car park. And the twins; giving birth to the twins. They came out naturally but I remember thinking this was a biological impossibility to do it twice in one morning. I worried I wouldn't be able to do it, I was scared they would be teeny tiny. They were, as it happened. They were both exactly five pounds each. I remember I could cradle one under each arm like loaves of bread.

It's all I can think about as I sit in the back of McCoy's car and he dodges the evening traffic to get us to the hospital. Tiny Ted, his fingers curled into my bosom to keep warm. Ted was always on the names list because Matt was adamant he wanted to call them Bill and Ted. They would have the most excellent adventures, he told me. Bill fell by the wayside but Ted stayed. He looked like a Ted. All these things flash through my head as we stop at traffic lights, rain bouncing off the tarmac outside. McCoy offered to drive us when Ben announced what was happening at the studio: a gesture I quickly took him up on. It turns out his driving is wildly erratic, without much lane discipline. But he's going to get me there, to my Ted. Ben holds my hand tightly in the back seat.

'Go through it again. Matt said he had a fever.'

251

We can't get through to Matt in the hospital so Ben is trying to sketch out what he does know.

'Just fever and a bad stomach-ache. Matt said he was on the floor, he couldn't even walk.'

I feel physically sick. Matt is a worrier, overly cautious about everything when it comes to health, but the thought of Ted being in pain and me not being there stakes at the very heart of me.

'Rash, did he mention a rash? Maybe he had a stomach bug?'

Ben shrugs but grips my hand tighter. Anything that has threatened our relationship or sought to come between us is forgotten. It all seems insignificant now. He stares at me for a moment too long, trying to work out my face or how I'm feeling. Because by this point in a crisis, there are usually tears and general hyper-emotionality. But there is something about me, something within my maternal side, that digs somewhere deeper. It is calm, powerful, it aches to be with my baby. The car stops suddenly and we're outside the main entrance.

'Both of you, go. I'll park up.' I run out of the car towards a maze of signs, arrows, and automatic doors, knowing I have no idea where I'm going. He's fine. I would know if he wasn't fine. I look down at my phone, flicking through the sixty-two unread messages that everyone from Matt and Dad to Donna tried to send.

Where are you?

Ted's not well. Trying to get him to see the GP.

I hate our GP. Seriously? On hold for a fucking age.

Fever is 40.5, going to the hospital on advice of 111.

Leaving kids with your dad.

Seriously, where the fuck are you? Studio said you left an hour ago.

Sending Ben to look for you.

'Jools.' I look up and it's Luella, shaking her head.

Normally she's hard-faced but she's soft with emotion. I've broken that façade through that common bond we share as mothers. She envelops me and I think about what McCoy told me earlier and squeeze that bit tighter.

'I told them I'd meet you here, you wouldn't know where you were going.' She starts marching as Luella does and I follow, trying to keep up. Ben links his arms into mine.

'Tell me everything.' She grabs my other hand.

'They think it's appendicitis. Matt has been with him every step of the way. He was frantic, he couldn't get hold of you so called me. I've dropped everything. I'm here for as long as you need me.' There is nothing in her face to say she still holds any resentment towards me. I hug her again to thank her.

'Donna and your dad have the other kids and I'll deal with the Beeb.' She stops at a curtain in a ward and turns to me. I don't have to see Ted, I can hear him – I draw the curtain back dramatically. Two nurses and a doctor hover over the bed and Matt's by Ted, holding his hand tightly. Matt closes his eyes in relief to see me and I can see they're red raw. Ted is screaming loudly.

'Daddy! It hurts! Don't … I don't want the needles. Please, Daddy! Please! I'll be good, I want to go home!'

Luella doesn't enter the cubicle but leads Ben away, who is already mid-sob. I immediately crouch beside the bed, grabbing Ted's arm and kissing his forehead. I cup his cheeks in my hands. I don't cry.

'Ted, sweets. It's Mummy. I'm here, I'm here.' I make hushing noises and wipe the tears from his face with my thumbs. I look him straight in the eye. 'Teddy, c'mon, I'm here …' He looks at me and starts sobbing.

'Mummy, it hurts …' he says. His body burns under mine and he drifts in and out of sadness and pain. I don't cry. The nurses and doctor step in.

'Mrs Campbell, I'm Carl, paediatric registrar.' I look at Matt who can hardly focus. 'I'm not sure how much you know but it is pretty important at this point that we get Ted into surgery. We are worried about rupture and the possibility of infection.'

I feel my breath, calm and steady. 'Then you do what you need to do. You have my full permission. Can we get him anything for the pain?'

'We are trying to insert a cannula but he's being a little resistant.' Matt is whispering in his ear but to no avail. He's a seven-year-old boy with a will of his own. This is scary, properly scary. To be in pain and surrounded by people you don't know. A nurse looks at me.

'If Daddy stays where he is, Mummy, can I get you to hold his other hand and we can do this?' I nod. I don't cry. I shield my body over his and let him rest his sweaty head under my chin. I flashback to Ted having his pre-school booster; Jake was a complete wuss and wailed through the whole thing. Ted looked down at the needle like an ant had crawled across him. Brave Ted. Another nurse holds down his legs as he kicks us away.

'Ted!' I raise my voice slightly and Matt stares at me. 'Listen to me, this will make you better. This will make the pain go away. I promise you. I really promise you. You need to be the bravest boy you can be. And I know you are, you are scared of nothing. I know you.'

This is my Ted who dives off three-metre-high climbing frames and who catches spiders in the bath and lets them out into the garden. He is my quiet, thoughtful boy who wakes me up to give me his last *Star Wars* stickers, who hugs me from behind when I'm chopping things at the counter. All my Ted moments from the past seven years run across my brain like a cartoon flick book. His body stops for a while and they manage to get a needle into his arm. He screams until the pain stops. He is pale and panicked, much like Matt who looks like he's about to throw up. I hug Ted as tightly as I can.

'See? Bravest boy I know.' He smiles faintly but I can't see his dimples so know it's only for my benefit. The doctor speaks up.

'We should get him down to theatre, they'll be waiting for us.' I nod. It's a blur of porters and clipboards as his gurney starts moving and we jog through the corridors with them. Ted's eyes are closed, protecting himself from the strip lighting and the stares of passers-by. I clench onto his hand the whole time, trying to make chit-chat the whole time so he can hear my voice.

'So, I think someone deserves the biggest present ever for this. What do you say, Daddy? I think this warrants the AT-AT Lego set.' Matt can hardly breathe, let alone talk.

'Yeah, sure thing.'

I squeeze his arm. Ted drifts in and out of consciousness. 'I'll share it with Jake, I promise.' I remember Ted has another half, his best friend, and the look both of them have when they're separated, like they're missing something. I picture Jake at home, wondering what he's feeling, half an empty bunk bed. Then Ted stops for a moment and winks at me. It's our thing. I wink back at him. We stop in a cold, sterile room, people with coloured shower caps stand around. A doctor approaches him.

'Ted, I'm Malik. We're going to put some special medicine in your arm ...' But Ted hardly registers him as he enters in and out of delirium. I lean over him, his body shuddering with fever and confusion. I put my face next to his.

'We'll be here afterwards, I promise you.' Matt is broken, his eyes tearing up as he kisses the top of his head. The nurse nods at me as his body goes limp and his breathing goes deep. I peel Matt away, locking him into an embrace. This is my boy. He's going to be fine. He's going to be fine.

As soon as we're escorted outside, Matt collapses to the floor in a ball to steady himself. I grab a handful of hair but he flinches and stands up.

'Where the hell were you? Do you know how many times I tried to call you? Text?'

'I was in the studio. You know it's a reception black hole.'

Stress leaves him angry and he's directing this towards me. I stare him down.

'We rang the studio but they said you were gone. We didn't know where you were.' I think about what I was doing, resetting some mango mousse. I was doing something ridiculous in the face of what's happening. I feel foolish, guilty.

'He had that tummy ache when he woke up.'

Matt eyeballs me. 'Ted has a tummy ache every day if he thinks it'll get him off school.'

'You sent him to school?'

'Christ, how was I supposed to know it was appendicitis?'

The implication is that I would have known, but I know that's not true either. I don't know why I'm expressing myself in this way and Matt doesn't either. We're both angry because we missed this. I was absent at a time when a child needs its parent most. I was irresponsible and should have been on call. Matt fobbed him off. He sent him into school thinking it was avoidance tactics.

'It's was fucking scary, Jools. One minute he's telling me he doesn't want to go swimming and I'm shouting at him telling him not to be a drama queen, then the next, he's on the floor. He was white with pain, he couldn't

256

walk, he was like a furnace. Do you know how awful that was for me? And Jake and Hannah are in tears … I don't know what the hell I'm doing and you … I couldn't reach you. I couldn't ask you what to do … you …'

'Matt,' I say softly.

And this is when he falls into me, holding me as tightly as he can, sobbing into my shoulder. And I cry. I lose my shit. I really properly cry.

'Mrs Campbell, Mrs Campbell.' A nurse puts her hand to my arm where Matt and I are curled around each other in the seating area. It's been a fraught couple of hours here, waiting, flitting in and out of panic, sleep, and worry. Ben and McCoy have kept us in coffees and sandwiches while Luella has managed to keep the onlookers and press at bay after we were spotted in reception. Matt and I are in some strange emotional paralysis whereby we will only be able to speak to each other when Ted is out of theatre. Instead, we cling to each other like scared monkeys. There was anger, but it's been replaced by the fact a little boy who is half him and half me needs fixing. Our kid.

'Ted is in recovery.' I immediately spring to attention. 'The operation went well, I'll get the surgeon to come and chat to you, but for the meanwhile, I think he'd like to see a familiar face.' I stand up. 'He's asked for Daddy.' I can't be offended, knowing Matt is equipped to deal with this, probably more so than me now the initial shock is over. The nurse leads him away. I sit on my own noticing a body hovering by the door of the waiting room. He pops his head around the door. His eyes are blotchy.

'I bought you some Maltesers.' Ben. I smile and beckon him over. He holds me in an embrace. 'That's good, right? He's in recovery, it means the operation went OK.' I nod. He opens the Maltesers and hands me one. 'Luella's gone to the BBC to cover you and make sure

257

work's sorted. McCoy said he'll call in some favours and get a guest judge on for tomorrow.'

His words fly over me. *Little Chefs* and contractual obligations couldn't be further from my mind. For the past two hours, little boys on operating tables were the priority.

'You're not bothered?' I fill my mouth with Maltesers, honeycomb stuck in my molars is a welcome distraction. 'Adam rang earlier to check in, he said he could come down if you needed a hand. Gia called as well … not sure how much she understood but I told her to wait for Matt's phone call. Do you know what the Italian is for appendix? *Appen-diche.*'

Ben is rambling, which is what he does in intense situations. That kid can talk until the cows come home and go to bed. Part of me loves him for filling the silence, another part can hardly process the words coming out of his mouth.

'McCoy's been good. He didn't want you to eat hospital shit so he went round the corner to a proper deli to get you food. He asked me what you liked. I told him you don't like egg mayo. Matt likes cheese. Was I right, I didn't even know if I was right? He even got stuff for me and Luella. I was a bit worried though, I know she doesn't like him so I thought I'd have to separate them but they were very civil. They had a chat. I was sitting right there. You know when people start talking and you think you shouldn't really be there, but if you leave, it would be even more obvious.'

Ben has this strange ability to be able to talk and eat at the same time without looking like a child who should have better manners.

'She calls him Tom, which is weird, but actually when you think of it, since he dropped the mockney schtick it suits him more. She didn't cause a scene because she thought it wasn't right. He said lots of clichés about abandoning her and always wanting to stay in touch. She showed him pictures of her kids and was very composed, posturing about how things worked out for the best. But she didn't hug him, he was going in for the hug and she totally turned her shoulder on him. I had a turkey sandwich. Did I mention he got me a sandwich?'

I nod. A million thoughts filter through my head. McCoy and Luella in a blank room, sitting down, staring at each other like an arty Sia video, conveying their emotion through the medium of dance. I'm proud of Luella for keeping her cool. I feel strangely calm towards McCoy being contrite and getting me to this hospital. I think about Luella's baby. I think about my baby. I picture Matt holding Ted in the same way he did when he was first born. This one is Ted, he said. He looks presidential and cuddly at the same time. I sigh with relief to know that at this very moment they are together and safe. I ache for my kids.

'I was a bit worried as I don't normally do bread with bits, let alone fruit, but McCoy said it would work and I was pleasantly surprised. He's seemed genuinely worried, you know. He's been here the whole time. And I don't think this has been on Cam's orders. I think he's trying to be nice.'

I turn to him as soon as he says Cam's name to gauge his reaction. He looks at me and kisses me on the forehead. He curls his body into mine.

'You were right about Cam. I don't like to tell you these things because it goes to your head.'

I smile. I'm not always right. At present, I'm lost in some grey space where maybe in the last six hours I've done something wrong. You can't help your kids getting sick, but I wasn't in the right place at the right time, I missed this. I got it wrong.

'I think I stayed with him for as long as I did as I wanted to prove you wrong. I knew he was a shitbag but sometimes you fall under the illusion that you can change someone or that you might be special.'

'You are special.'

'Special stupid, I was a mild flirtation at best. You call *me* a manwhore, he's in some weird open marriage. He does sex club things. Weird things that require invitations and masks.'

I'm glad he thinks that borders on something strange.

'I'm sorry I called you what I did. You deserve better. You've always deserved better.'

It's all I can muster up to say. Maybe this is the best place to have these sorts of conversations so emotion can't take over and I can't claim to have the upper hand. This is better, having Ben here and next to me. Not that it was going to end up any other way. Maybe that's the best thing about siblings. The fights you have that are nuclear and unlike any you'll have with anyone else but they are forgotten once the shit hits the fan. There's no need for apology, almost as if it's part of an unwritten contract.

'Move back in. The kids miss you. I miss you.'

He knows that's my way of apologising, to let him know how much he means to me.

'As much as I'd love to, I've moved into a communal house in Streatham.'

I turn to him, probably no more crowded than if he moved back in with us and probably greater licence to partake in light drugs and lie-in until lunchtime. I raise my eyebrows at him to question if he's making good life choices, but Annie's words echo in my head. He's a big boy now.

'My roommate is a fire-eater. And there's a trapeze in the garden.'

'You'll always have a place at mine, you know, even if

it means sharing a bunk bed with a twin.'

The weight of what I've said washes over me. He rests his head on my shoulder. 'Ted will be all right. This will be fine, Julio. A little hiccup.'

I bring him closer to me. Julio. Jewie. I think of his pet names for me. I've always called him Ben. We went through a phrase of Benson because he smokes like a chimney and liked to kiss boys in hedges. But he's always been Ben. My Ben. I look up to the door to see a surgeon smiling at me and nodding his head. I get up to follow him out of the room, my little brother holding my hand the whole way.

CHAPTER NINETEEN

'I don't get it Ted. How can there be so many Power Rangers?'

'These lots are Jungle Fury, there are space ones, and there are dinosaurs.' I consider myself to be quite an educated woman, but I can't seem to understand the difference. They're all in primary coloured Lycra catsuits and there's a lot of men wielding eighties' ponytails and bleached denim. But Ted seems to be quite involved, he knows their names, he knows exactly what's going to happen next. I'm teetering on the edge of a migraine but to see Ted alert, conscious, and happy keeps me in the room. We brought him home two days ago after a couple of days of doing shifts in the hospital, living on pull-out beds and relying on the kindness of strangers. Dad manned the fort. Ben and McCoy did the food runs, keeping us in posh deli fare and one day, they bought McDonalds for the adjoining cubicles. Say what you like, but there's a reason they're called Happy Meals. I found that out from McCoy. He who once chastised me for a mere fish finger.

Ted is almost back to himself. Now he is awake and conscious, he knows there will be rewards coming his way for bravery and he is loving the ice cream, *Avengers* stickers, and half decent Lego sets that fill his day. Thanks to the power of the media, even the builders have known what's been going on, so they come armed with Jelly Tots for him and boy magazines with flimsy toys and stickers that end up stuck to my newly painted bedroom wall. In

263

an attempt to keep him as absolutely still and static as possible, he gets to inhabit our bed most days and spends that time flitting between several different types of Power Ranger. God bless Netflix, else he'd be flinging himself off the bed and tearing his scar open. They had to open him up in the end and sometimes when I pull back the plaster and see the scar I flinch simply at the thought of someone cutting my baby. Of course, Ted wears this like a badge of honour. This makes him doubly hard especially in the eyes of Jake, whose biggest medical conquest to date had been falling head first on the drive and having his forehead super-glued together. But for his bravado, he has moments where he'll curl into me and seek comfort, a look in his eyes telling me that was fucking scary. I'm glad it's over, I'm glad I'm here, with you. There's a lot of winking.

'It's really itchy, Mum.' Ted's face is scrunched up into the shape of a prune and I get my fingers and claw them along his belly.

'I can't scratch it too much, just don't think about it. Focus on your ninjas.'

'They're samurais.'

'Same thing.'

My dad enters the bedroom. 'This might help.' He carries a giant bag of marshmallows and a bottle of Piriton. Never mind not having an appendix, I'll be glad if Ted has any more teeth after these next few weeks are over. Jake follows close behind him and launches himself onto the bed.

'JAAAAAAKKKKKEEE!' shouts the communal chorus of adults, but Jake and Ted both see the funny side and high-five each other, Jake pulling the covers to cosy up next to him.

'Ted, did you fart under there? OH MY GOD!'

Ted waves the duvet up and down. The boy is

definitely back. My dad looks over at them, chuckling.

'That's a boy's best joke, that is.'

Dad took charge of the little ones when Matt and I were yo-yoing between home and hospitals, keeping everything sane and tidy in our absence and making sure the builders were kept in tea and custard creams. He also did something I've only ever see him do twice in my lifetime. When he visited the hospital and saw Ted's half-naked body connected to all those machines and wires and bandaged up to the hilt, he cried. With relief, he told me. Because the last thing he'd ever want for me is to see my child hurt. Of course, that made me cry. And Matt. The lad who'd had his tonsils removed in the neighbouring bed didn't know where to look.

'So, Millie's down and when Han's done with her bath, we're going to watch a movie. And not these bloody people in the unitards, please.' Dad removes the mountain of clothes in the armchair in the corner to cosy himself, looking up to the ceiling, surveying the quality of the painting. This room is new and part of the extension. It feels alien, the faint smell of paint and new carpet lingers but to see it filled with three of my favourite men gives it life and light and all at once I feel the need to retreat, to huddle together with the family like a pack of bears and hide from the world. This used to be all I did, herd this family together under this roof, nourish and protect it. It was where I felt safest. But then I strayed from the pack, I wandered off, I did my own thing. And images of little crying children calling out for me, scared and confused, still haunt me and make me nauseated with guilt. I go over to Ted's side of the bed and cup his face. He glances over and sticks out his tongue, knowing I'm here to give him medicine. It's been a war of wills with the banana flavoured antibiotics.

Half the time we've had to missile it into his mouth with a syringe while he's being distracted by Matt. It's made us too aware of my exceedingly bad aim. Today, Power Rangers provides the distraction. I wipe his chin and stare at him for a moment too long. I think about all the medical dramas I've ever watched: *E.R* in the early nineties when Chicago would have been the best place to be ill because George Clooney and Goose from *Top Gun* would have been there to stitch you back up. But dramas where you'd see the worst happen: people not waking up from anaesthesia, a student surgeon nicking a major artery, a nurse giving the wrong dosage. Sometimes these stories have very different endings and this bed would have ended up cold and empty. The smallest cog would have disappeared from the machine and everything would have fallen to pieces. A huge lump forms in my throat. The what ifs. What did I learn about the what ifs? Sometimes they'll drive you round the fucking bend. I stare at his little mound of hair, curled atop his head like a Walnut Whip. Ted is very used to me having moments like this recently and rolls his eyes.

'I'm OK, Mummy. Stop being soppy. I love you too.'

Dad laughs in the corner of the room. Jake makes retching noises.

'Both of you smell.' Retching noises turn into raspberries. Hannah appears at the door, her hair plaited and onesie looking too small for her. She turns her nose up at the boys and lies across the end of the bed.

'Hannah, you love me, right?'

'Yep, why not?' She blows me a kiss and I see Jake gearing up to upend the duvet so she'll go flying. Dad puts his leg on the edge to prevent this happening. Hannah smiles and makes the shape of what I think is a heart with her hands. That'll do, Han. If anything good has come from the past week, it's that I've gone up in Hannah's estimations. I made it to my first swimming gala and I've been here, in the house, more. This is what she'd have every day, all of us here, the bears hanging around the pit. In fact, any child would probably love and benefit from such an arrangement, but maybe that's part of the joy and misery of families, that modern life gets in the way and we have to adapt to new routines, new roles. I kneel at the end of the bed next to Hannah and stroke her head.

'Did you do your reading?'

'Yep. Are you back at work tomorrow?'

'Yep.'

She smiles but knows that small window of time she had with me is over. We both feel confused and saddened. Tomorrow, I'll be back in rehearsals after a week off. Tomorrow, she'll be back under Matt's rule where she'll have to share one parent between four children again and not be allowed biscuits before dinner. I allowed for the biscuits.

'Do you think if both of you had been at home, then Ted would not have got ill?'

Her tone is serious and I rest my chin on the duvet so I can hear what she has to say next. The comment piques the interest of Jake and Ted, who turn the television down. Dad hears her too and flits between being touched and being in awe of a little girl with so much insight.

'Han, I think he still would have got ill. Appendicitis is one of those things. But I think Daddy and I feel a little guilty about how that day turned out.'

It's still unspoken between Matt and myself. We've sobbed and held each other and know that day was a complete and utter parenting shambles, but the good thing is that we can silently repair these things, we know we've done our best to make things better. Ted looks at the scars on his arms.

'Mummy has to work, Hannah, or we wouldn't have

money and then we'd still have to live with a big hole in our roof,' Jake informs us. I look over at him curiously.

'That's what Daddy told me. He had his turn working and now it's Mummy's turn.' Dad nods and pouts to hear such clarified thinking. 'And you have to let a woman go to work, otherwise it's sexy.'

'Sexist.'

'Yeah, that …'

I smile to think of the backseat car conversations that Matt's been having with his boys. Hannah seems resigned to the fact I may be less in her life and I feel a sharp pain in my chest to see her so crestfallen.

'But I'm still here-here. Right? I go to things. I'm here most evenings.' She smiles and I know exactly what she's thinking. You're not here for Friday fajitas. Daddy puts strange things in the fajitas like green peppers and tufts of coriander. You're gone for most of Saturday, one of the very few days I got to see you for the whole day. She hugs me, inviting Jake and Ted to participate. She kisses Ted on the top of his head and I melt a little. There is affection there even though they'd never openly admit it to each other. When I returned from the hospital that evening, she and Jake were huddled together in his bed, awake and holding each other. Jake looked lost. Hannah was wide-eyed in shock that there was the possibility of losing one of her troops.

'Well, you also need to talk to him about this macaroni cheese thing?'

I furrow my brow curiously. 'Ever since I said yours was better, he cooks trays of the stuff. It's getting boring.'

I giggle. It's not gone unnoticed. He's experimented with different kinds of cheese, added ham and cauliflower, used cream cheese and mustard, single cream and buttermilk. Foil trays of it line the freezer and he's been known to pop round Donna's house with the stuff.

All the while, Hannah jests that mine was better. In the madness, this feels like my biggest coup. Jake jumps at my shoulders and tries to climb them.

'Yeah, once he put leeks in it. They looked like bogeys.' He pretends to sneeze and inhale snot into his mouth.

'Jake!' I think about what would have happened if this had been the product of Jake's appendix rupturing. He's a drama queen, he would have milked this for months. He kisses me on the cheek to surprise me.

'I don't mind you working. I cut out your picture from a newspaper. When Daddy's being an idiot, I go upstairs and talk to it.'

This worries but heartens me in equal measure. Hannah and Dad laugh at him. He looks insulted.

'Does she talk back?' she giggles.

'She tells me I'm brilliant and I can have all the crisps I want.' Ted laughs, not too much because laughing still hurts. 'And she tells me to go on your bed and trump like a trooper.' I roll my eyes as Hannah launches herself at him. This is real life Power Rangers, like a live wrestling match. I hear the doorbell downstairs and look to Dad to maintain order. He picks them up like puppies and throws them back in the bed.

Downstairs, Matt is cleaning the kitchen, but stands there in rubber gloves telling me that answering the door is a near impossibility. I pull a face at him and answer the door.

'Hi, sorry, I know it's kind of late and I didn't want to wake your kids … ummm …'

Before me stands Miranda Scott. She of Tinder who left her husband and stuck her boobs in Matt's face. I can't be surprised anymore about who shows up at my door since everything happened with Ted. Most of what's turned up has been prompted by kindness. Luella has been here every day, even if it's just to bring milk. On the day we got back from the hospital, there were flowers, cards, and most surprisingly hampers from McCoy. And a hamper every day since with nice things like jam and joints of meat that have certainly altered Matt's opinion of him. I smile and note the sincerity in Miranda's tone.

'Miranda, hi …'

'It's just … I bought some things for Ted. I whipped round the football team and the kids chipped in and we got him some Lego and stuff … it's not much but …'

She's still the Miranda I remember from school and football, one of those mystical mums who have the time and inclination to apply fake tan, style their hair, and have a fully made up face every time I see them. The top is a little too low-cut for my liking, but hell, if I had assets like those, I'd be showing them off too. The gesture is sweet and completely out of the blue.

'It's really lovely, thank you. You should come in, have a cup of tea. Matt's here.'

She seems surprised at the invitation, as do I given the fact most of our downstairs is still laden with dust and plastic sheeting, but it felt wrong to just grab her offerings and leave her standing at the door like I was ungrateful. She follows me in and Matt pops his head around the door.

'Miranda? Hey, how are you?'

She air kisses him, looking slightly more flushed than she should be. Matt eyes me cautiously, wondering if this was a ruse to lure her into the house then stab her for flaunting her wares in my husband's face.

'Miranda and the Tigers got some things for Ted, it's really sweet. I invited her in for a cup of tea.'

Matt nods. 'Or something stronger? Jools and I have a Merlot open.' She smiles but shakes her head, a little confused. 'Or tea, we're good at tea too.' Matt understands where his duties lie and I pull a chair out for her at the kitchen table. The kitchen is still a bit of a cavernous hole at the moment; appliances hang out the wall haphazardly, paint samples line the wall. Still, it'd be better than sitting in the living room which acts as a makeshift store room piled high with laundry. Some people would come in here with shades of judgement, she doesn't seem to be one of them.

'How is Ted?'

'Upstairs, better than he was.'

'He can tell us he's hungry so we're taking that as a good sign,' adds Matt.

She laughs.

'How do you take it, Miranda?' I stop as he says it to think of the ways I want to laugh and kick out a double entendre myself.

'Just white, thanks.' Matt knows what's going through my mind and glares. 'We were really worried about him. He's a lovely boy. And I'm so glad it was appendicitis, not that I'm glad, but the rumour mill went into overdrive when we heard he been in hospital. Someone at school heard meningitis, then conjunctivitis, but I don't need to tell you about school mums ...'

I smile. There is so much to say in reply, but I want to stay gracious and ever so slightly cautious. Matt comes over with teas and malted milks. I swear that economy biscuit is in the foundations of this place.

'Oh, we know about school mums, don't we, Jools?' It would seem Matt is more than ready to partake in some gossip. I pull a face at him. Who are you and what have you done with my husband? I remember a time when he'd see a gaggle of women, pretend he'd heard the baby crying, then run and hide upstairs until everyone had left. His feet have entered the coven and he shall never be able to leave. I nod.

'Lizzy Farrow-Burns, you know her?' he says. I stuff a whole biscuit into my mouth to stop the swear words from falling out. I know her, I also know the things she's said about you. Matt shakes his head. Miranda nods slowly.

'The cocking bitchery is fantastic.' I choke on my biscuit. Cocking. People don't use that word nearly enough as an adjective. 'Do you know what she said about me when Tim and I separated? All that stuff about shagging me about.'

Matt and I are quiet as we know those rumours, we'd heard it from the horse's mouth and several others, too. We'd believed it, we'd shared it. The shame washes over us and we take giant swigs of tea that are far too hot and leave us biting our tongues.

'Listen, I have no shame. I'm a brassy girl and people can think what they want, but Tim and I are having a blip. No one's fault, nothing's happened. But we're not living together for the moment and for some reason that gives her licence to talk shit about me.'

She pouts her lips. What she says sounds like a massive admission to have shared with people she hardly knows, but she feels relieved to share the truth and stop the proliferation of lies. Do I tell her what I know?

'You've probably heard the Tinder version, right? Or the one where I shagged the work experience boy. Or maybe the rumour about how I've had my fangita pierced?' Matt spits out a bit of his tea and lets it dribble down his chin. We'd heard the first two.

'I'm sorry ... we had heard things but ...'

'But we all do. I lost weight and got a bit vain and people didn't like it. Tim certainly didn't. I'd heard at school that you and McCoy are having a baby and Ted just had a touch of the runs but you pimped it up to be this big thing to get press coverage.'

Matt's eyes widen. 'From Lizzy Farrow-Burns?'

'Who else?

'She likes the sound of her own voice, eh?' Matt adds. I'm secretly excited at him sat around this table. 'I mean, I don't really speak to her that much, but I found out she runs her own bookkeeping company, that her daughter's on her nine times tables and that her husband only buys German cars.'

'How?' I enquire.

'She announces these things, like she's got her own little soapbox and we need to hear it.'

Miranda laughs. 'Ugggh, have you seen Facebook with the boring lovey-dovey memes? Whatevs. Have you met Neil Farrow-Burns? All the fleece, am I right?'

I laugh because it describes the man to a tee. He owns a fleece of every colour for every occasion and in the winter has a matching fleecy hat. I await to hear of the day when the static shocks him into paralysis. She continues.

'She doesn't like me because she used to be me. We both worked in the City but she gave it up for motherhood and I didn't. She resents that. And she resents the success of anyone who's doing something with their lives that's bigger than her, like we're to blame for her life decisions.'

Matt sits there, enthralled. 'That's horrific. So that's the only reason?'

'Pretty much. And people like her have never grown out of being the bitches they probably were at school. They subscribe to petty gossip, clique mentalities, and believe the sun shines out of their kids' arses. I'm done with it. Don't even get out of my car these days.'

Matt nods, impressed that she has sifted through the crap that comes with the school gate and decided to hold her head up high.

'Jools gave her what for the other day,' adds Matt, still part of this conversation and stirring the pot.

Miranda smiles, 'Good for you!' She sips her tea. 'It won't stop her, though. I know her sort, the rumour mill will keep on churning. I'll keep getting tattoos and running wild like a bitch on heat, you'll still be McCoy's mistress and ignoring your mother because she abandoned you in a field in a box …'

Matt and I stare at her, mouths open. Especially to hear someone talk so casually about my mother like that. It is an eggshell topic in this house at least. She senses my discomfort.

'I read it in a magazine. I assumed it was wrong …'

'It is … there were no boxes …'

Matt laughs.

'It must be hard to have your life out in the open like that? People spreading rumours …' I tell her. She looks at me like I'm mad.

'Girl, it's a couple of women at the school gate. Nothing like what you've got going on. That's like my situation on steroids. I take my hat off to you.'

Perhaps we're not as different as we first thought. Yeah, my boobs pale in comparison in both size and pertness, but at the moment, we're topic du jour at the school gate. People are spinning us into these monsters of their own creation: mothers who have abandoned their broods to have mid-life sex crises (her) and spangly celebrity careers also involving sex (me). All the sex, all the gossip, all the lies created by those people on the sidelines, the ones my dad warned me about. The ones he told me would react to my circumstances in differing ways: some with support, some with kindness, others with downright rudeness. Whatever situation you found yourself in, whether good or bad, there was always ample opportunity to be spoken about.

'So, to clear things up, I'm not shagging Matt. Though I'm a bit shameless with the flirting.'

Matt laughs. 'I can vouch for that: the flirting and the non-shagging.'

'Well, I'm not shagging McCoy either.' She laughs, downing more of her tea.

'Then I say we move on. Anyways, I've exacted my revenge in the way I need to.'

Matt and I look at each curiously.

'That coffee fundraiser governor rubbish she does. Did you go?'

Matt shakes his head. 'It clashes with toddler swimming ...'

'Then you missed my special brownies. The ones I make every year, Lizzy loves them. It's the only time we ever talk because she wants to get my recipe. So I made her a special one, just for her in a box. With my pubes baked into it.'

There is no other reaction but to lean over, thank her, and hug her. Matt buries his face in disbelief and laughter.

'I hope she ate it and I hope they got stuck in her teeth.'

Why have I never spoken to this woman before? Why aren't we friends? She smiles, knowing she's done what she needs to level the playing field. It'll never be over, ever. These women will never change. All we can do is shrug off the lies and rumours. Bake our body hair into baked goods. Use elaborate, clever swearing to air our frustrations. To hell with them all.

'I don't mean to pry but you and Tim ...'

'... are working through some things. We need to for the kids. I've promised to take fewer selfies and I'm off the vino. That shit will get you into trouble.'

Matt looks mortified. 'I'm so sorry I offered you Merlot.'

'Oh babe, you weren't to know. Lovely tea, though. Your man's got skills.'

I laugh. She puts her hand into mine. 'But seriously, I am really relieved to hear Ted's all right.'

'Thank you, that means a lot.'

'And I know we don't see you at the gate anymore but I think you're fab. Most of the other mums do as well. Don't let a few jealous bitches get you down.' I smile, knowing that her being here and being so honest with me is reaching out. It feels awful to think I thought of her in any other way. Maybe she's teaching me a lesson about judging people solely on how they choose to interact with me and my family. To judge them by any other barometer of social hearsay is wrong. Dad walks in at that precise moment.

'Don't mind me, I'll be off soon. There's only so many times I can watch *Madagascar* and listen to that "move-it-move-it" song.' He spies Miranda and his eyes widen. He sticks his tongue out from behind Miranda and makes little ears with his hands. What the fuck is he doing? Oh my lordy, he's pretending to be a dog. Dogging. And points at her. Matt's tea goes flying out of his mouth. I notice Miranda has seen everything in the newly installed kitchen window and swivels around. I hold my breath.

'Yeah, on the A3, apparently. I'm Miranda. You should join us some time.'

Dad goes ashen with embarrassment but Miranda, Matt, and I burst into hysterics.

CHAPTER TWENTY

'So yeah, Nigella covered very well for you but are you sure you want to come back? Is Ed OK?'

Do you correct the Head of Programming of the BBC? That feels like correcting a headmistress and, back in the day, if I did I'd be lucky to see the playground for the rest of the term. I've been off *Little Chefs* for two live shows now and while Nigella did a wonderful job of covering, the general consensus was that the boys and their fathers stared at her breasts too much, making for quite uncomfortable viewing. Time to bring back my boring C cups ravaged by breastfeeding so they don't quite sit right in a bra anymore. Don't say his name is Ted, don't say his name is Ted.

'He's fine. Docs are really happy and he'll be back to school next week. It's the finals, it's important.'

'Well, thank fuck for that. Otherwise there would have been a filming clash and as much as I love Nigella, her rates are much higher than yours.'

I don't reply, thinking what those rates are. You mean I can get more for this gig? Nigella didn't hug the children nearly as much I do.

'The kids will be thrilled to see you. No show this week because of the football but rehearsals all of next week. Iris will email you over everything. Did Ed like my present?'

'Yeah, it was kind, thank you ...'

I hope I sound sincere. She sent over a giant Hulk that the boys think is the coolest thing ever, but we've had to

277

remove the batteries from as the noises he made scared Millie and to be honest, sounded like a grown man climaxing.

'My pleasure. I'll see you next week. Love to little Ed.' His name is Ted. And with that she hangs up. Luella bursts into the corridor.

'Well?'

'All good. I'm back.' She hugs me and drags me into the kitchen where everyone else waits. It's Sunday and to celebrate the end of the week, my son not dying, and general good friendship, we have Luella and her husband, Remy, Annie, and Chris around. I am cooking (yes, really), wine is flowing. It's a dinner party of sorts with added children upstairs, some sleeping, some glued to tablets, some trying to watch films they shouldn't be on Netflix. Luella pours me wine as the others gather to hear what happened on the phone.

'Yeah, done deal. I'm back for the finals.' Luella does a little jig. She was slightly worried that Nigella may have stolen my thunder (she's far more eloquent) but the chemistry with McCoy was lacking, which was part of the reason why the show worked. Remy comes over to embrace me tightly.

'Jools, this is great news.' I've only ever met Remy once, but there is a way the man says my name which makes me giggle. He goes in for the double air-kiss. Remy is the sort of man you expect to see with Luella. This is not a man who buys his clothes from a supermarket. He is perfectly preened and accessorised, with the sort of rock star chic which looks like he's been on a couple of comeback tours and could knock out a harmonica solo at any moment. With Luella's leather trousers and studded rings, they accessorise each other perfectly. Luella embraces me firmly then looks at me. Sure, there were things said and other things I did but

278

we're both here now. You are not just a publicist, a friend. You are a surrogate sister. Of course, we don't say these things out loud but we go in for another hug.

Luella was the superstar in all the drama with Ted. When she found a pap hanging around outside the children's ward, she called the police and threw a blueberry muffin at him. She managed the BBC perfectly, making sure McCoy had a guest judge for the week I wasn't there and making sure my privacy was fiercely protected. Matt's favourite line of the week? When a newspaper asked for an exclusive article and she told them that from now on, she was going to use their rag for her dog to shit on. She did this from my kitchen table because she was here every day. If not in the hospital making sure I was all right, organising transport, and muffin tossing, she was here rallying the troops, making sure kids were getting picked up and people were eating right. Matt said he even caught her cleaning the toilet once. Dinner was the least we could do for her and if anything, was a fitting way to make amends, celebrate modern medicine, and raise a toast to Phil who had finally laid the floor on the kitchen despite, we calculated, needing exactly five hundred and twenty malted milks (some covered in chocolate) to complete the task. But truth be told, this is an event long overdue. Not that Luella hasn't been in the kitchen before or partaken in the odd bottle of wine, but this feels like we're allowing our worlds to collide a little more.

Remy and her kids used to be almost hidden away because to involve them would be unprofessional and blur the lines of our relationship. Today she's let those defences down. I feel the urge to hug her again. I don't. Instead, I hug Annie, the other sister I invited because she demanded it. I forget how intrinsically linked she is to my kids and loves them like her own. She arrived with bags of presents for Ted and spent half an hour colouring with him before learning Power Rangers' names and sharing Revels with him in bed. She shed a little tear to hear the story of how he got so ill and drew Matt and I into an embrace as we told her what happened. Chris is here too. Benign Chris, who I've never minded but since Finn and things going awry, I am a little more cautious of him. I may not hug him. Not yet. The plan is to get them both plastered. New parents: there's little you can do for them sometimes bar offer them a free dinner with an option to pop the baby upstairs and plaster them with wine. Matt pours everyone a glass of wine and Remy, who doesn't look like he's averse to a tipple, leads the toast.

'This is good wine, Matt.' I nod to agree. Matt laughs.

'I think South African?' enquires Chris. Chris is as middle class as they come; he knows his wine, he drives an Audi, he wears Hollister.

'It's Italian for my French friend,' I blush. Remy roars with laughter. Thank fuck for that. Luella shakes her head and takes a large swig. We're both swiggers, none of that polite sipping and turning your teeth blue nonsense. Remy, Matt, and Chris turn to examining wine labels as Luella sits me down with Annie.

'So, Cam Jacobs?' I turn to her to gauge a reaction. Was that a question or an answer? Tommy fired him last week in the most spectacular fashion possible after it was discovered that he'd bribed nurses and kitchen staff to take photos of Ted in his hospital bed. We found out due to the strong moral fibre of individuals who approached us knowing it was a despicable act to even consider being involved in. I, in turn, told Tommy, who had no hesitation in firing him there and then after the live show I missed. Luella and I clink our glasses to small victories.

'How's Ben?' asks Annie.

'Surviving.'

'He deserves better,' says Luella.

'I told him that.' She smiles. She's always taken a shine to him, but we secretly know we'll miss him furnishing us with tea and chocolate from the vending machines.

'My sources tell me his husband is filing for divorce, so that'll be big. The fur will fly. Seriously, they have twelve Chihuahuas.'

'That's a shit load of fur,' says Annie.

It's rare for Luella to joke so I smile and top up her glass. My sources at the studio said McCoy's dressing down was legendary. Children were present, voices bellowed as far as the regional newsroom down the corridor, McCoy called him a 'fucking whore of the worst possible kind.' I think about the children and how it may be McCoy's turn to write some letters of apology. But it's done, we can bid a fond adieu to the parasitic Cam Jacobs and his puppeteering. I sigh with some relief to know he's gone, but worry for what will happen to McCoy. The problem is, he's always been a puppet and most likely not known what it's like to be anything else, to have his own choices considered or be an arbiter of his own fate. I wonder how Luella's involvement could have changed his life, but know better than to bring it up.

'Ummm, Jools, food burning …' Luella laughs as Matt ushers me to the hob to attend to my lamb. All these months trying to sell me as a chef to the public and I'm having trouble with oven gloves. If only my little chefs could see me now. I remove a large casserole from the oven. Not burnt. I'll pick those bits out. Annie comes and peers over my shoulder. 'It's called texture, babe.' Luella busies herself by bringing bread and vegetables to the table.

'You know, I think this might be the first meal you've ever cooked for me.' We look at each curiously. Sure, she's eaten my cakes, plenty of biscuits, but she doesn't lie. Back in the day, it was Gia who furnished this kitchen with her own brand of culinary genius.

'How have you denied her the pleasure for this long?' adds Chris, a participant in the experiment. I am pretty sure I once served Annie and him sliced ham and oven chips. But Luella lies.

'You came over that morning and I think I made you a bacon sandwich.'

She laughs, as does Remy. She didn't even have sauce. Inconceivable.

'Did she cremate the bacon?' asks Matt. I hit him with a tea towel.

'The smoke alarms may have gone off.' I shake my head at them, secretly crossing everything in hope that I seasoned the casserole properly. Maybe I should have added another stock cube. Matt serves up while I tear off some bread to soak up the alcohol.

'Remember that time you made jacket potatoes and you thought could leave them on a low heat overnight? You could've killed people with those things. They left holes in the bin bags,' adds Annie. Matt doubles over in hysterics. Luella looks horrified. People start to look at the lamb curiously. Matt tries it first to test the waters and put our guests at ease. Remy goes next. His reaction shocks.

'Jools, this is excellent.' Remy is still making me giggle with his pronunciation of perfectly normal words. It is? People around the table tend to agree. I'll take that. 'Lulu tells me we are planning a wedding. This is still happening?'

I have never heard her referred to as a small, Scottish singer before so the Lulu bit makes me smile, but yes, the wedding is still happening. I feel Matt grab my hand under the table.

'Yeah, in three months' time.' Recent events involving appendices, TV shows, and extensions have meant our concentration has shifted and the wedding has slowly lost priority. Not in meaning, of course, but in terms of the tulle-ridden production that Luella had in mind.

'I had another idea, you know ...' I wait to hear Luella's latest plans. 'Boat. A fleet of boats.' Matt looks at me, smiling. He's used to Luella's grand ideas, but I think this time she forgets we don't live in Cannes and the nearest place to launch a boat would be the cold, poo-coloured Thames. Annie and Chris look on curiously. They had one of those stately home affairs in Hampshire with embossed place cards and a choreographed first dance. I was there as bridesmaid, radiant in purple, but because the twins were only six months old, I was carrying quite a lot of baby weight so looked a little like a giant bar of Dairy Milk.

'Like rowing boats?' enquires Annie.

'No, like the Thames Clipper – we could elegantly sail down the river ...'

'While tourists throw things at them from the bridges,' says Chris.

'The lifejackets would totally ruin the pictures,' I add.

'And all their children in boats, it would look like the D-Day landings,' adds Remy. I laugh a bit unattractively.

'You're all spoilsports.' Remy leans into her and I get the first glimpses into them as a couple when their fingers brush against each other.

'Where did you two get married?'

It's a probing question, but not one that's unwarranted given they're here together.

'In France. We had the reception in my parents' house in the hills. Parfait.'

I realise he's not talking about a pudding and smile. Remy gets out his wallet.

'Remy!' Luella groans.

'This is my Lulu, on our wedding day, drinking wine under the stars.' It's the most perfect photo I've ever seen. Luella has longer hair, rolled into the back of her head and lined with giant roses. Her dress is slim vintage lace, her lips are crimson red – she doesn't wear shoes but sits on Remy's lap as he plants a kiss on her cheek, a glass of wine accessorises the final look. I have never seen Luella so happy, so relaxed. Luella rolls her eyes.

'See these candles? I lit twenty-three, one for every month she had been in my life.' Luella blushes and I hold my breath, mildly surprised that someone so matter-of-fact as her is with such a romantic.

'Luella, you look amazing,' says Annie. She smiles, almost embarrassed by the compliment.

'Yes, it was a good day, the best day.' Remy purses his lips to know he's been complimented and kisses her hand. I have all the more respect for him knowing how he probably mended a broken soul. I think about how they met, but don't want to mar the illusion of it being equally stylish and romantic, like in an art gallery or a case of mistaken identity at the Eiffel Tower. Remy helps himself to more food.

'This lamb is really excellent, Jools. Where do you buy your meat?' asks Remy.

Matt squirms in his seat.

'Ummm, all over, really ...'

I cough politely as Luella laughs. I can't lie for toffee and kick Matt under the table. 'It was bought for us by a friend. When Ted was ill, they sent over food parcels from some organic produce company thingy ...'

Matt looks at me, knowing that lying is not doing us any favours. Rue the day we'd ever have to stand up in court and present alibis for each other. But as soon as I say it, Luella knows.

'It's OK, you're allowed to mention his name. I told McCoy at the hospital it'd be a good idea. He didn't know what to do to help.'

Annie and Chris look a bit sheepish that disagreement may be brewing and stuff their mouths full of bread. You see, I had thought it a good idea to cook from one of McCoy's special hamper boxes. Matt wasn't sure it was the best idea, it'd be like serving tainted meat, but it would have gone to waste otherwise and I have to admit it's probably the quality of the meat as opposed to my skill level which has probably made this dinner what it is. I stare at the football-sized crumble on the counter made with rhubarb from said box.

Remy nods as McCoy's name is mentioned. He doesn't seem to bear a grudge or turn territorial but he holds his wife's hand tightly, letting us know he knows too. That is the wonder but also the beauty of Luella, the strength to have a secret like that and not let it chip away, to not take it to the press but let it fortify her in some ways is admirable. Sure, there is anger. I've seen the anger, how it's consumed and how she's laughed to see his downfall. But she never used the miscarriage to bring him down, to alter my opinion of him. I can understand why; who wants to relive that grief? But seeing her now, you get a sense she does it out of a loyalty she has for Remy and the family she has. If Luella is good at anything, it's compartmentalising her life. My kids, my job, my past, my now.

'Well, I think you're the bravest person I know for being in the same room as the fucker.'

Matt. Matt knows. Because I've told him. And Matt's a little tipsy so that means he has zero filter. Damn you, ya boozy Scottish twat. As soon as he's said it, Luella jolts a little in her chair. I stuff my mouth full of bread and look to my newly painted ceiling.

285

'Why brave, Matt?' she enquires.

Matt stares at his wine glass, knowing the wine has been his foe. Think on your feet, Campbell, you do it all the time when I ask you where the last Magnum went.

'Because, you know …' He gestures to her stomach with his eyes. Oh, Matt.

Luella looks at me, not quite smiling, not quite shocked.

'How did you know?'

'He told me.'

'*He* told you? What gave him the right?'

A quick glance to my left shows Annie and Chris looking like they're trying to work out a bad game of charades. Remy squeezes Luella's hand that bit tighter. Do we talk about this? Over lamb casserole? I can't quite read her eyes. I can't tell if this is too much, if a line has been crossed.

'It came up. I told him what I thought. Despicable behaviour.'

'I'd have taken him down. His star would never have risen if it were me. I'd have crushed his fucking bollocks,' Matt adds.

Someone, please take the wine off my husband. Luella smiles but it's resigned, polite. She looks over at Remy who affectionately puts a hand on the small of her back. For someone who is naturally so gutsy, so brave, it jars to see her so affected. She turns to Annie and Chris.

'I was with McCoy. I was pregnant and he left me. He didn't know. I was so angry, I didn't tell him. I geared myself up for motherhood. I was ready to rock it, actually. And at twelve weeks, no heartbeat and well, that was that.'

Annie puts a hand into Luella's. Her other hand grasps Chris' under the table. Till this day, I know their battle to have a child resulted in an unfathomable number of similar scans followed by teary phone calls to me from waiting rooms. Matt looks mortified and stares at me with his eyes wide open. What a way to kill a perfectly pleasant evening, dear husband.

'But like I've always said, different chapter. It did change me. Possibly for the better. I thought long before that I wasn't going to be a mother. I was young, self-absorbed, too selfish. Then the idea gripped me. And lo and behold, the future got rewritten and this impossibly cool Frenchman walked into my life.'

'That is me by the way, in case you were thinking of someone else,' interrupts Remy. We all laugh, gladdened the mood has been lightened.

'So not brave, Mr Campbell. Brave is soldiers going to war, people running into fires to save babies. Just a moment in the greater scheme of things.'

Remy raises his glass. 'To moments that change us ... and the lamb ... I think we should go back to the lamb.' I laugh at his attempts to lighten the mood further. Annie and Chris raise their glasses.

'We can drink to lamb,' I say, in mild shock that my cooking is toast-worthy, and hold my glass aloft.

But Luella is still quiet, almost subdued. Remy puts an arm around her. Perhaps the lamb is not as good as Remy has made out.

'Lulu?' he enquires.

'Ça va. It's just for so long there was this bilious hate. And now, it's been replaced by something else. I still can't quite work him out. I want to believe he's still the good man I knew, that he has worth. But ...' She fiddles with her wine glass. 'Matteo, I haven't asked you about your thoughts on McCoy.'

She says this knowing in Matt, she's always had someone who shared her opinion. Matt is mid-stuffing his mouth, which seems to happen far too frequently. I smile, watching him try to motor his way through his mouthful. He looks at me for help.

'Well, you know how I felt. Two years ago, when he was a pretentious cock then yeah, I disliked him greatly.'

Remy seems to think this a reasonable explanation.

'But I guess I learned that was an act, a deplorable one, but if you see how he is now, how he helped with Ted, how he jumped in and helped Jools with her brothers – there were some significant gestures that proved that he cared, that he wanted to heal the situation.'

'And you buy it?' she asks.

'I think I do.'

Luella takes her glass and downs the rest of it. Matt looks to me. Remy shrugs as if to say this is a regular occurrence in his house. She doesn't say anything because it feels like she doesn't have the words. Almost as if to say, yes, I'll spare killing him but I'm not quite sure what to do with him yet. Instead, she tears off a piece of bread and looks into that space where moments from your past sit, trying to work out where they fit now.

'And Annie? Chris? What do you think of him?'

Both of them shrug. 'I view him with a slight air of caution. He's not hugely nice to the kids on that show,' says Chris.

'Exactly, right? He should just be himself with them. I don't get the act. I still think something's up.'

'You have always thought that,' adds Remy. Luella gives him evils. 'Let go of all the suspicion, it's just a waste of your energy.'

If that statement had come from anyone else, it would lead to a fight, but Luella leans into hear what he has to say, as if he respects his opinion more than angling for a disagreement.

'You know, I often think of it like this. He's in the past and we all have people from our past that have fucked us over. True, most of these people fuck off and we never see them again, sometimes they haunt you like bad cheese. You deal, you move on. I never understood why Lulu held on to him for so long.'

Luella snarls at him slightly.

'When I met her, she used to sit there and smoke with her face like a withered plum and see McCoy in the papers and tap the pictures with her finger. Go to hell, McCockface.'

If Matt is the 'zero filter' drunk then I am your classic giggler. His impression of Luella is spot-on, down to the way she puckers her lips up in anger. Luella looks less impressed.

'Every time. I tell her to let go. In all aspects of her life, she is like a lioness. She is proud and amazing and kind but he is like this thorn in her side…for some time I thought she still loves him…'

Luella makes retching sounds.

'But I realise where the anger is from. It's because she is angry at what's he become. Never mind the baby she lost, the fact he tossed her aside. It is always sad to see someone change, to turn into a person you do not recognise anymore. My Lulu is one of the kindest people I know. I always think she hoped she could jump in and save him from himself. She cared.'

We all go a bit quiet. Because that sort of statement comes from a place of understanding, of love, of knowing someone better than yourself. Luella smiles at him, still a bit snarly, but squeezes his hand hard, running her thumb across his palm.

'She is not angry, really. I know angry women. I was married to one. Her name was Sandrine. She was the lead singer of a jazz ensemble and she used to bathe in milk because she was delusional and thought she was

Cleopatra. She used to beat me while I slept. We were married for two months.'

Matt is thrilled and horrified in equal measure.

'Full fat milk?' asks Chris. Chris and Matt are enthralled that Remy has obviously had far more glamorous dealings with women than either of them combined.

'That must have had an effect on your bath tub?' Matt adds. Never mind she beat the poor man, Matt. He's more worried about how the lactic acid would have destroyed the enamel. Remy looks perplexed by their questions.

'I don't know. But the smell was horrible. I should have known from our wedding day. She got so drunk she threw the cake at me. Like a discus. But then, c'mon, we've all dated our own brand of crazy? Non?'

Matt and Chris look almost embarrassed that they have no stories of equal dramatic worth. Poor Matt. Given the young age we got together, I think I never gave him the chance to spread his wings and date a few loons to spice up his dating history.

'No one here. I did date a girl who only ate Pot Noodles once for a whole week.'

I blush. Remy looks horrified. 'You mean the ones in the cup with the powder? Mon dieu, did she smell like fake chicken?'

'Yeah, so much so I married her.' Remy looks at me and laughs again, a huge laugh that sounds like our boiler coming to life. I like him. I like everyone in this room. Luella looks over at me and smiles. I'm still holding onto the fact that all of Luella's hate towards McCoy was just misplaced kindness. All the while, she cared. I'm not sure how I never worked this out myself. Remy is right, all her professional dealings, no matter how forthright, were always underpinned in doing right by me.

290

And so it adds a bit more to her story. A touch of detail to explain who and why she is. I may love her even more now. Wine glasses are refilled.

By 11.30, Chris has wandered off upstairs and fallen asleep with Finn and the five other adults downstairs are well and truly drunk. Remy has shown us a bit of Capoeira that he learnt after he spent a year in an artists' retreat in Brazil. He and Matt are doing drunken round kicks at each other while Luella and I shout at them to watch the crockery. Matt looks quite content. He's almost enthralled to have someone of such artistic leanings in his home. I always forget there is student bohemian Matt hiding away. He, who probably yearned for friends in adulthood who were artisan political dissidents and who he could have intellectual conversations with. This is probably more wanting given his days are spent with Ben and Holly's Little Kingdom. Annie props me up and stares at her phone to watch Chris curled around his baby boy using some fancy app. I peek over.

'So you and him?'

'We're working on things.' I think about Miranda Scott who was here only a few days ago and described her marriage to Tim in a similar way.

'Aren't we all?' Luella says languidly. Remy attacks my pepper mill and she makes a hand gesture and French guttural noise at him. He replies back with something equally throaty. 'Most marriages are a work in progress.'

'I thought we had things sorted, you know? I've been with Chris for eight years, he's fine with his nieces and nephews … I just …'

Luella snorts with laughter. 'I tell you, Remy was not instant father material. He had a lot of problems with the clean-up process – he still does. If Xavi or Clio throw up, he has to leave the house. I can be in the middle of a film set and I get calls from him about vomit clear up.'

'He stays at home with the kids?' asks Annie.

'It works well for us. The joys of him being a freelancer bohemian sort.' Luella senses she has questions brewing. 'When are you back at work?'

'Oh, not for a while but they've been asking and now comes that dilemma of balancing my career and Finn.'

'I went back when Xavi was three months old. It's hard. But I like working. I'm good at it.'

Annie sits up from her drunken slouch. 'Exactly, I like my job. I make a difference.'

'Then go back. Is Chris OK with it?'

Annie shrugs. 'I think so. We still haven't thought that far ahead.'

'Then have that conversation. Think about you, little Finn – you want him to have a mum in his life who's fulfilled. The best version of herself. Some mums do that by staying at home, some work, some do both. You work it out, just don't listen to the haters because everyone's got a fucking opinion.'

Annie and I sit there wide-eyed listening to her spiel. Both of us are figuring out new arrangements in working motherhood so her words ring with importance.

'Remy's mother still thinks I should be at home making sodding "confiture."Fuck that. I do right by my munchkins, I rock my job. Just go do your lawyer thing because from what I've seen, and I've met plenty of lawyers, you're quite good at what you do. There are proper bellend lawyers out there who don't know their heads from their arses.'

Luella is the sweary drunk. Annie, the emotional drink who takes in every word realising she's having a lightbulb moment in my kitchen. Luella was the best person to have this talk with her, which makes me realise I should have more dinner parties, bring more people together over lamb and rhubarb. Luella continues her pep talk and I marvel at how efficiently she handles life. I've met those kids, they seem relatively normal. She has good hair, rocks her job, and her husband is fantastically French and charming. I'd hate her if she wasn't a friend and I think about the crazy situation that brought us together. How we first met in this kitchen and she saved my bacon from the big, bad world of the media. I wouldn't be without her. She suddenly stops her conversation to flap her hands and grabs at her phone.

'Before I forget, you and McCoy ... I saw this the other day. Someone has knitted dolls of you.'

'For voodoo purposes?' Annie and her snort with laughter.

'No! Like fan dolls. I'll go on the Google and look it up.' She reaches for her phone and types in our names into the search bar. 'Yours was lovely, Tommy had yellow wool for hair.'

Blurry, trying to keep her eyes open, she smiles at me.

'Remy doesn't have a lot of friends, I think he likes Matt. Maybe it's a continental thing but we meet a lot of people and Remy sees through the bullshit instantly.'

I take that as a compliment. She stares at her phone but that pensive look returns. She presses buttons and scrolls quickly.

'Son of a shit whore, well, that's that. I knew Cam wouldn't take his firing lying down.'

Intrigued, Annie and I look over her shoulders, hoping she's not talking about something to do with me. Are the step-brothers back? Holy hell. A search for Tommy McCoy reveals a slew of headlines with pictures of Kitty's face and that of her most recent toyboy lover. Annie reads the headlines out slowly and dramatically.

KITTY'S BABY IS MCCOY'S!

KITTY: 'HE WAS AN ABUSIVE FATHER, HE'S NOT RAISING THIS BABY!'

MCCOY'S LOVER: 'HE LIED TO ME, I'M NOT MARRYING A LIAR!'

A small trickle of wine runs down my chin. Luella doesn't comment further and I realise this dilemma is extremely pertinent to her situation of old so know better than to comment. We read the facts, the commentary, in silence and I realise how this will totally flatten McCoy. Despite anything that went on before, I knew the McCoy now and the importance his kids had in his life This would completely reset all the progress he had made, it would destroy him. Luella looks at her phone with conversations from tonight obviously in the forefront of her mind. I think back to all the times she was jubilant about his demise; the split from Kitty, the empire falling apart. I always thought that jubilance was vengeful but now I know she just wanted him away from all those things that had changed him for the worse. This? This is is him having a huge bombshell dropped on him from very high above. This is evil Kitty back in his life once again.

'What do we do, Luella?'

She looks at me and shakes her head. She can't do anything. This is out in the open, like a missile fired and set to destruct. We're a neighbouring country, we'll have to wait and see if we're affected in any way. For now, we have to wait and see if we can salvage anything from the debris.

CHAPTER TWENTY-ONE

'Why are we here again?' Matt asks. I'm not entirely sure myself. It's been an important week at *Little Chefs* now we are down to the final four, and McCoy has missed every one of his promotional interviews and rehearsals. I rang, I left messages, I tried my best to reach out, but it all fell into the ether, leaving bosses angsty and rumours abound that he may be fired and they'd bring in Gordon Ramsay. So I panicked. One, Gordon and I would never get on, there was far too much shouty shouty going on and I'd spend all my time staring at his chin wondering if he'd had fillers, but two, I'll admit it, I was worried for him. The media went to town on McCoy after it was revealed that Kitty and he had a final fling before their divorce. It resulted in a pregnancy that she hid from him, but turned in her favour, trying to make it look like this was part of some abandonment and mistreatment of his family. Given he'd painted this picture of himself playing some bad boy chef, people had formed their own assumptions. Luella read the coverage closely and offered analysis and insider information. This was Cam Jacobs' doing – after being terminated by McCoy, he went to snuggle up to Kitty to get his revenge. Kitty's star on the wane, she wanted in on a piece of the action, keen to share some of the spotlight that her ex-husband had reclaimed. So they plotted his demise in the saddest way possible, via the media, unannounced. Boom.

Luella gave her insights into the matter, but I could tell she needed to leave it well alone and didn't want further involvement or to offer suggestions of how to remedy the situation. I didn't blame her, it was a frigging mess. I told her this affected us too. We were almost a duo, our conflict fuelled Little Chefs' ratings and without him, it'd be me flying solo and hugging random children as they cooked. Luella resisted. I could fly high without his help. Maybe his demise was meant to be, we'd aided in getting him out of it before, to do so again would make us look the fools. To make things worse, one paper had dredged up a picture of McCoy and I hugging outside a hospital, the implication being that I was involved and hinting that our relationship was more than professional. It was like pouring petrol on flames, she said. Best to let the fire die, not play firefighter. I then reminded her what Remy said, about her caring what happened to McCoy. She looked me in the eye at that point and told me she cared, about me. The only reason she stayed in the same vicinity as McCoy was to protect me. We hugged it out. She told me to ignore her husband as he was prone to talking out of his French arse.

'Are you sure we have the right place?' I nod and look at the house curiously. We'd managed to wrangle the address off someone at the production company. We drove, which was a mistake in itself as we spent most of the time on the North Circular fending off window washers and with me telling Matt he was in the wrong lane. But now we're here and there's a feeling that we're at the wrong house. Before us is a standard terraced townhouse set in a generic estate outside of Tottenham, not the sprawling mansions and eco lighthouses I'd seen him pictured with. This looks like something Matt and I would buy with its generic front door and faux gables. I stare at the windows for signs of life.

'Maybe he's left the country? I'd leave if the press were making me out to be some sort of monster.' Matt cups his hands and looks into the kitchen window. 'I'll say this, he might know how to cook but he's not keen on washing up.'

Matt shifts me one of his looks to tell me his patience is wearing thin. We've re-arranged childcare because of this and wasted time and petrol. He doesn't need our help. I look at my watch. I rap on the front door and ring the bell. Nothing.

'Maybe he's popped out for some milk? We could wait a bit?'

Matt gapes at the house then looks at me. I know why you want to do this, this is you being kind and trying to help. It's what you do.

'Half an hour then I'm out of here.' I smile and we head back to the car parked on the drive.

'We'll look like we're on a stakeout.'

'Or dogging.'

Matt laughs. 'In broad daylight, how brazen! Miranda Scott would be proud.' We settle back in the car and he opens up the Percy Pigs. This is our second pack. This is why I've never really lost my baby weight. 'Speaking of, I heard she got back with her husband. They showed up together at the last match and she's wearing high neck tops, put the puppies away.'

I look at him bemused. 'Really?'

'Donna confirmed it. Whatever happened, they got through it.'

'That's good, no?'

'Well, I see them both in a new light now. They've worked things out, changed, moved on, forgiven any past wrongdoing.'

We nod, knowing forgiveness and bygones have been an important feature in our lives recently. We inhale the rest of the sweets.

'Would you forgive me? If I went all celeb and started

shagging the manny?'

'We don't have a manny. Your dad helps us look after the kids.'

'You know what I mean!'

'Well, you'd be allowed certain celebrity byes. Tom Hiddleston, he's a handsome sod. I've seen how you look at him. If he offered it up, you'd be crazy not to.' I nod in agreement. 'Could I have Mila Kunis?'

I nod back. This feels like we're negotiating important contractual matters. Perhaps I should be writing this down. Celebrity shags permitted, protection to be worn at all times, no return to the fold in the event of crabs and intercourse is only to be consummated within four secure walls.

'I went to that Year 5 information evening, by the way. Your mate Lizzy was there.'

I roll my eyes. He laughs.

'You'll love this. She's got loads of campaign posters up for her next run of governor. Vote Lizzy Farrow-Burns!'

'Oh lordy.'

'Yeah, and someone's gone round with a marker pen and changed them all to "Lizzy's Flange Burns".' I choke on a sweet.

'Miranda?'

'Whoever's done it, I applaud them. Seriously, I've not said it yet but there's a certain torture involved with the school gate and playschool mornings and parties and politics. Well done for enduring it as long as you did.' I stare at him a moment too long and go to shake his hand, almost grateful for the acknowledgement.

'And soft play, don't get me started. I thought I was going to stab someone the other day. Those kids who go the wrong way up the slides incur my wrath.' Even more so to imagine him at the Monkey Maze. He flares his nostrils. He'd do it with a wooden coffee stirrer, I'm sure of it. Still, I am impressed Matt has made the effort.

'You go to soft play?' I laugh. If Matt is anything, he is slightly antisocial in tendency, which means he usually shies away from interacting with Joe Public. He and soft play go as well together as brown sauce and beetroot.

'Well, they have free Wi-Fi and the coffee in the one in New Malden isn't terrible.' Faint praise from someone who knows their Capps from their Americanos. I smile to think of Matt replacing me in these butt-cringingly awful situations where you had to make small talk and go armed with enough rice cakes to avoid meltdowns and having to pay out small fortunes. This was me once. This was what filled my days and what I used to tell Matt about.

'Well, don't go to the one in the industrial park. Ted had diarrhoea in the ball pit and the shame means I can't show my face there ever again.'

He laughs. I don't. It was one of those paralysing moments in parenthood where there were six children in there and their six accompanying adults froze, knowing there was a smell coming from those balls and one of our children was responsible. Ted's name being out in the open catches us both off guard. We still squirm over that incident, even though Ted is fine, the drugs have been administered, and he's back at school but there is still that residual worry that lingers. The sort that means every time one of the children cough, we watch them hawk-like and lavish them with unnecessary cuddles and Calpol. Matt holds my hand, knowing we are pondering the same thing, and we have a Ted moment, knowing any resentment we held for each other over the incident has now passed. We have our boy back.

'So, you being the all-singing, all dancing Harry Homemaker. I never told you, but you've got quite the

299

knack for it,' I tell him with a sideways glance. I see him beaming.

'Am I allowed to say I'm far better at it than you ever were?' I nod. Dare I say it, he's far more organised than me. He gets a perverse joy out of hoovering and the laundry is far more under control, but there is a sense of zen about him pottering about his house and organising his day.

'My mac and cheese is still better, though.'

He doesn't look too impressed. I smile slyly. I haven't told him my secret is a packet mix. I'm keeping that one up my sleeve for now.

'How do you always have food in the fridge?'

'Tesco delivery?' he says, confused. That really wasn't a complicated answer. But there is always milk in the house. When I was in charge, many an early morning was spent doing a slow jog to the petrol station on the corner.

'And you're happy? With this? What we have now?'

He smiles, because a couple of years ago, this was the question I was made to ponder when fame came a-knocking. I was happy with so many things in my life but there were always those niggles in the back of my brain that questioned how things came to be and whether there were other options. This arrangement we have now is new and untraditional, not because of our roles in the house, but because of this occupation of mine which sees me out of the house most of the weekend and not exactly working 9-5.

'You know, you did this job, *my* job, for ten years and can I imagine doing this for ten years? I don't know ... maybe not? But I have that option, that space to think about it and go do something else at a later date. I'm spending time with my kids. They know me, the real me, as opposed to tired commuter me who was grouchy and wore badly fitting suits. Plus, I have a much greater skills set now.'

'Such as?' I enquire.

'I can do French plaits, I know my phonics, and I can do crazy mad things with loom bands.'

'Loom bands are so last year.'

'Hush now. By the way, you know when the kids were in front of the telly and I used to criticise you and said they were watching too much? Yeah, I get that now ...'

I laugh. All is forgiven. There is a knowing look between us that despite taking this big leap into the great unknown, toying with celebrity, and coming away from what I know, that this has been good for us, for the family, for my marriage. This plan is not set in stone, I understand I've entered into a very fickle world and that people may not know who I am this time next year, but for now, Matt and I can say tentatively that this works. We've finished the Percy Pigs and sit there in silence, waiting for signs of life. Matt looks at his rear view mirror.

'There's a man in a bush over there.'

'Like a flasher?' Matt looks curious that my head swung around as quickly as it did and that my mind went straight to the perverse.

'Like with a camera. No wonder he's not answering the door. We probably look like a couple of loons too, sat here. Come on ...'

He gets out the door of the car and raps loudly on the front. 'Tommy, c'mon, we've come all this way, just open up so Jools can use your loo, otherwise she's going to piss on your drive. TOMMY!'

I sincerely hope the pap didn't hear, but I play along and pretend to jog from side to side. Matt rings the doorbell five or six times in that way we tell our boys not to do when visiting other people's houses. I see a neighbour come to the window.

301

'Matt, we're making a scene. Maybe he's not …' But the twitch of curtain gets my attention. I bend down to the letter box, hoping it will channel the sound of my voice better.

'It's me, Jools, please just let us in.'

A figure hovers in a doorway. All I can tell is that it's wearing pyjama bottoms.

'Are you really going to piss on my driveway?' Matt nods.

'Yes? Or no … we've come a long way. Please, Matt brought cake and beer and we just want to check you're all right.'

'What sort of cake?'

Matt finally speaks. 'Coffee and walnut.' The lock clicks open and the door opens slowly, a small gap for us to enter and for him not to be seen. I tiptoe in and hear a camera in the background snap into action. Matt turns around and gestures to it: a small reminder why he's not a celebrity. I glare back at him and enter the house quietly.

When we do enter, the sight that welcomes us is someone who could easily fit into the cast of *Lost*. That is some facial hair. The pyjamas are mismatched and stained and teamed with sports socks. There is silence. Even Matt, who has rarely been in this man's company or really met him formally, has nothing to say. Matt, who had an almost acidic hatred towards him, just scrunches his face up in sadness. Why kick him when he's down? He turns his palms up and rolls his hands up into fists, shaking his head. And tears. I remember those tears. It leaves me little choice but to embrace him, Matt's hand on my back almost pushing me towards him.

Five minutes of intense sobbing later and we've managed to lead McCoy into the living room and get him to sit down. The kettle is on, the cake is unpacked. Matt walks into his kitchen with that look of shock and despair that he used to have when I'd been cooking dinner and left a bomb site in my wake. I don't know what to say or do, especially as it's quite clear he's not wearing underwear so he really needs to make sure his mouse stays in the house. His house is almost as confusing as the mundane exterior. It's like he's just moved in; boxes line the corridors and there seems to be a lack of décor and furnishings.

'It's pretty fucked, eh? I thought Kitty was evil but this is a whole other level of evil, like Disney Queen evil.'

I picture her with comedy horns and purple eyeshadow. It works. I still have few words, hoping just having the chance to get thoughts off his chest may work.

'Cam's pulled all my legal representation so I have nothing to stand on. They'd worked to get me visitation and now I've had those rights revoked, she's poisoning my name again, zero access to the kids ...'

He swallows and inhales deeply. I've seen him like this before. This is Holiday Inn sad, tears he's shedding for his kids, kids he loves. Matt re-enters the room with a tray of tea and cake. McCoy swipes the cake and uses his hands to eat it like a small child.

'This isn't bad.'

Matt doesn't know whether to take that as a compliment, but looks at me and the very bare and sad room that we are sitting in.

'Who is representing you now?'

'No one, I'm doing this myself,' he says with the confidence of a drunk who says he can make the twelve-mile walk home from the pub on his own. 'I'll go back to what I do best, cooking and working on getting the kids back. That's the thing about this, you can stay in it for as long as you want and I don't need to prolong this bullshit any further. I've stayed for as long as I can tolerate.'

Matt nods, knowing that where we struck that good balance of celebrity on our terms, his world had been completely consumed by it. Celebrity claimed him and for the past ten years, it's almost as if he's forgotten who he ever was. He was talking of a back-to-basics, simple approach to his life where he'd have total control. It feels like he's reached a very edifying conclusion. I, therefore, am confused by the bedraggled tramp look he's chosen to adopt.

'My manners … I totally forgot to ask about Ted.'

Matt speaks up. 'He's good. He's home … and thank you for everything you did for us. The food packages were a kind gesture.'

'It was my pleasure. Super Ted. That's a good name for him.'

We all smile. That is the perfect moniker for the kid. Jake could be Spotty. I can tell Matt loves it and gives McCoy a look: a look that almost signals some form of truce between them, underlined by a mutual appreciation for eighties cartoons. God, I don't even know if these two have been formally introduced. Given their history, I wasn't sure how this would pan out, but I think they both know that moment where testosterone and ego could have got in the way has now passed. I look at his coffee table and see piles of legal textbooks. Crap, he's really doing this himself, isn't he? Matt notices too.

'So how long have you lived here?' Matt asks politely.

'Six months now. I know, it looks like a hovel and I need to get some people into decorate it but there's room for the kids and it'll look great once it's done. Did you see the green across the way?'

I nod. 'It'll be great, and you know, you have a plan, but you still seem a bit all over the place. You missed all

304

the *Little Chefs* rehearsals this week and ...' He closes his eyes.

'Shit, I know. Cam used to do my scheduling so I'm a bit all over the place and emotional and ...'

I look at Matt, who looks concerned at the lack of general organisation as he paws through papers and calendars on a pile on the floor.

'I mean I'll be there for Saturday and ...'

'... tonight?'

He looks at me blankly. I try to let him fill in the gaps. He doesn't.

'The TV awards thing. We're presenting an award with the finalists?'

He bites his bottom lip. He forgot. I thus realise the bedraggled tramp look is merely him being overwhelmed; he misses his children, the press reaction has been horrific. He's trying to act as his own legal representation, schedule his everyday, and just remember to put on underwear every morning. I imagined worse. I imagined recent events were going to having him recoil into a tiny, ball-shaped human again, downing gin and hallucinating that his wife was the pillow again. But he just needs some guidance, a kick up the arse, a wall planner. Matt is shaking his head.

'Seriously, McCoy, you need to get with the programme a bit.'

I cringe when I hear Matt say it as it's so direct, so forward. But it needed to be let out into the open. McCoy's shoulders slump.

'I'm shit, I know.' I shake my head. Matt continues.

'Well, yeah. You look like shit. This house looks like shit and you've let work go to shit, but you can make it better and it starts with you pulling your finger out your arse.'

God bless Matt with his Scottish accent and

phenomenal need to use as many swear words as possible. I lied before, I could definitely take on Gordon Ramsay. It's not like I've not had the practice.

'But tonight, I'm not ready. Kitty's going to be there, she'll be there with that reality gardening show she was part of. I need to …'

Matt turns to me. This was my badly thought-out plan, but time to lay it on the table.

'Well, we thought as much. So we've come prepared. We've got bags in our car. We've hired you a decent tux and brought all our stuff to get ready. Car will pick us up in exactly two-and-a-half hours.'

He looks at me in shock, a look I remember from a supermarket when I lectured him about making my own bread.

'Matt's right. If you want to do this yourself then what you need is a bit of courage. This is the perfect chance for you to show up to a public event and tell the world and Kitty to fuck off. You've done nothing wrong and it's important to your kids most of all that you show them that.'

He tears up to hear that bit about his kids and Matt marvels at the man's propensity to cry as much as he does. I told him he was a crier and herein lies the proof.

'But I don't how?'

'I brought a razor for a start,' Matt says. McCoy laughs.

'I contacted a friend, Annie. She's a family lawyer and she'll provide some advice.'

His mouth is agape.

'But why? I was pretty shitty to you. If it were my family, I wouldn't be doing this, what you're doing …'

Matt nods, knowing that's the first time he's been acknowledged in this and he commends the sincerity. We both shrug. I don't know why we're doing this, really.

306

Because as a wise Frenchman and his wife taught me, people in life do fuck you over but maybe it's how you choose to deal with it that's important. Life moves along and it becomes a measure of your experiences with people and how they change. You can be abandoned by your mother but that never resolves itself. She comes fleetingly back into your life without redemption. She never creates that space for you to forgive and forget. Your very best friend has a baby and you ignore her, misplace each other in your lives, but you find each other, you make it right. And then a celebrity chef ridicules you in the press, this bizarre celebrity he creates for himself serves to bring you down. But if anything, he makes you stronger and the more you get to know him, the more he interacts, he helps, the more he negates wrongdoing of the past. The relationship evolves. He becomes your friend. I look at him. I don't tell him, of course, but put a hand out to lever him off the sofa.

'It's because we're pretty awesome,' Matt informs him. 'And you're kind of my wife's TV husband. Without you, she's pretty dull on her own.' I laugh and punch him on the arm. Tommy smiles. And a moment where I realise he's not McCoy anymore. He's not that chef standing in a supermarket. I'm not that frazzled mum giving him what for. He's Tommy. My mate, Tommy.

CHAPTER TWENTY-TWO

'How in the mother of cock did you manage that?'

I love that being surrounded by Matt and Luella means I get to bear witness to some of the most inventive swearing known to man.

'Well, I learned from the best, obviously.'

Luella spies Tommy through the car window as he turns the lights off in his house. Matt and I weren't really sure what we were doing, truth be told. In any rom-com, it would have been a Chaka Khan music sequence where Matt and I had posh shopping bags, had gone to work on him with some rollers, tweezers, and nail polish and there would have been a grand reveal where we'd swing his chair round and the transformation would be complete. Instead, it was us with three IKEA sacks, sitting around waiting for his central heating to get the hot water going and me trying to put on some mascara and clearing Tommy's shaven bits of beard out of the sink.

He looked better for a shower and, given the beardy look is in, Matt managed to cultivate his facial hair so he looked less tramp and more Hackney trendy. If Matt and he had any umbrage with each other, it was gone now they had seen each other in their pants. Once we'd put him in the suit and found him some shoes to go with it, the turnaround was complete. It wasn't Chaka Khan-worthy, but it was better than the pyjama bottoms. We fed him some alcohol, the bit they don't show in the movies. Luella studies him closely for signs of weakness. The

309

truth is, we don't know how this evening will go. He might see Kitty, collapse to his knees, and have a nervous breakdown. I might fall in my stupidly high heels, taking down four small children with me, and show the world my Spanx. But coming out with us, taking that step into the big world, was better than loitering in his house forgetting what was supposed to come next. Tommy opens the car door and comes to sit in the backseat next to me. Matt is on the other side, Luella in the front. It's a tight if awkward arrangement, like when you were students and tried to get that extra person in without the driver knowing. Our driver is a small Asian man called Raj who likes showing us his teeth when he smiles, like he might be at the dentist.

'Lu, nice to see you again.'

She puts a hand up to acknowledge him. Raj takes this as his cue to drive on. Matt grabs my kneecap. In all this fuss, Matt was keen to point out that this is another posh night out for us. Are these date nights? We're not sure. I still have a fondness for date nights on the sofa, binge eating, watching TV, and drinking. Yet now we seem to be redefining the standards of our relationship and have these occasional nights out that involve layers of make-up and free alcohol which I now know to partake in with caution. Matt, again, carries off his suit with casual aplomb while I don a black, strapless dress and giant green earrings that make me feel like the Wicked Witch of the West but which Luella tells me go with my complexion. When did I turn the same colour as Yoda? My hair was put up six hours ago by a hairdresser called Maxi. Like Maxi Pad, I thought in my head and spent most of our appointment smirking. Even though it looks like it's casually put together, it is held together by half a tin of hairspray and a few dozen kirbigrips that would be sure to set alarms off. I put my hand over Matt's and squeeze. If this was a date, surely there'd be a chance for inappropriate groping. But not now. I'm thrown back to being eight and sitting between two brothers in the back of the car to stop them from fighting. I remember how much I hate sitting in the middle. Matt goes into his tux pocket and retrieves some Starburst.

'Tommy? Luella? Raj?' He offers the tube around. Everyone takes one and is polite. Possibly too polite as the silence is starting to deafen. I wait for Matt to offer me one, he looks at me and rolls his eyes. Tommy looks on curiously.

'She only eats the purples one so I have to eat them all until I find a purple one.'

He laughs, but looks pensive, knowing it's relationship quirks like this he once shared with Kitty. And the passenger in the front seat. I sensed this might be a difficult car journey, but configured the seating so Luella wouldn't have to look at Tommy. But not seeing her face is difficult. When she showed up, immaculate in a black flowing catsuit and a bright red lip, she looked like she'd seriously geared herself up for this meeting. She turns on the radio. Magic FM. Maybe some of Ronan Keating's greatest hits can dispel the tension. Matt turns to me and grimaces like he's in the throes of some severe aural pain. He reaches into his pocket.

'Can I say, I have brought us an aperitif for tonight's festivities.'

He reaches into a small plastic bag by his feet which seems to carry a number of tins. Please not a six pack of Fosters, Matt.

'So, they do mixed drinks in tins and I thought it'd be nice.'

I look at him with a scrunched up face. Yeah, if you're a fifteen-year-old girl on a bus going to the local nightclub on a Friday night. He senses my snobbery.

'Wine would be too much off a faff with glasses and stuff so I thought this was a good compromise.'

The ever-practical Matt. He throws a tin of ready mixed gin and tonic into my lap. What every girl wants on a date. And a straw, I'm touched.

'Sorry, didn't get one for you, Raj.'

'It is OK, Mr Campbell.' He gestures with his hands, still smiling.

'I got you a posh one, Luella as I know you're fancy. You get elderflower. And a straw too.' She reaches back to take it but swings her head around to the back seat to see Tommy take a big swig from his tin.

'Tom, slowly does it. Baby sips.' They look at each other and I realise there is significance in the familiarity of her tone. He raises the tin to her and she smiles and shakes her head. She faces ahead again. 'Jools, he's a lightweight with gin. Last thing I need you to do is have to prop him up on the red carpet.' Shit, gin. It was his Holiday Inn drink of choice. I look at him.

'Something to quell the nerves. I'll be good.'

Matt looks at him and digs a bit further in his plastic bag. I wonder if Brangelina do the same when they go to a special event. Does Brad stop off at a Tesco Metro? Does Angelina drink out of a McDonald's straw? 'I also bought some crisps. I upped the ante, it's a posh do ... I did Kettle Chips and nuts. Pistachios?'

'YES!' cries Tommy. There is a high-five and just like that, they have bonded over nuts. Luella goes into a panic.

'Raj, do you have napkins, lovely? Don't you dare get nut dust on Jools' black dress!'

She rifles through his glove compartment as Tommy arches his eyebrows. Matt heard it first and is already mid-giggle.

'Say again, Lu?' asks Tommy. 'Was that nut dust?' Luella refuses to look at us, but I see her shoulders vibrating with laughter. I shake my head as the men double up in fits of laughter. Was that a joke? About nuts. This suddenly feels like it's going well? I don't know any more. I take a deep swig of my drink and let the gin and sugar solution wash over me. Matt is wiping tears from his eyes and I suddenly feel very much like that older sister again. Luella has little time for laughing. She is not partaking in tinned alcohol party drinks but goes back to doing what she does best, which is checking things off on a clipboard.

'Jools, Heart will have some reporters about on the red carpet. I think Ant and Dec will let those kids loose, so big smiles for them. Your award is the first to be presented, if you can believe it, so they need you out back for a little run-through, nothing different to the notes I gave you.'

Matt and Tommy have very good nut shelling techniques and seem to be eating at incredible speed.

'Tom, please check your teeth before you get out of the car and please stick with Jools, hand on an appropriate place on her midriff please and lots of "you're so funny" looks.'

Luella's tone still sounds nervous, like Tommy may be a huge liability. She told me before that I could do this on my own and no one would be the wiser, that everyone had pretty much written Tommy off and wouldn't expect him to be there anyway. This would have been my chance to shine on my own and show the world I could fly solo. While the need to have him there was genuine, I fought my celebrity case. I interjected that Tommy there would create column inches and do wondrous things for our ratings, no? Luella then looked at me in a way she never had before. You're starting to understand this game, my little Padawan. She may even have looked proud. Still now, slightly shaky, she looks a little more cautious at what the night might bring. The car slows to a roll. Matt looks out of the windows as we seem to be caught in a rather large queue of black cars.

'Traffic?'

'The queue to get into the O2,' Luella says, looking at her watch. 'It's fine, it's just to make sure the right cars are going to the right places. Gives us some time to freshen up too. Jools, lean forward.'

I undo my seatbelt and she attacks me with a powder brush and gets out a small pot of Vaseline.

'Rub a little on your teeth. That's a strong lip and we don't want any on your teeth when the cameras have you in HD.'

I do as I'm told with Matt looking on like I'm slightly mad. Luella then touches up my lipstick with a brush and holds her face away from me. 'You'll do.' The car rolls forward slightly and the tumult of noise and lights outside starts to get louder. Luella studies the cars ahead and gets her phone out.

'OK, the *Little Chefs* kids are two cars in front, which is fantastic. If I planned this right, we all get out the cars the same time and it'll look like a big family portrait. Remember their names, please: Kai, Oscar, Erin and ...'

She looks at Tommy to see if he's been paying attention.

'Tia.' She nods, impressed he's passed that test. Nigella and Tommy had made the highly contentious decision on Saturday after pasta week. Commentators were furious that Shaun and his squid ink and crabmeat tortelloni didn't get through, but Erin nailed it with the flavours on the more mundane but equally as complicated four cheese lasagne. Either way, it was all apparently bloody tasty and whoever was going to win the finale would be hugely deserving and a far better chef than I ever was. Tommy chants the kids' names to himself as the car rolls forward again. Matt is still eating nuts, looking very casual about the whole event, knowing nut dust on his tux or teeth won't be half as important.

'And what happens after they present their award?' he enquires.

'Well, we can't just naff off ... we have to stay and mingle and enjoy the awards and there's an after-party in the club lounge, but trust me, you don't want to see soapstars drink. Bloody carnage. Last year I saw someone from *Hollyoaks* throw up in a Louis Vuitton clutch.'

I think about the *Little Chefs* launch party and about how that very well could have happened there. Tommy looks ahead and freezes for a moment. He darts his head in and around Raj's headrest.

'Lu ... read the number plate ahead for me ...'

She scans it and pauses for a moment. She sighs then calls an associate on the phone. Matt and I look at each other confused. 'Raj, is there any way we can veer into the right-hand lane, now?'

'But Miss Bendicks, you tell me to follow that other car ... I ...'

Tommy looks ill with worry, which may have been down to the cheap alcohol, possibly the over-consumption of nuts. Matt squints his eyes then whispers to me.

'The licence plate, read it ...'

I look ahead. KITKAT1.

'What like the chocolate?'

'No ...' says Tommy. 'Like my ex-wife.' Oh. Shit.

Luella is still on the phone. 'Tell the kids to stay in the car. I don't care what the producer is telling you ... keep those kids inside the ... shit ...'

I look ahead and see four little people get out of a black car. Oh, look at Erin in her little faux fur coat and Kai is wearing a hat, an actual trilby. They stand there holding hands and wave at the cameras. Tommy looks at me. I don't know what to say. Cars are at a standstill waiting for the traffic to clear before the next car rolls forward and Kitty McCoy comes strolling out to have her much wanted scene. He breathes slowly and deliberately like he might be having a panic attack. Red brake lights line the scene for as far as the eye can see. Matt squeezes my knee and whispers to me. 'Get out of the car. Now.' I look him in the eye. What? His voice gets louder. 'If we get out the car, now, before Kitty has the chance, we can avoid the drama. We can catch up with the kids and make our way down the carpet before Kitty has the chance to. You forget she's eight months pregnant, she'll be at a waddle ...' Matt forgets that at nine months I beat him to the fridge once to claim the last Cornetto. But he's right. Luella nods. I'm slowly panicked by the fact they may be asking me to jog in heels. Matt squeezes my hand. 'I'll hold your hand so you won't trip.'

'Wouldn't that be like pushing in?' I say, ever the polite Brit.

'No, it's frigging inspired. Go, go, go,' shouts Luella. Raj doesn't know what to do. I lean across McCoy and open the door. I won't say we get out gracefully or with much elegance. Tommy grabs my hand and pulls me up and I don't let go but lead the way, feeling like I'm pulling a child out of a crowded playground. You'll be fine, just don't lose sight of me and if anyone tries to push you off the roundabout, I'll have your back. I giggle as we speed walk with terrible awkwardness around Kitty's car and then literally jump in front of the waiting producers.

'We're here!' I exclaim. He casts his eye over the mad lot we seem to be.

'That you are,' he says into his headset. 'We have all the *Little Chefs* cast members, we are good to go.' I look down the crowd and Kai sees me, lets the others know, and they all come running up to us. Matt takes this as his cue to step to one side, but beams at me. I, for one, am glad he's here, but decided to leave the plastic bag in the car. Luella has her trusted clipboard and acts like sheepdog herder. Tia wraps herself around Tommy's bottom half, which completely takes him aback.

'We thought you weren't coming, Tommy.'

Tommy is still speechless, but keeps one eye on the stationary line of cars to our left. We all sidestep forward, dragging small children with us.

'You haven't been at rehearsals,' mentions Oscar.

Tommy looks at all these children, some of whom he hasn't been all that kind to, and looks immediately confused at their concern.

'I, ummm, it's been a busy time and ...' I notice cameras flashing at us and I am half confused at whether I should be doing my strange arm on my hip pose or entering into the conversation. We keep shuffling as a group, away from the cars with their tinted windows and surprises that lie in wait. Luella has her phone to her ear and signals for us to walk on. She and Matt have formed some sort of protective loop around us.

'You are all being very nice.' He starts to look suspicious. I shrug my shoulders.

Matt comes up behind me. 'I see Nando's.'

I love that this is his preoccupation. He's planned his meal already, hasn't he? I know that this is to make me relax in what has become quite a tense moment. Little Erin grabs my hand. I forget how stressful this may be, especially as all these photographers know her name and she doesn't know where to focus. I drag her along and think about my own children. I turn to smile at her.

'Erin, do I have anything in my teeth?' I show her my molars. She smiles. Someone definitely got a picture of that. Tommy looks over and realises how I'm playing this.

He takes Kai's hat and tries it on, posing for a comedy picture where they're pointing at each other and frowning. He looks at me and smiles. A producer arranges us in front of a backdrop with logos and asks us all to pose and smile. It's like the world's strangest family photo. Tommy comes over and gives me a hug. 'Thank you,' he whispers. That'll probably be caught on camera and skewed into a moment it's not, but I nod to tell him it's appreciated. I feel Luella's hand on my back and her whisper into my ear.

'You need to move. Now.'

I look over my shoulder. We've managed to move thirty metres down the red carpet but it still feels too close for comfort. A car door opens. A bright yellow shoe presents itself onto the floor. I feel sick.

What happens next is a blur. I stand there long enough to see Kitty get out of the car, flanked by Cam Jacobs (boo!) and in a cheap ploy for attention and sympathy, her eldest son, Baz. She's wearing a navy poncho-style dress that would be quite elegant were it not for the fact it skims her thighs and well, it's very possible you might be able to see her pregnant noo-nah if she bends over. Unlike our Little Chefs, Baz is a seasoned celebrity kid and waves to the cameras. But then he sees his dad. Tommy spies him too. Cam ushers Baz away and I see Tommy look a little lost. What do I do, what do I ...?

'Ben!'

I swivel around to see Ben in a tweed tuxedo, holding his phone and nodding to Luella. That would be the associate on the other end. Kai goes to hug him, probably on the sniff for sweets. He high-fives Matt.

'... Kids, I hear they have candy floss inside?' he claims animatedly.

'Last one in is a loser,' adds Matt. He even bends down and does the L-shape on his forehead. Oh dear, they're seriously doing this, aren't they? Because these are kids in ballerina flats and hi-tops. I have heels and again, you are expecting me to run. But I know what they're doing, they're moving us away from the melee and he knows what will make a child run. Sugar. Coloured sugar you can eat off a stick. My brother and husband may be geniuses of the highest degree. Matt looks at Tommy, who smiles back.

'Mate, are you telling me you want to race? Me?' I roll my eyes and laugh at the photographers. Luella smiles. 'Then a race it is.'

'Go!' They all sprint off in different directions. Flashbulbs almost blind me. Matt nearly runs into a *Gardener's World* aficionado and Tommy nearly loses a shoe, but they head off under the pretence that it's all fun and for the kids. Ben waves at me and blows me a kiss. Luella sidles up next to me.

'I'm glad you decided not to run. I'm not sure I gave you a bra that would support that movement.'

'Where is she?' I ask, smiling at a photographer.

'She's cosying up to the reporters. We can make a quick escape now.' But a small tug to my dress makes me turn around. Baz McCoy.

'Did you come with my dad? Where did he go?' I lie. I wasn't blinded before. I am now. Cameras bear down on us.

'Ummm, yeah, we all arrived in the same car. He's gone ahead. Baz, isn't it? I'm Jools.' He shakes my hand politely. Even Luella seems moved.

'I'd really like to see him later, is that all right? Mum says I can't but could you ...?'

Oh my deary dear. Kid, you're asking me this now? Cam Jacobs catches sight of our conversation and starts strolling over. I look at Baz and think about Hannah, exactly the same age, and I think about me, about how I lost a parent and was this same confused child, aching to see them again. I freeze, rooted to the spot to speak. Luella bends down to his level.

'Honey, go back and see your mum and I'll make sure this happens, OK? My name's Luella, I work for Jools. I promise.' He smiles and runs to where Kitty doesn't seem to have even noticed he'd left. I'm in awe of Luella's maternal instincts and calm. Baz could have been her child. This could have been very different. She makes sure he gets back to the safety of his group, but catches the eye of Cam who looks over. Luella holds his gaze and salutes him with one finger. It's at once assured and fierce. What was this about this being a nice night where we all got on? Luella's just fired a warning shot, clear as day. Boom.

Luella and I get into the O2 only for me to get whisked away into make-up and to prep for our award presentation. Little Chefs get reunited with chaperone parents. Matt did get his candy floss but there was decidedly little to no alcohol present to calm wretched nerves. This was deliberate, Luella told me. TV people are the worst when it came to free alcohol so they need to spoon feed it to us, little by little. It, however, made me ache for Matt's mixer drinks in the tin. It was frenetic; not a velvet curtained air of decorum about the place – just people shepherded into seats, stage managers checking lighting rigs, people telling us to read what was on the autocue. There was little to no time to properly steady myself given that I was within spitting distance of Dermot O'Leary (fist pump moment), or look over our shoulders to see from which direction the next shot would be fired. I was starting to feel like Whitney at the end of *The Bodyguard*. Where would Cam Jacobs swing out from? Had he bribed the cameraman to give me a double chin? Wait, did that mean Matt was Kevin Costner? I giggle as I stare at him and he pulls a face at me. God, that's the way he's going. He needs to cut his hair before it goes full-on Costner mullet. Luella hovers beside me as the arena fills with music and the lights go down. Tommy stands beside me, not nervous, just a little shell-shocked. From crying in pyjamas to this in less than four hours. I haven't spoken to him about Baz because I need him here, to focus, to participate in the next fifteen minutes or so. He suddenly gets a tap on the shoulder.

'Oh, Tommy babe! How are you doing?' It's Georgie Gale, her of the serviette dress. Tonight she's gone for some sheer creation that has conveniently placed bows over her nipples. I half want to cover the surrounding kids' eyes. Tommy looks surprisingly relaxed to see her and there are the customary air kisses. Georgie is obviously a bit wiser to this game as she looks suitably pissed and drapes her arms over Tommy's shoulders.

'This is going to go off ... you look amazeballs!'

'Thanks, babe!' There is a bit of light fondling and I try to distract the children with the fact there's a dog from *Britain's Got Talent* nearby. Georgie cups Tommy's chin.

'You were really nice to me. I'm sorry I didn't get to know you better.' Her hands reach to inappropriate places. Tommy peels her away.

'Presenting today, Georgie?' Little Oscar can't seem to take his eyes off Georgie's boobs. I snap my fingers before his face.

'Oh no, I'm here for my stint on *Big Brother*, we're up for Best Reality ... against that bint you used to be married to.' She does a bit of drunken cackling. Tommy is drawn out of the conversation for a while. Ben intervenes.

'Miss Gale, they're calling for you in wardrobe ...' They're not, but she won't know any different. Kai goes to stand next to Tommy and takes his hand. Kai's trilby sits at a jaunty angle on his head and he looks up at

Tommy hopeful, smiley. Tommy can't read it at all. You were the kid I was especially mean to. I tore you apart and still you stand here, holding my hand.

'I'm glad you came along,' says Kai.

Tommy nods. 'Really? I am sorry about all those things I said. I mean, you've pulled it out of the bag. You know that, right?'

Kai looks at him, shaking his head. 'Oh no, I know you didn't mean them ... Jools told us ... you're not mean at all. It's all an act, like Simon Cowell. She told us you fixed Callum's mousse and you buy sick people at the hospital McDonalds ... and if you did that then it doesn't make you mean ...'

He's rumbled. I'm rumbled. He looks at me.

'So let's bring them out, the finalists from Little Chefs: Kai, Erin, Oscar, and Tia and their judges, Tommy McCoy and Jools Campbell!'

CHAPTER TWENTY-THREE

Tommy: Thank you O2 and thank you, Dermot! How are we, National TV Awards?

ROARS OF APPLAUSE AND GENERAL CONTENTMENT

Tommy: And who's watching the final of *Little Chefs* this Saturday?

MORE ROARS OF APPLAUSE.

Tia: So, awards shows should be like a really nice cake …

Kai: They should look good …

Erin: Be brimming with fresh talent …

Tia: And have lots of tasty bits.

(Seriously, who wrote that shit?)

Jools: So the *Little Chefs* family are here tonight to present the award for Best Newcomer.

Kai: Are we like a family, Jools?

(Seriously, why is this being drawn out? I can feel myself cringing.)

Jools: Well, I guess that makes me the fun mum?

Tia: And I think we all know who's the grumpy uncle …

MCCOY TO PULL A FACE (to his credit, he does.)

Erin: Which must mean we're your four talented and amazing kids, right?

Tommy: …

I look at Tommy. It's his line. Shitshitshit, someone brought up his kids. He has four kids, I have four kids. These aren't our kids. Why are they looking at me?

Jools: Of course, you obviously get it from me … So we have a lot of awards to get through tonight. Let's have a look at these nominations.

ROLL VT

OPEN ENVELOPE

ALL: And the winner is RUTH WALKER for *THE CHESTNUT WARS*.

(Cue mad applause, a very glamorous woman in a backless grey dress sashaying onto the stage to gush, cry, and thank God. Cue me moving stage right, dragging children and a shell-shocked Tommy off the stage. Job done.)

By the time I get Tommy backstage, Matt and Ben are waiting with alcohol that Matt apparently acquired off Georgie Gale.

'You spoke to Georgie Gale,' I ask.

'She's speaking to anyone with a penis at the moment.'

'And currently in a toilet with someone from *TOWIE*,' Ben tells me. 'Which reminds me, the bloke I fancy from *EastEnders* is over … there …' and with that he runs off into the crowd.

I take a swig from the paper cup as Little Chefs hug me and run back to parents to go and enjoy watch the show from the front. I am a bag of nerves. It is unfathomable at the moment what can set Tommy off and it's like watching a boiling pot set to foam over. Knowing Kitty is nearby also keeps me on edge. Luella jogs over to me.

'Good save, Campbell. But I expected nothing less.'

She stares at Tommy, who stands there looking like he's been slapped.

'Tom ... stay with me.'

He looks at her and they have a moment of knowing, of forgiveness, maybe? I breathe slowly through my mouth and take another swig. Is that vodka? Is it bad I can't tell anymore and am just glad it smells like something that could take the edge off? Geez, this could be laced up to the hilt with something dodgy and I'm not sure I would care. Luella is talking Tommy through his mild moment of panic. And I get a glimpse of the fact she does care, really. However, I'm starting to hate my altruistic streak that served to give this man a lifeline he's not using to his full advantage. Just when I think he's clawing it back, something stops him in his tracks. Matt stands in front of me and pushes strands of hair from my eyes. He shows me a text on his phone from Annie.

YOUR GIRL DID AWESOME. FINN AND I LOVE THE HULK EARRINGS! NEXT YEAR I WANT TO BE THERE, SHE BETTER TAKE ME OR I'M NEVER SPEAKING TO HER AGAIN xxxx

I smile and ache to hug her. Multiple texts from Dad, Gia, and Adam also sit there.

'You did good. I saw it on the monitor. Now, do you want to go and take our seats?' To be honest, I'm not sure. Maybe because I'm starting to realise we have another hour left of this and I'm really quite hungry, but it's been one of those evenings where the desire to sit trussed up in my Spanx and giant earrings is not hugely appealing. I want to cling onto Matt. In a onesie. On a sofa. He reads it and we hug it out. Let's just get Tommy home.

'Daddy!'

Or not.

325

Matt looks up at me as a ten-year-old boy runs into Tommy's arms and he bundles him up.

'Baz, dude. It's so good to see you.' It's hard not to shed a tear at this. At a dad studying every inch of his son's face, at a son so joyous to see someone he loves, someone he obviously hasn't seen for a while. Matt and I can't claim to know much about their relationship, but we recognise this as parents. Luella looks around and bends to their level.

'Tom, I can try and find you a private room if you want ...'

Luella looks like a meerkat, carefully scanning the room, knowing the media are just around the corner and what's happening here doesn't need to be party to that sort of intrusion. I grab Matt's hand, thinking of our own kids. At home, with Dad – hopefully watching the awards show and not Power Rangers. Tommy is beleaguered with emotion and won't let Baz go.

'How are the others? Is Ginger better, I heard she had a cold ...'

'She's OK, but we want to see you. All the visits to your house stopped and we don't get it ...'

It's hard not to watch. A hand falls on my shoulder. Ben. He's seen what's happened from across the room. 'What the hell, is that his son?' I nod. We stand there and form some sort of protective shield as passers-by try to get a glimpse of the action.

'Baz, it's just really difficult at the moment, but you know Jools, she has a friend who's a lawyer and we'll sort something out really soon and ...'

'I seriously doubt that,' announces a voice. Cam Jacobs. God, you smarmy, loathsome git. Really? 'Baz, we told you not to go off like that.'

'You're not my dad.' I can't hide my glee as Cam is dressed down by a ten-year-old. Cam's grimace tells me

326

dealing with children is not his forte. Ben stares him down, but he manages to avoid his gaze. Punch him, Ben. In the balls. You have my full permission.

'There are legal precedents in place. If you want to see your father, you need to do it through the appropriate channels.'

Tommy is a hair's breadth away from having one of his breakdowns, though I can't read this pent-up emotion as rage or sorrow. Don't cry, Tommy. Now is not the time. Matt steps in.

'You're talking about a kid here. Let him talk to his father and maybe keep your fat Yankee oar out of it?'

Oh Matt, please don't insult (or punch) the American with the capacity to sue us. Cam smiles slyly.

'Oh, it's Mr Campbell, the kept man. Have you been allowed out of the cage this evening?'

Jesus H. Arsebiscuits. Rise above, dear husband, rise above. Ben senses he's set to simmer and drags him away. Cam puts a hand on Baz's shoulder, who shrugs it away.

'Don't touch my son.'

'*Our* son.' Kitty appears almost like a shadow cast by the moonlight, which is no word of a lie given her very pregnant size. 'And after all your behaviour, it was decided that you were not allowed anywhere near him.'

'You know exactly what the courts said, unless you want me to call the police.' Cam smiles, appearing vindicated. I can't believe they'd talk so carelessly with a small, confused child in their midst. Tommy looks defeated, but stands calm, unearthing some sort of energy to deal with this. He bends down to talk to Baz.

'Soon, bud, I'll sort this soon.' Baz has tears in his eyes. I can't help but be moved. I have no leverage here, neither does Matt. A voice pipes up.

'What did you do to him?' It's Luella, a soft-spoken version of her. 'He was never Tommy. He was Tom and he was a good bloke and you got your claws in him and gripped tight and you turned him into something unrecognisable. You used him. Shame on you for belittling him in front of his own son.'

And now my tears roll because I know how Luella didn't want to get involved, but she is here saying all these things that take courage, that take heart. Tommy looks at her and his eyes mist over.

'And who are you?'

'Luella Bendicks.'

They eye each other up, not completely sure if they know the significance Luella holds in Tommy's life. 'Well, I don't know if you're his new publicist, but "Tom" should know better. It's no wonder I'm keeping him away from this baby.' She cradles her bump and I scan down to her legs, free of the cellulite and cankles that reigned through my own pregnancies. I watch as Tommy studies her bump.

'How far along are you?'

'Not that it's any of your business, but eight months.'

He stares at her and then at Baz, who still clings to his father. 'Baz, mate. There's a candy floss machine around the corner. Go knock yourself out.'

'Refined sugars at this hour, Tommy, seriously?' Baz doesn't need persuading and disappears quickly.

'Lying about your pregnancy, seriously?'

Matt and I step back a little. Luella seems to have disappeared. And Ben. Why was I not paying more attention? Are they all right? Has Luella run off crying? Has Ben gone off to vomit at the sight of seeing Cam?

'Lying? Why would I lie? We had sex eight months ago, just before the divorce went through, remember? I mean, I have every reason to regret it, but you know how sex works, right? The other four times I conceived your children, you were there, right?'

Matt squeezes my hand in a way that tells me if I ever spoke to him like that, some proper bitch slaps would be forthcoming. Tommy is for once still, almost apathetic. Unlike Cam, who can't wait for the punchline.

'But you said it was that other bloke's kid,' Tommy says. 'You told the magazines ...'

'I panicked. I didn't want to be a single mother.'

'A lying single mother.'

'Why am I lying?'

In that moment, he turns to me. I'm not sure why. He gives me a look as if to say, I know what I have to do. Breathe through the diaphragm, find something inside of you that wants to fight for what's important. You are the tiger. He smiles. I nod.

'Because, dear Kitty, after Ginger was born, I had a vasectomy.'

And there it is, the final bullet in his chamber. The one he'd had hiding all along. Boom. Shake the fricking room. Cam looks at Kitty, disappointed. Matt and I are wide-eyed in shock. She did lie! Given the tendency Tommy has to be a big ball of emotion, we marvel at how he stands his ground. And I smile because he's realised this is about looking after his kids. And when your kids are involved, you dig deep, you find that calm, that instinct to fight for them. Ted taught me that much. Still, I'd be throwing some serious shapes if I had that hiding up my sleeve.

'No, you didn't. I would have known ...'

'I knew after Ginger you kept lying about being on birth control so I took matters into my own hands. DNA tests will prove it. And the fact you're a liar and an unfit mother.'

I hear laughing behind me and turn to see a small crowd has formed. Stood in front is Ben, his arms linked with Georgie Gale, who is seriously off her very pretty face. You know because the sheer part of her dress has moved so her left nipple is exposed. I look to Matt, whose eyes are drawn to it like a magnet. To be honest, I look too – more reminiscing about when my nipples looked like that as opposed to the sad, droopy coat hooks they've evolved into. Ben smiles, knowing he's brought along a very secret weapon. Georgie pushes her way past me and goes into a drunken hug with Tommy.

'Unfit, was that? How old are you, Georgie? Like twenty? Really appropriate, Tommy …'

I'm not sure what to do. Is Georgie helping? Do I get Matt to help out and peel her away? I glare at Ben. I go to approach her but Luella re-appears and holds my arm back.

'I'm twenty-five, actually.' Ooh, it's a stand-off of bitchy faces. Georgie reaches over and wipes some lipstick off Tommy's face. 'Sorry, lovey.' Cam doesn't look impressed as he knows he set these two up for publicity so doesn't believe there's a threat.

'Because Tommy and I dated for a bit and he was lovely to me … but I know you dated at least two of my co-stars … though dated might be an exaggeration … if it had a knob, you were on it.'

Or maybe there is. Georgie laughs. 'Toms, you need my help supporting you, you know where to find me. Don't let this bint get in the way of you seeing your kids.'

A person next to me is scribbling down every word and I realise they might be press. Another has a camera phone out. This will no doubt be on YouTube soon and gossip news outlets across the land. This is primo stuff. I know because once upon a time, that was me. In a supermarket. I wasn't wearing a bra either, but I didn't look like Georgie. It was how it all started. Press start to swarm them and Tommy looks at me and smiles. I've got this. I've realised where I need to be and how I'm going

330

to do this; my way. Sure, if it were the case, you'd know he'd have donned a Batman outfit and swung from every bridge in the land to see his kids, but today he broke through a wall and got back in the game. Luella and Ben watch their handiwork. Ben looks over at Cam, gesturing to him with his little finger about the apparent size of his cock. Cam does nothing but glare. Ben and Luella grab each other's hands and do a salsa.

Beside me, a little boy re-appears with a cloud of candy floss as big as his head, jumping to see over the crowd of adults.

'Where did my dad go?' he asks me. Matt and I bend down to his level, also in a concerted effort not to get involved.

'He's talking to some people, you can stick with us for a minute.'

'Sure ...' He offers us some candy floss and we don't refuse. I roll it into a ball and let the sugar dissolve on my tongue. Geez, now I remember why my kids go a bit doolally when they eat this. You see a lot of Tommy in Baz in the same way Hannah looks more like Matt than I do. I like having that picture of him in her features, always have done.

'I watch your show on iPlayer sometimes ... you're really good.'

I'm a little taken aback by the genuine nature of his words.

'You should keep doing it,' he tells me.

'Maybe I will.'

'You've been nice to my dad too. Thank you for looking after him.'

Matt smiles to hear that last bit and puts an arm around me. A harried Kitty emerges from the crowd and he pulls a frog face at me. 'I've got to go or she'll be moody.'

Baz waves at us before he runs off and Matt and I look

at each other, smiling. There's a sense that McCoy has managed to pick himself up, things have been resolved, small victories have been won. But we're out on the other side of celebrity, we're not sure how things might pan out but we've survived. And it's a wonderful feeling of euphoria mixed with facing the unknown that overwhelms me. And it's a good feeling that makes me want to high-five everyone in the room. I don't. I just put my hand out, waiting for Matt to find it. Yeah, we got this.

Later that evening, there seems to be only one way to celebrate this euphoria and that's a Nando's.

'Seriously, Matt, a whole chicken.'

'I haven't eaten since this whole thing started. I am famished.'

I lean into him and whisper, 'Just don't go overboard with the spice. I'm not dealing with your Nando's farts all night.'

He laughs. Ten years of marriage mean I can say things like that to him without blinking an eyelid. I might work that into our vows. Tommy surveys the menu and looks baffled. Never mind earlier, now the whole world and their mothers have their camera phones out. McCoy in a Nando's and getting his peri-peri on for the first time.

'It's all chicken. It's KFC without the batter and Colonel Sanders.'

'And this is a problem, why?'

'What if I don't want chicken?'

'Seriously, if you come here and order halloumi, the whole deal's off. I'm disowning you. Don't order for Luella and Ben – they've gone for drinks with Georgie.'

To sign her up, negotiate some terms, and celebrate a night of stunning publicity masterminding. Despite being off her face, Georgie was impressed by Luella and was keen to get on board; a huge signing for her given Georgie just agreed to be in the next *Transformers* movie. She was also impressed by a publicist who with one hand could sort out her exposed nipple problems. Tommy still pores over the menu. The girl behind the till is having a bit of a fangirl moment and can't speak to either of us. I suspect we may be part of her Facebook status this evening. A queue is forming.

'Sorry, he's a newbie. Look, I'll order for him. Wings platter with corn on the cob, chips, and coleslaw and spicy rice. Let's go for medium on the chicken and two free refill drinks.'

He looks at me. I sometimes have trouble getting my own cues out for the show with that much dexterity. I give him a look. Don't come in somewhere like Nando's and take the piss. He smiles and gets out his wallet. Matt looks like this night is properly ending on a high.

We take away our chicken and find a bench overlooking the Thames to break garlic bread and gnaw on our peri-peri.

'Tommy, I can't believe you've never had a Nando's.'

Tommy is still not convinced. 'There is a Five Guys over there. Quality burgers, handcrafted shit. Seriously?'

'There's a Harvester over there ... and ...?'

'What's a Harvester?' Matt and I are questioning everything and stare at him. But we are hungry, feral hungry. Matt and I are past caring about what we're eating. That bit of candy floss we stole off Baz has not even vaguely hit the spot and all that's carrying the alcohol is a few nuts. Matt verges on the edge of proper little boy hungry where he might have a full-out tantrum and leave me. I need to quell the desire to chuck up. Overpriced, on trend burgers are not the priority. Tommy stares at us quietly as we sit on the bench like feral tramps and Matt tears off bits of chicken with his hands, caveman-style while I line my dress with napkins. I won't lie, this scene has been well-practised over the years whether we've been out with the kids and not been able to face the prospect of a sit-down meal or had a night out and needed post-booze sustenance. Tommy should just be lucky we're not taking him to Station Kebabs around the corner. Chips, garlic sauce, chicken tikka naan. The drunk parents' feast of choice.

'Chicken wing?' He sighs and dives in. There is a look about him that he might be enjoying this but won't admit to it.

'Is this chicken organic?'

'Shut up, McCoy.'

We sit in silence, digesting every detail of the evening, slowly. Tommy realises this is just the start of an epic battle. Kitty was now riled, exposed for the liar she was, but Tommy had put her in her place. He'd have to fight Cam along the way but he was ready. I'm still here. So is Matt.

'Thank you,' says McCoy.

For making him eat Nando's on a bench? He looks pensive, more than anyone should be when eating chicken.

'For getting me here. For telling me what needed to be done.'

I'm not sure how to reply so I nod quietly. Matt has devoured half his chicken with such impressive speed that I wonder if there's a career in this for him. Professional eating. We could move to Vegas. I've seen how this boy inhales pasta. He smiles, delirious amounts of joy.

'So your wedding, your second wedding. Have you decided what's happening with that?'

Matt smiles. Given how happy he looks, I'm half tempted to shift the reception to Nando's. Free refills on frozen yoghurt, people! But he looks over at me and smiles.

'We're going back up North … to where it first happened. Big field near Leeds and some yurts and the kids running about …' Matt puts a sticky peri-peri hand in mine. Despite Luella's best efforts, this felt like the option to run with. No magazine deal, no croquembouche, no swans. Just everyone we love in one space, a dance floor, kids without shoes, Matt not dressed as a Beefeater but most likely in jeans.

'You're coming, right?'

Tommy looks at me curiously like this invitation is born out of courtesy rather than choice, but deep down this feels genuine. It'd be weird not having him there.

'Bring the kids, make a weekend of it. Anyway, I need someone to make my cake.'

He smiles broadly. 'What are you serving for food?'

'Fish finger pies. Individually sized, of course.'

He laughs, little splinters of chip falling out of his mouth.

'May I suggest a hog roast?' Matt and I nod, also an option. 'And a cheese wedding cake. I know an artisan fromagerie who can help you out …'

I veer between cheering and knowing Tommy is turning foodie again. Cheese, yes but you can buy that shit from Sainsbury's at half the price and I wouldn't know the difference. Matt doesn't care, coleslaw mayo around the sides of his mouth. I go to wipe at it with my thumb. Heavens know why I chose him. Tommy tears into some corn on the cob.

'So Nando's … really?'

'Shut up, McCoy.'

'And your family eats this a lot?'

'It's just an occasional treat. It's Nando's.'

He pulls his lips back across his teeth.

'I mean, it's comfort food. You don't have a comfort food?'

He looks at me and sighs. I want to question the sort of man who has never sought infinite amounts of joy from a Nando's, a whole packet of Jammy Dodgers, Hula Hoops you eat off your fingers, a jam doughnut, a bowl of custard. A fish finger sandwich. We jolt through a feeling of déjà vu. Tommy smiles and I elbow him, probably a little too hard, but he takes another chicken wing, shakes his head, and the three of us sit there, watching the lights bounce off the Thames as boats drift in and out of the piers.

EPILOGUE

What were you doing when you were ten? I was wearing leggings with loops that went under my feet and had quite the collection of My Little Ponies. I rocked a shell suit. I remember them because Dad bought us three of the same from a local market stall in the same colours as the Union Jack that made us look like a Eurovision act. Did I cook when I was ten? I possibly could butter toast. And warm up soup.

Because I've just seen a ten-year-old make his own profiteroles. He stirred that flour like a bastard into his butter/water mixture, piped that shit, and now they're cooling in front of me. Perfect little hollow spheres of pastry.

'It needs to come away from the sides of the pan,' he told me. I nodded. Of course it did, otherwise it would have exploded and mutated into something else? I marvelled at the intensity in this kid's face, the way he could have cooked any old dessert for this finale. I would have opted for a trifle (shop-bought custard, naturally) but he decided to go for a stack of choux pastry with edible flowers and salted caramel Crème Pâtissière. You go, kid! I'm not sure what was more edifying here – the fact that this kid knew far more than me about baking/cooking/food in general (I usually try and stop my kids from eating flowers), or the fact that this kid was Kai: he of the solidified chicken casserole, reduced to a snivelling wreck in round one. Of course, I take sole responsibility for him being here. If I hadn't given him the title of Head Chef that week, his confidence would have taken a complete nosedive and he'd have slunk away to the shadows thinking the worst. But I re-wrote the script. I told him the whole time that he had this. I've taught him fuck all about cooking but I taught him something about brushing off the flak and getting back up again. I have a feeling this is why they brought me on board. Because I buy my profiteroles in. We all do, right?

'So how do you salt your caramel, Kai?'

Tommy looks at me, trying to shake his head off camera.

'Ummm, I add salt.'

Well, that's me told. I high-five him as that's what I do with all the kids in the slim hope it'll make me trendy and relevant but also gloss over my faux-pas. At least it's better than when I asked one of these kids why his cauliflower rice didn't have any actual rice in it.

I stand back and watch the set as Kai, Erin, Oscar, and Tia stand behind their counters, the atmosphere unfeasibly tense given that they're kids. Their families standby and, in a new twist, are caged in areas with automatic sliding doors. The doors open every fifteen minutes and a new family member is allowed onto set to assist and then has to run back to their pen. It's set up to add pace and excitement but in the back of my mind, I am fearful for some of the grandparents who lack pace and appropriate footwear and thus risk not getting back in time, or worse, being eaten or losing limbs to the strangely aggressive automatic doors. That would make the headlines surely. *Granny eaten by door in BBC show finale*. All the remaining contestants seem to have the steely ninja focus of children you know are really good at spelling and will probably go on to break some balls in life. It was of little surprise to see Erin here. Erin plays violin and has a purposeful way of putting on her oven mitt like she's donning boxing gloves. We've already spoken about my

338

little fighter, Kai but there's also Tia; great sense of humour and always hugs the person sent home each week. Her family all wear T-shirts with her face on them. Oscar always brings a small tear to my eye. He sought solace in the kitchen after losing his dad to cancer. Every week, his family bawl their eyes out telling us how proud they are of him. This, in turn, makes me cry and dole out hugs to everyone involved which, in turn, makes the viewers cry and tune in every week. The fact is, he could serve me a bowl of cereal and I'd vote him through every week. I think about him and instantly want to let him win. But I have a soft spot for Kai. Erin will no doubt pull this out of the bag. Tia's already told me her favourite joke and made me belly laugh. (Why did the chicken go to the library? To get a 'buk-buk-buk.') But there has to be a winner. Someone's got to choose. Shit, that's me, isn't it? I knew there'd be a downside to being a judge. The time away from home, the pressure on my family, having inner crises of confidence again about who I am, what I am, who I love. But this is the hardest thing: having to choose a kid that's the best. There is no way to do this. I wouldn't choose between my four. They're all perfect for the amazing things they achieve, but also in their imperfections. Maybe I need to take a stand and tell these kids they all won. Yes, there is an element of competition in life and in what we do, but you should all embrace the freedom of childhood. Learn that life is also a collaborative effort where we work together for the common good. We are winners! This should be my parting words. I can dole out high-fives, we can embrace in a collective circle. But then they'd need prizes. I have a feeling the BBC would make me pay for them. And possibly not ask me back.

But then they wouldn't be able to do that. I will be back next spring. The contract was signed three hours ago before we went to air. The show has been a hit and they're keen to replicate its success having sold the format to eight different countries, including the USA, who will replace me with a country singer who made a killing out of selling her own brand of organic fruit leather but has seven children who all have names starting with the letter K, including one called Kiaora. Like the popular eighties' juice drink. Of course, I was a big bag of nervy nerves three hours before this kicked off. So much so I retched repeatedly into my dressing room sink before they applied my prerequisite five layers of make-up. But Luella sensed this was all a bit of an ambush to catch me off-guard while I was in a state of panic so she intervened quickly. She went through that contract like a boss. She even brought highlighters. I heard all sorts as the make-up girl Polyfilla'ed my chin. Financial compensation for promotional work, cuts of related cookbooks, and most importantly, assurances that the judging panel would stay the same. No dragging in bloody Kitty McCoy as some sort of ratings booster. It's a deal. We shook hands, I signed paper. That's that.

'What do you think? I think Tia's onto a winner with the roulade. That's some technical skill and I love that's she using matcha ...'

Tommy has sidled up next to me, his hand against his chin as he surveys the room. Matcha is green and related to tea in some capacity but I don't ask for clarification. He'll be back, as we take on the televisual world as the new dynamic duo in town. Him with his panto villain act, stern and serious, while I do the anxious mama stance with the encouraging perma-smile, willing everyone on to do their best. Something tells me we will be asked to do comedy photo shoots involving us pointing at each other. A camera appears in front of us, expecting us to talk.

'I like that's she sticking with fish. Her sea bass from last week was the dish of the series for me.'

'*En papillote.*'

'Yes, Mr Chef.' I salute him. The cameraman's shoulders shudder with laughter. Tommy gives me evils.

'But Kai, choux pastry. Risky for a finale. I think they look underdone, they'll be soggy in the middle.'

Tommy has continued to be quite harsh with Kai in what he secretly has told me is his way of charting a believable relationship between the two of them, so when Kai does pull off, it makes his success all the sweeter. Kai is wise to his game, admirable for not letting it get to him but secretly, there are times I wish he'd stick his middle finger up and give him what for. I will, and always have, got Kai's back.

'But for the main, he's made his own venison sausages. I like a good sausage ...'

Wow. I've said that, haven't I? Someone's going to make a GIF, aren't they? Tommy flares his nostrils, trying to hold back the giggles. He can't. So he turns his back to the camera, pretending to terrorise the amateur chefs instead. Tommy. Mr McCoy. He's not had a good week. He and Kitty are going at it, full bore in the press and it's not been pretty. Tommy has managed to clear his name of being a wife-beater and bad father but the battle to spend quality time with his kids is on. As for Kitty, it turns out that Georgie was right; she did get around after leaving Tommy, properly around the block stopping off at many beds along the way. Ones of married men, ones of younger men, and ones whose occupants recorded proceedings resulting in a sex tape which shows she has a penchant for making horse sounds when she's in flagrante. But Tommy is showing a focus that was lacking. Now he has an end game, he knows what's important, and found his mojo. He's signed a lease for a new pub around the corner from his new pad. He can serve his foodie chef malarkey and it can be head-to-toe organic and overflowing with heirloom tomatoes and pomegranates. But it will be his choosing, his venture. He's invited Matt and I to the opening. We'll go to support him. But I've told him I'm eating nothing out of a flower pot or anything that involves 'foam.'

'Ten minutes left, kids!' I shout out, reminiscing about when I used to shout that upstairs, reminding kids that the school run would be leaving soon, with or without them. I look over, off camera. The Campbell kids are here. Usually we leave them out of this but there's a wrap party where there'd be free milkshakes, so it felt rude not to partake. Hannah gives me a thumbs-up while the twins seem to be mid-fight, which is being refereed by Ben and Matt who hold them back like little warring drunks. Where is Millie? No eyes on Millie! Make sure she's not biting through cables! Hannah looks so tall. When did she get so big? She stands next to Clio, Luella's youngest who is also here for the freebies. Luella's brood are now our extended media family. It was all thanks to Remy and Matt, who've become dad pals. It would seem women are far more complicated creatures when it comes to forming friendships. For men, a similar taste in beer and Stevie Wonder was all it took.

Luella said that Remy talked constantly about how Matt was the only Brit he'd ever met who knew his cheeses and wore Vans without looking like an idiot. Matt, in the meanwhile, harped on about Remy's creativity and how their kids had that cute bilingual thing going on which made him feel worldly and cool by association. It was a man-crush match made in heaven. When I talk about extended media family though, I also talk about the other four kids in the room: Baz, Mace, Clementine, and Ginger stand about watching their dad in action accompanied by Marigold, the nanny. It's good to have them here, to know they are not being paraded in front of a camera but here to see their dad and support him. He winks over at Mace, who winks back in that way that kids do where it looks like they use their whole face to control the one eyelid. My heart smiles. Jesus Christ, these kids are winners! Prizes for everyone! But seriously, where the hell is Millie? Matt looks at me. I do some strange sign language that to anyone else would look like I'm doing a bad version of the Macarena but Matt knows instantly. Please make sure she hasn't wondered into an oven. He smiles and I stop for a moment. He knows.

A puff of dry ice suddenly appears on stage, the automatic sliding doors open, and family members mill out to help their kids while others are herded back into their pens. I eye the giant automatic doors, praying they've been constructed to health and safety requirements. Oh dear, they've released Oscar's grandfather, who's like a dad to him. Shit, don't cry. Not now. Tia's aunt moves to her work station but is chopping the wrong herb. I think Tia asked her to chop some parsley. I am 75% sure that is coriander. I sidle over.

'I think that's coriander, Aunty Meg.'

Aunty Meg looks cautiously at me. Tia is mid-roll of her roulade.

'Parsley is the one that tastes like grass, coriander tastes like soap.'

My foodie wisdom knows no bounds. Tia's Aunty Meg looks at me like I'm either planning sabotage or speaking the truth. She starts sniffing everything. I glance over at Kai, who's adding something gold to his profiteroles. Erin is turning out a flan. Tommy comes to stand next to me.

'So who are we giving this to?' he whispers.

'Traditionally, shouldn't we taste the food first?' I inform him.

'Erin needs this the most but the public will never forgive us if we don't give it to Oscar, and I have all that stuff with Kai ...'

'I believe this should be about the food.'

'Wow, fame has changed you, Campbell.'

I elbow him in the ribs and he moves along to harass Erin about whether her potatoes are cooked through. Maybe it should be Oscar and his shin of beef. Shit, I don't know. There is salted caramel. There is Tia and her matcha and white chocolate roulade. Erin has done something with duck. I wouldn't know where to start. Cook it like chicken, no? I watch as the scene gets more hectic, pans are boiling. God, there are kids everywhere. I stand perfectly still. We have impressive frying pan pyrotechnics in one corner that in my house would signal that I am burning things, causing our smoke alarms to get their weekly testing. Why am I here again? I burn stuff. I still don't know what quinoa is exactly. Isn't it just couscous in disguise? I don't even know where to start with choux pastry. Oscar seems to be mopping his brow and has gone a little beetroot from excitement. The clock ticks down perilously, second by second. I stroll over to him. Don't cry, Jools.

'How's it going, little man?'

Oscar has always been one of little words. 'He lets the food do the talking' was what most TV critics said, but I know part of it was being pushed into the spotlight and not knowing how to cope with it. That and the dad thing. Shit, keep it together. The people, the lights. I get why it's all a bit much. I bend down to his level.

I whisper into his ear. 'You're doing so well. Your dad would be super proud of you ... you know that, right?' I don't collapse in a flood of tears but I wait to see his eyes crease up. His lovely little smile. There. Will he win? Who knows anymore. Erin's duck looks burnished and crisp. Kai's profiteroles stand tall and glossy. All of Tia's family are cheering and chanting her name. Aunty Meg still stares at herbs wondering if she got this a bit wrong. Two minutes left on the clock. I take my place on a neon spot that emits an unusual amount of dry ice that has possibly been borrowed off a *Doctor Who* set. Tommy stands next to me and playfully punches my arm.

'We did it,' he whispers.

'Well, the kids did it. We just stood around and tasted stuff. I put on half a stone polishing off desserts.'

He laughs. 'Same again next year then?'

I nod. We're legally bound by contract but I have a feeling I might want to come back. To do it again, all over again for as long as the BBC will allow. I survey this new scene which has become my day job for now. Kids mill about frantically, adding their finishing touches to plates and trays of food. Kai, remember that garnish at the end of your bench! Oscar, don't trip over your apron! I want to hug them all. Must stand rooted to my allotted spot. Family members are shepherded back into their pens. A floor manager runs past me with a clipboard muttering something about fish slices. I feel like I should be doing something to help. The washing up, maybe?

'Oscar's won, hasn't he?' I say badly out of the side of my mouth.

McCoy laughs. 'I thought you said we had to taste the food first?'

'I'm just making conversation.'

'You're such a sucker for a sob story. Well, bring on judging because I'm fighting Tia's corner. I think she's nailed this.'

'It's on, McCoy.'

'Bring it, Campbell.'

He laughs. And a final smile. This hasn't been too bad, eh? Of course, I did this for the cheque, really. It was like a really cool part-time gig that helped me find myself and paid for the new roof. And it's been fun. But this was always more of a gamble for McCoy. I'm strangely proud of the fact he clawed his way back and I was the person who gave him a leg-up. So maybe he's the winner in all of this. And just this once, I'm content to let him claim that glory. A camera slides in front of us and we immediately put on our TV faces.

'Erin, are you really sure those potatoes are done?' he calls across the studio. Erin, who is plating up, is not the sort to suffer fools regardless of age or media standing so she rolls her eyes in the manner of a teenager who's been asked to pick their clothes off the landing. I smile. If that makes McCoy the annoying TV dad then I must be the TV mum. Super Mum. Or Souper Mum if you will. How very foodie of me. I like soup. And I'd look damn fine in a cape.

'5-4-3-2-1. And that's it! Step away from your plates. We are done ...'

346

Follow the adventures of

SOUPER MUM

By KRISTEN BAILEY

For more information about
Kristen Bailey

and other **Accent Press** titles

please visit

www.accentpress.co.uk

A

For more information about

Kirkus Kelly

and other Accent Press titles

please visit

WWW.ACCENTPRESS.CO.UK